THE BLACK HILLS

This Large Print Book carries the
Seal of Approval of N.A.V.H.

THE BLACK HILLS

WILLIAM W. JOHNSTONE
WITH J. A. JOHNSTONE

WHEELER PUBLISHING
A part of Gale, a Cengage Company

GALE
A Cengage Company

Farmington Hills, Mich • San Francisco • New York • Waterville, Maine
Meriden, Conn • Mason, Ohio • Chicago

Copyright © 2019 by J. A. Johnstone.
A Hunter Buchanon Novel.
The WWJ steer head logo is Reg. U.S. Pat. & TM Off.
Wheeler Publishing, a part of Gale, a Cengage Company.

Wheeler Publishing Large Print Western.
The text of this Large Print edition is unabridged.
Other aspects of the book may vary from the original edition.
Set in 16 pt. Plantin.

LIBRARY OF CONGRESS CIP DATA ON FILE.
CATALOGUING IN PUBLICATION FOR THIS BOOK
IS AVAILABLE FROM THE LIBRARY OF CONGRESS

ISBN-13: 978-1-4328-6316-6 (softcover)

Published in 2019 by arrangement with Pinnacle Books, an imprint of Kensington Publishing Corp.

Printed in Mexico
1 2 3 4 5 6 7 23 22 21 20 19

The Black Hills

CHAPTER 1

As the supply wagon rocked and clattered along the old army road west of Tigerville, Dakota Territory, Hunter Buchanon heard the light thumps of four padded feet and looked into the buttes to his left to see a coyote leap from a trough between two bluffs and onto the chalky slope above the trail.

The brush wolf lifted its long, pointed nose and launched a chortling, yammering wail toward the brassy afternoon sky, causing Hunter to set his jaws against the tooth-gnashing din.

Hunter drew back on the reins of the stout Missouri mule in the traces. As the wagon lurched to a grinding halt, he frowned up at the nettled coyote.

"What is it, Bobby Lee?"

As if in reply, the beast turned to Hunter and mewled, yipped, and lifted each front foot in turn, fidgeting his distress. Hunter had adopted the coyote two years ago, when he'd found it injured up in the hills above his family's horse ranch just west of where Hunter was now.

The pup had survived an attack by some raptor — an owl or a hawk, likely — but just barely. The pup, while only a few weeks old, had appeared to be on its own. Hunter had suspected its mother — possibly the rest of its family, as well — had been shot by ranchers.

He had taken the pup home and nursed it back to health, feeding it bits of rabbit and squirrel meat and dribbling goat's milk into its mouth from a sponge, and here it still was after two years, close by its savior's side, though Hunter had assured the friendly but wily beast it was free to venture back into the wild, its true home, whenever it pleased.

Hunter wished he'd learned the coyote's language over their months together, but while they communicated after a fashion, there was much that was mysterious about Bobby Lee. However, the apprehensive cast to the coyote's gaze could not be mistaken. Trouble was afoot.

As if to validate Hunter's suspicion, something made the air shiver.

A veteran of the War Between the States on the Confederate side of that bloody conflagration, Hunter Buchanon was all too familiar with the spine-shriveling, mind-numbing sound of a deadheading bullet. The slug kicked up dirt and gravel just inches from the troubled coyote, which squealed and ran.

An eyeblink later, the rifle's ripping report sounded from a butte over the trail to Hunter's right.

The ex-Confederate cursed and hurled himself off the wagon seat — all two-hundred-plus pounds and six-feet-four inches of the twenty-six-year-old man. He rolled fleetly off a shoulder and hurled himself into the brush along the trail just as the mule, braying wildly, took off running straight up the trail, dragging the wagon along behind it. Dust from the buckboard's churning wheels swept over Hunter, offering him fleeting cover.

He scrambled out of the brush and scampered straight up the bluff Bobby Lee had been perched on.

More bullets chewed into the bluff around his hammering boots, the rifle cracking angrily behind him. Breathing hard, Hunter lunged quickly, cursing under his breath. Though a big man, he was nearly as fleet-footed as he'd been when as a young Rebel soldier he'd run hog-wild behind Union lines, assassinating federal officers with a bowie knife or his Whitworth rifled musket with a Davidson scope, and blowing up supply lines — quick and wily as a Georgia mountain panther.

He'd been in his early teens back then, still wet behind the ears, but he'd become a backwoods warrior legend of sorts — as revered and idolized by his fellow Confederates as he was feared and hated by the Bluebellies.

Those days were over now. And while he might have still been fleet enough to scamper up the butte ahead of the bushwhacker's bullets, and scramble behind a tombstone-size boulder as another bullet smashed into it with a screeching whine, he had no gun on his hip to reach for. Even if the mule, old Titus, hadn't lit out with the wagon, there was no rifle or shotgun in it. The only knife he had on him was a folding barlow knife. He could feel the solid lump of the jackknife now in the right pocket of his buckskin trousers.

The barlow felt supremely small and inadequate as another bullet screeched in from the butte on the opposite side of the trail and smacked the face of the boulder.

The rifle's hammering wail echoed shrilly.

"Law, law!" Hunter muttered. "That

fella's really out to trim my wick!"

He jerked his head down as yet another bullet came screeching in and smashed the face of the boulder with another hammering crash.

"Hey, you with the rifle!" Hunter shouted. "Why don't you put the long gun down so we can talk this out like grown-ups?"

The shooter replied by hurling another bullet against Hunter's rock.

Hunter cursed to himself, then shouted, "Is that a definite no or a maybe?"

Again, the shooter replied in the only language he cared to communicate in.

"All right, then," Hunter said under his breath. "Have it your way!"

He waited for another bullet to smash against his covering rock, then heaved himself to his feet and dashed straight up the butte. He covered the fifteen feet in three long strides, crouched forward, keeping his head down, trying to make himself as small as possible.

He hurled himself up and over the butte's crest as a slug tore hotly along his right side, tracing the natural furrow between two ribs.

Hunter hit the butte's opposite slope and rolled halfway to the bottom. When he finally broke his fall, he winced against the burn in his side and lifted his left arm to see the tear in his linsey-woolsey tunic.

He jerked up the garment, exposing his washboard belly and slab-like chest as well as the thin line of blood the bullet had drawn across his side, about halfway between his shoulder and waist. Not a wound, just a graze hardly deep enough to bleed, but it ached like six bee stings.

"Son of Satan!" Hunter exclaimed. "What in the hell is this fella's problem?"

Was he after the mule? The wagon? Possibly the ale Hunter was hauling to town to sell in several Tigerville saloons? His father, Angus Buchanon, was a brewmaster, using old Buchanon family recipes his own father had carried over from Scotland to concoct a dark, creamy ale that was much favored by the miners, prospectors, and cowhands in and around this neck of the Black Hills.

Something told Hunter the shooter wasn't after any of those things. Just a sense he had. The man seemed so damn determined to kill him that maybe that was *all* he wanted.

Time to find out.

He knew a rare but vexing regret that he wasn't armed. He knew he should keep at least a six-shooter in the wagon. This was wild country, after all. Populated by men nearly as dangerous as the wildcats and grizzlies that stalked these pine-clad hills, elk parks, and beaver meadows east of the Rockies.

But he'd had his fill of guns and knives . . . of killing . . . during the war. Just looking at a pistol or a rifle or even a skinning knife conjured bloody memories. After Appomattox, he'd sworn that he would never again raise a gun or a knife against another human being. Not carrying a weapon when he wasn't hunting was his way of trimming his chances of having to break that promise to himself.

So far, he'd made good on that promise.

So far . . .

Reacting more than thinking about the situation, a trait that had held him in good stead during the war, Hunter heaved himself to his feet and took long, lunging, sliding strides to the bottom of the butte, loosing small landslides in his wake.

He followed a crease between buttes back to the west. When he figured he'd run a good fifty yards, he made a hard left turn between another pair of low buttes.

This route took him back to the trail, which he crossed at a sharp curve shaded by cottonwoods. Pushing through low cottonwood branches, he hightailed it into another crease between the chalky bluffs on the shooter's side of the trail.

He climbed the shoulder of another low butte and paused in the shade of a lightning-topped pine.

On one knee, taking slow deep breaths, his broad, muscular chest rising and falling deeply, his mind worked calmly. The shock and fear he'd known when he'd heard the rifle's first crack had dwindled. The old natural instincts and battle-tested abilities moved to the forefront of his warrior's mind.

He had no weapons. No traditional weapons, that was. But he had an enemy who apparently wanted him dead. His own mind recoiled at the notion of killing, but there was no point in denying the fact that whoever was out to kill him needed to be rendered unable to do so.

Hunter picked out a rock that fit easily into the palm of his right hand. Working the rock around in his hand like a lump of clay, he scanned the high crest of a bluff just ahead and above him on his right. That was the highest point of ground anywhere around. It likely gave a clear view of the old army trail. It was probably from that high point that the bushwhacker had hurled his lead.

Hunter tossed the rock up and caught it, steeling his resolve, then moved quickly down the slope. He was trying to work around behind the ambusher when he spied movement out the corner of his left eye.

Stopping, crouching, he swung his head around to see a man — a man-shaped shadow, rather — walk out from the butte's far end, directly below the high, stony, pine-peppered ridge from which the bushwhacker had probably fired at Hunter. The man, carrying a rifle in both hands across his chest, dropped down below a hump of grassy ground and disappeared from Hunter's view.

Hunter sprang forward, running across the face of the steep bluff, about ten yards up from the bottom. There was a slight ridge at the end of the bluff, and Hunter stayed behind it, running almost silently on the balls of his worn, mule-eared boots into which the tops of his buckskin trousers were tucked.

He gained the base of the slight ridge, slowly climbed.

Near the top, he got down on one knee, swept a lock of his long, thick blond hair back from his eyes, and cast his blue-eyed gaze into the hollow below. His belly tightened; his heart quickened.

The man was there. A big, bearded man with a battered brown hat. He was hunkered down behind a low, flat-topped boulder, a grimy red bandanna ruffling in the slight breeze. He cradled a Winchester repeating rifle in his thick arms tufted with thick, black curls. The stout limbs strained the sleeves of his red-and-black-checked shirt beneath a worn deerskin vest.

Hunter couldn't see his face. The man's head was turned slightly away. He was looking in the direction of the trail, searching for his quarry. There was a wary set to his head and shoulders.

The man knew who he'd been shooting at. He was aware he'd made a grave mistake by not sending those first shots home. He knew that a Buchanon would not tuck his tail and run. At least, not run *away.* Armed or unarmed, having sworn off killing or not, a Buchanon would run *toward* trouble.

If one of Hunter's brothers — the younger Tye or the older Shep, or even their one-armed father, old Angus — were in Hunter's position now, this man would already be dead. None of them subscribed to Hunter's pacifism. Of course, neither Tye nor Shep had fought in the war. Old Angus had fought in the Georgia state militia, and he'd lost an arm for his trouble. Still, the old mossy horn wouldn't give up his rifle until they rolled him into his cold, black grave.

16

Hunter rose a little higher on his knees. He raised his right arm, adjusting the rock in his fingers, preparing for the throw. His gut tightened again, and he drew his head down sharply. The man had turned toward him.

Had he heard him? Smelled him? *Sensed* he was here?

Hunter lifted his head again slowly, until his eyes cleared the top of his covering ridge. The man's face was turned slightly toward Hunter, looking off toward Hunter's left. Hunter still couldn't get a good look at him. The man's hat brim shaded his face. If Hunter jerked his head and shoulders up to throw the rock, the man would see him and likely shoot before Hunter could make the toss.

Damn.

The familiar patter of four padded feet sounded.

The man turned his head sharply back to his right, away from Hunter.

Bobby Lee leaped onto a low boulder down the slope below the shooter. The coyote lifted its long, pointed snout and sent a screeching din rising toward the brassy summer sky.

"Why, you mangy bag o' fleas!" the bushwhacker raked out through gritted teeth.

He raised the Winchester to his shoulder, aiming toward the yammering coyote.

Hunter raised his head and shoulders above the ridge, drew his arm back, and thrust it forward, throwing the rock as hard as he could.

CHAPTER 2

Hunter's aim was true, as it should be after all his years of killing squirrels, gophers, rabbits, and sometimes even turkeys with everything from rocks to spare bullets. A Buchanon was nothing if not thrifty.

The rock thumped sharply off his stalker's head.

The man yowled and fell forward, cursing and rolling down the grassy slope toward where Bobby Lee danced in zany, manic circles atop his boulder. Hunter leaped to his feet and ran. He jumped the boulder behind which his stalker had been crouching, and continued down toward where the man was still rolling, flattening grass and plowing through a chokecherry thicket.

The man rolled out the other side of the thicket and came to rest at the slope's bottom, about ten feet from where Bobby Lee stood atop the boulder, glaring down at the bushwhacker, baring his fangs and growling. The man had lost both his hat and his rifle during his fall, but now as he pushed onto his hands and knees, shaking his head, his thick, curly hair flying, he slid his right hand back for the Colt .44 still holstered on his right thigh.

From behind the man, Hunter grabbed the gun, ripping free the keeper thong from over the hammer and jerking the weapon from its holster.

"Hey!" the man said, turning his head to peer behind him.

Hunter recognized that broad, bearded face and the cow-stupid, glaring eyes reflecting the afternoon sunlight. Also reflecting the sun was the five-pointed badge pinned to the man's brush-scarred vest.

"Chaney?" Hunter said, tossing the man's gun away. "What in blazes — ?"

But then Deputy Sheriff Luke Chaney was suddenly on his feet, moving fast for a big man with a considerable paunch and broad, fleshy hips. Dust and dead grass coating him, he wheeled to face the taller ex-Confederate. From somewhere he'd produced a Green River knife; he clenched its hide-wrapped handle tightly in his right hand as he stood, crouching, a menacing grin curling his thick, wet lips inside his dusty, curly, dark-brown beard.

The Green River's steel blade glinted in the afternoon sunshine.

"Come on, Buchanon," Chaney said, lunging toward Hunter. "They say you Reb devils got some fight in you — even if you don't wear a gun!"

He slashed the Green River knife from right to left and would have laid open Hunter's belly if Hunter hadn't leaped back. The Green River's razor-edged blade had come within an inch or even less of doing just that. The knowledge caused a burn of rage to rise up from the base of the ex-Confederate's back, spreading across his shoulders and blazing in his clean-shaven cheeks.

Hunter faced his opponent, crouching, arms spread, ready to parry Chaney's next assault. "What the hell's this about, Chaney? What's your beef with me?"

Chaney curled his mouth in a sneering grin, then lunged, slashing with the knife. Overconfidence was the man's Achilles' heel. He'd just retreated from another attempt at eviscerating Hunter when Hunter sprang forward, kicking upward with his left boot, the toe of which smashed against the underside of Chaney's right hand.

There was the dull snap of breaking bone.

Taken by surprise, Chaney gave a hard,

indignant grunt. The knife flew out of his hand, arcing sharply up, flashing in the sunlight before landing not far from where Bobby Lee now sat on the boulder, watching the fight with a devilish glint in his long, yellow eyes, a low whine of apprehension issuing from deep in his chest.

Chaney grabbed his wrist and bellowed, "Damn you, Reb devil — you broke my wrist!"

He stood there, knees buckling, crouched over his injured hand, as Hunter walked wide around him and scooped the knife up out of the tawny grass. He brushed off the knife and started to turn, saying, "Now suppose you tell me what —"

He stopped when he saw Chaney coming toward him like a bull out of a chute, head down, eyes glinting malevolently, a sinister smile tugging at the corners of his mouth. Hunter stepped to one side. Chaney plowed into Hunter's right chest and shoulder, gave a yelp, and stumbled away.

Bobby Lee lifted his head and sent a warbling cry careening skyward.

Dazed by Chaney's assault, Hunter swung around toward where Chaney stood six feet away, his back to Hunter. The deputy sheriff was leaning forward as though he were looking for something on the ground. Hunter looked at his own right hand.

He was no longer holding the knife. His hand was slick and bright with fresh blood.

Chaney turned to face Hunter. The Green River was sticking out of Chaney's belly, the handle angled down. Doubtless, the knifepoint was embedded in the deputy's heart. Reacting instinctively when Chaney had bulled toward him, the old warrior instincts coming alive in him, Hunter had dropped the knife handle slightly, angling the blade up toward his assailant's heart.

He'd killed countless Union soldiers that way. Only, he'd done so consciously. He'd killed Luke Chaney without thinking.

Hunter's heart thudded as Chaney stared at him in wide-eyed horror.

The deputy had both his big, bloody hands wrapped around the knife handle protruding from his belly. He took one stumbling step backward, wincing slightly as he tried to pull out the knife. He opened his mouth as though to speak, but no words made it past his lips.

Chaney's eyes rolled up in their sockets. His chin lifted and he tumbled straight back to the ground with a heavy thud and a breathy chuff as the air was punched from his lungs. He lay still.

Yipping softly, Bobby Lee dropped down

off of the boulder, ran over to Chaney, and hiked a back leg, sending a yellow stream dribbling onto the dead deputy's forehead.

Hunter stared in shock at the dead man.

He raised his bloody hands, stared at them. A million images of bloody death flashed through his mind all at once. The screams and wails of the wounded and dying, the concussion of hammering Napoleon cannons and howitzers, the crackle of musket fire.

Hunter felt as though he'd been kicked in the head. His legs buckled. He dropped to his knees. Sagging back onto his butt, he stared at his blood-washed hands.

He was still sitting there maybe ten, fifteen minutes later, staring at his hands. Bobby Lee lay beside him, calmly chewing burrs out of his mottled gray-brown coat. Suddenly, the coyote lifted his head and sniffed, twitching his ears. Then Hunter heard them too — hoof thuds rising in the distance.

Bobby Lee mewled softly, staring off toward Hunter's right.

Hunter felt inert, unable to react though warning bells tolled in his head.

The hoof thuds continued to grow louder until the rider appeared, swinging through a crease between the buttes. She turned her head toward Hunter and Bobby Lee, and drew back on the reins of her fine buckskin stallion. Sunlight glinted off the long, dark-red curls cascading like amber honey down from her man's felt hat to spill across her shoulders.

Annabelle Ludlow batted her heels against the buckskin's flanks, and the gelding galloped forward until the girl drew back on the reins again and sat for a moment, staring down in horror at Luke Chaney lying dead in the tawny grass. She was nineteen years old — a rare beauty with emerald eyes in a fine, smooth, heart-shaped face lightly tanned by the sun. She wore a calico blouse and tight, badly faded and frayed denim jeans, the cuffs of which were pulled down over her men's small-size western riding boots, which she wore without spurs.

The boots were as worn and scuffed as any cowpuncher's.

A green-eyed, rustic beauty was Annabelle Ludlow, with long slender legs and womanly curves. A rich girl to boot, being the daughter of one of the wealthiest men in the Hills. By looking at her you'd think she was the daughter of a small shotgun rancher whose wife sold eggs to help make ends meet. Annabelle didn't believe in flaunting her riches, and that was only one of the many things Hunter Buchanon loved about her.

"I was airing Ivan out nearby," she said after nearly a minute had passed. She'd named her horse Ivanhoe, after the hero of a book she loved. "I heard the shots. What happened?"

It was as if she'd whispered the query from a long ways away. Hunter had barely heard her.

As he sat there on his butt in the grass, in his mind he was a thousand miles east and more than ten years back in time, and he was pulling his bowie knife out of the wool-clad belly of a young Union picket. It was late — one or two in the morning — and he'd been sent to blow up several supply wagons along the Tennessee River, using the Union's own Ketchum grenades. Those wagons were heavily guarded, and the young man he'd just killed had been one of those guards.

There'd been a clear half-moon, and the milky light of the moon shone in the young soldier's eyes as Hunter, his hand closed over the private's mouth to muffle any scream, jerked him over backward from behind. He pulled the bloody knife out of the young man's belly and found himself staring into a pair of impossibly young, anguished, and terrified eyes gazing back at him in silent pleading.

26

The soldier was tall and willowy. He had the body of a sixteen- or seventeen-year-old. But the face, speckled with red pimples, and the wide-open eyes were that of a boy a good bit younger. Hunter dragged him almost silently back into the woods along the river, the water lapping behind him. The soldier's body seemed impossibly light. He did not struggle with his killer.

He was bleeding out and dying fast.

Hunter lay him down on the spongy ground and slid his hand away from the young man's mouth.

"Oh God," the boy had wheezed, drawing air into his lungs. "Oh God . . . I'm . . . I'm dyin' — ain't I?" It seemed a genuine question that the boy answered himself. "I'm dyin'!"

Hunter stared down at him. He'd killed so many almost without thinking about it. That's what you had to do as a soldier. You had to numb yourself against killing. You killed for the greater good. You killed for the freedom of the Confederacy, to stamp out the uppity Yankee aggressors. But as much as he wanted to ignore the innocent eyes staring up at him this moonlit night along the Tennessee, he found his mind recoiling in horror and revulsion at the fear he'd inflicted, the life he'd just taken.

27

The boy had whispered so softly that Hunter could barely hear him.

"Ma an' Pa . . . never gonna . . . see 'em again. My lovely May!" The boy's eyes filled with tears. "We was gonna be married as soon as I went home!"

Hunter felt as though it were his own heart that had been pierced with the knife he kept honed to a razor's edge. He looked at the blood glistening low on the young soldier's blue-clad belly, wishing that he could take back what he'd just done, return this horrified soldier's life to him. Return Ma and Pa to him, and the girl, May, whom he loved and intended to marry.

Horror and sorrow exploded inside of Hunter. He dropped the bloody knife, grabbed the young man by his collar, and drew his head up to his own. "I'm sorry!" he sobbed. "I'm sorry!"

The young man stared back at him, twin half-moons floating in his eyes as though on the surface of a night-dark lake. The soldier opened his mouth as though to speak, but he couldn't get any words out.

Pain twisted his face. His lower jaw fell slack. His eyes rolled back until all Hunter could see were their whites.

The soldier's raspy breaths fell silent, and his chest grew still. Hunter released him and he fell, lifeless as a sack of grain, to the ground.

"I'm sorry," the Confederate heard himself mutter.

But then it wasn't the young Union soldier lying before him in the light of the Tennessee moon. It was Luke Chaney lying sprawled in the tawny grass of the Black Hills, blood glistening brightly in the light of the afternoon sun.

Annabelle knelt beside Hunter, her hand on his thigh, gazing into his eyes with concern. "Hunter? Hunter, can you hear me? Hunter!"

CHAPTER 3

Hunter slid his gaze slowly toward his girl. He'd been only vaguely aware of Annabelle's presence, but now as that moonlit night of so long ago mercifully dwindled into the past, he was aware of her worried green gaze on him.

He placed his hand over hers, atop his right thigh. He found modest comfort in the warmth of her flesh. "I'm all right."

"Where were you?"

Hunter shook his head and winced against the throbbing in his temples. He leaned forward, pressed his fists against his head as though to knead away the pain that normally came at night, on the heels of his frequent nightmares.

"You were back with that boy you killed," Annabelle said, placing a comforting hand on his shoulder. "With the young Union soldier."

Hunter pressed his hands to his temples

once more, then lifted his head and cast his gaze toward where Chaney lay in the grass. Bobby Lee lay ten feet from the body, in a scrap of shade offered by a cedar branch. He was staring at Hunter and mewling deep in his throat with concern.

"What happened?" Annabelle asked again.

"I was on my way to town with Angus's beer. Sidewinder ambushed me." Hunter turned to her, grabbed her arms, and squeezed. "I swear, Annabelle. I didn't mean to kill him. I kicked the knife out of his hand. I walked over to pick it up. As I turned, he ran into me. I must've —"

"Shhh, shhh." Annabelle wrapped her arms around him, hugging him. "It's all right. He gave you no choice. I heard the shooting from the next ridge north. He was out for blood, obviously."

Annabelle pulled away from Hunter and gazed guiltily into his eyes. "This is my fault."

He frowned. "What're you talking about?"

"I caught him following me again the other day. I was driving a wagonload of supplies up to the men manning my father's line cabin on Beaver Ridge. When I topped a hill I saw Luke following me from about a quarter-mile back. I pulled the wagon off the trail and waited. When he rode up, I

31

threatened him with my Winchester.

"I swear, Hunter, I was so mad to find that vermin dogging my heels again, after I had refused his marriage proposal in no uncertain terms, that I almost shot him right then and there! I told him once and for all to leave me alone, or I'd shoot him. And . . ." She dropped her eyes demurely. "And I made the mistake of telling him that when I married, you'd be the one . . ."

Hunter smiled and placed a hand on her cheek. "Well . . . I kinda like the sound of that myself."

"I do too." Annabelle kissed his hand. "But I'm afraid that might be the reason he ambushed you here today. Why you had to kill him."

"Well, whatever the reason," Hunter said, turning to Chaney once more, "he's dead."

"I'll ride over to the mine and tell my father. He'll know what to do."

Luke Chaney's father, Max Chaney, was a business partner of Annabelle's father, Graham Ludlow. Chaney had wanted his thuggish son to marry Annabelle, and had tried to arrange it with Graham Ludlow. Ludlow wouldn't hear of it. It might have stressed his and Chaney's business partnership, but Ludlow had set his sights on higher fruit than the ungainly, foul-mouthed, and whore-mongering Luke Chaney.

The man Ludlow wanted for his future son-in-law was the somewhat prissy but well-bred and well-heeled son of an Eastern railroad magnate currently working to build a railroad that would connect the Black Hills with Sydney, Nebraska. The young man's name was Kenneth Earnshaw, and he'd graduated the previous fall from none other than Harvard University.

"No," Hunter said, grabbing Annabelle's arm before she could walk back to her horse. "No, I'll take care of it. Chaney's Stillwell's deputy. I'm going to take him on into Tigerville and tell Stillwell what happened."

"That's crazy, Hunter!"

"Telling what happened out here ain't crazy. It's the only thing to do."

"Stillwell will sic his other cutthroat deputies on you! He'll kill you!"

Some called Frank Stillwell a lawman-for-hire. In other words, he was a gun-for-hire who sometimes wore a badge. A couple of years ago, Tigerville and the hills around it had been a hotbed of bloody violence. This was right after General George Armstrong Custer had opened the Hills to gold-seekers in 1874, despite the Hills still belonging to the Sioux Indians, as per the Laramie Treaty of 1868.

Men and mules and horses and placer mining equipment poured up the Missouri River from Kansas and Missouri by riverboat and mule- and ox-train, and the great Black Hills Gold Rush exploded.

Naturally, crime also exploded, in the forms of claim-jumping and bloody murder as well as the stealing of gold being hauled by ore wagons, called "Treasure Coaches," southwest to Cheyenne, Wyoming, and the nearest railroad. Tigerville was on the Cheyenne-Custer-Deadwood Stage Line, and the coaches negotiating that formidable country were often preyed upon by road agents.

For those bloody reasons, the commissioners of Pennington County, chief among them Annabelle's father, Graham Ludlow, brought in Stillwell and the small gang of hardtails who rode with him, also calling themselves "lawmen." Max Chaney got Luke a job as another of Stillwell's deputies, and the big, gun-savvy, boorish Luke fit right in. Bona fide crime dwindled while the death rate went up. It was still said in these parts that you couldn't ride any of the roads spoking out of Tigerville and into the surrounding hills without coming upon Stillwell's low-hanging "tree fruit" in the form of hanged men.

Men hanged without benefit of trial.

Many of those men had once fought for the Confederacy. It seemed that most of the "tree fruit" Stillwell "grew" hailed from the South, which wasn't one bit fishy at all, given Stillwell's history of being second-in-command of one of the worst Union prisoner-of-war camps during the Civil War and having a widely known and much-talked-about hatred for the warriors of the old South.

"He won't kill me, Anna," Hunter said, sounding more confident than he felt. "Not even Stillwell or his tough nuts will kill an unarmed man. Not in town in broad day-light, anyways." He glanced at Chaney again, and flared an angry nostril.

"At least fetch your pa and your brothers. You need someone to back you in town, Hunter."

He shook his head stubbornly. "Pa an' Shep an' Tye would only come armed. It'd look like we were spoiling for a fight. Knowin' Pa an' Shep like I do — they'd likely start one. A fight is what I'm trying to avoid."

Anna glowered up at him, said softly, "Just bury him out here." She glanced at the dead man. "Toss him into a ravine and kick some

35

dirt on him. It's better than what he deserves."

Hunter placed two fingers on her chin and gently turned her head toward his. Her green eyes glistened in the sunlight. "You know that's not how I do things, Anna."

"Oh, I know it's not. And that's why I love you. But I don't want you to die, Hunter. I love you and want to spend the rest of my life with you, you big Southern scalawag!" She rose up onto the toes of her boots, wrapped her arms around his neck, and kissed him passionately. Hunter returned the kiss, basking in the comfort of the girl in his arms.

Finally, he eased her away from him.

"Can I borrow Ivan to fetch my wagon?"

"You know you can."

"Obliged." Hunter walked over and grabbed the buckskin's reins. He swung up into the saddle and galloped off in the direction from which Anna had come.

He found the wagon not far up the trail. The mule, Titus, was too lazy to have run far. Angus's beer kegs were still secure in the box, stacked against the front panel and tied down with heavy ropes.

Hunter stepped off the buckskin's back and into the wagon. He tied Ivan to the tailgate and climbed over the beer kegs into the driver's box. A few minutes later he swung back into the buttes south of the trail and saw Annabelle sitting on the ground not far from Chaney's slack figure.

Bobby Lee lay close beside her, his head on her thigh. She stroked the coyote affectionately. The coyote gave his tail intermittent, satisfied thumps against the ground and blinked his long yellow eyes slowly, luxuriously.

Hunter gave a wry snort. His coyote friend appeared to be appropriating the affections of his gal. It seemed sometimes that most all the males in the county were in love with Annabelle Ludlow. Hunter couldn't blame them. She was a rare, striking beauty, and a girl of heart and substance. If he got his way — and he was determined to — he was going to marry the girl, and he and she were going to raise a whole passel of young'uns right here in the Black Hills, on a wild horse ranch of their own.

If he had his way, and the girl's father didn't get his . . .

Trouble was likely afoot in that regard, but Hunter didn't want to think about Graham Ludlow at the moment. Right now he had his hands full with Sheriff Frank Stillwell.

Annabelle was no hothouse flower. Despite Hunter's protestations, she helped him haul Luke Chaney over to the wagon and dump him into the box. Most girls would have been stricken with the vapors over such a task. Annabelle merely scowled down at the dead man, her disdain for him plain in the set of her fine jaws, then brushed her hands on her jeans when they were done with the job.

"Don't worry about me now," Hunter told her, taking her once more in his arms. "I'll be fine."

"At least take my Winchester." Anna glanced at the carbine she always carried in her saddle scabbard.

"No. Going in armed will only be asking for trouble. Like I said, don't worry, now."

Annabelle sighed in defeat. "I am going to worry about you," she said with crisp defiance, gazing up at him, her green eyes as clear as a mountain lake, a wry humor crinkling their corners. "When you're finished, you meet me at our usual place so I can make sure you're still of one piece."

"And if I'm not?"

Annabelle pursed her lips angrily and reached up to snap her index finger against the underside of his hat brim. "Everything better be in its rightful place. I'll be checking!"

Hunter chuckled. He kissed her once more and climbed into the wagon. Bobby Lee was already mounted on the seat to his right.

Hunter turned the wagon around, pinched his hat brim to his girl standing gazing up at him admonishingly, fists on her hips. He rattled on past her, threaded the crease between the buttes, and swung onto the main trail.

A half hour later, a nettling apprehension raked chill fingers across the back of the ex-Confederate's neck as the town of Tigerville appeared before him, sprawling across a low dip of tawny ground surrounded by the narrow spikes of pine-clad knolls that sloped from higher ridges toward the town. The hillocks and natural dikes seemed to be pointing out Tigerville to weary travelers who, having journeyed this far off the beaten path, had lost hope of finding any hint of civilization at all out here in this vast, rugged, pine-bearded and gold-spotted country east of the Rockies.

Tigerville, named after the now-defunct Bengal Mine, was far from the howling hub of boisterous humanity that was Deadwood, fifty miles north. But Tigerville was no slouch in that regard either. Now as Hunter rattled and clomped down the town's main street, he was surrounded by the din of player pianos, three-piece bands, and laughing women disporting their wares from boardwalks and the second-floor galleries of sporting parlors, of which Tigerville had several of note.

Men of all sizes, shapes, and colors, including blacks and blanket Indians, crisscrossed the street still muddy from an earlier rain, some with frothy ale mugs in their fists and/or painted ladies on their arms. There were miners, prospectors, cowpunchers, market hunters, railroad surveyors, soldiers from the local cavalry outpost, as well as cardsharps, run-of-the-mill rowdies, grubline-riding tough nuts, and confidence men.

The buildings were mostly wood-frame and false-fronted business establishments with more than a few of Tigerville's original crude log cabins and tent shacks remaining to give testament to its humble roots.

The King Solomon's Mine, owned by Graham Ludlow and Max Chaney, sat on the high ridge to the east of town, like the castle ruins of some vanquished lord overlooking the humble dwellings of his unwashed subjects. Gray tailings stretched down the mountain below the mine, around which was a beehive of activity including men at work with picks and shovels, hand-cars rolling in and out of the mine portals, thundering ore drays traversing trails switch-backing up and down the mountain's face, as well as the constant, reverberating hammering of the stamping mill in its giant timber frame at the base of the ridge, behind the barrack-like, wood-frame mine office.

Hunter turned his attention to the street before him. The office of the county sheriff was on the east side, roughly two-thirds of the way through the half-mile length of Custer Avenue. Hunter angled Titus toward the jailhouse, and felt another cold-fingered massage of apprehension.

Sheriff Frank Stillwell was tipped back in a hide-bottom chair on the front porch, his five-pointed star glistening on his brown wool vest. His high-topped black boots were crossed on the rail before him. As Hunter turned the mule up to the hitching rack fronting the sheriff's long, unpainted, wood-frame office, Stillwell's mud-black eyes turned to regard him with customary malignancy.

CHAPTER 4

"Well, well — Hunter Buchanon. To what do I owe the pleasure?"

Sheriff Stillwell was slowly peeling a green apple with a folding knife. A barred window flanked the sheriff on his left. The long, narrow, mustached face of Buck Fowler, one of Stillwell's deputies, peered out for a moment, then disappeared.

The front door opened and Fowler, working a wad of chaw around inside his left cheek, stepped onto the porch to Stillwell's right. Fowler, a potbellied man in his early forties, slid his hands inside his brown suit coat, tucked his thumbs behind his suspenders, and glanced down toward his boots. He hung his head as though in shame, then opened his lips slightly to let a long, wet string of chaw dribble out of his mouth.

The tobacco plopped onto the porch between his boots.

The man lifted his long, ugly, pockmarked

face toward Hunter, and the mustached mouth shaped a jeering grin.

Hunter looked at the porch floor beneath Fowler's boots. The man was standing on a worn, torn, soiled, and rag-thin Confederate flag, which Stillwell had tacked down fronting his office door. The Confederate-hating sheriff used the flag as a mud mat — or, in Fowler's case, a spittoon. Stillwell had been using the old Stars and Bars as such since he'd taken office nearly two years ago now, after a rigged election, openly insulting and mocking each and every born-and-bred Southerner and ex-Confederate soldier residing in Pennington County.

Those he hadn't run off, that was.

Fowler had drawn Hunter's attention to the flag now as if Hunter hadn't already known it was there. As if he and every other Southerner in the county didn't know that Frank Stillwell and his deputies used the Stars and Bars, Old Dixie, the Rebel Flag — the guidon for which so many Brothers of the Southern Confederacy had made the ultimate sacrifice — to scrub the mud and horse dung from their boots.

"Hidy, Hunter," Fowler said through a jeering grin, his wet, tobacco-stained lips glistening in the sunlight angling beneath the porch's slightly pitched, shake-shingled

43

roof. "What brings you to town? Say, you got your pappy's beer in the wagon there, do ya?"

"That's right. And I got somethin' else in the wagon." Hunter looked at Stillwell, who was holding the apple and his knife up close to his thickly mustached mouth, squinting his eyes and furling his black brows, really concentrating on his apparent endeavor to remove the peel in one long, continuous curl. "That's what I come to talk to you about, Sheriff," Hunter added.

Stillwell stopped peeling the apple to extend his mud-dark gaze toward Hunter. Holding the apple and the knife very still before his chin, not wanting to tear the peel, he slid his eyes toward Bobby Lee sitting to Hunter's right, and scowled, his waxy cheeks flushing, his mean eyes crossing slightly in anger. "That beast right there is pestilence. Vermin. You oughtta take it off in the brush and put a bullet in it!"

Bobby Lee made a low growling noise deep in his chest and shifted his weight from one delicate front foot to the other, yellow eyes flashing indignantly.

Hunter said, "It ain't Bobby Lee I came here to powwow about."

"Oh, it ain't Bobby Lee you came here to powwow about," said Stillwell, his words

44

thick with mockery. "Well, then what did you come here to powwow about, Buchanon?"

"Luke Chaney."

"Luke Chaney," Stillwell said, continuing to slide the sharp edge of his knife along the surface of the apple, making quiet snicking sounds. "What about Luke Chaney? I ain't seen Luke for hours. You seen him, Buck?"

"Not since early this mornin'. He was eatin' *huevos rancheros* over at the Chinaman's place." Still standing on the flag, with the fresh brown stain between his boots, Fowler grinned and rubbed his belly. "Best beans and eggs I ever ate, and I lived three years in Mexico."

"No kiddin'?" Stillwell removed the coiled peel, inspected it carefully, then tossed it over the rail and into the dirt fronting the porch. "I don't believe I've ever partook of the Chinaman's *huevos rancheros.* I will remedy the matter soon, see what all the fuss is about."

Bobby Lee leaped out of the wagon, ran over and picked up the apple peel, giving it a few nibbles before dropping it back into the dirt with a snort, then leaping back into the driver's seat beside Hunter.

Both Stillwell and Fowler eyed the coyote

as though it were a pile of fresh dog dung up there on the seat with the ex-Confederate.

"Pestilence," Stillwell snarled.

"Absolute vermin," Fowler added, scowling at the beast that sat with its snoot in the air, eyes half-closed, sunning hisself. The pock-faced Fowler looked at Hunter. "Good Lord, Buchanon — don't you know all them beasts is good for is a winter coat?"

Hunter held the deputy's gaze for a moment, suppressing the rage that was flaring in him, keeping his expression calm, implacable. Sliding his gaze to Stillwell, he said, "Chaney's in the wagon. He's dead."

Stillwell had just removed a slice of the apple with his knife. Now, holding the slice atop his knife blade, he scowled at Hunter curiously. He repeated what Hunter had just told him, as though by repeating it he could better understand it.

"What?" Fowler said, stretching his lips back from teeth that were as narrow and pointed as picket fencing.

"You'd best have a look," Hunter said, his cautious gaze glancing off the two long-barreled Colt Peacemakers strapped around Stillwell's waist and then at the two Remingtons thonged low on Fowler's thighs.

Stillwell and Fowler shared a befuddled

glance. Stillwell jerked his head to indicate the wagon. Fowler lowered his hands to his sides and stepped down off the porch. He walked over to the side of the wagon and peered inside.

"Glory hallelujah," he said, turning darkly to Stillwell. "It's Luke, all right." He slid his belligerent gaze to Hunter. "Gutted like a fish!"

Stillwell's face remained expressionless. He sucked the apple slice off his knife blade and chewed. Buck Fowler stepped back away from the wagon and drew one of his saw-handle, nickel-washed .38-caliber Remingtons, aimed the revolver at Hunter, and clicked the hammer back.

"Easy, now," Stillwell said, chewing. "Go easy, Buck. We don't know what happened" — he slid his hard-to-read gaze to Hunter still sitting atop the wagon beside the coyote — "yet."

Hunter turned his head to sweep his gaze along the street on which most of the activity had come to a somber halt. Apparently, word had gotten around this end of Tigerville that Hunter Buchanon had come to town with more than his pappy's beer in his wagon. Men were filing slowly out of the town's dozen or so saloons and sporting parlors, some carrying sudsy beer mugs in their fists, a quirley or a cigar smoldering between their fingers, interested scowls on their faces.

Stillwell's deputies had gotten word, as well, it appeared. Hunter saw at least a half dozen of them now, most in shabby suits sporting five-pointed silver stars, elbowing their way through the crowd and slowly converging on the wagon from various points along the street, heads canted to one side, glowering toward the wagon. A few carried rifles. A few others carried sawed-off, double-bore shotguns. They were a small army of hammerheaded cutthroats, and most of Tigerville lived in fear of them.

Hunter heard the crowd whispering and muttering, boots softly crunching horse apples and gravel as the curious onlookers made their way over from their respective watering holes and shops, the whisperings and grumblings growing ever-so-gradually louder and more heated as the crowd, including Stillwell's deputies, drew closer to the wagon and could see, or thought they could see, who it was Hunter had hauled into town.

Hunter turned to Stillwell. "He ambushed me out by Eagle Butte. I was unarmed. I didn't mean to kill him. It was an accident."

The deputies were shoving their way up

through the crowd, closing on the wagon from Hunter's right and left. The crowd made way for them, stepping back, giving them room, not wanting to take a bullet if it came to a lead swap.

Stillwell cut a quick, flat glance toward Fowler, then sliced off another bite of the apple and sucked it off the knife blade. He chewed slowly, ponderously.

"Accident, eh?" Stillwell said, placing his finger on the nub of his chin and sliding a foxy glance not only at Fowler but at the other deputies now standing in a ragged semicircle around the wagon. "Hmmm."

"Yeah," Fowler said, pacing his own finger on his dimpled chin. "Hmmm."

A funereal silence dropped over the street. The only sounds were the barking of a distant dog, the piping of birds, and a whore getting a workout behind an open window somewhere along the street to the south. For a hundred square feet around Hunter's wagon, you could have heard a frog fart.

Hunter stared at Stillwell.

The sheriff swallowed another apple slice, drew a breath, and raised his voice officiously. "Mr. Buchanon, were there any witnesses to this purported bushwhacking you allege that Luke Chaney affected on you, and/or were there any witnesses to your murder . . . er, uh, *killing by accident* of said Mr. Lucas Chaney?"

"No."

"Well, then," Stillwell said, flicking a speck of dust from his right trouser leg, then turning to his senior-most deputy, "I don't see how we can hold him, Deputy Fowler. I suppose we should hold a — what do you call it again?" He snapped his thumb and index finger to nudge his memory. "A coroner's inquest. Yes, that's it — an *inquest.* But I see little point in wasting the taxpayers' hard-earned money or time on such busy nonsense when there is very little reason for me to believe that any more light could be shed on the subject — there being only Mr. Buchanon here to tell the story, which he's just done."

Glaring at Hunter, Fowler flared a nostril.

A deputy now standing beside Fowler said, "You mean to tell me that he can kill Chaney and suffer no consequences at all?"

"That ain't right, Sheriff!" Fowler agreed.

"That's the way the law works, I'm afraid," Stillwell said, slowly shaking his head in mock frustration. He looked at Hunter. "Mr. Buchanon, do you swear that you told the truth here today?"

"I do," Hunter said with a resolute nod. "It was an accident."

"Tell me how guttin' a man like a damn fish is an accident!" shouted a deputy on the other side of the wagon from Fowler. He was a seedy, stocky, heavy-shouldered man in an opera hat and holding a double-barreled greener on his shoulder.

"Luke wasn't no bushwhacker!" said another deputy. The one beside him nodded while another man, an apron-clad Yankee shop owner named McGee yelled from the stoop fronting his shop, "No, sir, he weren't!"

Hunter leveled a look at Stillwell. "Tell these men to stand down, Sheriff. Chaney ambushed me. I was unarmed. I circled around him, laid him out with a rock. Didn't hurt him bad, just dazed him. He pulled a knife. I kicked it out of his hand. When I went to pick it up, he came running at me. I turned and the knife went in by accident."

"By accident, my ass!" bellowed the deputy standing with Fowler. Hunter thought his name was Junior Edsel, a gunman from Oklahoma. He had two gold front teeth and a naked lady tattooed on his neck.

Stillwell continued to stare at Hunter, one-half of his mouth curved in a jeering grin. "You're gonna need to write out and sign an affidavit."

51

"A what?"

"An affidavit. So we got it down on paper what happened. You know — to make it all official. Oh, and there's a filing fee."

"A filing fee?"

"That's right. Standard procedure. We gotta pay someone to file it, don't we? Fifty dollars."

"Fifty dollars? I told you I didn't mean to kill the son of a — !" Hunter stopped himself, his cheeks afire with rage.

Stillwell couldn't suppress a smile as he cut his eyes around his deputies and the townsmen flanking him — Yankees, mostly — from whom more angry murmurs rose.

"I just meant," Hunter said, getting his wolf back on its leash, "that I don't see any reason I should have to pay a filing fee. If I'd just left him out there, which I could have done, there wouldn't be any filing fee. Besides, I don't have fifty dollars."

"All right, all right," Stillwell said with phony amiability, striding up to the porch rail and hiking a hip onto it. He dug a half-smoked stogie from his shirt pocket. "Maybe we can work something else out."

"What?"

Stillwell lifted his chin to get a better look inside the wagon behind Hunter and Bobby Lee, who was growling deep in his chest again, as though the coyote were having as hard a time as Hunter was keeping his passions in check.

"Is that your pappy's famous ale back there?" Stillwell asked.

CHAPTER 5

Hunter glanced over his shoulder at the six ten-gallon kegs of freshly fermented, coal-black ale stacked in two rows of three each, and secured with heavy ropes. Several saloons in Tigerville had standing orders for the stuff — even some owned by Yankees. In fact, over the summer, old Angus couldn't make the grog fast enough to keep up with demand.

"That's Angus's ale, yes," Hunter told Stillwell.

"Damn." Stillwell drew a long breath, sniffing the air. "I swear I can smell it from here!"

"What about it?" Hunter asked, trying to stop imagining his fists smashing the sheriff's face until it looked like a ripe tomato smashed against a rock.

Stillwell slid his cunning gaze from the crowd, which he was working like a veteran thespian, to Hunter. The crowd of deputies and townsmen waited in silence. So did Fowler. So did Hunter. Hell, even Bobby Lee appeared to be waiting for the sheriff's next words.

"I'm thinkin' we might be able to settle this whole complex problem of the affidavit and the filing fee in a much simpler, friendlier, small-town fashion. How about you turn over one of your pappy's kegs to me, and we'll call the matter resolved? You know, there ain't much I like about ole Angus Buchanon . . . or your brothers . . . or you, as a matter of uncontestable fact."

Stillwell's eyes hardened briefly as they stared out at Hunter, but he was quick to soften his demeanor again with an ironic smile. "But I gotta admit I have a weakness for that rancid ole Confederate's black Scottish ale — a fact I find hard to admit right out here in public, but admitting it I am, doggone it." He gave a mock-fateful sigh.

Several of the men around the wagon chuckled.

"Well, it is good ale," one of them said, keeping his voice down as though it were something he, too, were ashamed to admit.

Hunter looked at Stillwell. "You want a keg of ale."

Stillwell only smiled.

"If I turn over a keg of ale, you'll forget

55

about the filing fee and I can go on about my business?"

Stillwell lifted his chin. "Soldier to soldier — absolutely."

Hunter studied him. Something told him it wasn't going to be that simple. Still, handing over a keg of his old man's ale was a hell of a lot simpler and cheaper than filling out some official document and paying fifty dollars to have it filed — if that was even how things worked. Hunter didn't know, but he had a feeling Stillwell was full of mule fritters, which was typical for a Yankee. Most of them had it oozing out both ends.

He shrugged a heavy shoulder and jerked his chin toward the ale. "All right, help yourself. One keg."

"I'd like you to fetch it for me."

Hunter stared at him. Stillwell stared back at him, chinned dipped slightly. The game continued. The mockery. Hunter could hear the snickers of the other men around him. Buck Fowler had lowered his revolver. He stood with the big popper hanging low by his side, his other fist on his hip, grinning in delight at Hunter, reveling in the sheriff's takedown of a former Confederate.

Stillwell beckoned. "Bring it on up here — a fresh keg of Angus Buchanon's famous ale. I can taste it now. Whoo-eee. Even warm, it'll cut the summer heat!"

Hunter stared at Stillwell, who grinned back at him.

Hunter glanced at the heavy-shouldered, hatchet-faced deputies standing around the wagon, also grinning. They held rifles or shotguns. Six-shooters bristled from their hips or from holsters thonged on their thighs.

Hunter's cheeks and ears were as hot as a blacksmith's forge. Still, a little humiliation was a whole lot better than bloodshed. If he made a misstep here, not only would he likely pay the price with a hefty fine and time in jail — and possibly a necktie party held in his honor — his father and brothers would probably feel Stillwell's heat as well.

He wouldn't put Stillwell past trying to make them complicit in Chaney's death and going after them with hang ropes too.

Hunter drew a ragged breath as he rose from the wagon seat. He glanced down at Bobby Lee, who returned his dubious look, flicking his bushy gray tail like an anxious cat.

"Stay, boy," Hunter told the coyote, who gave a low yip.

Hunter stepped back into the wagon box. He untied the ropes from the heavy steel rings in each side panel, then leaned down and picked up one of the ten-gallon kegs. Straightening with a grunt, he set the keg on his right shoulder. He stepped over the side of the wagon and dropped to the street.

Buck Fowler stepped back, making way for him, grinning, rising jubilantly up onto the toes of his boots and hooking his thumbs behind his suspenders, thoroughly pleased at the spectacle that Stillwell was making of an ex-Confederate, one of the hated Buchanons no less.

Hunter knew that there were a few ex-Confederates in Tigerville, but they were badly outnumbered by Yankees, and they were wisely making themselves scarce. There was no point in a street fight that would likely turn into a lead swap faster than a whore could shed her pantaloons.

Hunter would carry the beer keg into Stillwell's office — a small price to pay, relatively speaking — and be on his way, leaving no more blood in his wake.

Hunter mounted the porch steps, aware of all eyes on him. He crossed the porch and stopped, staring down at the Confederate flag tacked down with rusty nails. His heart skipped a beat, and a fresh burn of anger rose into his ears. He looked at Stillwell, who was still sitting with one hip on the porch rail, smiling with pugnacious

58

satisfaction at the big blond Rebel with the keg on his shoulder.

Stillwell had lit his stogie. Slitting his eyes, he exhaled a long plume of smoke toward Hunter.

No one said anything. No sounds issued from the street or even from the town beyond it. The whore's cries had faded; the dog had stopped barking. Not even any birds were chirping.

It was as if everyone in Tigerville — men and animals alike — was aware of the pageant being played out here this afternoon — the takedown of one of the hated Buchanons, though no one had any reason to hate them except for the side they'd taken during the war.

The deputies fronting the sheriff's office were waiting to see if Hunter would walk on the flag — the flag he'd fought and nearly died for, the flag he'd seen so many of his brethren make the ultimate sacrifice for. There was no way not to walk on it unless he wanted to step back and take a running leap, which would only further humiliate him and buy him even more chips in Stillwell's game.

Hunter drew another breath and, staring straight ahead, strode forward. He'd just stepped onto the flag and was about to step off, when Stillwell said, "Wipe your feet."

Hunter stopped, whipped his head toward the lawman, narrowing one eye. He could feel a vein off the corner of that eye throb almost painfully.

Stillwell's own face flushed now in anger. He straightened, spread his boots shoulder-width apart, and hooked his thumbs behind his cartridge belt, narrowing both dark eyes. "You wipe the dung from your boots before you enter my office, Reb!"

Several deputies snickered. One said something too softly for Hunter to hear. Someone was cackling delightedly under his breath and behind his hand.

Hunter's heart thudded.

Stillwell's eyes blazed at him.

Hunter looked down at the flag beneath his boots. Between his boots lay the freshly smeared plop of Buck Fowler's chaw.

Hunter shifted the keg's weight on his shoulder, drew another calming breath, then shuffled his boots, giving them a cursory wipe on the flag he'd almost died for more times than he could count. Chest burning with barely containable rage, he strode over the threshold and into Stillwell's office as the crowd roared with laughter behind him.

Hunter set the keg on Stillwell's desk, then headed back through the door and out onto the porch.

"Now, that, gentlemen, is what is known as a galvanized Yankee," Stillwell yelled. "Let's give him a big round of applause!"

The crowd exploded, laughing and clapping, all jeering eyes on Hunter as the big ex-Confederate cast one more parting glare at the laughing Stillwell, then strode down the porch steps and swung toward his wagon.

"One last bit of business." Buck Fowler raised his Remington and took aim at Bobby Lee sitting on the wagon seat. "Time to rid Tigerville of vermin!"

Hunter swung to his left and buried the toe of his right boot in Fowler's crotch. Fowler screamed and, jackknifing forward, triggered his Remington into his own right foot. As the deputy dropped the smoking Remy and clamped both hands over his smashed privates, Hunter slammed a savage left roundhouse against the man's left ear, flipping him over sideways and leaving him howling and writhing in the fetal position.

"Get him!" one of the deputies shouted.

Two men lunged ahead of the others, swinging their fists. Hunter sidestepped and ducked the fist of Junior Edsel. He hammered the man's face three times quickly — twice with his right, once with his left —

turning the man full around and sending him sprawling into three deputies running up behind him.

Vaguely aware of Stillwell laughing uproariously behind him, Hunter dodged another fist and buried a hard right in a soft belly, just above the large brass buckle of a cartridge belt. More deputies came at him. His pacifism turning to ashes beneath the fire raging inside him, he bulled forward to meet the onslaught, swinging his fists, twisting, turning, pivoting.

His knuckles smashed jaws and noses and eyes and hammered bellies.

Fists battered him, as well, though he was only vaguely aware, for the old battle berserker was awake inside him.

He was as big or bigger than the men attacking him. Bigger, tougher, angrier. They'd pushed him too far, and now they were paying the price. He would likely pay later, but for now . . . *oh, the sweet bliss of rage!*

Hunter shrugged a man off himself and pivoted to his right in time to see Bobby Lee leaping onto the shoulder of a man moving toward Hunter, leveling a sawed-off shotgun. Snarling, Bobby Lee sunk his teeth into the man's neck. The man screamed and whipped the coyote off his shoulder, triggering both barrels of the barn-blaster skyward with a howitzer-like explosion.

Bobby Lee gave a shrill screech and ran.

Hunter leaped on the man's back, driving him to the ground and smashing the back of his head with his fists. Two others grabbed Hunter's arms and hoisted him to his feet. Three others took turns hammering Hunter without mercy, with fists and rifle butts. Between blows, Hunter saw a big, mustached deputy named Merriman bound forward, raising a Buntline Special and clicking the hammer back.

"Step back, boys!" the big man shouted, thrusting the Buntline's long barrel toward Hunter's face. "I'm gonna finish the varmint!"

Merriman's head jerked sharply to one side. Blood and bone matter spewed from above his left ear. He staggered away, triggering the Buntline into the belly of one of the other deputies, making him howl like a poleaxed bull.

The gut-shot deputy dropped to his knees, screaming. The two men holding Hunter released him, and Hunter fell to his butt in the street.

The deputies were looking around, wondering who'd fired the shot that had killed Merriman, who now lay belly-down in the dust with only half his head intact, unmoving. Fowler was still in the fetal position, venting his anguish over his smashed oysters and ruined foot. It was as though he and the gut-shot deputy were in a contest to see who could yell the loudest.

Otherwise, the street was quiet until a voice familiar to Hunter's ears yelled, "Drop those weapons, you mangy cayuses, or there's going to be more blood shed here today!"

Hunter, still on his butt, cobwebs from the beating he'd taken floating around behind his eyes, shuttled his gaze to the livery barn on the opposite side of the street from Stillwell's office. Behind a rain barrel on the building's left front corner hunkered a willowy scarecrow of an old man with a gray beard and long gray hair flowing down from his battered gray Confederate campaign hat.

Old Angus Buchanon aimed his prized '66 Winchester, known as the Winchester "Yellowboy" for its brass receiver, over the top of the barrel. Though only one-armed, he could shoot as well as any two-armed man.

"You heard the old rapscallion!" shouted another familiar voice. "Drop your guns and step back away from my little brother's

64

wagon, or we'll fill you so full of lead you'll rattle when you walk!"

CHAPTER 6

Hunter turned his head to his right to see his older brother, Shepfield Buchanon, standing against the high false façade of Scanlon's General Merchandise, clad in fringed buckskins and aiming his own Henry .44-caliber rimfire repeater toward the group around Hunter's wagon.

Shep was a big man, as big as Hunter, but he had more flesh on him than Hunter did — a good bit more. Close-cropped, sandy-brown hair was concealed by his cream sugarloaf *sombrero.* Bushy sideburns trailed down both sides of his broad, fleshy face, and a full mustache mantled his mouth.

He stood with one boot cocked forward, holding the long, octagonal-barreled Henry straight out from his right shoulder. He hadn't fought during the war — he'd stayed home to keep their small farm out of Yankee hands and to tend their ailing mother — but he was as good with a rifle as Hunter or any other man on the frontier.

Neither was he too shabby with the horn-gripped Remington New Model Army revolver holstered low on his right thigh or the bowie sheathed on his hip.

"What Pa an' Shep said!" shouted the youngest Buchanon brother, Tyrell, who lay prone on the roof of the harness shop to the right of Stillwell's office.

The left-handed twenty-two-year-old was aiming down the barrel of his own cocked Winchester carbine, narrowing his left eye beneath the brim of his battered, funnel-brimmed Stetson. Tye's long, straight, dark-red hair dropped to his narrow shoulders clad in a loose-fitting linsey-woolsey tunic. He wore a single cartridge belt crisscrossed on his chest, and a stag-butted, hand-carved Colt angled for the cross-draw on his right hip. Scraggly whiskers, the butt of much brotherly and fatherly ribbing, drooped from his chin.

"You're surrounded!" bellowed Angus Buchanon from behind the rain barrel, above the continued yelling of the gut-shot deputy and Buck Fowler. "Drop them irons or die! I ain't gonna tell ya *one more time*!"

The deputies looked around at each other. They turned to Stillwell, who stood above the steps of his office porch, the cigar smoldering in his left hand, his right hand draped over the grips of his holstered Peacemaker. His face was a stony mask in which his dark eyes were set like two lumps of charcoal.

The gut-shot deputy's cries had been dwindling. Now they fell silent as he lay back in the street and shivered out his ghost. Fowler finally stopped bellowing as well. He turned his pain-racked gaze toward Stillwell, whom all the other deputies were staring at, awaiting orders.

The townsfolk had retreated to the boardwalks. Some had slipped inside the shops and saloons to avoid any lead that might be swapped. Those remaining on the boardwalks looked cautious, wary.

"Don't do it, Stillwell," Hunter said. "Tell 'em to drop their guns."

Stillwell glared straight across the street at the Buchanon patriarch, old Angus. He slid his gaze to Shep standing on the roof of the mercantile. From Shep he looked at young Tyrell lying atop the harness shop, aiming down the barrel of his cocked carbine, waiting.

Even from the ground near the wagon, Hunter could see a forked vein throbbing above the sheriff's nose. The man's jaws were set hard in mute fury, and his cheeks were mottled red.

Finally, stiffly, he lifted his hand from his Colt, leaving the hogleg in its holster. He thrust his hand forward, bunching his lips and wrinkling his nose as he pointed at Angus behind the rain barrel. "Kill those Rebel trash!"

A deputy near Hunter snapped his rifle to his shoulder, aiming toward Angus. He was rewarded with a third eye drilled through the dead center of his forehead. He was dead before he hit the ground.

"Ah, hell," Hunter muttered as the other deputies went to work, snapping rifles down from atop their shoulders or clawing six-shooters from their holsters, shuffling their feet, pivoting on their hips, and trying to draw beads on the rooftop Buchanons.

Three or four of the deputies might have gotten off shots, but it was mainly the three armed Buchanons who were popping caps. Orange flames lapped from the barrels of their long guns. Their bullets screeched through the air over the wagon to smash flesh and pulverize bones. It appeared to Hunter, looking on in mute horror, that every bullet his father and brothers hurled from their corresponding rooftops hit its target.

The deputies danced bizarre death jigs,

two almost hooking arms as though they were going to do-si-do together before they were thrown backward off their heels to hit the street in two dusty, bloody messes.

One man fell wounded and crawled for the safety of a wagon parked in front of the mercantile. Another bullet careened in from a rooftop to drill the back of his head. He plopped down to his face and belly three feet from the wagon's left front wheel.

"I'm done!" rose a man's shrill cry amidst the thunder. "I'm done! I'm done — ya hear? I'm done!"

Hunter turned to see the man standing over near the post office, thrusting his arms straight up in the air. Hunter thought his name was Stanley. Charlie Stanley, a wanted pistoleer from Texas. It was widely known that most of Stillwell's men had paper on them.

"I'm done!" Stanley bellowed at Angus. "Don't you shoot me!"

Angus gazed down the smoking maw of his Yellow-boy at the tall, lean deputy, who wore a filthy red bandanna around his neck and a black hat with a fresh hole in the crown. A flesh wound had drawn a red line across the outside of his left leg clad in gray denim.

Shep and Tyrell held their fire, staring

down at the deputy thrusting his hands in the air as though reaching for a ladder to heaven.

Stanley turned toward Stillwell, who was standing where he'd settled before the shooting had erupted. The sheriff's features were hard and pale. He held both hands straight down at his sides. His cigar smoldered where he'd dropped it on the step near his left boot.

"I'm done!" Stanley yelled at the sheriff. He glanced at Shep and Tye and then shifted his fear-bright gaze to Angus and yelled, "You Buchanons are pure mountain crazy!"

He ran over to where a mouse-brown dun stood tied to a hitchrail. He ripped the reins from the rail, clambered into the saddle, reined the horse into the street, turned it north, and put the steel to it. The horse whinnied shrilly and lunged off its rear hooves.

A gun roared behind Hunter. He whipped his head around to see Stillwell standing atop the porch of his office, extending his Colt straight out toward the fleeing deputy. The Colt bucked and roared three more times. The fleeing deputy screamed as he flew forward over his horse's pole.

The horse buck-kicked fearfully. The

deputy rolled down over the mount's right withers, hit the street, and rolled in a billowing dust cloud.

One of the dun's rear hooves clipped the man's head with a dull thud, and the horse continued galloping north, screaming. The deputy lay in a twisted, bloody pile in the sifting dust.

"Hold it, Stillwell!" Shep warned from the mercantile roof, aiming down his Henry's barrel at the sheriff.

He must have thought that Hunter would be Stillwell's next target, since Hunter was the nearest Buchanon. He'd been wrong. Stillwell glanced from Shep to Hunter. He stood glaring for a moment, mute with rage, then swung around, holstered his pistol, crossed the stoop, and disappeared inside his office, slamming the door behind him.

"Hunter!" Angus yelled as he rose from behind the rain barrel. "You all right, son?"

Hunter only vaguely heard him. He was looking around at the dead men lying in growing blood pools. The only deputy alive was Buck Fowler, who remained in the fetal position, writhing miserably, pressing his hands to his crotch and cursing under his breath. Hunter could smell the blood and the viscera of the dead men around him, the rotten-egg odor of cordite. He'd never wanted to smell that stench again.

Flames of rage began igniting again, rising up from the small of his back, as he turned toward the sheriff's office.

"Coward," he snarled through gritted teeth. "You coward, Stillwell!" he shouted. "This was your fight, Stillwell! You started it! Get out here an' finish it!"

He looked around. A Schofield revolver lay in the street beside one of the dead deputies. Hunter picked it up, wiped the blood, dust, and horse manure from its barrel, and opened the loading gate. Four pills remained in the wheel. That was enough.

"Hunter!" Angus bellowed behind him.

Ignoring the old man, Hunter strode with grim purpose toward Stillwell's office. He was halfway there when young Tye walked out from behind the harness shop.

"Hunter, what . . . where you . . . ?" He stopped and frowned curiously as Hunter mounted the steps of the sheriff's porch.

Hunter crossed the porch, tried the door. Locked.

Hunter stepped back and rammed his heavy left shoulder against the cottonwood door. It cracked down the middle but didn't open. Hunter stepped back again, and again he heaved his shoulder against the door. This time the door burst open in two halves, wood slivers flying from the frame, the locking bolt clattering onto the office's wooden floor.

Hunter stopped when he saw Stillwell standing in an open doorway before him — the doorway to the cellblock. The sheriff aimed his Colt straight out from his shoulder, bunching his lips in fury.

Hunter lurched back behind the building's front wall just as Stillwell's revolver roared once, twice, three times, the bullets hammering the inside wall opposite of where Hunter crouched, one slug screeching past him through the door to plunk into the street.

Hunter jammed the Schofield around the doorframe and fired into the office. His bullet flew wide as Stillwell gave a startled cry and ran from Hunter's right to his left, angling toward a glass window at the back of the room.

Hunter fired two more rounds, and then Stillwell dove through the window in a shower of screeching glass. Hunter bounded across the room. Through the broken glass, he saw Stillwell gain his feet and run straight out away from the office.

The cellblock was on the L-wing, to his right. Several prisoners, including a couple of females, laughed and jeered through their barred, glassless windows, one man shouting, "Stillwell, you yaller dog — I never knew you could run so fast!"

"Hey, Stillwell — where's the fire?" bellowed one of the females.

"It's in his drawers!" yelled another.

Another man said, "Look at Stillwell imitatin' a jackrabbit!"

Hunter poked the Schofield through the broken shards jutting around the window frame. He purposefully pulled his shot wide, not wanting to shoot even Stillwell in the back. He was just venting his spleen. His bullet plumed dirt just inches off Stillwell's hammering boots.

The sheriff bulled through some brush, leaped into a wash, and disappeared.

Behind him, the prisoners yelled and whistled, laughing raucously.

"Hey, Buchanon — that you?" one of them called.

Hunter slid his gaze to the third barred window from the cellblock's far end. "That you, Clancy?"

"Sure enough. Bring the key, will you?"

Hunter thought about it. Clancy was a good ole boy from the 'Bama hills, probably locked up for drunk and disorderly and ordered to pay a hefty fine merely because he was born in Dixie. Since there was no one to tend the jail, with the bulk of Still-well's deputies lying dead in the street and the other, Fowler, in no condition for anything but a long convalescence, it would have been a crime to keep prisoners locked in the cellblock.

Who knew where Stillwell had gone or whether he'd return? The man's pride had likely taken quite a hit.

Hunter took a key ring hanging from a ceiling support post and strode down the cellblock corridor. Prisoners to either side erupted in cheers, thrusting open hands through the bars. Hunter chose one large, scarred hand at random to offer the key to.

"Thanks, Buchanon!" said the man to whom the hand belonged — Rascal Willis, a burly ore driver who worked for Ludlow and Chaney at the King Solomon. "I owe ya a beer!" He looked badly hungover — his hair was matted and tangled, and both eyes were black and swollen from a recent brawl.

"Turn 'em all loose — will ya, Rascal?"

"Yeah, yeah, sure — hey, what happened out there in the street? We heard the shootin'!"

Hunter had already left the cellblock and was heading for the door hanging in pieces from its frame. He paused to lean down and rip up the Confederate flag that Stillwell had been using as a mud mat. He balled it up and shoved it into Stillwell's potbelly stove, giving the old guidon the proper disposal it deserved.

As he stepped out through the broken door, he heard one of the prisoners yell in the cellblock behind him, "I don't know for sure, boys, but I got me a feelin' ole Stillwell got a goodly dose of the Buchanon boys!"

The prisoners laughed and gave a raucous Rebel yell.

CHAPTER 7

Hunter dropped down the steps of the porch fronting Stillwell's office. His father, old Angus, and brother Shep waited in the street near the bottom of the steps.

Sixty-three years old, Angus was a leathery, sinewy old-timer with a full head of thick, coarse gray hair and a long bushy beard one or two shades darker than the hair hanging down from beneath his old Confederate campaign hat.

His eyes, set deep in sun-seared sockets, were the same frosty blue as Hunter's. He wore a buckskin shirt and canvas breeches held up with snakeskin galluses. A potbelly swelled the front of his shirt, and his shoulders owned a definite slouch.

Still, there was a rough-hewn ruggedness about the elder Buchanon, whose friends back home had called Reb. His left sleeve was rolled and pinned up close to the stump. A corncob pipe and canvas makings sack jutted from a breast pocket.

"Did you fix that badge-totin', green-horned devil?" he asked his middle son.

"No," Hunter said, stepping into the street before the two men facing him.

"You all right, Hunt?" Shep asked.

Two years Hunter's elder, at six-feet-three he was equal in height but with a goodly portion of excess tallow. Hunter was all muscle. Shep excelled at blacksmithing and gunsmithing, and had the roast-size hands and thick neck to show for it. He held his Henry repeater on his shoulders, and his left gloved hand was closed over the stag-butted grips of his Remington.

Shep moved up close to scrutinize Hunter's face. "They gave you a good working over, they did." He grinned suddenly, which was Shep's way, his brown eyes flashing a boyish glee. "They ain't in any condition to do it again."

Hunter didn't share in his older brother's easy nature. Especially when it came to killing. Hunter didn't hold it against him. Shep had missed out on the killing fields of the war, but he hadn't had it easy at home, tending the farm as well as seeing to young Tye and their ailing, bedridden mother, who'd died from consumption the year before Hunter and Angus had returned — a fact that still caused Angus to sob himself to sleep at night.

"Anna sent for you, I'd fathom," Hunter said.

"That girl's smarter'n a half dozen of you," Angus said, narrowing his eyes in reproof at his middle boy. "You don't deserve her, an' I never thought I'd say that about a Yankee girl."

"I'm sorry you had to come."

"Well, the point is we had to, little brother," Shep said, though there was nothing "little" about Hunter Buchanon. "If we hadn't, it'd be you lying out there instead of Stillwell's deputies."

"I know," Hunter said grudgingly, glancing at the dead men once more. Turning back to his father and Shep, he said, "This is only the start of trouble — I hope you both realize that."

"Trouble from where?" Angus said. "Hell, Stillwell's cut 'n' run, and his deputies are saddling golden clouds and sailin' off to the great beyond. All except Fowler, that is, an' he's a damn fool."

"Yeah, well, Stillwell's not dead, and there's more men from where these men came from." He glanced at the dead deputies. "Besides, Stillwell's got friends in high places."

He turned to look toward the King Solomon Mine office and diggings to the east. Graham Ludlow and Max Chaney had brought in Stillwell, who'd done a good job protecting their interests. They weren't likely going to take it sitting down that their Yankee sheriff had gotten his hat handed to him by four ex-Confederate misfits from the western Hills.

Especially when one of those misfits was courting Ludlow's daughter against the elder Ludlow's wishes.

"Pshaw — it'll all blow over in no time," Angus said with hollow optimism.

Hunter wasn't so sure about that.

Again, he looked at the dead men. The town sawbones, Dr. Norton Dahl, had come into the street with his black medical kit, probably having heard the crackle of gunfire from his office on the other side of town.

The thirtyish, somewhat bedraggled, bespectacled medico was now tending the cursing and grunting Buck Fowler, who was casting dark, threatening glances toward the three Buchanons standing out front of the sheriff's office. Meanwhile, the prisoners emerged from the cellblock, blinking against the sun and slapping Hunter on the back as they headed into the street to inspect the dead deputies before heading off for drinks

81

in the Tigerville saloons.

Hunter saw that Luke Chaney now lay in the street with the rest of Stillwell's men. After dumping Chaney unceremoniously into the dirt, Young Tye had taken the wagon over to one of the saloons that had ordered ale from Angus, and was offloading a couple of beer kegs. That's where the youngest Buchanon brother was now, accepting cash payment from the apron-clad Silver Dollar proprietor, Ralph Richmond.

"You shouldn't be goin' around unarmed, boy," Angus told Hunter now, gently but gravely, knowing they'd been over this ground before but hoping that after today his stubborn middle boy would listen to reason.

"It wouldn't have done me any good here, Pa."

"It would have given you a fighting chance!" Angus said, losing his temper. "You're as muleheaded as your mother was, and that's sayin' somethin'!"

"I know it is." Hunter walked over to the old man, several inches shorter than he, and planted a kiss on Angus's craggy, bearded cheek. "Thanks for saving my hide, though I know I don't deserve it."

Angus flushed and turned away, customarily embarrassed by any show of affection while also basking in it.

Hunter turned to Shep and repeated himself. "Thanks, brother."

"We didn't do it for you," Shep said, his eyes sparkling again with amusement. "We were worried what your girl would do to us if we . . ."

He let his voice trail off as the thudding hooves of a galloping horse sounded.

"Speak of the devil," Angus said as he turned to see Annabelle Ludlow galloping hell for leather down the middle of the main street, from the south.

She was approaching at a fast clip atop her buckskin, Ivanhoe, her dark red hair bouncing on her shoulders, eyes wide and fearful. When she got close to the dead men lying sprawled in the street fronting the jailhouse, she drew the buckskin to a skidding halt and looked around, surveying the scene of battle, likely wondering if Hunter himself lay among the dead.

When she swung her head toward the jailhouse, her green eyes showed instant relief. Hunter stepped around his father and Shep, and walked over to where Anna sat astride the sweaty, dusty Ivan.

"Oh, Hunter," she said softly. Her expression changed to one of guilt, and she winced a little, turning her mouth corners down.

"Are you . . . angry?"

"At you?" he said. "How could that be? You saved my ornery hide."

She looked at the dead men again and gave a shudder of revulsion. "This is my fault."

"Hell, no, it ain't," Hunter said. "It's Chaney's fault. And Stillwell's. None of these men needed to die here today. Stillwell's a damn fool, and he should be among them."

Annabelle swung down from her saddle. She winced again as she walked up close to Hunter, who towered over her, and stared up into his face.

Gently, she touched fingers to his battered cheeks. "They gave you a good working over, didn't they?"

"Looks worse than it is."

"You need some raw meat for that eye, salve for your lips."

"Later."

Hunter walked over to where his father's and brothers' horses were tied to a hitchrail in a break between the mercantile store and a ladies' dress shop. He snagged the reins of Tyrell's Appaloosa from the rack and swung up into the saddle.

"Pa, have Tye drive the wagon home, will ya?" he said as he galloped past his father and brother, heading back toward Annabelle. "I'm gonna borrow his hoss!"

"All right," Angus said, staring after him speculatively. "You don't be late for supper now, son," he called with irony. "Be dark soon!"

"Come on," Hunter said to Annabelle, who scowled up at him curiously.

"Where we going?" she asked.

"I got somethin' to show you."

"I've already seen it," Annabelle said as she swung up onto the buckskin's back, her eyes flashing coquettishly. "And I was right impressed."

Hunter grinned and snorted. He turned the Appy south.

Annabelle followed him at a wild gallop out of Tigerville and into the countryside beyond. Bobby Lee loped out from the break between buildings he'd been soothing his nerves in, and followed them, a gray-brown ghost crackling through the brush along the trail.

A half hour later, after by turns walking and trotting their horses as the afternoon sunlight waned, casting long shadows out from the pine-stippled hogbacks rising around them, Hunter and Annabelle reined their horses to a halt on the third of three consecutively higher benches rising just north of the main trail.

Hunter stared up past yet a higher fourth bench toward a small, weathered log prospector's cabin hunkered at the base of a limestone ridge that resembled a giant pileup of large boulders fused together by ancient lava. Brush and a few hardy trees grew out of the clefts and furrows between the rocks that jutted two hundred feet toward the gradually darkening sky.

The cabin was on open government range; Hunter had stumbled upon it unexpectedly several years ago while out hunting. The cabin had probably been built by one of the first white prospectors to illegally hunt for gold in the Black Hills.

Though old, it was still relatively weather-tight and supplied with a working sheet-iron stone, a table and a few chairs, shelves for food, and a comfortable cot. Hunter figured the prospector who'd built the structure had abandoned it when he'd either been chased out of the Hills by the Sioux or he'd mined all the gold out of the mountain behind it.

Hunter and Annabelle had put the cabin to good use after they'd met not far from here, when they'd both been out riding in the Hills, looking for game, and their love had blossomed. They often met here secretly, away from the prying eyes of Annabelle's father and her foppish brother, Cass, to spend a long afternoon now and then in the best way known to both man and beast — making love.

The cabin was their trysting place, known only to them, and their love play was what Annabelle was obviously thinking about now as she turned a devilish, glittery-eyed grin to Hunter and said, "Well, I guess I know what you have on your mind, Hunter Buchanon!"

"I'll do you one better than that!" Hunter batted heels against the Appy's ribs and galloped on up the incline through pines and firs and a few scattered aspens.

"What could be better than that?" Anna called behind him, laughing.

Hunter galloped around behind the cabin and over to the base of the rocky ridge flanking it and which now threw thick, purple shade over the cabin and the forested bench around it. In the valley below the cabin and through which the trail from Tigerville snaked, appearing like a thin cream ribbon from this vantage, sunlight lay like molten copper in a long, deep mold.

As Anna galloped up behind him, Hunter swung down from the saddle and dropped the Appy's reins.

"Follow me!"

"I've *been* following you," the girl said, stepping down from her buckskin's back. "Where are we going?"

Hunter leaped onto a narrow trail that twisted around the boulders comprising the ridge, steeply climbing. "Almost there!"

He climbed maybe twenty yards up the ridge, angling sharply to his right. He stopped at a thick pile of brush. Many rocks of all shapes and sizes were strewn down the steep slope, making a large pile at the bottom around and over which small trees and more brush grew, nearly concealing the old prospector's mine tailings.

Hunter quickly removed the brush that he'd piled against the slope until the mine portal lay revealed before him. He'd piled the brush there to conceal the mine entrance from anyone else snooping around the cabin.

"What are you doing, Hunter?" Annabelle asked, deeply puzzled but also amused.

"Come on!"

"Where?"

"In here!"

Annabelle stopped and stared up at the splintery cross- and side-beams of the portal, hand-adzed from pine logs. The right side-beam was cracked down the middle and the upper beam sagged on that side.

Anna punched the side-beam with the back of her right hand. "Are you sure this will hold? Looks little more substantial than a matchstick!"

"Ah, hell," Hunter said, punching the side-beam himself and taking Annabelle's hand. "That'll be there for the next hundred years. Come on!"

He'd just started to draw her into the mine when a chortling wail sounded. Annabelle gasped. She and Hunter turned to see Bobby Lee sitting on the slope below the mine, snout in the air, his bushy gray tail curled around him.

Again, the coyote yammered.

"What is it, Bobby?" Hunter called.

"Someone's out there," Annabelle said uneasily. "Someone must have followed us out from town."

Hunter stepped out of the mine and looked around. He shrugged. "I don't see anyone. I kept a pretty close eye on our back trail too." He paused, looked around again.

Bobby Lee stared at him ambiguously, moaning in his throat.

"He's just nervous from all the shooting in town." Hunter took Annabelle's hand

again, drew her into the mine. "He'll let us
know if there's real trouble. Come on."

CHAPTER 8

As Hunter led Annabelle down the dark tunnel that smelled of mud and stone, Anna looked around at the crudely chipped walls and ceiling, braced by occasional wood supports like the portal, and made a face. "Aren't there bats in here?"

"Oh, a few. Likely still asleep. If we move quiet-like, we won't wake 'em." Hunter squeezed her hand reassuringly. "Come on. Keep close. It's only dark for a little ways."

Hunter was tall enough that he had to remove his hat and crouch to keep his head from scraping the ceiling. Slowly but with resolute purpose, he strode forward into the darkness, holding Annabelle's hand in his left hand, his hat in his right. The air was cooler in here, dank and rife with the stench of mushrooms and bat guano.

"Stinks," Anna said, following on his heels, their feet occasionally colliding.

"You'll forget about the smell in a minute."

"I doubt it."

"Trust me."

She gave a snort but also squeezed his hand that clutched hers, letting him know that she did, in no uncertain terms, trust him.

Maybe thirty feet ahead, a shaft of dim light angled down from the ceiling. Hunter moved toward it, occasionally stumbling over a rock that had fallen from above or out of one of the walls, between the bracing pine timbers. When he came to where the light spread a murky, watery pool onto the cave floor, he stopped.

Anna was so close that she ran into him, giving a little gasp.

"End of the trail?" she asked dryly.

"End of the trail."

Hunter released Annabelle's hand and turned to the wall on his right. The light came from a cleft running clear up through the ceiling to the top of the mountain. The original prospector had probably used it as an airshaft. The light made visible several rocks set low in the cave wall.

Hunter dropped to a knee, wrapped both hands around one of the rocks, and, bunching his lips with effort, pulled it out of the wall. When it slid free he set it down, then removed two more rocks roughly the size of a wheel hub, and also set them down on the cave floor.

"Now I just have to hope no rattlesnakes slithered into my hole while I've been away," Hunter said, turning sideways to the hole and thrusting his left hand inside.

"Hunter . . ." Anna said cautiously.

"Oh!" he cried, snapping his mouth and eyes wide in mock horror. "One's got me! It's got me!"

Anna gave a startled scream, then slapped his shoulder. "You idiot! I hope it fills you full of poison!"

Hunter gave a raking, snorting laugh and pulled his arm out of the hole. His hand was wrapped around the neck of a burlap pouch roughly the size of a ten-pound bag of sugar.

"What on earth . . . ?" Annabelle said.

"Hold on."

Hunter set the pouch down against the base of the cave wall and reached into the hole three more times, pulling out three more burlap pouches around the same size as the first one. He looked at Annabelle, who knelt beside him, sliding her curious gaze between the pouches and Hunter.

Hunter smiled enticingly, then picked up

one of the pouches and scuttled over to where the light slanted directly into the cave from above. "Come here."

Anna scuttled over to him. She knelt just across from him, on the other side of the shaft of weakening, pale-salmon light.

"What's in those?" she asked in a voice hushed with awe, as though she had already anticipated the answer.

Hunter grinned at her again, then untied the rawhide binding the neck of one of the bags. He dropped the hide, opened the bag, and dipped a hand inside. He pulled it out, opened it palm up.

Gold dust glittered in the light angling down through the shaft.

Annabelle gasped. She stared wide-eyed up at him, her lower jaw hanging, the gold dancing in her eyes. "Is that . . . is that *pure gold*?"

"About as pure as it comes, Annabelle."

"Where did you get it? Did you find it here in the mine?" She glanced around the tunnel.

"I panned it."

"What?"

"I panned it out of a wash about a mile from here. An underground spring busted out the side of a ridge. Blasted gold out with it, for almost two hundred yards along the wash. I found it when I was helping Kinch Early brush-pop strays a couple of falls ago." Early was a neighbor to the south of the 4-Box-B Ranch whom Hunter occasionally hired out to when Kinch, who also hailed from Dixie, was shorthanded. Most men in the Hills preferred to look for El Dorado than wet-nurse beef on the hoof, so it was often hard for ranchers to find capable hands.

"I've been panning it a couple of days a week, mostly at night after ranch chores and supper. This is what I got so far. Pa an' the boys think me an' Bobby Lee are just out running around the mountains, looking for artifacts like old arrowheads an' such, like I used to do back home . . . before the war. I haven't told 'em. Shep goes to town and gets liquored up from time to time . . . shoots his mouth off."

"How much is there?"

"A little over thirty thousand worth, I 'spect, figuring on the current rate. Maybe closer to forty by now."

Annabelle stared at him, her lower jaw hanging. "Why didn't you tell me?"

Again, Hunter grinned. "It's our secret, Anna — yours an' mine."

She frowned. "What do you mean — *our* secret?"

"This gold's our stake, Anna." Hunter paused, licked his lips, then dropped the gold back into the sack. "There's a ranch for sale west of the 4-Box-B. It's been for sale a couple years now. I know the man selling. He's having trouble finding a buyer because everyone around here is more interested in gold than rangeland, cattle, and hosses. But the man, Orrin Johnson, has a weak ticker, an' he just wants to go back down to Texas and retire.

"Pa and the boys an' me have trapped broncs on his land. It's good range — stirrup-high brome and needle grass, good water, nice high ground for the summer, a spring-fed creek with plenty of cottonwoods for winter cover, and a roomy lodge house with a big, fieldstone hearth. It sits high on the top of a low bluff. You can see for miles in every direction. Four bedrooms upstairs. A kitchen and parlor I'd get lost in! They're both one big room with heavy wood an' leather furniture an' such. Orrin an' his sons — all four of whom ran off to be either lawmen or outlaws — built most of it themselves — back when they weren't fightin' Injuns. I figure we could run a whole passel of young'uns in the upper story, an' . . . ." Hunter let his voice trail off. "Anna — are . . . are you *crying*?"

He reached up and brushed a tear from her cheek with his thumb.

Anna sniffed and, eyes averted, brushed her hand across her nose. She sobbed.

"Anna, I don't understand . . . what's wrong? Don't you . . ." The thought was almost too painful to be considered. "Don't you want to marry me?"

Anna looked up at him, tears flooding her eyes. "Hunter, don't you know by now you don't need to buy my love — with gold or anything else? I love you, you big galoot. I don't care how rich or poor you are!"

"Well . . . I . . . I just thought . . . you know, considering how you were raised . . ."

"In spite of how I was raised, I could live very happily for the rest of my life in that old, mouse-infested cabin with you. I could raise a whole passel of your boys an' girls there, and die there, and be just as happy as I would be in that big ranch house you just described."

Hunter shrugged, smiled crookedly. "Well . . . this'd make everything a whole lot easier, though — don't you think?"

Anna laughed through her tears and threw herself into his arms, wrapping her arms around his thick neck.

"So . . . you'll marry me?"

"Of course, I'll marry you!" She pulled

her face away and beamed up at him, placing her hands on either side of his face. "I was *born* to marry you, Hunter Buchanon. I will be proud to be your wife and bear your children. But . . ." She frowned, shaking her head. "Why now?"

"Because of the trouble, I reckon. I reckon I just realized how short life can be. I also realized that I need to get farther away from Tigerville. Johnson's ranch is twenty miles west of the 4-Box-B. Our supply town would be Roseville. We wouldn't have to have any more dealings with Tigerville, but I'd still be close enough to the 4-Box-B to help Pa and my brothers out, if they need it."

Anna kissed him, then smiled up at him once more, running her fingers through the sweat-damp blond hair curling behind his ears. "Sounds like a plan. Why wait?"

"What about your pa?"

Annabelle sighed. "He's not going to like it. You know he wants me to marry Kenneth Earnshaw. I told him I wouldn't, and I guess we're at a Mexican standoff, as the saying goes. But I'll tell him tonight that I'm going to be your wife, and he's just going to have to get used to the idea.

"He will, I think. In time, he'll get used to it, come to accept it. I'm his only daughter, and he wants grandchildren, after all. I doubt Cass will be getting married any time soon, though I wouldn't doubt it a bit if, knowing how Cass likes to sow his seed, that my father has a few — or more than a few — grandchildren running around these hills. Born to several different mothers, no doubt. Most of the sporting variety."

Cass Ludlow was known throughout the Hills as a firebrand and ladies' man. Clad in gaudy Spanish-cut clothes, he gambled and rode through the Hills displaying his gun prowess. Having been born with a silver spoon in his mouth, he'd never held an honest job.

It was said that he also rode the long coulees, holding up stagecoaches and rustling beef — mostly just for fun and because he liked the camaraderie of other young men who fancied themselves owlhoots — but he'd never been arrested. That was probably due to the fact that he was Graham Ludlow's son, and no one wanted to make accusations they might suffer for. Ludlow had a good many hardtails riding for him, and they, like Stillwell, had always protected the mine owner's interests, whether they were business or personal interests.

Or a little of each.

"Right," Hunter said. "Why wait? Let's meet here tomorrow. Say, around noon? I'll leave the gold here 'til then. It's safe here, and it's close to the Cheyenne trail. We'll ride down to Cheyenne and exchange the dust for silver certificates . . . and get hitched. We'll take our time riding, sleeping out under the stars."

He wasn't too worried about Stillwell gunning for his father and brothers at the 4-Box-B. He had a feeling that while he might not have seen the last of Frank Stillwell, he'd seen the last of him for a good long time. It would take months or longer for the lawman-for-hire to form another small army like the ones he tended to have backing his play.

Besides, after Stillwell's display of cowardice, Hunter wasn't sure he'd find any more men willing to throw in with him.

Hunter hadn't realized before what a coward the man was. He'd no doubt try to exact his revenge, and when he did, Hunter would be standing with his father and brothers against him. They'd be ready.

"Noon tomorrow," Annabelle said, throwing herself into Hunter's arms once more, kissing him long and deep. She pulled away and stared gravely into his eyes. Her voice was soft, warm, intimate. "But first . . . I think we should celebrate with a visit to the cabin."

Hunter looked at the sumptuously beautiful girl before him . . . this girl who'd promised to spend the rest of her life with him . . . and he felt a warm stirring low in his belly. He cleared a knot of lust from his throat. "I couldn't agree more . . . Mrs. Buchanon."

"Oh, I like the sound of that," she said, rising, taking his hand and lightly raking her fingers across his palm.

CHAPTER 9

Stillwell bulled through the brush behind the sheriff's office, thorns ripping the sleeves of his black frock coat, and fell headlong into the dry wash tracing a jagged course through the heart of Tigerville.

He rolled wildly, groaning, gasping, dropping his pistol, and smacking his head on a rock as he hit the wash's dry, sandy bed. He could still feel the menacing nudge of the last bullet Buchanon had slung at him, which had nipped the edge of his left boot heel.

He could still hear the mocking laughter and the jeering howls of his prisoners.

He knew the wash ran along behind his office, but in his haste — in his terror — he'd forgotten about everything except his deputies lying dead in the street behind him, and the savage look on Hunter Buchanon's face as the big ex-Confederate had busted into his office like a blood-hungry

102

grizzly out to tear him limb from limb and clean his bones.

Stillwell had never known such fear. It had possessed him like some demon out of Indian legend. It had been as though he were watching some cowardly stranger run screaming across his office and hurl himself through the window in the rear wall, then scramble madly to his feet and sprint off for the safety of the wash while his prisoners howled and yipped like a pack of moon-crazed coyotes behind him.

Stillwell sat up, leaned back against the cutbank.

Buchanon . . .

Remembering that unhinged look in the Confederate's eyes, Stillwell scrambled back up the cutbank and edged a look over the top. He shot his frightened gaze through the brush back toward the rear of his office from which the prisoners' yells were still sounding. He expected to see the big South-erner striding toward him, a pistol in his hand, that kill-crazy fire in hiseyes.

Thankfully, the yard behind the jailhouse was empty. Buchanon was still inside.

Stillwell lowered his head. He had to catch his breath. His heart hammered insanely against his breastbone. He was bathed in sweat. Fear sweat.

Christ!

For some reason, he became aware that he wasn't wearing his hat. He felt naked without it. Naked in his fear. He peered down the slope. No sign of the felt topper. He looked through the brush toward his office again.

The hat lay in the yard outside his office, amidst the glass from the window peppering the sage and tufts of buck brush. Amidst the glass he'd broken out of the window when he'd fled. Fled like the most cowardly of soldiers on the field of battle.

The hat lay there, crown up, tilting off a sage plant, taunting him, jeering him every bit as loudly as the prisoners yelling through the barred windows of the cellblock.

Stillwell cursed and crawled back into the ravine. He was like a whipped, chicken-thieving dog. Fear was still alive inside him. He couldn't deny it. It wouldn't budge.

He shook his head, trying to clear the cobwebs, the terror, and looked around for his Colt. It lay beside a rock, half covered with dirt. He picked it up, brushed if off. His hands were shaking. He cursed his hands, the demon fear inside him, and opened the revolver's loading gate. He shook out the spent cartridges and replaced them with fresh from his shell belt.

Having a fully loaded weapon made him feel a little better. Not much but a little.

He glanced up toward the lip of the wash. The prisoners had fallen silent.

He considered his next move.

Maybe he should go back up there, confront Buchanon, the man's father, and two brothers . . .

"No," Stillwell said aloud, his heart quickening again, cold fear spurting through his veins, oozing out his pores. "No, no . . . no."

The Buchanons could wait. He had to compose himself. He had to rid himself of the fear that was a living beast inside him. When it was gone and he'd returned to the man he knew himself to be, then he could sit down and think out a plan to exact his revenge and reclaim his dignity.

What he needed now was a drink.

He glanced once more toward the lip of the wash and then slid the pistol into its holster. He trudged heavily down the wash to the south. When he'd followed a bend to the east, he climbed up out of the wash and shambled along a path that skirted an abandoned prospector's cabin. He walked straight south through the sage and scattered bits of trash. Wood frame houses, stock pens, shanties, and whores' cribs slid past on both sides of the horse- and foot-path.

The Gypsy tarot card reader, Madame Marcollini, stood outside her wood-framed tent, smoking an opium pipe. She was a round-bodied Italian with a prune-like face gaudied up with too much lipstick and rouge, her thick, black hair swept back under a purple turban trimmed with an ostrich feather.

Wearing a dress of dyed sackcloth and fur-trimmed slippers, she leaned against her tent's doorframe, drawing on the long, slender pipe, then exhaling slowly, dreamily. The cloying odor of the midnight oil reached Stillwell's nose, and he wrinkled his nostrils against it.

On a low table by the door lounged a cat with golden eyes and long, charcoal fur.

"Care for a reading, Sheriff?" the Gypsy asked.

"Go to hell, you old devil," Stillwell said, and continued trudging through the sage, toward a line of large business buildings looming straight ahead, their backsides facing him, abutted with piles of split firewood.

Behind him, the Gypsy laughed very quietly and raspily as though in collusion with the dark demon inside of the sheriff himself.

Stillwell made his way over to the rear of the largest hotel in town — the Dakota Territorial — in which he kept a room. Since the hotel was on the opposite end of town from the jailhouse, he hoped that no one here had yet gotten word about the shootout. If you could call it that.

It had been a bloody massacre. One in which Stillwell had taken no part except to back-shoot one of his own fleeing deputies. Otherwise, he'd run.

Humiliation burned inside his head as he entered through one of the large, barrack-like structure's two rear doors. This door opened into one side of the large kitchen in which two black cooks and one old Sioux cook clad in white smocks and chef's hats were tending bubbling pots and kneading biscuit dough. They glanced at Stillwell with dull-eyed interest and then resumed their work, indicating that they were probably ignorant of the festivities on the other end of town.

Relief eased some of the tension that made his shoulders ache. So far, so good.

He pushed through the swinging door into a hall that extended past the main, carpeted stairs rising to the hotel's second and third floors. Ahead was the hotel's large, well-appointed saloon with its heavy, round wooden tables, a gambling layout to one side, and a large, ornate horseshoe bar coming up on Stillwell's left.

As he'd both hoped and expected, the saloon was sparsely populated this time of the day. Only a couple of tables were occupied — maybe eight men total — and they appeared deeply involved in conversations that had nothing to do with the massacre. At least, they didn't seem to be talking about Stillwell. A couple of men glanced toward the sheriff, but they were fleeting glances. They did not stare.

That relieved Stillwell a little as well. He wouldn't linger here. He just wanted to get up to his room. First things first.

He turned to the bar. Hank Mitchum was just coming around from the far side of the mirrored island bar with a crate of liquor bottles in his big, fat hands, his puffy face flushed from exertion. Now the bartender stopped and stared at Stillwell in surprise.

"Frank!"

Mitchum knew. Stillwell's pulse quickened.

"Bottle, Hank. The usual. Then I want you to do me a favor."

Mitchum just stood at the end of the mirrored island, gazing at Stillwell with concern and . . . something else. What? Amusement?

Was that mockery building slowly in the beefy bartender's dark-blue eyes?

"Jesus, Frank, I heard about —"

"Shut up!" Stillwell glanced behind him to make sure no one at the occupied two tables was listening. He hardened his jaws as he leaned forward and glowered at Mitchum. "A bottle, Hank. The usual. The good stuff."

"All right, Frank. All right."

As Mitchum set his crate on the back bar counter and tramped off in search of Stillwell's preferred coffin varnish, Stillwell grabbed a notepad and a stubby pencil from off the bar to his left, and slid it toward him. He flipped through to a clean leaf, quickly scribbled a note, ripped it out of the pad, and turned it facedown atop the bar.

He brushed his fist across his nose, glanced behind him once more. He'd caught one of the men staring at him. The man sat at a table not far from the large, open arched doorway to the hotel lobby. Four others sat at the same table. The man in question was big and broad shouldered, with curly red hair, a thick red neck, and arms like those of an ape.

As his gaze met Stillwell's, he turned his head quickly away and rejoined the conversation at his table.

Stillwell narrowed his eyes at him, suspicious. Slowly, anger kindled in him. It was a good feeling. It shoved away a little of the fear that still had his knees feeling like mud.

The man who'd been staring at him — his name was Willie Jackson, a mule skinner and part-time shotgun guard for the Cheyenne to Deadwood Line — glanced at Stillwell out of the corner of his left eye. Jackson's pitted, sunburned cheeks flushed slightly as he quickly returned his gaze to the others at his table. He leaned forward to say something to the man sitting directly across from him, and both men laughed quietly.

"Here you go," Mitchum told Stillwell, setting a fresh bottle of Maryland rye onto the bar and prying up the cork with a jack-knife. "Fresh bottle, just came in."

"Put it on my tab," Stillwell said, grabbing the bottle as well as a glass off a near pyramid. He turned the glass up and carelessly splashed whiskey into it, overfilling it so that a good bit of the rye washed over the sides.

"What the hell happened out there, Frank?" Mitchum asked. "I heard that all of your —"

Stillwell had tossed back half of the whiskey. Now he glared sidelong at Mitchum, who stood regarding him with his mouth open, his words cut off in mid-sentence, the question lingering in his eyes.

The sheriff slid the scrawled note over to the barman. "Take that over the Western Union office. Have the telegrapher send it out pronto. You can add that to my tab too."

Mitchum turned the note faceup and then scowled up at Stillwell, shocked. *"Dakota Jack?"*

"I didn't say you could read it, Hank. I told you to send it." Stillwell threw back the last of his rye, then grabbed the bottle off the bar and stuffed it into his coat pocket. "When you get back, tell Jane to haul water up to my room. I want a bath." Jane Campbell was the pretty young saloon girl and dancer Stillwell had staked a claim to.

"A *bath?*" Mitchum looked at him as though he'd suddenly grown a second head. *"Now?* Your men are layin' dead out in — !"

"Yes, now!" Fury exploding in Stillwell, he grabbed the bartender by his shirt collar, jerked the man's large, beefy head toward him. "A bath, goddamnit, Hank!" the sheriff shouted, his words echoing around the cavern-like room. "Why are you still here? I thought I sent you over to the Western Union office!"

He gave the barman a violent shove.

Mitchum staggered backward, red faced. He got his feet settled, then straightened his collar and stared indignantly across the bar at Stillwell.

The sheriff was suddenly, dreadfully aware that silence had filled the saloon. He looked into the back bar mirror. All heads in the room were turned toward him.

The burn of embarrassment rose in him.

Quickly, stumbling a little over his own feet, he moved away from the bar. He kept his eyes from the men sitting at the two tables. Keeping his head down, wanting to run as fast as he could, he compelled himself to take one step at a time as he slowly climbed the stars, brushing his left hand across the banister. He had his right hand on the bottle in his coat pocket.

God, how I need another drink!

Silence welled from below and behind him until a snickering voice said, ". . . ran like a donkey with its tail on fire!"

Men snorted their laughter.

Halfway up the stairs, Stillwell stopped.

He could hear his heart beating in his ears.

Slowly, he turned to face the room.

The snickering stopped. The men who'd been laughing at the table near the doorway to the lobby glanced uncomfortably toward Stillwell. They cleared their throats, brushed fists across their mouths or noses, sipped their beers, drew nervously on cigars or cigarettes.

Stillwell dropped back down the stairs. His held his chin down. His eyes were dark as coals under his high, bulging forehead. He crossed the room slowly and stopped at the table near the door.

All five men sitting there stared up at him now. The laughter was gone from their eyes. It had been replaced by incredulity tossed with a goodly portion of apprehension. All eyes flicked toward the big, handsome Colt Peacemaker residing on the sheriff's right thigh and over the ivory handle on which his right hand was draped.

Willie Jackson sat with his back to Stillwell, but he had his head turned and was looking up at Stillwell now, a half-smoked Indian Kid cigar smoldering between the thumb and index finger of his right hand. His thick lips set inside a tangled, dark red beard twitched an edgy, cowering smile.

No one at either table now said anything. All eyes were on Stillwell. Mitchum remained behind the bar, staring warily toward Stillwell and the five men at the table near the lobby.

Stillwell looked at Jackson staring up at

him with drink-glassy eyes. "What's so funny?"

"What, uh . . . what's that?" Jackson said.

"I asked what's funny?"

Jackson glanced at the man sitting directly across from him — Bernard Wise, a crony of Jackson's who worked as a farrier for the stage line but also sold meat to local eateries from game he shot in the Hills.

Jackson turned his head to stare back up at Stillwell. A single sweat bead trickled into his beard.

He hiked his thick left shoulder. "Noth-nothin', Frank."

"Sheriff Stillwell."

"Wh-what's that?"

"It's Sheriff Stillwell."

"Yeah, right — Sheriff Stillwell."

"I'm going to ask you again," Stillwell said, keeping his voice very low and taut. "What's so funny?"

Jackson's lips twitched another nervous smile. "Like I said . . . *Sheriff Stillwell . . .* nothin's funny."

"Look, Frank," Bernard Wise said, rising from his chair, hands up, palms out, "you got no truck with us. We was just talkin' about what happened down the street."

"That's all we was talkin' about, Frank," Jackson said, slowly, carefully. "Just chewin' over the news is . . . *wait, wait, hold on, Frank!*"

Jackson leaped up out of his chair.

Stillwell had clawed his .45 from its holster and raked the hammer back.

"I told you the name's Sheriff Stillwell, you big, ugly, filthy son of a mule!" The big Colt bucked in the sheriff's hand, lapping orange flames across the table.

The Colt roared three times, all three bullets plowing into Jackson's chest and sending the man stumbling backward, grunting and screaming as blood spewed out the exit wounds in his back. He fell backward over a table behind him, rolled across it, smearing blood across its surface, and dropped to the floor with a heavy thud on the table's other side.

Bernard Wise cursed shrilly as he reached for the old Remington holstered on his right hip.

He didn't get the Remington clear of its holster before Stillwell emptied his big Colt into Wise's chest from point-blank range. The roaring hogleg was so close to Wise that the man's shirt caught on fire.

As Wise twisted around and flew backward onto the table he'd been sitting at, and from which the other men scrambled, heading out the door, flames engulfed him, licking up from his chest and filling the room with fetid smoke.

"Good God!" Mitchum bellowed.

The barman came running out from behind the bar, wielding a bar towel. He brushed past Stillwell to bat the towel at the chest of Bernard Wise, who lay back down atop the table, on cards and shot glasses and scrip and specie, twitching as he died.

"Jesus, Frank — what's got into you?" Mitchum cried, dousing the last of the flames with the towel and wrinkling his nose at the stench of cordite and burning flesh and blood. "You're gonna burn down my place an' half the town!"

"Just wanted to make myself clear," Stillwell said, backing away from Mitchum and the men he'd just taught lessons they'd never forget. *Don't mess with Frank Stillwell.* He glanced at the men at the other table. All stared at him, frightened and speechless.

Stillwell kept backing toward the stairs. "The name's Sheriff Stillwell. No one best forget that."

Stillwell dropped the smoking Colt back into its holster, swung around, placed his hand on the bottle in his coat, and headed up the stairs.

CHAPTER 10

Annabelle Ludlow trotted the buckskin along a bend in the two-track trail northeast of Tigerville. It was good and dark, the sky sprinkled with stars, and she was late getting home to supper.

An owl hooted in the pine-studded hills rising darkly on her left, but it wasn't the owl that caused her to pull back on the buckskin's reins. When the horse stopped, Annabelle curveted the mount and swung her head around to stare along her back trail.

She'd heard something. She'd heard it before, roughly fifteen minutes ago, after she'd skirted the town of Tigerville and had swung the buckskin onto the trail to the Broken Heart, her father's ranch. She wasn't sure what the sound had been then or now, but it had sounded strange. Unnatural. Not a sound made by any forest creature.

It came again now very faintly — the soft clink of a spur or possibly a bridle chain. It hadn't originated along the trail behind her but on a hill to the north of the trail, on her right now as she looked back.

Annabelle's heart quickened. "Hello?"

Nothing. Just the sound of the slight breeze scratching branches together and brushing the tall, tawny grass growing thick along the shoulders of the haystack buttes.

Very faintly, a horse blew from the same direction from which the other sound had come.

The buckskin looked back and gave a shrill whinny, shaking its head and rattling its own bit and bridle chain.

"Easy, boy, easy," Annabelle said, patting Ivan's withers reassuringly, though she herself was feeling a good bit of apprehension.

She looked up the hill on her right and called, "Is someone there?"

Still nothing. Chicken flesh rose along Anna's arms and across her shoulders, and it wasn't because of the chill that had descended over the Hills soon after the sun had set. She felt as though someone were watching her, staring at her from the concealment of the darkness shrouding the near butte.

"Who's there?" Anna called, putting some steel in her voice now.

Again, nothing.

But she could feel those eyes on her. Ogling her.

Suddenly, a horse whinnied. A shadow moved atop the hill. The shadow separated from the hill itself and the tall pines peppering it. The shadow took the shape of a horse and rider.

The horse reared, lunging up off its front hooves, which it clawed at the sky. It whinnied again, and its eyes shone blue with reflected starlight while the rest of the mount, including its rider, remained in the concealment of silhouette.

The horse dropped its front hooves back to the ground. The rider reined it sharply to the right, away from Anna and the buckskin. The horse galloped off across the top of the bluff and disappeared down the other side, the thudding of its hooves fading gradually until the girl could hear only the natural night sounds of the forested mountains once more.

Annabelle's heart raced, skipping beats.

Who on earth . . . ?

She pointed the buckskin up the trail and batted her heels against its flanks. The horse was obviously as chilled by the shadow rider as Anna herself had been. Ivan shot straight up the trail, pinning his ears back. Knowing his own way home, he automatically swung off the main trail onto the secondary one, which led to the ranch yard, and galloped up and over the last hill.

Beyond Anna lay the lodge of her father's Broken Heart Ranch halfway up the distant, low opposite hill, two hundred yards beyond. The sprawling house's lamplit windows showed soft umber glows in the heavy darkness, as did the small windows of the bunkhouse down the hill to its left.

The bunkhouse sat near the hay and stock barns, corrals and other outbuildings, including a blacksmith shop, springhouse, and summer kitchen — all shadowy figures in the night. The lowing of cattle sounded from the surrounding hills, and the cool night air was rife with the aroma of summer-cured hay and the not unpleasant smell of cow and horse dung. At least, such smells were not unpleasant to Annabelle Ludlow, who'd been born and raised on the Broken Heart and who'd been riding horseback since she was five years old, having taken to horses the way "lambs take to their mother's tit," as her father once put it.

The buckskin galloped under the ranch portal whose wooden crossbar bore the

Broken Heart brand as well as the Ludlow name. When she'd halted the sweaty, blowing horse at one of the stock barns, Annabelle turned the buckskin over to one of the two Mexican hostlers still working in the barn and adjoining corral by the soft glow of two railroad lanterns.

"Give him plenty of oats, will you, Carlos?" Annabelle said, patting Ivan's long, sleek snout, then pressing her lips to it. "He's had a long day."

Ivan switched his tail affectionately.

"Sí, señorita," the hostler said, leading the horse away.

Anna shook her hair out from her collar and headed along the path toward the house, removing her fringed riding gloves. Her mind was still on the shadow rider who'd spooked her. She stopped and turned back to the hostler.

"Carlos?"

The man, who'd just led the horse up the ramp and through the barn's large double doors, turned back to Anna, he and the horse now silhouetted by the flickering lamplight behind them. The second hostler was forking out a stall, pitching the hay and dung into a large wooden wheelbarrow.

"Are any of the hands still out on the range?"

Carlos shrugged a slender shoulder. "No, I don't think so, señorita. You know how the cook's triangle brings them all in, and none have left since supper." The hostler's white teeth shone in the darkness. "None that I know of, anyway, and I've been here all night."

"Okay," Annabelle said. *"Gracias, Carlos."*

She swung around and started again for the main lodge that sprawled atop the hill to the southeast. She'd wondered if the shadow rider had been one of the Broken Heart hands. For several years, ever since she'd started filling out her riding pants and blouses, she'd been aware of the lingering scrutiny of her father's men.

Mostly, the hands favored her with harmless and understandable attention in the form of playful ribbing. They were unmarried men, after all, and she was a young woman blessed with the kind of face and figure men paid attention to.

Some of the hands, however, occasionally showed her a little too much attention — the kind of sheepish interest and prolonged, dark stares that made her feel uneasy. There were one or two such men on her father's payroll now.

She wondered if the shadow rider might have been one of them. She'd have to keep her eye out for him, though she didn't want to get anyone fired. Her father had been, to her mind, a little too quick to fire those men whom he felt were crowding Annabelle a little too closely. On the other hand, she didn't want to have to keep looking over her shoulder every time she took her horse out either.

But, she reminded herself, in the light of very recent events, she wouldn't have to worry about any of her father's men for much longer. The Broken Heart had been a wonderful place to grow up, but she was a woman now. She was about to be married. Soon she'd be living in a house of her own a good ways away from here with the man who was shortly to become her husband — Mr. Hunter Buchanon.

She muttered the name as she walked up the steps of the lodge house's broad, wrap-around veranda. "Mrs. Hunter Buchanon . . . Mrs. Buchanon . . . Mrs. Hunter Bu—"

"Well, well, well — look what the cat dragged in."

Annabelle gasped and stopped dead in her tracks, slapping a hand to her chest in shock. "Cass!" she exclaimed. "What in the hell do you think you're doing — giving me a fright like that?"

123

"What was that you were sayin'?" her brother, Cass Ludlow, asked her. "I couldn't quite make it out."

Cass sat in one of the several wicker chairs positioned about the porch. He was five years Annabelle's senior, and her only sibling. The only one who'd made it through infancy and the war, that was. Cass was a handsome young man. Most would say devilishly handsome, with dimpled cheeks, a cleft chin, and high, tapering cheekbones. He was a ladies' man, but he attracted all the wrong ladies.

He dressed a little like a Mexican *caballero,* in a red shirt with gaudy Spanish-style embroidering and ruffling down the front, and bell-bottom, deerskin trousers. A concha-studded shell belt encircled his waist. A fancy, horn-gripped .44 was snugged into a hand-tooled leather holster tied fashionably low on his right leg. His crisp, sand-colored Stetson with brightly beaded band hung on his right knee.

In his hand was a glass. Light from the curtained window behind him reflected in it. Tequila perfumed the cool night air of the porch.

"I wasn't saying anything."

"Oh sure, you were. Something about *Buchanon,* wasn't it?"

Annabelle started toward the lodge's front door. "Be quiet, Cass. I'm not in the mood for your —"

"Out kinda late, aren't ya? Pa's been holdin' supper."

Anna stopped, her ears warming a bit. Facing the door, she said, "I . . . I got turned around in the hills north of town. It hardly ever happens to me, but —"

"Oh I see. That must've been *after* you rode out of town with Hunter Buchanon."

Annabelle turned to him, the warmth of her chagrin spreading throughout her face. "What?"

"Oh sure — I seen ya with my very own eyes. I was in town too. In a room with a view, shall we say?" Cass grinned, his dimples filling with shadows. His eyes flashed with amusement in the lamplight flanking him.

Anna knew what kind of room Cass had been in. She'd worried that friends of her father might have seen her in town with the Buchanons and gotten word to her father, making not only trouble for her but possibly more trouble for the Buchanons as well. She'd been right to harbor such fears. Her own ne'er-do-well brother had seen her.

"Does Pa know?" she asked in a soft voice touched with dread.

"I didn't tell him."

Relief washed over her. "Thank you, Cass." Annabelle started toward the door again.

"Max Chaney did."

Again, Annabelle stopped with a gasp. She turned to her brother, mouth half-open, her chest rising and falling heavily as she breathed.

"He . . . saw?"

"Nah, he was up at the mine. Pa was here at home, preparing for a guest. Chaney got word up at the mine that Luke had been hauled into Tigerville dead as last year's Christmas goose. Not only that but *all* of Stillwell's deputies had been kicked out with cold shovels, to boot!"

Cass chuckled and shook his head in amazement. "Max rode down to get a look at his poor misbegotten son and get him over to the undertaker's. That must've been when someone in town told him that you was in town only a few minutes ago with Hunter Buchanon . . . and them other three no-account hillbillies from the Rebel South!"

Cass grinned and threw back several swallows of tequila.

"Oh no," Annabelle said, dropping her

stricken gaze to the porch floor between her boots.

"Oh, it gets better," Cass said, thoroughly enjoying himself.

"What . . . what . . . do you mean?"

"Chaney rode up here, blubberin' an' cryin' over his dead no-account boy. He told Pa all about it . . . includin' the part about you ridin' out with that big blond Confederate devil, Hunter Buchanon. Headed for God knows where an' *doin' what?*"

Cass laughed again and then indicated the door with his tequila glass. "Oh, Pa's waitin' on ya inside. I'm sure he'll tell ya all about it. Only, he might wait 'til tomorrow. Remember that guest of Pa's I told you about?"

"Yes."

"Well, he's still here. He's in yonder. I doubt Pa will want to talk about any of this nefarious stuff regarding his purty, virginal daughter — whose reputation, of course, is above reproach — until it's just the two of you together. The two of you together with a bullwhip!"

Cass threw his head back, laughing uproariously.

He stopped abruptly when the front door opened.

Annabelle jerked her head toward it. "Pa!"

Graham Ludlow stood in the doorway, holding the stout oak door half-open. The tall, broad-shouldered, potbellied man studied her through gimlet eyes for a good five seconds before his big face, chiseled out of solid granite with a liver-spotted doorstop nose, drew up in a too-bright smile. "Here she is! The princess herself! Annabelle, what's been keeping you? I hope you're all right, darling. I have a surprise. A very special guest!"

Ludlow, clad in gray denims and hickory shirt beneath a black leather vest and bolo tie, stepped back, drawing the door wider.

Cautiously, like a girl walking into a leopard cage, Annabelle stepped over the threshold, doffing her felt hat and shaking her hair back behind her shoulders. She stopped just inside the foyer overlooking the lodge's large, sunken parlor area furnished in heavy, leather furniture including bookshelves and hand-carved tables.

Her father's and brother's game trophies adorned the walls. Every mammal that had stalked the Black Hills within the past thousand years was represented. Even a stuffed wild turkey and an albino moose.

But what . . . or whom . . . Annabelle's eyes were riveted on was the diminutive, impeccably attired young man just then rising from a quilted leather sofa near the flames dancing in the fieldstone hearth.

"What a pleasant surprise — eh, my dear?" intoned Graham Ludlow, sliding his coldly smiling eyes between his daughter and her wealthy young Eastern suitor, Kenneth Earnshaw.

CHAPTER 11

Annabelle's heart turned a somersault.

As she stood staring in shock at young Kenneth Earnshaw looking back at her from the parlor, where he stood ramrod straight in front of the crackling hearth, he smiled fawningly and gave a courtly dip of his chin, his spectacles glinting in the firelight.

"Annabelle," he said in his resonate orator's voice — a voice made for battling other attorneys, imploring judges, and lecturing juries — "what a pleasure it is to see you again."

He was a short, slender young man with a boyish face still a little plump with baby fat he would likely never outgrow, and an almost feminine mop of carefully combed, strawberry-blond hair, with sideburns of the same color, and a thick, bushy strawberry mustache. His carefully trimmed goatee did little to obscure the fact that his chin was weak.

He was dressed to the nines in a black swallowtail coat over a silk white shirt and paisley vest adorned with a gold watch chain. Round, steel-framed spectacles perched on his delicate nose. Pince-nez reading spectacles dangled from a black ribbon pinned to his lapel. Tweed trousers were stuffed into the tops of polished black riding boots that rose nearly to his knees.

"Kenneth," Annabelle said, swallowing down the slight obstruction in her throat. She slid her gaze to her father, who stood to her left, smiling nervously down at her. Looking back at young Earnshaw, she said, haltingly, "I . . . I'm afraid . . . I . . . I don't know quite what to say . . ."

A small V appeared in the skin just above the obviously puzzled young Earnshaw's compactly conservative nose sprinkled with small, light freckles.

Graham Ludlow broke the uneasy silence with a nervous guffaw. "Well, tell him you're delighted to see him, Annabelle!" He gave his daughter's shoulder a not-so-gentle shove. "Go on over there and let him kiss your cheek!"

Ludlow laughed again, too loudly, nervously.

Annabelle found herself dropping down the three steps to the sunken parlor, but it seemed as though someone else were steering the ship. Her feet were filled with lead, and she felt as though a strong, hot hand were splayed across the back of her neck, squeezing.

"Hello, Kenneth," she said as she slowly, haltingly crossed the room until she found herself standing before the young man who was roughly as tall as she was, his shoulders hardly any broader. She extended her hand to him, wanting to forestall anything more intimate.

"The honor is mine, sweet Annabelle." Ignoring her hand, young Earnshaw leaned forward, placed his hand on her arm, and pressed his brushy, moist mouth to her cheek, which made her innards recoil.

Straightening, smiling at her again, customarily obsequious, he said, "I see you're surprised."

Annabelle tried to smile, but her mouth wouldn't cooperate. She knew she must have looked stricken, like someone getting bad news about the fate of a family member. "I can't tell you how . . . how . . . *surprised . . . I . . . am.*"

She glanced at her father again still standing by the door, smiling a little too broadly, nervously. Cass now stood beside the elder Ludlow, drink in hand, grinning like the cat that ate the canary. He thrust a boot back to close the heavy door with a *bang!*

"*Pleasantly* surprised, one would hope," Earnshaw said to Annabelle, gently imploring.

Annabelle stared at her unexpected guest, then turned to her father once more.

"No," she heard herself saying, shaking her head slowly. "No, Kenneth. I'm sorry. But it's not a pleasant surprise at all."

"What?" Earnshaw said, canting his head and frowning, as though he thought he'd misheard her.

"You know what, my pet?" Graham Ludlow said, clapping his big hands together loudly and wringing them together, changing the subject. "I think what you need is a quick bath and a change of clothes. Then we'll go ahead and sit down to supper. Chang has been keeping the food warm long enough. I bet you're a little sunburned and tired."

To Earnshaw, he said, "The girl just needs some food in her belly, that's all, Kenneth. She's always cranky when she's hungry! Ever since she was yay-big! You go on upstairs, now, Annabelle." He turned to their middle-aged Chinese cook, Chang, standing in the doorway between the parlor and the dining room, looking confused in his crisp white smock. "Chang, heat some water for Annabelle's bath. Chop-chop!"

"I'll take the bath, Chang," Annabelle said, then, turning to her father and Kenneth Earnshaw, added, "But I won't be sitting down for supper."

As Chang shuffled off, glancing warily over his shoulder, Graham Ludlow said, "What on earth are you talking about? Kenneth came all this way from the East Coast just to see you, Annabelle. He's done with school, he's gone to work for his father's railroad — a very big, important position, I might add — and he's come all this way to ask you a very important question!"

To Earnshaw staring at her hang-jawed, she said, "The answer is no."

"Wha-wha-what?" Earnshaw shuttled his exasperated gaze to Ludlow. "What in God's name is going on here, Mr. Ludlow?"

"I'm telling you *no,*" Annabelle said, firmly, confidently. "I'm telling you both *no.* I won't marry you, Mr. Earnshaw. I tried to make myself clear on the subject in the letters we exchanged and the last time you were here, with your father."

She looked at Ludlow, who was flanked now by Cass. The younger Ludlow leaned back against the wall, laughing into his hand

134

as though at the funniest joke he'd ever heard.

"I told you both no," Annabelle told her father. "Now, I suppose I could play along with the charade this evening. I could take my bath and dress myself in some frilly, silly gown. I could sit down for supper with you and then join you on the porch afterward, where you would take my hand, get down on one knee, profess your love for me, and ask for my hand."

Anna shook her head, scowling from her suitor to her father and then back again. "I see little point in keeping up such a farce, especially since you both seem incapable or simply unwilling to take no for an answer. You are both bound and determined to believe that I will be your wife, Kenneth. But I will not. I've promised myself to another."

"Who?" Earnshaw demanded, his face suddenly red and bloated with outrage.

Annabelle turned to her father, whose slab-like face was a mask of exasperation, his eyes wide and hard.

"Hunter Buchanon," Annabelle said proudly, holding her chin in the air. "I've loved him for nearly two years now. I've known since the first time I met him that we were meant for each other. I am truly sorry, Kenneth. I've never returned your feelings for me, though I hardly see how you could feel much of anything for me at all since we've seen each other a total of three times, each time no longer than a few hours.

"I think that if you were honest you'd admit that you don't really love me at all. You only feel forced into this union by both of our fathers. Such a marriage would be nothing more than a business relationship between *them*."

Anna shook her head with defiance, casting an accusing glance at her father, who appeared to have turned to a statue. A statue with eyes carved out of pure, mute rage.

"I will have no part of that," the girl continued. "Especially since Hunter is the man I'm in love with." Turning to her father again, she said, "He's asked me to marry him. We're eloping tomorrow. It wouldn't have to be that way if you'd accepted him. We could have been married here. But I know that's not going to happen. So I'll be riding out of here before noon. I hope you can accept that, Pa. I'm old enough to make my own decisions."

She glanced once more at young Earnshaw, who now seemed as lost for words as her father was. "Please forgive me, Kenneth. And please excuse me."

Anna swung around and headed for the carpeted stairs at the back of the room. She stopped halfway to the top, then turned around. Both her father and Earnshaw were staring after her, as though they were both in some sort of trance.

Cass had disappeared into the kitchen during the height of the dustup, probably searching for a fresh tequila bottle.

"I truly am sorry," Annabelle said, meaning it.

She swung around again and hurried to the top of the stairs.

Once inside her room, she closed the door and pressed her back against it, blowing out a long sigh of relief. She was still standing there several minutes later, trying to calm down, going through the entire, embarrassing scene in her head, feeling guilty but also relieved that her secret was out in the open.

And that she'd made her intentions clear.

A soft tap came on the door. Recognizing Chang's tentative knock, she drew the door open. The Chinaman had brought up a long, copper tub and a bucket of water.

Anna sat on the bed while the Chinamen poured the bucket of hot water into the tub, which he'd set on the wooden floor at the foot of the canopied bed. He fetched two more buckets of hot water from the kitchen and then hauled up a bucket of cold water and another of hot, for rinsing, which he left sitting on the floor beside the steaming tub.

Bowing, eyeing the girl warily, incredulously, the Chinaman shuffled back out of the room. He poked his head back in to say, "Miss Anna want supper? Here?" He smiled, showing the gap where he'd lost a front tooth. "I bring. No problem, I bring. Girl must eat. Especially if girl getting married tomorrow."

He snickered, then looked quickly, cautiously behind him, making sure none of the other men in the house were near enough to have heard him.

Annabelle smiled at the Chinaman, whom she considered a close friend and even a confidant at times. "I don't think I could eat a bite after all that."

"I bring plate anyway, leave here." Chang patted the top of the dresser to his left. "Just leave." He shrugged exaggeratedly. "You eat, no eat. Up to you." He smiled, winked, pulled his head out, and closed the door.

Annabelle got undressed, sank into the tub, and slowly, pensively washed herself. She was so deep in thought that she was only vaguely aware of Chang opening her door just far enough to set a plate of food on her dresser before slipping quietly back out again. Her nerves felt like bits of frayed yarn.

She felt guilty for what she'd done to her father and Kenneth Earnshaw, but she wouldn't have had to reject young Earnshaw — as well as her father's wishes — if both men had taken the time to listen to and heed her previous, more discreet objections to their plans.

Instead, they acted as though they'd made her mind up for her, and there was nothing she could do about it. As though they were refusing her all say in the matter of her own life, her own love and happiness. As if they, being men, knew what was best for her, and she, being a silly young woman, did not.

Finally, Anna's emotions overwhelmed her. She sank back in the tub, resting her elbows on its sides and leaning her head forward against the palms of her hands. She sobbed, her shoulders quivering.

She was still sitting there, naked in the tub, sobbing into her hands, when footsteps thudded loudly on the stairs. They grew louder, approaching her room. Anna turned her head to stare at her door and then gave a startled scream, crossing her arms on her bare breasts when her father burst into her room, face swollen to the size of a bright red pumpkin with fury.

"Pa!" she cried.

"How dare you humiliate me like that!" Graham Ludlow roared, pointing an outraged finger at the end of his extended arm, leaning slightly forward at his thick waist.

"Pa!" Annabelle cried again, drawing her knees up closer, trying to make her naked body as small as possible in the copper tub.

"And I don't mean just about young Earnshaw either!"

"Pa, I'm bathing!"

"I know where you were earlier, young lady. And I know who you were with. You were seen in town . . . and riding *out of town* . . . with the ex-Confederate ne'er-do-well who butchered my business partner's son!"

"Luke ambushed Hunter! Hunter was unarm— !"

"And you know who I heard it from? Max Chaney himself! By now, the whole town likely knows that the daughter of Graham Ludlow is the . . . the . . . the . . . *whore* of Hunter Buchanon!"

"I'm not a whore!"

"A whore of that Union-killing Rebel!"

Enraged now herself, Annabelle twisted

around in the tub to face her father. She slapped her hand down hard against the side of the tub. "I don't care what side Hunter fought in during the war! I don't give a damn about that horrible war! It's over. I love Hunter and we're going to ride to Cheyenne and be married whether you like it or not!"

"How dare you tell me you don't give a damn about the war! You lost a brother in that war!"

"It's over, Pa!" Annabelle was fairly screaming, her fury a wild thing inside her. "Hunter and I are going to be married, and you just have to accept it or you'll never see me again!"

Ludlow stared down at his daughter, his own emotion burning in his eyes. His nostrils expanded and contracted. Bulging veins throbbed in his forehead.

Slowly, he shook his head, hardening his jaws and gritting his teeth. "No daughter of mine will marry any man who fought for the Confederacy. *Who killed Union soldiers, like your brother, for the Confederacy!* I forbid it. You think you can turn your back on me — the man who raised you in the lap of luxury, bought you every damn horse you wanted, educated you in the finest schools in the country. But you can't."

141

"Pa, I appreciate all you've given me."
Annabelle sobbed, tears rolling down her
cheeks. "It's true, I've had a wonderful life.
But that doesn't mean —"

"It means exactly what I say it means. It
means that you will marry the man I tell
you to marry. The man you will marry,
whether you like it or not, is Kenneth Earnshaw!"

"No, Pa! Why can't I get through to — ?"

Ludlow threw his hand up, silencing her.

He shook his head slowly, his eyes now
bleak and dark with menace as he gazed
down at her. "You may be strong, Annabelle. You may be stubborn. But you're also
spoiled. Spoiled and foolhardy. Keep in
mind that what I do I not only do for myself
but I do for you as well."

Annabelle studied him, foreboding weigh-
ing heavy in her. "What's that supposed to
mean?"

Ludlow sniffed, swallowed, seemed to
compose himself. He jerked down the bottom of his cowhide vest and lifted his chin.
"Now . . . I sent Kenneth to town. Obviously, he's upset. But he promised to return
tomorrow night. I assured him that things
will go far differently . . . far *better* for both
of you . . . tomorrow night."

He paused, filled his broad, lumpy chest

with air, let it out through his nose. "You think I don't, Annabelle. But I know what is best for you. I know what the world consists of. You don't. You've been sheltered from it. But I know what is best. You remember that."

Ludlow swung around and left the room, leaving the door standing wide behind him.

"You only know what is best for you!" Annabelle screamed behind him.

Her only response was Ludlow's heavy, resolute tread descending the stairs.

She lowered her head to the side of the tub and cried.

CHAPTER 12

Annabelle finally washed the tears from her face, then climbed out of the tub, grabbed a towel off a chair, and, holding the towel, walked over and closed the door. She toweled her hair and brushed it and then dropped a nightgown over her head.

For a long time, she paced the room, moving from one end to the other, her mind swirling. This wasn't exactly how she'd expected the time leading up to her wedding day would be.

But there was no point in feeling sorry for herself. She was about to marry the most wonderful man she'd ever known.

Her father didn't want her to marry Hunter Buchanon. But, while Annabelle appreciated the more-than-comfortable childhood Graham Ludlow had provided, she was not going to allow him to force her into marriage with a man she didn't love. Providing Annabelle with a luxurious home and a happy childhood despite the premature death of her mother from a heart ailment did not mean her father had bought and paid for her entire life.

He could not dictate how she lived her adult life, or with whom she would live it.

It was wrong of Annabelle's father to forbid her to marry the man she loved and to compel her to marry a man she did not love merely to boost his business relationship. Wrong, plain and simple.

While guilt still nibbled at the edge of her consciousness, Annabelle felt resolute. By the light of a single, guttering lantern, she packed traveling clothes as well as her mother's wedding dress into two carpetbags. She set the bags by the door, ready to go at first light. She'd get an early start in the morning, before her father rose. She didn't want them to get into another row like the one they'd had last night.

Having made up her mind that she was doing the right thing, and deciding that eventually her father would see it that way, too, and might even come to accept Hunter Buchanon as his son-in-law, Annabelle's anxiety eased. The calming of her nerves allowed hunger to rise in her. She carried the plate of now-cold supper over to the bed, tucked her bare legs under her, Indian-style, and ate Chang's delicious food with relish. She finished the entire plate of roast beef, mashed potatoes, and garden-raised green beans, and swabbed the last of the gravy with one of Chang's buttery biscuits.

Sated, buoyed now by a warm optimism and eagerness to be in the arms of her lover once again, to finally start a life with Hunter on a ranch of their own, she climbed into bed and drew up the covers. For a long time, she lay awake, pressing away the persistent fears and doubts with fantasies of what her and Hunter's life would be like. She imagined all the little ones they would have running around their ranch house, and watching her boys growing tall and strong like their father, riding off with Hunter on dewy summer mornings to tend their range.

Annabelle chuckled delightedly into the palm of her hand. Imagine Hunter panning for gold these last two years, building a stake so they could marry! And without mentioning a word!

Knowing she had to sleep, she stopped indulging the voices and images washing through her head. She focused on emptying her mind. She needed to sleep. She had a big day ahead. She took several deep, slow breaths.

Try as she might, it seemed to take forever

to quiet herself down. She wasn't even aware of having slept before she realized that she must have nodded off at least for a time. Suddenly, it was nearly dawn. She could tell by the faint milky light brushing the night outside her window, and the piping of morning birds.

She tossed the covers aside, rose, and started dressing. If she left now, she'd likely arrive at the cabin well ahead of Hunter, but she couldn't wait. She was too anxious and excited to start her new, married life. Also, she didn't want to wait around here at the Broken Heart. She wouldn't put it past her father to physically impede her from leaving.

She stepped into her boots, donned a fringed buckskin jacket and her crisp felt Stetson. She picked up her carpetbags and reached for the door. The knob wouldn't turn. She looked at the lock. The key was gone.

Annabelle tried the knob again.

Locked.

During the night, someone — who else but her father? — must have stolen into her room, removed the key from the inside lock, and locked the door from the outside. Damn him!

Why hadn't she heard? Maybe she'd slept

longer and more deeply than she'd realized.

Anger burned inside her. She stepped back from the door and turned to the window on the opposite side of her bed.

"Don't worry, Pa," Annabelle said cunningly, under her breath. "I'm every bit as much Ludlow as you are."

As a young girl, when she couldn't sleep, she used to sneak out that window, climb to the ground, and take long, dreamy walks along the creek, imagining that she were Lady Rowena awaiting her very own Ivanhoe to save her from Cedric of Rotherwood's plans to marry her off to the vile Lord Athelstane.

She hadn't realized how prophetic such imaginings had been! She'd used the window because her father, who'd lived out here when the Sioux had been a constant threat, had forbidden her to leave the house alone between sunset and sunrise. She didn't think her father had ever discovered her secret escapes — if he had, there surely would have been hell to pay — and that should work in her favor this morning.

Quickly, she hauled her bags around the bed to the window. She set them on the bed, quietly opened the window, and looked out.

All clear. Nothing moved but the flickering shadows of birds on the wing.

The faint periwinkle wash of the pre-dawn shone over the eastern hills. Annabelle could smell the smoke from the cook's breakfast fire emanating from the bunkhouse, but the hands didn't usually head to the barns and corrals until after they'd eaten, which wouldn't be for another half hour. Anna hoped the cook's dog, Farley, was off hunting rabbits in the hills, or her goose might be cooked . . .

Quickly, she tossed her bags onto the kitchen roof slanting six feet beneath her window. Fortunately, Chang and her father wouldn't rise for another hour, and both their rooms were a good distance from Annabelle's. Cass's room was right down the hall from hers, but if the young firebrand hadn't gone to town to slumber with the percentage girl of his choice, he was likely three sheets to the wind and wouldn't rise until mid-morning.

Graham Ludlow had long ago ceased trying to get Cass to do an honest day's work. He'd not banished him from the ranch because he'd already lost one son in the war. One useless son was better than no son at all.

With customary agility, Anna slithered through the window and dropped lightly onto the kitchen roof. She tossed the carpetbags to the ground, on the far side of Chang's pile of split and stacked cordwood, then dropped herself to the woodpile. From there, she leaped to the ground, gathered her bags, and jogged around to the front of the house and then down the hill toward where the barns and corrals were slowly taking shape in the dawn's misty shadows.

She could see a light at the near end of the bunkhouse, but that would only be the cook brewing coffee and preparing breakfast. The hands were likely sound asleep. They usually stayed up late playing cards.

Anna slipped into the stock barn, finding it so dark that she lit a lamp hanging from a ceiling support post. Quickly, she went into the adjoining corral and roped Ivan, the buckskin. She led the horse into the barn, saddled it, hooked the handles of her carpetbags over the horn, and strapped her bedroll and her saddlebags containing a few trail supplies behind the cantle. She also strapped her saddle scabbard, containing her Winchester saddle ring carbine, over her right stirrup. She used the long gun for hunting and for protection, if needed.

She led the horse outside and was about to step into the saddle when she remembered she'd left the lamp burning inside. You never left an unattended flame in a barn full of hay. She led the buckskin over to the corral, tied it to a rail, then walked back into the barn. She moved to the lamp and was about to turn down the wick when she heard the sound of boots crunching hay and straw down the alley ahead of her.

Looking in that direction, she saw a man-shaped silhouette moving toward her, staggering slightly.

Annabelle's heart thudded.

Cass stepped into the watery sphere of lantern-light. He wasn't wearing a hat, and his hair was mussed. Hay and straw clung to it. Obviously, he'd slept in one of the empty barn stalls, as he often did when he wanted to drink beyond the prying eyes of their father, or when he'd gotten home late from town and was too drunk to negotiate the path to the house.

Cass studied her, squinting his eyes at first, as though having trouble making her out in the weak light. Suddenly, his mouth shaped a grin, dimpling his cheeks. "Oh-oh!" he said. "Oh-oh! Oh-oh! Does Pa know you're out here?" His words were badly slurred. He must have been drinking most of the night, and he was still pie-eyed.

"Be quiet, Cass!"

He dragged his boot toes around his sister to peer out the two open doors behind her, turning toward where she'd tied the buck-skin.

"Oh-oh!" he cried again, swinging back around to face her, grinning delightedly. "You got your bags packed, li'l sister!"

Anna gritted her teeth and looked beyond him toward the house. "Cass, be quiet! Please don't say anything. Just go back into your stall and lay down before you fall down!"

She tried to walk past him, but he grabbed her arm and turned her sharply toward him.

"D-don't think I can do that, li'l sister."

"Let me go, Cass!"

She jerked her arm out of his grip, but he lunged toward her, grabbed it again. He shoved his face up close to hers. His breath was warm and fetid with liquor, appalling her.

"What do you think you're gonna do? You really think you're gonna marry that Gray-back . . . that Johnny Reb? You really think you're gonna marry up an' raise a family with that no-account Southern hillbilly?"

Annabelle looked at his hand on her arm. "Let me go, Cass."

"Tell me somethin', li'l sister," Cass said, leaning even closer to her. "You been shackin' up with that big Grayback, ain't ya?" He grinned lewdly.

"That's none of your business. Let me go!" Anna pried her brother's fingers from around her right arm, but he quickly grabbed her left one with his other hand.

"You got a baby in your belly?" Cass pressed his free hand to her stomach. "That the problem? Huh? That why you feel like you gotta run off with that Confederate privy rat?"

"Cass!" She slapped his hand away and looked at him in horror. She'd never seen him like this. This angry. This enraged. Crazy with fury.

Cass stepped back, pulled a bullwhip down off a ceiling support post from which it hung by a nail. "Maybe Pa's right. Maybe you are a whore."

Cass made a circular motion with his hand, uncoiling the whip, the braided black leather growing longer and longer as it turned through the air beside him, whistling malevolently. Gritting his teeth, Cass snapped the snake in the air beside Anna's head. She felt the air curl against her cheek, like a demon's kiss. The popper at the whip's end snapped sharply, loudly, causing her ears to ring.

Anna screamed and jerked back, horrified.

"Cass! Stop this! You're drunk!"

153

Cass popped the blacksnake again, stumbling toward her, his eyes strange and dark — as menacing as those of any nightmare specter.

"Cass!"

"I'm gonna whip you like the traitorous whore you are, Anna! Somethin' Pa should've done a long time ago!"

"Cass, stop!" Anna screamed as she stumbled back against the ceiling support post from which the lantern hung from a nail.

"Traitorous whores get whipped 'til there ain't a stitch of clothes left on 'em!" Cass laughed maniacally, then flung the whip handle back behind his shoulder, the deadly blacksnake uncoiling in the air behind him. As he snapped his arm forward, gritting his teeth, Anna flung her hand up, grabbed the bail of the lantern, and ripped it off the nail.

"Nooo!"

At the same time that blacksnake lashed into her left arm, biting painfully through her coat, she flung the lantern forward. It smashed against Cass's left temple. Burning coal oil spewed like a dragon's breath, dancing across the side of Cass's head and spreading onto the floor beyond him. The carpet of fresh straw instantly caught fire.

Cass bellowed as he dropped the whip and fell to his hands and knees, swatting at the flames smoking on the left side of his head, burning his hair.

Anna fell back against the support post, gasping. The flames were building around her and Cass, who lay belly-down now before her, folding his arms around his head and writhing. Soon, he'd be engulfed.

"Cass!" Anna cried, crouching over him, tugging on his arm. "We have to get out of here!"

He pushed up onto his knees, howling, making no effort to flee the flames.

Anna ran forward, tugging harder on his arm. Finally, Cass complied, crawling forward on hands and knees. She half dragged him out into the yard, away from the smoke now roiling out the front doors. Inside, flames danced thickly, crackling and roaring.

Anna stared into them, shocked and horrified, her mind still trying to comprehend all that happened in the past two minutes.

The screams of frightened horses caromed through the building roar of the flames, penetrating Anna's stunned consciousness. She bolted forward and, mindless of the hot flames licking at her, the smoke watering her eyes and making her lungs ache, she ran down the barn alley.

There were two stalled horses, one on

each side of the alley. Both were being doctored — one for saddle galls, the other for a swollen fetlock. They were pitching and rearing, the flames showing orange in their eyes.

Quickly, Anna opened the stall doors and hazed both animals back toward the front of the barn. The horses followed a curving, dark, smoky path through the flames until they were outside, galloping, screaming, and buck-kicking off into the misty dawn shadows.

Anna followed the mounts' path through the building fire and stumbled out between the gaping doors that were also limned now with snapping flames. Near Cass, she dropped to her knees with exhaustion and drew several draughts of fresh, cool air into her burning lungs. Tears oozed from her stinging eyes.

"Fire!" a man called. "Fire! *Fire!*"

Anna turned to see a bulky, apron-clad man running toward the barn from the bunkhouse. The cook continued running toward the barn, bellowing. Several other men, half-dressed, stumbled out of the bunkhouse, looking around groggily.

"Get the water buckets!" one of them shouted. "Water! Water! Hurry!"

Anna looked at Cass. He lay belly-down

in the dirt and ground horse apples of the barnyard, moaning. The hair on the left side of his head was burned away, and the skin was scorched.

"Oh my God!" a familiar voice shouted.

Anna looked toward the house. Her father was running toward the barn, Chang following from about ten yards back. Ludlow was clad in a red plaid bathrobe, long-handles, and deerskin slippers.

He stopped suddenly and stared incredulously toward his son and daughter. Cass still lay belly-down, arms folded over his head, moaning and writhing. Graham Ludlow looked from Anna to Cass and then back to Anna.

"What . . . ?" He stumbled forward, thick gray hair in his eyes that reflected the burning barn's dancing flames. He glared at Anna, his eyes now cast with accusing. "What . . . have . . . you . . . *done?*"

Anna stared back at him. She wanted to explain, but she could find no words. Her mind was still reeling from Cass's assault. Besides, what would be the point? She just wanted to get the hell out of here.

She looked at the buckskin tied to the corral, dancing and whickering fearfully as smoke from the barn roiled around it. Anna heaved herself to her feet, ran over to the mount, ripped the reins off the top corral slat, and swung up into the leather.

"Get back here!" Ludlow bellowed, running heavily toward her, the robe winging out around him. "Get back here, damnit, Anna! Where do you think you're going?"

She turned the horse out from the corral, glanced at her father once more, then swung Ivan to the southwest and gave him his head.

"Anna, get back here!" Ludlow shouted behind her.

The horse gave a shrill whinny, rose off its front hooves, dropped back to the ground, and bolted off its rear feet, heading for the ranch portal and the gradually lightening hills beyond.

CHAPTER 13

Annabelle galloped to the crest of a steep rise west of the ranch, stopped the buckskin, and looked back.

It was full dawn now, but the sun was still twenty minutes away. The orange glow of the burning barn was like a sun itself, pulsating in the gauzy, purple shadows of the long slope upon which the lodge house sat.

Anna wasn't all that unhappy about the barn. No horses or people had been inside, and her father's men would be occupied for the next couple of hours fighting to contain the fire, which they would likely do. The well was near the barn, and she could see the caterpillar-shaped line of the bucket brigade stringing out from the well to the fire.

By the time her father's men took to her trail, it would be cold, and she and Hunter would be well on their way cross-country to

Cheyenne. Revulsion and humiliation swept through her as she remembered Cass in the barn. She probably should have left him in there to burn alive, a deserving punishment for a man so wicked. Quickly, casting the bleak, angry reflections aside and turning her thoughts instead to the prospect of seeing Hunter soon in the old prospector's cabin, she booted the buckskin on down the trail.

The horror of the past several hours would seem a distant memory as soon as she saw the man she loved again. Nothing would stand in the way of her and Hunter's happiness.

She pushed Ivan on down the trail, but not too hard. They had many miles to cover today. As she loped past the hill on which she'd spied the mysterious rider, another chill spread across her shoulders. She wondered if the mysterious horseman could have been Cass, then quickly nixed the idea.

There was no way he could have gotten back to the Broken Heart ahead of her. When she'd seen him on the porch, he'd been quite drunk; he'd obviously been sitting there awhile.

All Anna knew was that she'd feel mighty glad and relieved to be safely in Hunter's arms. It would be nice to get away from the

Hills for a while even though they planned to be gone only long enough to be married. They had to get back to the Hills so Hunter could buy the Johnson ranch, and they could start a life together as husband and wife — a good distance from the Broken Heart and the corrupt town of Tigerville.

An hour after she'd left the ranch, Anna put the buckskin up across a shoulder of a forested hill, outcroppings of mossy rocks jutting around her. The trail wound up and over the hill's brow and then along a twisting path through thick pines and aspens. When the trees peeled back behind her, her heart lightened.

The cabin sat before her, hunkered at the base of the high, rocky ridge that contained the old prospector's mine. Sunlight angled through the pines behind her, limning the weathered shake roof spotted with tufts of green moss.

It was still early, not yet eight o'clock. Hunter wasn't due to arrive for several hours. Anna's nerves were still frayed from what had happened at home, but maybe she could get a few hours' sleep . . .

Wait.

Something was wrong. Someone was here.

Sniffing the air, Anna looked at the rusty stovepipe jutting from the cabin's roof. A thin tendril of gray smoke unfurled just above the pipe, dispersing in the barely sunlit air. Anna could smell the tang of burning pine.

She looked around for a horse. There were none.

She turned back to the cabin, frowning. "Hunter?" she called tentatively. "Hunter, are you here?"

The buckskin lifted its head sharply, snorted uneasily.

Hooves thudded heavily down the slope behind Anna. She whipped her head around with a start. A man sat a horse in the tree shadows about forty yards down the hill, partially concealed by the pines.

He was gazing up the slope toward the cabin. Anna couldn't make him out in the murky morning light and dense shadows.

Hipped around in her saddle, one hand on the cantle, she called, "Hunter?"

She waited. The horseman continued to stare at her in menacing silence.

"Hunter?" Anna called, slowly waving an arm. "Is that you?"

The watcher jerked his horse around, a big black, and galloped down the slope, weaving through the pines and aspens, the black's hooves kicking up gouts of morning-damp forest duff and throwing it back behind him.

"Hey!" Anna called, heart thudding. "Who are you?"

Hooves thudded softly in the thick forest duff.

"Hey!" Anna yelled, whipping the buckskin around. *"Stop!"*

She booted the buckskin down the slope and onto the watcher's trail. As she gained the bottom of the slope, her stalker who was now her quarry disappeared over the top of the next hill.

"Come on, boy!" Anna urged the buckskin.

She had a feeling he was the same man she'd seen on her ride to the ranch the previous night. She wanted to know what he wanted, why he was following her.

She shot up and over the top of the hill. The rider was now galloping along the bottom of the next ravine, heading off to Anna's right. She swerved the buckskin in that direction. As she gained the bottom of the slope, the other rider disappeared around the shoulder of a low, pine-sprinkled ridge.

"Stop!" Anna shouted. "Who are you? What do you want with me?"

She leaned forward over the buckskin's pole, urging more speed. Ivan leaped a deadfall pine. As she rounded the shoulder of the ridge, she spied the other rider galloping straightaway from her, fifty yards distant, hatted head bobbing as his black galloped hard, leaping over and swerving around obstacles.

Anna followed the man up and over another hill and then along another, narrow ravine sheathed in pine brush and firs leaning close over the trail down which water from a nearby spring trickled. A few yards ahead, the trees disappeared on Anna's left, the ground dropping away into a deep canyon.

Something flew toward Anna from her right side. She screamed as the man crashed into her, driving her out of her saddle.

As the buckskin continued galloping straight on down the trail, Anna hit the slope with a loud grunt and a *whoosh* as her breath was pounded out of her lungs. She rolled several times, then came to rest on her belly, facedown in the thick, tawny grass.

She sensed quick movement to her right. Then someone jerked her around by her coat collar. She gasped as a large, red fist started toward her in a blur of fast motion. It stopped inches from her chin.

"Anna?" a familiar voice said.

"Hunter!"

■ ■ ■ ■

Hunter unclenched his fist and dropped his hand. Anna stared up at him, her green eyes round and bright with fear.

"Oh God, Anna — are you all right?"

She winced and fell back onto her elbows. "I . . . I think . . . so." She frowned curiously. "You're . . . early."

Hunter smiled. "Couldn't wait."

Anna smiled back. "Me too."

"Oh, honey," Hunter said, looking her over, running his hands down her legs extended out before her, probing for broken bones. "Is anything broken? Jesus, I didn't mean to . . ." He let his voice trail off and shook his head in disbelief at what he'd done. "I . . . I thought you . . . were the one chasing . . . you. I mean . . ."

"It's okay." Annabelle smiled, her cheeks flushed, chest rising and falling sharply as she breathed. "I'm all right." She looked back up along the ridge. "Did you see him — the other rider?"

Hunter shook his head. "I didn't get a good look at him. I heard you yelling, so I took off after you. I saw two riders. I thought since you were yelling, you must have been the one being chased." He ran his hands down her arms. "Oh, Anna — are you sure you're all right, honey?"

"I'm all right." Suddenly, she threw herself into his arms, pressing her mouth against his thick neck. "Oh, Hunter!"

He held her tightly. "It's all right, honey. It's all right. I got you now."

Her body quivered as she sobbed against him, holding him tightly around the neck.

"What did he do, Anna?"

She shook her head slightly. "Nothing. He was just watching me." She pulled away, looking up at him, tears dribbling down her cheeks. "He just gave me a fright, that's all." She gazed up at him. He sensed there was something more she wanted to say, that there was more bothering her, but she was having trouble finding the words or was reluctant to speak them.

"What is it, Anna? What's wrong? Are you sure he didn't do anything to you? Are you sure I didn't hurt you?"

"Oh, Hunter — so much has happened. I don't want to go into it right now."

"What?" Hunter said, shaking his head curiously. "I don't understand. What all has happened?"

She stared up at him, eyes flooded with tears.

"It's your father, isn't it?" he said, hardening his jaws in anger. "I bet he made trouble."

"No." Anna shook her head, tossing her mussed hair back behind her shoulders. "No, it's not that. I'll tell you later." Suddenly, her eyes were cast dubiously, and she wrinkled the skin above the bridge of her nose.

"What is it?" Hunter said.

"That rider." Anna looked back up along the ridge before returning her gaze to Hunter. "He found the cabin. He must have spent the night there. Or part of the night, anyway. I saw smoke lifting from the stovepipe."

Hunter thought about that, shrugged. "Probably just some drifter who needed a place to spend the night." He grinned. "Who cares? We won't be needing that shack anymore. Soon, we'll have a house of our own."

Anna returned the smile, but an edginess returned to her gaze.

"Can you stand?" Hunter asked her, taking her hand. "Let's fetch the gold and hit the trail. What do you say?"

Annabelle beamed back at him. "I say I love you, Hunter Buchanon!" She wrapped her arms around his neck and kissed him with deep affection.

Hunter returned her kiss with a heartfelt one of his own. Then he ran his fingers through her long, thick red hair and brushed his thumbs across her smooth, suntanned cheeks. He frowned. "Is that . . . fire ash . . . ?"

"It's nothing," Anna said. "Let's fetch the gold and head for Cheyenne."

Hunter helped her back up the steep slope to the narrow trail at the top. She moved a little stiffly at first but then got her step back and was able to climb without assistance. He fetched his own horse and the mule he'd brought along for hauling the gold to Cheyenne. The mule was rigged with a wooden pack frame and heavy canvas panniers.

Hunter's mount, one of several in his string but also his favorite, was a fine charcoal stallion he'd named Nasty Pete for his wicked streak. He left the mule with Annabelle and then he and Nasty Pete ran down the buckskin, returning Ivan to where Annabelle waited where he'd left her.

"Where's your trusty sidekick?" Annabelle asked.

"Bobby Lee? Left him at home. I don't think he'd get on well in Cheyenne."

"No." Anna laughed. "I don't think Cheyenne is at all ready for Bobby Lee."

Hunter swung down from Nasty Pete's

back to help Annabelle onto the buckskin, but she ignored his offered hand, saying, "Save your strength for your wedding night, Hunter Buchanon. You're gonna need it." She flashed a coquettish smile at him, then swung lithely into the leather.

Chuckling, feeling the warmth of desire low in his belly, Hunter stepped back up onto the grullo, and, leading the mule by its lead rope, headed for the cabin. He rode up the last ridge and drew up in front of the shack, noting the thin, gray smoke curling from the chimney pipe. Like Anna had said, someone had made the cabin home for the night.

Just some drifter, most likely. Nights got cold in the Hills even at high summer. Hunter didn't begrudge anyone a warm night's sleep. Frightening his girl, though, was another thing altogether. That put a burr under Hunter's saddle blanket. He wished he'd gotten a better look at the man. On the other hand, maybe it was best he hadn't . . .

He turned to Anna drawing rein beside him. "You sure you're all right, honey?"

She drew up her mouth corners and narrowed her eyes, which sparkled with warmth. "Fine as frog hair split four ways." It was one of old Angus's many colorful expressions. "Now that I'm back with you, my love."

Hunter smiled and swung down from Nasty Pete's back. "You wait here. I'll be back in a minute with your dowry." He winked at her.

"Uh-uh." Annabelle stepped down from the buckskin. "I'm right by your side, Hunter Buchanon. From here on out."

As Hunter led the mule back along the base of the ridge wall, Anna clung to him closely, hooking her arm around his, pressing her hip against his thigh as they walked. As they approached the trail that meandered up the ridge wall, Hunter stopped abruptly.

He stared up at the mine mouth.

"What is it?"

Hunter dropped the mule's reins and ran forward. He leaped onto the slope and sprinted along the trail that angled through the brush and rocks. At the cave mouth, he stopped, his heart turning somersaults in his chest.

Someone had removed the brush he'd used to cover the mine entrance. It lay piled to each side.

"Oh God!" Anna said, coming up behind Hunter and closing a hand over her mouth.

Hunter glanced at her. "Doesn't mean

anything. Maybe the fella you saw was the old prospector who carved the mine in the first place. Maybe he's thinking about working it again." He paused, his words sounding wooden even to his own ears. "That's probably all it is."

Heavily, he moved into the mine, doffing his hat and crouching. He moved blindly through the stygian darkness, wanting to run but, knowing there was rubble strewn here and there about the floor, he held himself back. He heard Anna's footsteps behind him.

As he approached the thin shaft of light that marked the niche into which he'd cached his gold, he slowed his pace even more. His boots grew heavy. He sensed what he would see before he even saw it.

Or saw *them,* rather — the rocks behind which he'd stowed the gold.

They lay strewn about the base of the mine wall, leaving the cache itself as dark as an empty eye socket. Slowly, his knees threatening to buckle from shock, he shoved his left hand into the hole. He didn't need to. He knew what he'd find. He found it, all right.

Nothing.

Nothing but air and gravel and the solid chiseled rock of the cave wall.

The gold was gone.

Suddenly a voice, sounding like a shout from the top of a well, caromed toward Hunter and Annabelle from the direction of the mine entrance. "You two lovebirds might as well make yourselves at home!"

Annabelle gasped. She grabbed Hunter's arm.

Hunter whipped his head toward the round circle of gray-green light that marked the cave's entrance. A slender, murky figure stood there, holding something.

The man raised whatever he was holding. There was a thudding sound as he smashed what appeared a stick — maybe a pick handle? — against the rotting side-beam of the crumbling portal frame.

" 'Cause home is what this place is gonna be for a long, long time!"

Frank Stillwell's jeering voice rocketed around the mineshaft, bouncing off the stony walls.

The sheriff laughed loudly as he continued rapping the pick handle or whatever it was against the portal's rotten side-beam.

"No!" Hunter shouted.

Leaving Annabelle, he took off running.

The rapping continued. He could hear Stillwell grunting with the effort.

"Stillwell!" Hunter bellowed. "You son of a — !"

Hunter's boot clipped a rock hidden by the darkness. He hit the mine floor hard, skidding forward on his belly. He looked up. Stillwell was laughing as he hammered the pick handle against the portal beam. The top beam was sagging and dirt and gravel was dribbling down to clatter onto the cave floor fronting the sheriff.

"Stillwell, no!" Annabelle screamed as she ran past Hunter.

Hunter heaved himself to his feet. Anna was ten feet ahead of him. He could see her silhouette against the light of the cave entrance. Beyond her, Stillwell stepped back, shouting, "See you in hell, lovebirds!"

Hunter reached forward. "Annabelle, stop!"

He grabbed her as the portal beam collapsed and the light at the end of the tunnel was snuffed like a doused flame.

CHAPTER 14

Annabelle screamed as darkness filled the mine shaft.

The scream was nearly drowned by the thunder of the cave-in. Hunter held her tight against his chest and closed his eyes against the dust billowing over them on a wave of warm air smelling like earth and pine from the timbers. He braced himself as he heard the timbers above and around him groan, threatening to give.

If that happened, he and Annabelle would be crushed. The mine would be, as Stillwell had termed it, their home for a good long time.

A sarcophagus.

Finally, the rumbling dwindled to near-silence. A few more rocks clattered onto the pile now blocking the mine entrance and onto the floor behind it. Then full silence. The air was so thick with dust that Hunter could barely breathe. He could feel Annabelle convulsing in his arms, gasping.

"Come on!"

Hunter took her hand and led her back toward where the weak light angled down from the crack in the ceiling, near his stolen cache.

"The air should be fresher here," he said.

They both lifted their faces toward the crack and drew in the cleaner air filtering down through the natural flue.

Hunter looked toward the dark mass of the cave-in. "The dust will settle in a bit."

Annabelle drew another deep breath of the relatively clean air and looked up at him, her eyes glassy and round with terror. "And then what?"

Hunter looked around, feeling the walls and ceiling closing in on him. "Yeah," he said, drolly. "Good point."

Hunter looked up at the crack in the ceiling through which the light angled. He probed the crack with his fingers. It was only about five or six inches wide, varying by degrees along its length cutting across one corner of the ceiling and into the wall. "I wonder how wide that flue is farther up."

"You mean, you think we might be able to crawl up through that crack . . . and get out?"

"It's a thought."

"Not a very good one." Annabelle moved back and slumped down against the opposite wall, drawing up her knees, wrapping her arms around them. "I think . . ." She paused, licked her lips. When she continued, her voice was thin, trembling. "I think we're finished, Hunter. I think that rat Stillwell has killed us."

"Don't say that." Hunter looked at the crack and then back toward the mine entrance. At what had been the mine entrance but which now was a severalton pile of raw ore and splintered pine timbers. "We're just gonna have to dig through that . . . that's all."

Whatever optimism and calm he was feeling was shattered when a thundering crash sounded from the direction of the cave-in. More dirt and rock tumbled out of the ceiling.

"Oh God!" Annabelle cried, closing her arms around her knees and lowering her head, bracing herself for death.

Death under tons of dirt and rock.

Hunter hurried over and sat down beside her, wrapping an arm around her, drawing her toward him. She pressed her cheek against his chest and trembled as the thunder gradually died.

More dust wafted thickly.

When the debris had settled and the rumbling had ceased, Hunter gave Anna a reassuring squeeze. "Stay here."

He rose and, stepping out of the dim light, moved into the darkness toward the debris pile. He reached into his denims pocket for a small, tin matchbox. He slid open the cover and snapped a lucifer to light on his thumbnail.

The flame sputtered, flickered, shedding a fluttering circle of amber light. The debris pile lay just ahead. Hunter slid the match flame close and then up and down, from side to side. His belly tightened. He didn't like what he saw.

It appeared that a huge, slab-shaped chunk of granite had broken out of the ceiling. It was sandwiched by smaller rocks, dirt, gravel, and pieces of framing timber. What he was looking at was essentially a solid wall of debris. There was no way to move that slab of granite. Which meant there was no way through the debris. No way to get out by way of the mine's entrance.

The entrance was sewn up tight as a heifer's ass in fly season, as old Angus would have said.

Hunter was on his third match, studying the blockage in a stubborn belief that there must be some way to squirrel through it, when boots crunched behind him. Annabelle walked up to squat beside him, facing the pile.

"Doesn't look good, does it?" she asked.

Hunter shook his head. "No. I don't think we're going to get out this way."

He let the match drop and flicker out on the dark floor, and turned to gaze behind him, beyond the weak ray of gray light.

"There's not a back door, is there?" Anna asked quietly in the eerily dense silence.

Hunter shook his head. "I've checked out the whole tunnel. It goes on for maybe thirty more feet and ends in solid rock."

They stood in silence together, shoulder to shoulder. Their breathing was the only sound until Anna said, "Does anyone know we're here?"

"I haven't told anyone about the shack . . . or the mine. I told Pa an' Shep an' Tye about us eloping together, but I didn't mention where we were meeting up today. Just that we'd be home in a few days."

"Just out of curiosity," Anna said after a while, "what was their reaction to what you told your father, Shep, and Tye?"

"About us runnin' off to get hitched?" Hunter grinned. "Pa said he was mad because he wanted to marry you himself."

"That old devil!"

"Shep wanted to ride over and snatch you away from the Broken Heart last night, bring you back to the 4-Box-B for a good, old-fashioned, wedding-night hoedown."

Anna laughed.

"Tye thought it was a good occasion to tap one of Angus's kegs. So that's what we did. Even after several glasses of the old man's ale, though, I couldn't sleep for thinkin' about today."

Hunter wrapped his arm around her again and pressed his lips to her forehead.

"They don't mind you marrying a Yankee girl?" Anna asked him.

Hunter smiled. "Not this one. Those three ole Rebels don't hold nothin' against a pretty girl. Especially one so nice, like you are. And who can ride a horse as well as you do. They've never known a pretty, rich Yankee girl who don't put on airs . . . and knows horses. Old Angus still can't wrap his mind around the fact you don't ride sidesaddle!"

They laughed briefly.

Anna pressed her head against his shoulder. She didn't say anything. After a time, he felt her shuddering, and then she sniffed quietly. She was crying.

"Oh, Hunter . . ."

He took her hand in his. "Come on over here. Let's sit down."

He led her back into the light angling down through the crack in the mine ceiling. He helped her sit down against the wall opposite where the cache had been. He sat down beside her. They both drew their knees up toward their chests.

"We could have had such a wonderful life together," Anna said. "Even without the gold. We didn't need gold to make us happy." She looked up at him through watery eyes. "Or rich."

"No," Hunter said through a long, fateful sigh. "It would have helped though. We could have bought old Johnson's ranch." He paused, shook his head. "That damn Stillwell."

"How do you think he knew about the cabin?"

"I don't know. He must have followed us out from Tigerville yesterday. It's the only way I can figure it. Must've been spying on us. Seen us walk into the mine."

"Unless he paid a visit to the tarot card reader in Tigerville — Madame Marcollini."

Hunter gave a droll snort.

"He was probably watchin' us in the cabin," Anna said thickly, giving another jerk of revulsion.

Hunter thought about Stillwell ogling them through a window, and ground his back teeth in barely bridled rage.

"He must have overheard our plans, spent the night there in the cabin, waiting for us to return. Right now he's probably heading for Mexico . . . with our gold."

Anna lowered her head to her knees and gave another bereaved sob at their fate.

"What happened, Anna? Back at the Broken Heart. What made you so upset? I could see it in your eyes."

Anna lifted her head, sniffed, and brushed a hand across her nose. She shook her red hair back, then told him about the dustup with her father and Kenneth Earnshaw and then her run-in with her brother Cass in the barn earlier this morning. About the fire.

"If we ever get out of here," Hunter said, grinding his molars again, "Cass is gonna get his hat handed to him."

Anna looked at the pile of debris humped darkly on their right. "I think he's safe," she said finally.

"I reckon so," Hunter had to admit, studying the debris himself.

"Hunter?"

"Yes, honey?"

"Just know I love you, and there isn't another man anywhere I'd rather die with deep in the earth's bowels."

Hunter knew she'd meant it seriously, but for some reason they both found it funny after she'd said it. They laughed together, raucously for a time, shuddering against each other. Deep down they were both just trying to distract themselves from the grimness of their situation, but laughing felt good. It tempered their fear — for a short time, anyway.

When their laughter dwindled, Hunter drew Anna to him again, kissed her forehead, and held her tightly in his arms.

They sat in the thick, stony silence, breathing together, for a long time.

Hunter gentled Anna away from him and gained his feet, crouching to keep his head from scraping the ceiling. "I just can't let it go, damnit," he growled. "There's gotta be a way out of here!"

He looked around.

"If we could both lose some weight — I mean, a lot of it," Anna said, "I guess we could climb up through that crack."

Hunter looked at the narrow crack zigzagging across part of the ceiling. "Yeah."

"Give us a few days without food."

Hunter shoved the fingers of his left hand into the crack. He shoved his entire left hand into the crack, rage burning in him.

He pulled against both sides of the crack at once, spitting out through gritted teeth, "If I could just . . . !"

"Hunter, honey. Please, stop."

"Damnit all anyway!" Hunter kept applying pressure against both sides of the crack, desperation boiling in him.

"Hunter!" Anna cried, rising to her feet. "Stop! You're gonna hurt — !"

She screamed and leaped back as a tombstone-size boulder came falling out of the wall to crash onto the mine floor with a resounding thud, breaking in half. Hunter leaped back with a grunt as another slab of limestone, about half as large as the first, also fell out of the ceiling. It landed on the toe of his boot, and he hopped on the other boot, cursing.

"Damn my crazy Rebel hide!" the big ex-Confederate intoned, hopping on one foot while holding the other one in both hands. "Why can't I let well enough alone?"

"Hunter."

Anna's tone was odd. He set his injured foot back down and looked at her. She was staring up at the ceiling, her lips parted, eyes wide. Her emerald-green eyes sparkled like a sunlit summer meadow as light shone into them.

Hunter turned to the gaping hole the

dislodged boulders had left in the ceiling. The hole was roughly four feet by five feet in diameter. Hunter's lower jaw hung. His heart quickened, his veins tingling with racing blood. He stepped slowly up to the gaping hole, peered into it, crouching and tipping his head far back on his shoulders so he could probe it more deeply with his gaze.

Mostly, he could see the stone sides of the cleft glowing gold and salmon with mid-morning sunlight. He couldn't see an exit from the chasm, for the natural flue seemed to angle back against the mountain, but the sunlight was coming from somewhere. And the chasm appeared as big around as the hole in the ceiling was.

He looked at Anna. She looked back at him, her rich mouth slowly shaping a hopeful smile.

Hunter donned his hat and poked his head into the hole. The cleft twisted off to his left and then climbed upward, where the sunlight was even brighter. Hunter's heart beat even more optimistically. There was open sky up there. Had to be. All he and Anna had to do was climb up through it.

Hunter lifted his arms up through the hole. He bent his knees and bounded up off his feet, smashing his elbows down against the bottom of the cleft, hoping to hell more

184

rock didn't give way. He began hoisting himself up, grunting and praying the rock wouldn't give.

So far, so good.

He drew his legs up into the cleft that was rife with the smell of fresh air, the tang of pine, and the verdant aroma of summer leaves. He'd forgotten how wonderful the summer air smelled. He'd never take it for granted again.

On one knee, he thrust his left hand down through the hole.

"Come on, Anna!"

Anna stepped up to the hole, smiling. She thrust her hand into Hunter's. He pulled her up through the hole.

"Come on!" he said. "Watch your step!"

He began climbing up through the cleft, setting his boots down on lumps of rock jutting out of a belly of stone bulging on his right. Using his hands, he pulled himself up by similar small bulges and dimples. He and Anna climbed up and around this bulging belly, and there it was just ahead and above — a large, round circle of blue sky containing a slice of lace-edged, puffy white cloud.

Hunter scrambled up out of the hole, which was a deep crack sheathed in wiry brush and rocks at the very top of the ridge. Setting his boots in a cleft among the pale rock, he reached down for Anna's hand and pulled her up onto the crest of the ridge.

For a time, they just sat there, side by side, speechless with thankfulness. In awe at how close they'd come to doom. They looked around at the pines jutting around them. Birds flitted here and there. Several crows fought raucously in a branch behind them.

Squirrels chittered.

The breeze raked across the top of the ridge, caressing them.

The world was new and beautiful.

Finally, Anna turned to Hunter, smiling broadly. She held out her hand. Hunter took it, kissed it, squeezed it.

"Now what?" Anna said.

Hunter looked around once more, filling his broad chest with deep draughts of precious air. He heaved himself to his feet and leaned forward to brush off his denims.

"You wait at the cabin. I'm going to pick up Stillwell's trail. I'm going to run him down and get our gold back. And then you and I are going to head down to Cheyenne just like we —"

Hunter stopped. Anna was looking around, frowning, eyes thoughtful.

"What is it?"

"I heard something."

Hunter waited.

A crack sounded from somewhere in the hills behind them. A rifle crack.

That wasn't unusual. Many people in this neck of the hills hunted game.

But then there was another crack. Another one sounded close on the heels of the previous one. Then more and more rifle reports crackled off to the northwest, one after another.

"That's not just someone after a deer," Hunter said. He stared toward the northwest, as did Anna. Half to himself, he said, "The 4-Box-B is over that way."

"Oh God."

Hunter turned to her. She stared darkly in the direction from which the rifles were crackling now furiously, as though a battle were being fought in those piney ridges.

Anna turned to Hunter. "My pa's men. I bet Pa sent them after me. After *us*. They probably figured they could find us at the 4-Box-B. Oh, Hunter!"

Hunter's heart leaped into his throat. He imagined his father and two brothers being ambushed like he himself had been yesterday by Luke Chaney. Only, Angus, Shep, and Tye would be confronting a whole lot more rifles than Hunter had. Graham Ludlow had a good twenty, thirty men on his payroll, and many of them were better than good with a shooting iron.

"Come on," Hunter said, taking Anna's hand. "Let's find a way down from here and get back to our horses!"

CHAPTER 15

Graham Ludlow stood at the bottom of the footpath climbing the rise to his sprawling, timbered lodge house, staring at what remained of his stock barn.

All that was left was a large, smoldering pile of smoking rubble. The roof had collapsed a half hour ago. Even before that, Ludlow had known the building was a goner, as engulfed in flames as it was even before his men could form a bucket brigade stretching from the skeleton-like Halladay Standard windmill, whose tin blades clattered in the warm morning breeze to Ludlow's right.

His men, tired and weary, covered in soot and sweat, had let the brigade unravel a few minutes ago, when most of the flames had finally been doused. Now most of them stood around, eyeing the charred, smoking, glistening wet remains warily, wearily. None was fully dressed. Most wore only their

189

wash-worn longhandles and boots. A few donned hats. Three or four had managed to pull on pants and suspenders before charging out of the bunkhouse nearly an hour ago now, to the cook's screams of "Fire!"

Two men were walking around the barn's perimeter, dousing the last of the flames cropping up here and there amidst the ruins.

Now C. J. Bonner, Ludlow's foreman, finished talking to the bulk of his men gathered off the barn's right front corner. As the men began trudging back to the bunkhouse to get cleaned up and to partake of their delayed breakfast, Bonner walked toward Ludlow.

The rancher himself was still clad in only his long-handles, deerskin slippers, and bathrobe, which was fire-blackened and reeking of smoke. Ludlow had joined the brigade after he'd watched his daughter, Annabelle, gallop out of the yard, riding off to marry that damned Confederate . . . after he and Chang had gotten Cass, his badly injured son, into a bed in the house, where Chang was still tending him while they awaited the arrival of the doctor from Tigerville.

"Well, that's about all we can do, Mr. Ludlow," Bonner said, walking up to stand beside the rancher and turning to face the smoldering ruins. His voice was like gravel raking through a sluice box. "We got her contained, and I reckon that's the most we can do at this point. She's a goner, that's for sure." He squinted an eye at his employer. "You know how a fire like that can spread. Lucky it didn't take out the other two barns, the bunkhouse. Hell, sparks might've winged it up to the main lodge . . ."

Bonner, a slender, long-limbed, gimlet-eyed horseman with close-cropped hair and a drooping blond mustache, let his voice trail off sheepishly. Ludlow now looked at him, riled by the man's not-so-vaguely accusing tone that let Ludlow know just who was responsible for the fire in the first place. The rancher's daughter, of course. Thereby involving Ludlow himself, who should have kept a tighter rein on the headstrong filly.

At least, that was the implication.

"I'm well aware of the possible calamity here, C.J.," Ludlow growled.

He thought he saw the foreman's broad, thick shoulders tighten slightly as the man stared at the smoldering ruins.

Still, Bonner wasn't ready to let it go. He glanced at the thicker and older Ludlow again and said, haltingly, "You . . . you want me to get the boys saddled up, an' . . . you know . . . maybe pay a visit over to the Buchanon ranch?"

"No. That won't be necessary."

Ludlow stared at the remains of the barn, an intoxicating mix of emotions churning inside him — rage at the loss of the barn, exasperation at what Annabelle had done to Cass. Humiliation at her involvement with Hunter Buchanon behind Ludlow's back, despite his strictly forbidding her to see the Grayback. More rage and exasperation at where she was going at this very moment, at what she intended to do.

Marry up into that clan of scoundrel ex-Confederates.

He also felt stupid. Gullible beyond belief. He should have known she was meeting up with the Buchanon son on the sly. She'd mentioned having met him on one of her rides through the Hills, a couple of summers ago.

Maybe Ludlow did know, deep down, that she was seeing that Reb. Maybe he hadn't wanted to admit it to himself. He knew how stubborn Anna could be, not unlike himself in that way, and that it was damn near impossible to change her mind about any damn thing, much less a young man she'd set her hat for.

In the past, Ludlow had been proud of his daughter's spirit. What's a horse without some pitch? She was tough, hardy, and strong willed. She was her father's daughter. Like her mother, she was smart and she was beautiful.

Now, however, she'd gone too far. She'd humiliated her father. He'd allowed her to win smaller battles in the past. Maybe he'd been saving himself for this larger one. She wouldn't win this one. Ludlow couldn't allow that to happen. Not if he wanted to retain any of his hard-won respect from the other tough men in these Hills, not to mention the other investors in both his ranch and his mine.

Annabelle was going to marry whom her father told her to marry, by God. And that certainly wasn't one of the unwashed Southern clansmen who'd killed her brother. She was going to have a very public wedding, and the groom would be Kenneth Earnshaw, despite his mealymouthed, nancy-boy demeanor and cow-stupid eyes, for he was the son of Ludlow's valued business associate, Ferroll Earnshaw, who was helping Ludlow build the first spur railroad line into the Black Hills and which would make him and the Earnshaws — Mr. and Mrs. Kenneth Earnshaw, included — the wealthiest people in the Territory if not the entire upper Midwest.

"No, that won't be necessary, C.J.," Ludlow told his foreman now. "That nasty boil on my backside is likely in the process of being lanced even as we speak."

Ludlow looked at his sun-seasoned, blond foreman, and curled an ironic, telling smile.

"Oh, I see," Bonner said, nodding his understanding.

It was well known that Ludlow had more men than the ranch hands riding for him. He and Max Chaney had hired some of the toughest men in the territory to guard their ore shipments to Cheyenne and to perform other sundry affairs that were part and parcel of surviving as a businessman in this savage place and during these unscrupulous times.

No bona fide law had yet found its way into these Hills, which had been home to the kill-crazy Sioux only a few short years ago. That meant every man was law unto himself.

"Get the men ready to drive that southern herd over to Hat Creek, C.J.," Ludlow said. "On the way back, make sure no squatters have set up housekeeping on that tributary to the Little Steven. It might be government graze and officially open for homesteading, but unofficially I say it isn't. If those square-heads from Minnesota are back, go ahead and hang the father and the oldest boy. It isn't like we haven't warned them. Tell the mother to be grateful for the children she has left and to head back to Minnesota. That's where they belong!"

"Yes, sir, Mr. Ludlow," Bonner said, giving a two-fingered salute. "I got me some new hemp that needs stretchin', I sure do!" He gave a devilish wink. Pulling up his sagging britches, he strode in his somewhat stiff, bandy-legged horseman's fashion over to the bunkhouse.

Ludlow had just started in the direction of the main lodge to check on Cass when the clatter of iron-shod wheels rose on his right. He stopped and watched the black, red-wheeled single-seater chaise roll in under the portal, then angle toward him and the path leading to the main lodge.

Doctor Norton Dahl sat in the front leather seat, leaning forward, elbows on his knees, reins in his gloved hands. His black medical kit was perched on the seat beside him.

The sawbones stared at the smoldering barn ruins, frowning curiously, then turned to face Ludlow as he rolled the buggy past the rancher and over to one of the three iron hitchracks about halfway up the hill to the lodge, in the shade of a sprawling box elder.

"I hear you got trouble, Ludlow," Dahl said as he drew the roan to a halt fronting one of the racks and engaged the wagon's brake.

Ludlow had sent a man, Roy Finnegan, into town to fetch the doctor for Cass. He saw Finnegan now, galloping around a bend in the trail, a hundred yards distant but closing fast. He'd likely stopped for a snort or two in a Tigerville saloon, thinking he could catch up to the doctor before Dahl reached the Broken Heart.

The rancher snorted his self-directed reproof. You can't send an Irishman to town and not expect him to throw back a shot or two of Taos lightning. Ludlow continued up the path toward the lodge, Dahl falling into step beside him. "He's in a bad way, Doc. Burned pretty bad on his head. For the love of God, half his hair is gone!"

"What the hell happened?" Dahl asked. He was a seedy-looking man in his late thirties. He had long, stringy, sandy hair and an untrimmed mustache and goatee. He was too pale, and he was scrawny and smelled bad, as though he rarely bathed, and he gambled and whored too much. The Tigerville whores were free as long as he tended their sundry health problems — pregnancy and Cupid's itch being at the forefront of their afflictions, not to mention the occasional stabbings by drunk or otherwise disgruntled clients.

Some said that Dahl himself had a couple of orphans running around the Hills.

His cheap wool suit was rank with sweat and spilled ale and tobacco smoke, causing Ludlow to wince but also to remind himself that there were many men in the Hills, maimed from mining accidents or the bloody skirmishes drunk miners were forever getting into, armed with picks and shovels, who would otherwise be dead if not for Dahl's creative ministrations.

"The hand you sent for me said something about Miss Ludlow . . . ?" the doctor probed as, breathless from the climb from the yard, the rancher led the sawbones up the veranda's broad front steps.

"Blast Finnegan!"

Ludlow stopped and rammed his fist into his open palm. He glared back down the hill toward the corral in which the Irish hand was just then turning out his lathered mount.

"I told him to keep his damn trap shut about that. He was to fetch you out here and keep his damn mouth shut. Probably shot his mouth off in the saloons too. By now it's halfway around the Hills!"

Ludlow turned to the sawbones, who stood two steps below him, cowering a little. "Uh, sorry about that, Mr. Ludlow. Rest assured I myself am rather good at keeping secrets. A man in my line has to be. You'd be surprised who in these Hills is on tincture of mercury for the pony drip." He gave a wry smile. "You know what they say — a night in the arms of Venus leads to a lifetime on Mercury!"

He snorted a laugh. Ludlow could smell whiskey on his breath.

The rancher cursed, then led the sawbones into the house, up the stairs, and down the carpeted hall. Cass's bellowing curses emanated from behind a closed door on the right side of the hall, directly across from Ludlow's own room, at the end. The rancher cast a look at the key still in the lock of Annabelle's closed door, and muttered another oath of his own.

Devil child. And all this time he'd thought she was just headstrong.

Ludlow threw open his son's door and moved into the room, drawing the door wide for the doctor, who doffed his hat and threw it onto a chair. Cass lay writhing on the bed before the door, belly-down, holding his arms up around his head as though shielding himself from further injury. Chang hovered over the young man, on the bed's far side from the door, trying to apply ointment to the side of Cass's head.

Cass cursed and howled every time the stocky Chinaman tried to smear arnica on the burn that had turned the left side of his head, including his ear, to ground burger. Pus already dribbled from the gaping sores.

"Get away from me with that poison!" Cass bellowed, turning his head to glare at the Chinaman. "It burns like hell's fires!"

"Thank you, Chang," said Dahl, moving up to the bed, holding his medical kit in both hands before him. "I'll take over now."

Chang gathered his medicines onto a tin tray and shuffled toward the door, pausing to bow before his employer. Chang glanced from Ludlow to the howling young man flopping around on the bed, then returned his dark, bleak-eyed gaze to the rancher and shook his head.

He shuffled on out of the room, muttering under his breath.

"Look at me, Doc!" Cass intoned, lifting his head so Dahl could get a look at him. "Look at what she did to me! That Rebel's whore!"

"Cass, I'll have none of that!" Ludlow

walked over to the bed's far side, wincing at the grisly spectacle of his once-handsome son's ugly, oozing head. "You stop with the foul language! Stop slandering your sister!"

"She's a Rebel's whore, Pa! You an' I both know it! If your hands don't kill both of 'em, then I will!" Cass turned to Dahl, who'd set his kit on the bed and was crouched over the young man, staring distastefully down at his head. The doctor stretched his lips back from tobacco-stained teeth.

"How bad is it, Doc?" Cass asked. "Will my hair grow back? Will I heal an' look normal again?"

Dahl continued to stare down at the young man's head.

Slowly, he shuttled a dark, foreboding look toward Ludlow and then stiffly opened his medical kit. "Oh . . . oh . . . I've seen far . . . far worse burns than this," he said, though his tone was hardly reassuring.

Ludlow turned away and drew a ragged sigh, hardening his jaws against his own fury.

All that Cass had had going for him was his looks. The boy was cow-stupid and lazy. But at least he had thick, curly hair and a dimple-cheeked smile, which had attracted the women, even though he seemed to prefer percentage girls for some reason.

Ludlow had been sure, however, that sooner or later the young firebrand would settle down and let his father marry him off to one of Ludlow's business associate's comely daughters.

Now, however, the rancher doubted that would happen.

Ludlow had seen what a bad burn could do to a man's face. Cass's looks were gone for good, which meant he had nothing. He'd likely be living right here in the house, a ghost of his former self — an ugly specter — confined to his room, from which all looking glasses would be banished.

Unable to listen to his son's unmanly howling any longer, Ludlow left the room and went downstairs.

He walked out onto the veranda. He fished a half-smoked cigar from a pocket of his robe, scratched a lucifer to life on the porch rail, and touched the flame to the end of the stogie.

Taking the peppery, bracing smoke deep into his lungs, he looked toward the southwest, in the direction of the Buchanon 4-Box-B spread.

A grim, hard smile tugged at his mouth as he imagined the current course of events in that direction.

Chapter 16

Hunter and Annabelle had found their horses and Hunter's pack mule spread out along the forested slope fronting the old prospector's cabin, grazing with their reins drooping. Hunter had left the mule, knowing the animal would follow him home at its own pace.

He and Annabelle had swung up into their saddles and taken off at a hard gallop for the 4-Box-B. Now as they closed on the ranch, Hunter could hear the shooting clearly. The rifle cracks and echoing rips rose from the other side of a pine-studded haystack butte just ahead.

Movement caught Hunter's eye ahead and on his right, and he jerked his head to see a dun shape leap onto a rock beside the trail.

"Bobby!" Hunter cried.

The coyote sat atop the rock, fidgeting and mewling, deeply troubled. He gave three quick, yammering yips, then leaped down off the rock and fell into pace beside Hunter's and Annabelle's galloping mounts, stretching out low to the ground. Leaning forward over their galloping horses' polls, Hunter and Annabelle exchanged dark glances.

Hunter swung his horse up the side of a high bluff on his left. Near the top he stepped out of the saddle and ran up to the crest of the bluff, doffing his hat as he dropped to his knees. Annabelle scuttled up beside him while Bobby Lee held back with the horses, sitting down in the shade of a chokecherry shrub, thick tail curled forward, mewling anxiously.

Hunter peered over the top of the bluff and gazed down through thick, columnar pines and firs. The 4-Box-B headquarters lay in a grassy clearing below, in a hollow surrounded by pine-studded buttes. It was a humble place, consisting of a handful of hand-adzed log buildings, including a single barn and several corrals and a round breaking corral with a snubbing post. The main house sat on the opposite side of the yard from the butte atop which Hunter and Annabelle hunkered.

They were facing the rear of the barn and blacksmith shop, Angus's brew shed, and the springhouse. Smoke fluttered up from the blacksmith shop's brick chimney, hanging thick and blue in the still air. Earlier this morning, Shep must have fired up his forge and was likely making repairs to the hay rake he'd been working on yesterday, when Hunter had started for town with Angus's ale.

Shep must have been in the shop this morning when the attackers had struck.

Now two bodies lay in the yard between the barn and the long, low, log-walled, shake-roofed dwelling that was the Buchanon ranch house. They were spread out about twenty feet apart, one lying in front of the blacksmith shop. Even from this distance, Hunter could tell the body in front of the shop was Shep. It was larger than the other one, and clad in the thick, brown leather apron Shep always wore when he was at work at his bellows and forge.

Something long and slender lay several feet away from Shep. Likely Shep's prized Henry repeater. The eldest of the Buchanon boys never strayed far from his rifle.

The other body, nearer the house, appeared to be that of Tyrell. Even lying splayed out on the ground, one leg curled beneath the other, the body was long and slender. The boy's long red hair shone in the sun.

Neither Shep nor Tye was moving.

The men who'd shot them and were continuing to exchange fire with the cabin were moving around in the brush behind and between the barn, corral, springhouse, and blacksmith shop. There were a dozen, at least.

Hunter could see six or seven men, but smoke puffed from more guns than that, the puffs indicating that the attackers had formed a ragged semicircle around the front of the cabin. One man appeared to be trying to move around behind it. He was in the pines to the right of the ranch yard, shooting as he darted behind trees.

Old Angus was returning fire from the broken-out windows of the cabin, moving from window to window, smoke puffing first from one and then from another. Between shots, Hunter could hear the old, one-armed Rebel cussing a blue streak. Hunter couldn't hear what he was saying from this distance of a hundred yards, but he knew Angus well enough to know he was giving his attackers holy hell.

Hunter's heart was racing. Tears were oozing from his eyes and dribbling down his cheeks. He looked again at Shep and Tyrell lying motionless in the yard, Shep likely having run out of the blacksmith shop when the ambushers had opened up on the cabin. Tyrell, young and hotheaded, had run out of the cabin to return fire. His own rifle lay near his outstretched right hand.

"Oh God, oh God, oh God . . ." Annabelle intoned, staring in shock down the bluff toward the shoot-out. If you could call it that.

It was a bushwhack, pure and simple.

Hunter rose quickly. "Are you packing your carbine?"

Annabelle turned to him, her eyes now filling with tears. She looked at him imploringly. "Please, don't. You're outnumbered, Hunter."

Hunter gave her a pointed, commanding look. "Stay here. Whatever you do, Annabelle, don't go down there."

She merely gazed up at him through tear-flooded eyes. She didn't say anything. She knew what he was going to do, and there was nothing anyone could do to stop him.

He ran down the slope so quickly that he frightened the horses already made jittery by the crackle of the gunfire. He bounded up to the buckskin, shucked Annabelle's Winchester carbine from its leather scabbard, then grabbed his grullo's drooping reins and swung up onto Nasty Pete's back.

Instantly, he went galloping off around the

shoulder of the bluff, bulling through grass and brush. Then he was fairly flying down the front of the bluff, giving Nasty Pete his head, the horse weaving around pines and leaping through shadbush and wild currant shrubs.

The horse bottomed out on the floor of the hollow in which the ranch lay, and loped through the stirrup-high brome toward the rear of the barn. None of the bushwhackers had yet spied Hunter. They were too busy flinging lead at old Angus in the cabin.

Hunter saw one just then moving back through the broad gap between the barn and the blacksmith shop. He was moving toward Hunter but he was preoccupied with reloading the Winchester in his hands.

Hunter recognized him. He was one of Ludlow and Chaney's bullion guards — a big man with a full beard and a floppy-brimmed canvas hat, twin bandoliers criss-crossed on his chest. Furlong was his name. He'd once prospected on a place near the 4-Box-B.

Hunter aimed Nasty Pete straight toward him.

Hearing the grullo's thudding hooves, Furlong looked up. His eyes grew so wide that Hunter could see the whites clear around them. Hunter took the grullo's reins in his teeth. He racked a cartridge into the Winchester's breech, aimed quickly, and fired, punching Furlong straight back off his feet.

He rolled, howling.

Jerking the reins in his teeth, Hunter swung Nasty Pete right, then pulled back, momentarily stopping the hard-breathing mount. A man was just then turning from the barn's far rear corner, his eyes snapping wide as he started raising his own Spencer carbine.

Another bullion guard.

Another *dead* bullion guard.

Hunter's .44-caliber round blasted a quarter-size hole through the guard's forehead and blew the back of his head into the brush behind him, like spilled paint. *Dead* before he could scream. *Dead* before he hit the ground.

The next man too. He'd just lifted his head above a pile of timber scraps leftover from when the Buchanons had built their headquarters, and Hunter tattooed his cheek.

The man hadn't finished dropping before Nasty Pete was bounding along the rear of the barn. Hunter swung the horse sharply left, galloping up the side of the barn toward the front. Two shooters were hunkered up at the front of the gap, facing the cabin. Another man lay dead behind and between them, likely sporting one of old Angus's own bullets in his brisket, which oozed dark red blood.

One of the men ahead of Hunter cursed as he turned sharply to see Hunter storming toward him. "Behind us!" the man screamed, and took a bullet through his right shoulder, another through his throat.

Hunter didn't have time to shoot the other man. Nasty Pete was moving up on him too fast. Hunter let the horse hammer him straight down to the ground and then stomp him a few times, turning his face to strawberry jam.

Hunter booted the grullo out into the yard, pausing to look around. He couldn't see anyone on his right. Smoke puffed from several guns on his left, however, those slugs hammering the front of the cabin.

A rifle report sounded from the lodge, telling Hunter old Angus was still kicking, still fighting. As Hunter swung Nasty Pete hard left and began racing toward where he could see other bushwhackers hunkered around the yard, Angus gave a screeching wail:

"Hunter, what in the hell you doing, you crazy son of Satan? Get off that catamount an' take cover!"

But then the shack was back behind Hunter's right shoulder, and he was recocking Anna's Winchester and taking aim at a man hunkered behind a rain barrel off the corral's left front corner, just beyond the barn.

"Get him, boys!" one of the bushwhackers shouted beneath the thunder of rifle fire. "Blow that Rebel devil off his hoss!"

Hunter recognized the voice of Luke Chaney's old man, Max Chaney. He didn't bother looking for him. He'd find him sooner or later. In the meantime, he shot two more men who'd been hunkered down inside the corral, hurling lead from over rails or around posts. He killed one outright, only wounded the other.

As the wounded man fell back, clutching his shoulder, Hunter jerked back on Pete's reins, ejected the spent cartridge, and tried to seat fresh.

No doing.

The Winchester was empty.

As lead screamed toward him, all the bushwhackers now training their sights on him, he hurled himself off the grullo's back and rolled toward the corral. As he did, he picked up a rifle discarded by one of the men he'd shot, pumped a round into the action, and, lying prone, snaked the Winchester over the corral's bottom slat.

The man he'd only wounded was crawling toward the rear of the corral, cursing.

Hunter shot him in the left buttock, evoking a shrill howl.

Bullets hammered the dirt around the big ex-Confederate, spraying grit in his eyes. One grazed his left leg.

He rolled up on his left shoulder and extended the rifle, throwing lead at three more shooters bearing down on him from the yard's east side, hunkered in the dun brush or behind the scattered pines and aspens lining a dry creek bed. One man threw his rifle straight up in the air as the bullet punched him backward. Another cursed and rose up out of the brush, staggering forward and yelling and firing his rifle into the ground in front of him.

Then the bullet that had emptied his belly dropped him to his knees. He lay shaking his head and blubbering.

As a bullet cut a hot line across Hunter's neck, he dropped the third man he'd fired at, with a second shot. That bullet hammered the man's head straight backward on his shoulders, making his hat fly high.

Hunter rose onto a knee and began triggering lead toward the puffs of powder smoke rising from the tall grass and from

211

behind a pile of brush he and his brother had cut from the yard behind the cabin, to make room for a vegetable garden.

More men screamed and howled. Several ran.

One shouted, "Fall back! Fall back to the horses!"

That was Max Chaney again.

Hunter saw the old reprobate hightailing it through the brush off the near corral's rear right corner, heading toward a grove of aspens in which Hunter could now see horses tied to a long picket line. Several other men were also running toward the horses. He thought two of the running men looked like Luke's two brothers — Billy and Pee-Wee.

The ambushers' rifles had fallen silent now as most of the bunch made a hasty retreat.

Hunter ran forward. When he gained the front corner of the corral, he pumped another cartridge into the Winchester's action, raised the rifle to his shoulder, and aimed at Max Chaney's thick, retreating figure. He narrowed one eye as he gazed down the barrel.

The old buzzard deserved a bullet in the back. He was no better than a chicken-stealing dog, after all. In fact, he was an insult to chicken-stealing dogs.

It was a long shot at a hundred and fifty yards, but Hunter had taken longer shots during the War of Northern Aggression albeit with a Whitworth, designed for such long-range shooting.

He led Chaney a hair, centering the Winchester's sights on the back of the man's head, up near the crown of his bowler hat. He drew a breath, held it, squeezed the trigger.

A half a blink later, Chaney turned his head and his fat, tan, bearded face to look behind him. As Hunter's bullet rammed home, Chaney's head jerked forward, and the old man flew headlong into the brush.

"Pa!" one of the two Chaney boys yelled.

Both younger Chaneys ran over to where Max Chaney flopped in the tall grass near the horses.

Hunter lowered the rifle and smiled grimly as the two Chaney boys converged on their old man and dragged him forward. They cast wary, panicked looks behind them.

A muffled rifle report sounded from inside the cabin behind Hunter. Old Angus wasn't firing out the front. He must have been firing out the back, at someone trying to flank him.

Hunter ran south around an old corral

and a big, L-shaped pile of split cordwood, and then over toward the cabin. He stopped and dropped to a knee beside a boulder.

A man was hunkered behind another boulder just south of the cabin and near the small vegetable garden Hunter had dug and in which pumpkins grew thick and tangled and corn was hip-high. Powder smoke jetted from a rear window of the cabin. The bullet ricocheted off the boulder behind which the flanking attacker was hunkered.

As the ricochet screamed around the hollow, the flanker rose and snaked his rifle over the top of the boulder, aiming toward the cabin, at old Angus. Hunter didn't let him get off a shot. Hunter's bullet plowed through the man's left shoulder, twisting him around and dropping him.

Hunter rose from behind his own boulder and walked forward. His jaws were hard, his eyes like cold blue marbles at the bottom of a deep lake.

The wounded flanking attacker flopped around, groaning. He turned and saw Hunter striding toward him with grim purpose. The man's eyes snapped wide, grew dark with dread.

He stopped flopping around and, half sitting, he thrust a gloved hand out toward Hunter in supplication. His name was

Gavin Mulgavery — another ore guard. He was short and thick around the waist, with short blond hair and a blond beard and one wandering blue eye. He wore two pistols in shoulder holsters on the outside of his brown leather vest.

He didn't reach for either hogleg.

"Don't shoot me!" he bellowed. "Please, don't —"

Hunter stopped and fired the Winchester straight out from his right hip, the bullet ripping through the man's wide-open mouth to punch a fist-size hole through the back of his head, leaving him stretched out flat on the ground, quivering as the life quickly left him.

Walking slowly forward, his face set as hard as a plaster mask, Hunter shot Mulgavery again . . . again . . . and again. Until the Winchester's hammer pinged benignly against the firing pin.

The padding of four little feet sounded.

Hunter watched Bobby Lee run up out of the brush behind the cabin. The coyote stopped near the dead man, gave a low snarl, showed his teeth, and hiked his back leg on the dead man's head.

CHAPTER 17

Bobby Lee sat down before Hunter, lifted his long, gray-brown snout, and hurled several baleful wails skyward.

Hunter stared down at the dead Mulgavery, wishing he could kill the man — all of these men — all over again.

Ragged breaths sounded behind him. He wheeled, raising the Winchester with both hands. He checked the motion, lowered the rifle. It was old Angus standing in the window to the left of the cabin's rear door.

The old man's head was bare, his long, gray hair hanging in sweat-soaked tangles to his shoulders clad in a wash-worn balbriggan top and suspenders. Coarse gray hair curled out from between the old garment's unbuttoned front flaps, from the old man's bony, liver-spotted chest.

Angus's cold blue eyes were on the man Hunter had just sent to hell in a hail of hot lead. The elder Buchanon was breathing

216

hard, and he was holding his only hand to his right side, from which blood bubbled up around a bullet hole about six inches above the waistband of his patched dungarees.

"He dead?"

Hunter nodded. "He's dead, Pa."

"He the last of 'em?"

Hunter looked around. "I think so. The rest lit a shuck, tails between their legs." He stepped forward, toward the broken-out window in which his stooped, grizzled old father — looking older and more grizzled now than ever — crouched, staring out. Pain shone sharp in Angus's eyes.

Physical pain. Mental pain.

"How bad you hit, Pa?"

Angus slid his gaze from the dead man to Hunter. His left cheek twitched, and tears glazed his eyes.

"Shep," he muttered, upper lip quivering, a tear dribbling down his gray-bearded cheek. "Tye . . ." He stumbled backward against a dresser — he was in his own back bedroom — then turned and ambled heavily toward the bedroom door to the hall. "Gotta . . . gotta see to my boys!"

"Pa, hold on." Hunter dropped the rifle and walked toward the lodge's back door. "You're bleedin' bad, Pa!"

He grabbed the latch handle and pulled,

but Angus had barred the door, which had been hammered repeatedly with bullets, from the inside. Having hailed from a war-torn country, and having heard about the viciousness of the Sioux before they'd all come west as a family, they'd built the humble log house as stout as a military fortress, with thick walls of native timber heavily chinked and with loopholes bored through the doors.

Through one hole Hunter could see old Angus stumbling off down the hall toward the front of the cabin, intent on reaching Tye and Shep lying out in the front yard.

Hunter hurried around the side of the lodge, Bobby Lee trotting along behind him, panting. He reached the front just as old Angus burst out the lodge's stout front door and limped onto the porch, stooped forward, pressing his hand to the wound in his side.

"Oh!" the old man cried, seeing Tye lying about ten feet off the broad, timbered veranda's front steps. More tears dribbled down Angus's ashen cheeks. "Tyrell!" he called as he stumbled down the five steps.

Hunter reached up and wrapped his arm around the old man's waist, or Angus would have collapsed. Hunter knew there was no way to get the man to sit down, so he kept his arm around him, keeping him from falling, as Angus shuffled out to where Tyrell lay on his side, red hair splayed out on the ground beneath his head.

"Ty-rell!" Angus fairly bellowed as though ordering his son to rise and get to work. "Ty-rell!" he yelled again before dropping to his knees and staring down in horror at his youngest son, who lay bleeding from a half dozen bullet wounds.

Hunter dropped to a knee. He stared down in shock at his dead young brother. Tye had probably seen Shep shot after their oldest brother had run out of the blacksmith shop, likely after their ambushers had started yelling threats and shooting.

Hunter doubted that Tye had gotten off a shot himself, as no empty cartridge casings littered the ground around the young man's body or his rifle lying near his outstretched right hand. One bullet had drilled poor Tye in the neck. He'd taken two to the chest, near his heart. One had smashed into his hip while the other two had been punched into his right thigh.

The boy's eyes were half-open as he lay staring sightlessly at the ground. A fly lit on his bottom lip.

While old Angus rested his hand on his son's body, hovering over him, sobbing, shoulders jerking, Hunter brushed his fingers over Tye's eyes, closing them. Then he rose and walked over to where Shepfield Buchanon lay in front of the blacksmith shop.

Shep lay on his back, limbs akimbo. He'd taken two shots to his chest. One had likely pierced his heart, the other his left lung. Another had grazed the outside of his left knee.

The two in the chest had done him in.

Three cartridge casings lay in the blood-splashed dirt around him.

Hunter dropped to a knee, placed a hand on his oldest brother's shoulder. Sorrow was a living, breathing thing inside him. His heart had been torn by a giant, razor-edged knife. The rage of the unbridled berserker he'd known only a few minutes ago had made way for his grief.

It would return later. He knew himself well enough to know that fact.

When it did return, he would welcome it.

He had tried to live a peaceable life. The men from Tigerville — Stillwell, Ludlow, the Chaneys — hadn't let him. And, because they hadn't, and because of what they had done here today, they would all die as bloody as Tyrell and Shep.

"Good-bye, big brother," Hunter said

now, raking the words out on a long, bitter sigh. "Sleep well. You were a good man. You deserve a good rest. And . . . know that you'll be avenged."

The thunder of hammering hooves sounded from behind the barn. Instinctively, Hunter reached for Shep's Henry repeater. He rose, both hands on the rifle, ready to cock it and bring it up. He lowered it when Annabelle galloped out from the break between the barn and the blacksmith shop.

She checked the buckskin into a skidding halt just outside of the break and looked around. Her frightened eyes found Hunter. Her gaze raked him, checking for wounds. Satisfied he'd been grazed a few times but not seriously wounded, she dropped her gaze to Shep before sliding them over to where old Angus was still crouched over Tye, bawling.

Bobby Lee sat near the old man, yipping softly, miserably.

Annabelle sat the buckskin stiffly, in silent shock and disbelief, as Angus climbed to his feet and shambled over to where Hunter stood by Shep.

"Shep!" Angus wailed. "Shepp! Nooooo! Oh God, *noooooo!*"

He dropped to his knees and threw himself over his oldest son's body, wailing, sobbing,

221

and cursing.

Annabelle swung slowly down from the buckskin's back. She dropped her reins and walked over to Hunter. She stared up at him, tears filling her eyes.

She had no words. There was nothing to say.

She merely moved against him, pressed her cheek to his chest, and wrapped her arms around his waist.

Hunter held her very tightly as he stared down at old Angus crouched over Shep.

Bobby Lee moved over to sniff the body of young Tye, yipping softly, voicing his own sorrow. He walked over to circle Shep, Angus, Hunter, and Annabelle several times, howling faintly, wailing.

Then the coyote sat in the very middle of the yard and sent a long mournful howl rocketing toward the heavens.

"Come on, Pa," Hunter said after a time, placing his hand on the old man's quivering back. "We gotta get you inside, see to that wound."

Angus shook his head. "Leave me here. Leave me with my boys."

"Pa, you'll bleed out."

Angus ground his forehead against Shep's bloody chest. "I don't care!"

"Pa!" Hunter jerked his father up by his lone arm. "I'm your son too. I'm alive. You are too. Shep and Tye are dead" — his voice quaked with emotion — "an' there's nothin' we can do for 'em now except bury 'em. But I need you to stay alive. For me."

Angus stared back at him. For nearly a minute, it was as if the old, grief-stricken ex-Confederate wasn't sure who he was looking at. His son's blood stained his forehead, like a tribal tattoo. His tear-flooded eyes clarified somewhat, and he gave a slow dip of his chin. He ran his big, arthritic hand down his face and glanced at Shep once more.

"All . . . all right."

Annabelle hunkered down close to old Angus, and she and Hunter gently pulled the old man to his feet. They turned him toward the house, each supporting one side. Angus hadn't taken more than three steps before he gave a ragged sigh. His head went back, his eyes rolled up in their sockets, and his knees buckled.

"I got him," Hunter said, stooping low and picking the old man up in his arms. Angus was as light as a scarecrow. Frighteningly light. "Let's get him inside."

"I'll heat some water!" Annabelle ran toward the cabin ahead of Hunter, swerving wide around Tye and taking the lodge's veranda steps two at a time.

Hunter carried Angus inside and laid him down on the leather sofa in the parlor, which was just inside the front door and off the main entrance hall, to the left of the kitchen. The halved-log stairs to the second story were straight down the hall, ten feet from the door.

Hunter ran upstairs for cleaning rags and bandages and then hurried back down to find Angus looking ghostly pale and quiet on the parlor's sofa, beneath the old Rebel flag they'd brought with them from Georgia and tacked on the wall with countless animal skins and Hunter's mother's water-colors of idyllic Georgia farm scenes from before the war.

Bobby Lee sat on the braided rope rug in the middle of the room, holding his own brand of coyote vigil.

Hunter stopped halfway across the room, near Angus's handmade chair carved from native Black Hills wood, cow hide, and deer antlers. Angus lay so still that he didn't appear to be breathing.

"Pa?" To Hunter's own ears, his voice sounded like that of a little boy. A frightened little boy. "Pa . . . ?"

Angus didn't move, didn't make a sound.

Hunter moved forward, feet heavy with dread.

He dropped to one knee before his father, placed a hand on Angus's bony chest, over his heart. "Don't you die on me, you old Rebel!"

He pressed his hand down harder on Angus's chest, desperately wanting to feel a heartbeat. But then Angus opened one eye half-wide and snarled, "Don't you worry." He coughed a little and drew a reedy breath. "I'm too mean to die!"

"You old sod," Hunter said in relief. "You had me goin'."

"I'm not gonna die 'til I see whoever sent those bushwhacking hardtails hanging from one o' them long, tall pines in the bluffs over yonder." Angus pointed a crooked finger. "I ain't gonna die 'til we throw a necktie party in that devil's honor!"

Bobby Lee yipped as though in agreement.

"That would likely be my father."

Hunter and Angus looked over to see Annabelle standing in the doorway to the hall, holding a small tin tray in one hand and a whiskey bottle and a bone-handled knife in the other.

Annabelle glanced down, sheepish, then moved forward to kneel beside old Angus.

"What beef would Ludlow have with me?" Angus looked at Hunter. "I thought it was Stillwell . . ."

"It's a long story, Mr. Buchanon. I'll tell you all about it in due time. At the moment, we have to tend this wound, get the bleeding stopped."

Angus cursed and looked at Annabelle, scowling. "How many times I told you, girl, you're not to call me Mister!" He gave a weak laugh and lay his head back against the sofa. "Do I look like a 'mister' to you?" His smile broadened. "I'm a nasty ole Rebel from the hills of north Georgia." He exaggerated his Southern accent, pronouncing the last two words "Nothe Joj-ahhh."

Annabelle was cutting the old man's shirt away from the wound. She paused to uncork the whiskey bottle and offer it to him.

"Best have you a sip, Mister . . . I mean, Angus . . ." Annabelle smiled.

Angus wrapped his hand around the bottle. "And here it ain't even noon." He winked up at Hunter. "You'd best marry this girl soon, boy. Yankee or no Yankee, I'm liable to snatch her away from you."

"I'm working on it, Pa." Hunter cut a lopsided smile at his girl, who returned it.

Angus took several long pulls from the bottle. As Annabelle began to dab a dry towel at the bloody wound, tears came to his eyes once more, and he sobbed. "Oh . . . my boys. My dear dead boys!"

He glared up at Hunter kneeling beside him, holding the bloody shirt while Annabelle cut it away with the knife. "We got us a reckoning, boy! We got us some revenge to serve up colder'n a Dakota snowstorm in January!"

CHAPTER 18

When Hunter and Annabelle had finished cleaning the wound and sterilizing it with the little whiskey Angus left in the bottle before he passed out, Hunter picked his father up in his arms and carried him back to his room behind the kitchen. They undressed him down to his red cotton balbriggans, which too many washings in stout lye soap, cooked with wood ash from the Buchanon stove grates, had turned a sickly shade of pink, and tucked him into his bed.

An ambrotype photo of Angus and his wife, Hunter's mother, taken in Chattanooga on their wedding day, kept watch from a bedside table. The two young faces, bearing expressions of customary formality for the times, seemed to mock and jeer the unconscious old, one-armed former soldier lying passed out and snoring on the large, lumpy bed that fairly swallowed his spindly body.

"You think the bullet went all the way through?" Hunter asked Annabelle as she tucked the covers up close around Angus's chin.

The old man's deep snores resounded throughout the room.

"I think so. At least, that wound in his back looks like an exit wound to me."

Being the only woman out at the Broken Heart, Annabelle had often assisted the cook in administering to the medical needs of her father's injured men over the years — even those who'd taken rustlers' bullets and needed faster attention than waiting for the doctor in Tigerville would allow. "I think we've done all we can for him. We cleaned the wound, got the bleeding stopped, and sutured it."

She glanced at Hunter standing beside her staring down at his father. "Now we just have to try to keep his fever down. If it gets up too high, we're probably going to need Dahl to look at him."

Hunter turned to the door. "I'll fetch him now."

Annabelle grabbed his arm. "Hunter, if you ride into town now, you'll ride into an ambush."

"I know how to ride in without bein' seen. I can ride out the same —"

229

"Dahl's likely got his hands full. You said you think you wounded Max Chaney and sent another four or five of his men back to town in the same condition." Annabelle shook her head, her eyes grave. "You'll never even reach Dahl, Hunter. I think Angus will be all right if we can keep his fever down. If not, you can fetch the doctor tomorrow."

Hunter stared worriedly down at Angus.

Annabelle squeezed his arm. "I'm sorry, Hunter. I should have known my father would send his men here. After what happened at the ranch . . ."

Hunter looked at her. "I didn't see any Broken Heart men in that pack, Anna. Those men were led by Chaney and his two sons. I don't think your pa had anything to do with it."

"He may have not sent any of his ranch hands, Hunt," Annabelle said, "but my father was part of what happened out there. He and Chaney head up the ore guards. They were sent here because of both Chaney and my father. He would have sent his own men, but he probably didn't because he and Chaney had already decided to send the ore guards, and likely men in town loyal to the Chaneys."

She shook her head slowly, dreadfully. "I'll go to my grave knowing that . . . knowing that your brothers were killed . . . your father wounded . . . because Luke Chaney got some crazy idea in his head that I —"

"Don't even say it, Anna." Hunter grabbed both of her arms and turned her toward him. "For the final time, none of this is your fault. It's the fault of the men who killed Shep and Tye."

Hunter stared at her levelly. "If one of those men is your father . . ."

He knew he didn't need to finish the sentence.

Annabelle tightened her jaws as she stared back at him, her eyes as hard as his. "My father deserves what he gets."

"Even if it comes to lead?"

Keeping her eyes on Hunter's, Annabelle dipped her chin. "Even if it comes to lead . . . or a hang rope."

"All right, then," Hunter said, pressing his lips to her forehead and moving to the door. "You keep an eye on Pa, will you? I'm going to go tend my brothers."

"Leave old Angus to me." Annabelle gave a weak but genuine smile, turning to where the old man snored beneath the covers. "I'll take good care of this old Confederate." She turned to Hunter again, and the smile stretched her lips a little more. "Just as I intend to take care of his son."

■ ■ ■ ■

The next morning, at dawn, Hunter sunk a spade into the sandy ground at the bottom of the freshly dug grave.

With a grunt, he pulled up the shovelful of earth and gravel, and tossed it up and over the wall of the grave. He heard the flecking thuds of the dirt hitting the side of one of the two coffins he'd hauled up here to this hill southwest of the ranch yard in the supply wagon.

One of the coffins serving as the final resting place of one of his two dead brothers . . .

Dead brothers.

He still hadn't gotten his mind wrapped around the notion yet. His heart knew it. Maybe it didn't understand it. But it knew it. It had been torn in two by the knowledge.

His mind, on the other hand, felt as dull as wood and heavy as stone. At times, he felt drunk. At other times, he felt so sober he thought he would go mad. That's why he'd been up here for the past two hours, slowly, methodically, thoroughly digging the graves. To distract himself from the hard, cold facts of the recent events, and to bleed off some of the sap of his rage so his head wouldn't explode.

Bobby Lee sat beside the grave, yipping softly from time to time, mincing his delicate front feet. Bobby occasionally looked at Hunter working in the grave, his yellow eyes soft with sadness. The coyote mewled softly as though sympathizing with Hunter's sorrow, offering comfort and moral support.

Hunter had started on the graves just after midnight, after spending the several previous hours building the coffins from lumber old Angus had intended to use for a new workbench in his brewing shed. Hunter and Shep had whipsawed the one-by-twelve-inch boards from a giant fir at the edge of the ranch yard that the wind had toppled earlier that summer. Last night, Hunter had used a crosscut saw to adjust the lumber to the lengths he'd needed for the coffins. He'd planed the boards, nailed them together, and built lids that fit snugly enough to keep out predators.

Around midnight, by the light of a single, guttering lantern hanging in the barn, he'd laid the bodies, wrapped in animal skins from Shep's and Tye's own beds, into the coffins. He'd taken one last, long, lingering look at his brothers and then nailed the lids down tight. He would have liked to give his father another chance to say good-bye, but he didn't have time. He sensed a storm brewing in the form of more men coming.

He had to bury his dead and make plans for a possible war. A battle for sure, but possibly war.

Another damned war. Out here where he and his father and brothers had come to start a new life, far away from their last war.

As during the last one, there was no time for funerals.

Breathing hard from the digging, Hunter looked around at the grave. It was a good five feet deep, edging toward six, its bottom relatively level. He stooped to pluck a stone protruding from one corner, and tossed it out. Satisfied the grave was to his liking, he tossed the shovel out of the grave and placed his hands on its edge, intending to hoist himself out.

Bobby Lee hunkered low on his belly and peered down at the grave's bottom, which the gradually growing light of dawn had not yet found. The coyote looked up at Hunter standing over him, Hunter's feet still in the grave.

Bobby Lee gave a quiet, mournful howl, then scuttled closer to Hunter, rose onto his hind feet, and licked his master's cheek, the tongue small and rough but warm with shared sadness and kinship.

"Thanks, Bobby Lee," Hunter said, running his hand down the lean coyote's thick-furred body. "I appreciate that."

The coyote gave a moan, then padded over and lay down beneath the wagon.

Hunter hoisted himself out of the grave — one of two sitting side by side on the crest of this hill that now so early in the morning was all blurred edges and misty shadows. He turned to the coffins and felt the perpetual lump in his throat tighten. He glanced at each wooden box in turn, smelling the pine resin from the freshly cut wood.

His brothers were in those boxes. They shouldn't be. They'd both been young men, with long lives ahead of them. Taken away by Max Chaney and probably Graham Ludlow, as well, in response to Hunter's having killed Luke Chaney in self-defense.

And because an ex-Confederate had fallen in love with Ludlow's daughter.

Hunter drew a breath, brushed a tear from his cheek.

"All right," he said, prodding himself into action. He couldn't dally up here. He had a long day ahead.

He'd tied ropes around the coffins. Now he used those ropes to lower the boxes into the graves, dropping to his knees, grunting with the effort, the muscles in his sculpted forearms bulging, the ropes burning his well-calloused hands. When he had the coffins settled into their respective resting places, he straightened, mopped sweat from his brow with a handkerchief, grabbed the spade, and began tossing dirt into the holes.

A grim damn job, burying your brothers. He'd buried plenty of men during the war — men to whom he'd felt as close as brothers. But never an actual brother.

Sorrow mixed with the rage inside him, but he kept it on a tight leash.

For now . . .

He filled in the graves and mounded each with rocks. Later, he'd erect stones at the head of each.

He'd just finished arranging the stones tightly enough that he didn't think the wolves or wildcats could dig through them, when he heard the whine of door hinges from the direction of the cabin. He looked down the hill to the northeast to see a slender figure step out of the cabin's back door, thick red hair spilling down over Annabelle's slender shoulders.

She walked out away from the cabin and angled up the face of the hill. When she was a hundred yards away, Hunter could see that she was holding something in each hand. As she came nearer, he saw the steam from the two stone mugs rising in the pale air.

She came around a twisted cedar and stopped. She stared down at the two graves, the dawn breeze gently rippling the long strands of her hair that were beginning to glow now as the sun peeked its head over the eastern horizon.

Still staring at the graves, she said in a voice thick with emotion, "You've had a long night."

"Wish it was longer," Hunter said, toeing a stone. "I feel like I'm racing the clock."

"You think more men will come."

Hunter nodded.

Annabelle came forward, extending one of the two chipped stone mugs in her hands. "Take time for some coffee. I'm frying some eggs and bacon and cooking some beans. You have to eat."

Hunter took the mug.

"Pa?" he asked her.

"He made it through the night," Annabelle said. "I've been keeping the fever down with cool cloths. I changed his bandages a few minutes ago. It didn't look like his wound had bled during the night. So far, so good."

"You've had a long night too."

"It's the least I could do."

Hunter blew on the surface of the coal-black coffee, then sipped and smacked his lips. "You cook good mud, Mrs. Buchanon."

"That's about the extent of my kitchen skills, I'm afraid. I think I burned the beans."

Hunter walked up to her, kissed her cheek. "I'm glad you have a fault or two. I got a few myself."

She reached up and slid a lock of his long, thick blond hair back behind his ear. "No, you don't, Hunter. You're perfect in every way." Her eyes flickered, her gaze wavering. Brushing her fingers down the side of his face to his neck and then on down his broad chest, she said with a sadly pensive air, "I wish we could have been married. You know . . . before all this . . ."

Hunter took her hand, kissed it. "There'll be time. Afterward."

She looked up at him darkly. "Will there?"

"There will be, Annabelle." He cleared his throat and tried to sound more certain than he actually was. "I promise. There will be."

She tried a smile but it didn't reach her eyes or even get close. She turned away as though not wanting him to sense the doubt she was feeling. He reached up, laid a finger against her chin, and turned her face back toward his.

"Annabelle, I want to get you an' Pa to a safe place. Safer than this."

She frowned. "Hunter, we can't move Angus. Not yet. That wound could open up."

"I know it's a risk. But the place I got in mind isn't far. The house ain't safe. There's only you an' me to defend it. Our enemies could surround us and easily burn us out. We need high ground. Defensible ground. *Hidden* ground. Trust me, I learned a few things during the war."

"Then what?" Annabelle placed her hand on his forearm and squeezed. She no longer tried to hide her consternation. "Say we reach defensible ground. Then what do we do? We can't hold that high ground forever, Hunter. Eventually we'll run out of food, ammunition . . ."

"We won't need to hold it because they won't find us there. At least, not right away. While you tend Pa, I'll be off . . ." Hunter let his voice trail to silence, searching for the right words to convey his plan without unduly upsetting her.

"Off doing what, Hunter?"

On the other hand, Annabelle Ludlow was no shrinking violet. She was as tough as most men Hunter knew. "While I'm off doing what I did in the army. Bringing the war to the enemy."

"Bringing the war to the . . . ?" Annabelle cut herself off, gazing up at him in shock. "Hunter, my father has between twenty and thirty men on his roll. The Chaneys have many friends in these Hills! They might even call in the federal law — the U.S. Marshals!"

"Annabelle I don't know what else —"

Hunter stopped. He'd spied movement out the corner of his left eye. He whipped his head around, sucked air down his throat.

Bobby Lee barked three times, sharply.

Riders were moving along the wagon road from the west, heading toward the ranch yard. They were a couple of hundred yards away, just now entering the bottle neck in the forested hills at the head of the box canyon in which the 4-Box-B lay.

The sun was climbing above the opposite horizon from the riders, striping the hills and the yard with shadows and coppery light. The riders themselves were in shadow, though several of the lead men appeared to be waving white flags.

"Now what?" Annabelle rasped, staring wide-eyed toward the men nearing the ranch yard.

"I think we're about to find out." Hunter swung around and headed for the wagon.

"Come on!"

Bobby Lee barked and ran ahead of them.

Chapter 19

Annabelle leaped up onto the wagon beside Hunter, and Bobby Lee plopped down between them. Hunter reined the mule around the two freshly mounded graves, heading back down the hill. He entered the yard as the approaching riders passed under the ranch portal at the yard's west edge, near Angus's brewing barn.

Hunter pulled the wagon up to the cabin's rear door, set the brake, and leaped to the ground. Annabelle was close behind him as he pushed through the back door and stepped into the hall. He turned to his left. Angus's door was cracked.

Hunter opened it wider, poked his head into the bedroom. Angus lay much as Hunter had last seen him, flat on his back under the mounded quilts, his frail, age-gnarled body consumed by the large bed, beside the photograph of his much younger self and much younger bride.

His mouth opened wide as he snored.

Hunter glanced at Annabelle. "Stay back here with him, will you?"

"No." Anna shook her head, frowning. "I want to be with you."

"I'd like that, too, honey, but if he wakes up and sees those men in the yard, he's liable to start shooting, start something that maybe doesn't need starting."

Anna pulled the corners of her mouth down and nodded. "Right. Okay."

As Hunter continued down the hall toward the front of the house, Anna called, "Hunter, be careful!"

Hunter threw up his arm in acknowledgment.

He hurried to the front door, beside which he'd left Shep's fully loaded Henry repeating rifle. He rammed a fresh round into the breech, then pushed open the door and stepped out onto the broad front veranda. The riders were just then reining their mounts up in the yard, slightly to Hunter's left and about thirty feet out from the house.

Bobby Lee ran out from the corner of the house, barking at them angrily, hackles raised.

"Stand down, Bobby!"

The coyote wheeled and ran over and sat

down at the foot of the veranda steps, growling.

There were around seven men. A wagon now clattered up behind them. It was the undertaker's buckboard wagon. The undertaker and his idiot son sat hunched in the driver's box. The undertaker stopped the wagon behind the horseback riders, then cast his wary gaze through the riders' sifting dust toward the cabin, where Hunter walked up to stand atop the veranda steps, resting the Henry casually atop his right shoulder, his hand wrapped around the neck, finger curled through the trigger guard.

His heart thudded heavily, hotly, as he eyed the seven horseback riders sitting their dusty, sweat-lathered mounts before him. Three men sat out front of the others. Those three were none other than Graham Ludlow himself and Luke Chaney's two brothers — Billy and Jason, or "Pee-Wee," as he'd been called all his life.

The origin of the nickname was unknown to Hunter. While not as big a man as Luke was, Pee-Wee wasn't all that small. However, he owned the small pig eyes and rabid demeanor of his older brother, now deceased. But then all the Chaneys had the thuggish temperaments of Brahma bulls.

Ludlow and both Chaneys held rifles with

white handkerchiefs tied to their barrels.

The four other saddle-mounted men were common townsmen, none particularly known for his cold-steel savvy. They were friends of the Chaneys, loyal also to Ludlow. Yankees, of course. Two wore thick beards; the two others wore mustaches. All wore angry scowls but they also looked hesitant, fearful.

Not Ludlow, however. He looked as angry as Hunter felt. The rancher — Annabelle's father — was the best attired of all of them in his fleece-lined buckskin vest, bolo tie, black whipcord trousers, and pearl-gray Stetson. He wore a big Colt on his hip, and he held a fine Winchester butt-down against his beefy right thigh. His horse was a handsome dun with three white socks. It was dusty and sweaty but its eyes were bright. It looked like it could gallop all day.

No one said anything for nearly a minute. The only sounds were the horses blowing and whickering and shifting their hooves. One of the men — a barber by the name of Glavin — snorted up a chunk of phlegm from his throat and hacked it into the dirt beside him.

"We're not here for trouble," Ludlow said finally, but he didn't look like he was all that averse to the notion, his blazing eyes riveted on Hunter, who in turn stared back at him with his own brand of barely bridled rage.

"What are you here for, then?" Hunter said tonelessly.

"The dead. Their friends have come for them. They want to load them into the undertaker's wagon."

Hunter hadn't done anything with the men he'd killed yesterday. They all still lay where they'd fallen. Scavengers had likely chewed on a few of them overnight. The hills around here teemed with carrion-eaters of all kinds. They were almost as dangerous as some of the men in the Hills.

"They can take what's left of them," Hunter said, curling his upper lip in a defiant, jeering sneer.

"No trouble?" Ludlow said tightly.

"I wasn't the one that started the trouble in the first place, Ludlow." Hunter looked at the Chaney brothers sitting their horses to the rancher's left. "Luke Chaney was."

Pee-Wee Chaney thrust an arm toward Hunter, poking an accusing finger. "You shot Pa up bad, you weasel! He damn near lost the whole side of his face! Turned his right eye to jelly!"

"Blinded!" added Billy Chaney, a wad of chaw making one brown-bearded cheek bulge. He poked at his own eye. "Blinded in that eye!"

Hunter didn't respond to that. At least, not with words. He just stared gimlet-eyed at the two Chaneys while he opened and closed his hands around the cocked Henry. Both Chaneys looked cowed by his silence, the steeliness of his blue-eyed gaze. They knew they didn't have much of an argument. They knew Hunter had lost two brothers here yesterday.

Killed in a gutless ambush.

"We're not here for that," Ludlow told the two Chaneys while keeping his eyes on Hunter. "We'll deal with that later. Right now, we're just here for the bodies." He paused, staring at Hunter, his gaze a little apprehensive now. "You'll yield?"

"I'll yield today," Hunter said. "Fetch your dead. What the scavengers left. They're nothing but vermin to me. I was going to drag 'em into a ravine. Feed for the wildcats."

"That smart-ass Grayback son of a bitch," growled a man flanking Ludlow, glaring at Hunter.

"I yield today," Hunter said. "But if I ever see another man on the 4-Box-B who don't belong here, I'm gonna kill him. No questions asked. No warning. No nothing. Then

I'm gonna feed him to them wildcats. They're hungry too."

Pee-Wee Chaney, who wore a bowler hat, a pinstriped shirt with a poet's collar, and suspenders, looked as though his head was about to explode. "Just who in the holy hell do you think you . . . ?"

"That's enough!" Ludlow admonished him.

The rancher glanced behind him at the others, then jerked his head to indicate the dead men around the yard. As they rode off, the wagon rattling along behind them, to gather the dead, Ludlow turned to Hunter.

"My daughter?"

"What about her?"

Ludlow drew a deep breath, puffing up his chest. "She's here, I take it." He cut his embarrassed eyes toward the Chaneys, who sat their saddles stiffly, tensely glaring at Hunter.

Hunter didn't say anything. He stood atop the porch steps, holding the Henry on his shoulder, one boot cocked before him.

"Send her out here, damn you!" Ludlow finally bellowed, standing up in his stirrups, his face bright red now in the sunlight angling over the hollow from the east. "Send her out here now! She is going home with me!"

The Chaneys looked at the rancher in wide-eyed surprise at his passion. The other men, just now loading into the wagon the three men whom Hunter had shot between the barn and the blacksmith shop, turned toward him now too. Ludlow cut his eyes around in humiliation, then eased himself back down in his saddle.

Boots thudded behind Hunter. The heavy-timbered door opened and Annabelle stepped out. She had a pistol wedged behind her wide black belt, and she held one gloved hand over it now as she stepped up to stand beside Hunter atop the porch steps.

"Annabelle!" Ludlow said, flaring his red nostrils. "You're coming home with me!"

Annabelle let the man's order hang there in the yard between them, losing its teeth with each second that passed.

"I am home," she said finally, with quiet defiance.

"What are you talking about?" Ludlow looked around, his thick gray-brown brows beetled with incredulity. "This is not your home!"

"It is now."

"Nonsense."

"This is my home until we have a ranch

of our own, Hunter and I. He's my man. I'm his woman."

Ludlow switched his gaze to Hunter. "This man has one boot in the grave! Do you know how many men he killed? He's a killer! That's all he is! That's all he'll ever be!"

Hunter's gut tightened at the accusation. At one time, he'd believed that himself. Maybe now after yesterday he still did . . .

Through gritted teeth, Annabelle said, "He was defending his home. Those men you and Chaney sent killed his brothers and wounded his father."

Ludlow's pursed lips were a knife slash across the bottom half of his face, beneath his bushy gray mustache. His eyes fairly glowed with raw fury. "Do you know what you did to your brother? You should see him. He's badly burned, and the barn is no more than ashes!"

"He took a blacksnake to me!" Annabelle fairly screamed, bending forward at the waist.

That jolted Ludlow slightly back in his saddle. Both Chaneys looked at him, more surprise showing in their cow-eyed gazes. Ludlow's horse must have sensed its rider's roiling passions. It crow-hopped slightly, whickering, so that the rancher had to draw up tight on the reins to prevent it from throwing him.

Ludlow kept his shocked, exasperated gaze on his daughter. "That's a lie!"

"He said I was a traitorous whore, and he was going to whip me naked!" Annabelle repeated, her voice less shrill this time. "My own drunken waste of a brother tried to bullwhip me in the barn. I hit him with the lantern to repel the sick snake, as I would do to any man who tried to do that to me. I should have let him burn up in the fire. It would have been no less than he deserved."

"That's a lie!" Ludlow bellowed, cutting his eyes at both Chaneys regarding him hang-jawed. Again, he had to bring the dun under taut rein. "That's a filthy lie!" To the Chaneys he said, "Don't listen to her. She's crazy. She's as crazy as her mother ever was." To Annabelle again, he said, "Your brother may be many things, but Cass would not bullwhip his own *sister*! How dare you make that accusation, Annabelle! How *dare* you!"

Keeping her own taut voice low with barely restrained fury, Annabelle said, "I never want to see him again. As for you, Pa — after you sent men to kill the man I intend to marry, to kill his whole family and likely to burn his ranch — I don't ever want

251

to see you again either. I'm going to bear Hunter's children. We're going to have a whole house full. And I promise you this: Not one of them will ever hear your name. Not once. Your name will never pass over my lips again. They will be Buchanons only — without the taint of the Ludlow name."

Ludlow's eyes blazed even brighter. With quiet, savage menace, he said, "You ungrateful trollop. *You ungrateful lying trollop!*"

Annabelle sidled up close to Hunter, wrapped both her arms around his left one, and gave a cold smile. "This trollop stands with her man. When you send more men, I'll be fighting against them. I'll be fighting against you, Pa. And Chaney. And Stillwell. And anyone else. No matter how many."

She paused. Hunter felt her draw a deep breath as she leaned against him.

"You started this war," she said. "It will be my man and I who finish it."

Again, Ludlow's anxious horse turned a full circle, arching its neck and its tail. As it did, the rancher swiveled his thick neck to keep his blazing eyes on his daughter. He puffed up his cheeks and opened his mouth to speak, but he seemed to be at a loss for any more words with which to parry the dressing down he'd taken from his daughter.

"So . . ." he sputtered, gritting his teeth

and tugging on the dun's reins with his black-gloved hands. "So . . . so be it!" He lowered his fiery gaze to the dun's head. "Damn you, horse!" Lifting his eyes again to Annabelle and Hunter, he shouted, "You will rue this day!"

With that, he glanced once more at the Chaneys, said, "Stay with the wagon!" Then he gave the dun its head, and horse and rider galloped back across the yard of the 4-Box-B headquarters. It galloped under the portal and around the northward curve in the wagon trail, passing between two rows of aspens whose leaves now glittered green and gold in the summery light of the rising sun.

Man and rider disappeared into the low hills before the thunder of the dun's hooves dwindled to silence.

Pee-Wee and Billy Chaney stared at Annabelle in shocked silence.

"Why don't you two help the others gather your dead?" Hunter told them in a voice taut as piano wire. "Then get the hell off the 4-Box-B — for the last time!"

The Chaneys looked at each other, then did as Hunter had ordered. When all the bodies had been recovered from the brush and trees around the headquarters, the undertaker turned the wagon back onto the trail, heading westward out of the yard. The townsmen, stained with the blood of the fallen, their horses jittery from the smell of so much carnage, followed the wagon.

Several men looked warily back over their shoulders at Hunter and Annabelle before passing under the portal and then galloping out of sight.

Hunter looked down at his girl. At his woman. She looked up at him. Color had climbed into her cheeks.

His own heart thudded heavily, warm blood pooling in his belly.

"Let's go inside," he said thickly.

Annabelle squeezed his hand. "Let's."

CHAPTER 20

As the dun galloped hard in the direction of Tigerville, Graham Ludlow felt a tightness grow in his chest.

It was like a clenched fist of fury, swelling and swelling, sending sharp waves of pain up into his left shoulder and down that arm. The arm grew heavy and sore, so that he had to let it flop down over his leg. He gritted his teeth against the pain.

He drew back on the dun's reins, bringing the horse to a leaping halt, dust billowing up from behind.

Ludlow leaned forward over his saddle horn, drawing sharp breaths through his teeth. Each breath caused more pains to shoot up from that clenched fist in his chest, into his shoulder and down his arm until the arm felt like a raw nerve hanging stiffly at his side.

"Oh hell," he muttered thickly, looking down at his claw-like hand, which he could not get to open. "Oh hell . . . am I . . . having a . . . *heart attack?*"

The ground spun around him. The low hills spotted with pine forest pitched this way and that. Thin dark curtains rippled in front of his eyes.

A stream gurgled off to his left. Suddenly, he was both cold and hot and very thirsty. Cold sweat streaked his broad, fleshy face.

He slid down from his saddle. As he put weight on his left foot, the ankle gave. He cursed and threw his right, gloved hand — the only one that worked — toward the dun, trying to break his fall. His fingertips only brushed the saddle.

He plopped heavily into the middle of the trail on his butt and rolled onto his right side, his left side partly paralyzed.

He groaned, cursed again, heaved himself up into a sitting position, and cradled his sore left arm in his lap.

"She's . . . she's killing me," he wheezed. "That girl is killing me . . . slow. The lies." He ground his back teeth until he could hear them cracking. "The lies she told in front of the Chaneys!"

He pondered that. He pondered how the news would spread, Ludlow's daughter nearly bullwhipped — the punishment of a disloyal whore — by her ne'er-do-well brother. Word would race like smallpox around the Hills, infecting everyone. "Hey everybody!" someone would yell in one of the Hills' many saloons. "Guess how Cass Ludlow ended up with nearly half of his face burned off? Took a blacksnake to his own sister an' she got the better of him!"

Roaring laughter, and then someone would yell, "Brother an' sister, huh? I thought that was just a Southern thing!"

More roaring laughter.

The rage and humiliation seared through the rancher from head to toe and then back again. His eyes burned. He lay back in the trail and drew deep, even breaths, trying to relax. Gradually, the fist in his chest unclenched and his left hand did as well. The pain in his arm abated.

He sat up, blew a long sigh of relief. He shook out his arm and opened and closed that hand several times, until the entire arm felt nearly normal again.

He clambered to his feet and walked heavily through the brush to the stream. He lay belly-down on the edge of the bank, doffed his hat, and dunked his head into the rippling water, opening his mouth, swallowing great gulps of the cold water, feeling its cooling freshness push through him, easing the tension in his mind and body, clearing his head.

Finally, he sat up. He rubbed the water out of his hair, set his hat back down on his head. He sat there for a long time, looking around, thinking.

His eyes turned dark again.

They thought they'd gotten the better of him, those two.

The ex-Reb and Ludlow's own daughter.

They thought they had him in a whipsaw. In a way, he supposed they did — what with the lie Annabelle had told. The one about Cass. The lie about Cass that the Chaney brothers had overheard and would soon spread if they weren't already spreading it to the other men who'd ridden out from town to collect the dead. The Chaneys after hearing Annabelle's story — her lie! — would make a laughingstock of Ludlow himself. Casting a blight over his name.

The big, lumbering rancher slowly gained his feet, his big belly jiggling over the silver buckle of his cartridge belt. Standing, he regained his balance, drew a deep breath, and adjusted the set of the hat on his head.

Let them think what they wanted. In truth, the joke was on them. Ludlow had figured to leave the Buchanons alone as long as Annabelle had returned to the Broken Heart with her father and made amends to her brother as well as promised never to see that big ex-Confederate ever again.

But she hadn't done that. Too bad. She was only hurting herself. Hurting the Buchanons.

She'd been right about one thing. She and her so-called man would be finishing the war, all right. But one of them would be finishing it toe-down while the other one would be dragged kicking and screaming back to the Broken Heart, where once and for all she would learn her rightful place. She would obey her father's wishes and marry Kenneth Earnshaw.

Ludlow spat to one side, feeling satisfied. Confident. Hopeful.

He might have to endure some humiliation in the meantime, but in the end he would be the last one standing . . . and laughing.

He flexed his left hand a few more times, then walked back out to the trail where the dun stood grazing. He mounted up with considerable effort — still feeling a little light-headed and short of breath, like a small crab was lodged in his chest just beneath his brisket — and put the horse into a trot toward Tigerville.

Reaching the outskirts of Tigerville, Ludlow

checked the dun down to a trot. Even now at mid-morning the main artery meandering through the sprawling, haphazardly arranged village was choked with horseback riders and wagons. There were also the obstructions of timber piles standing here and there along the sides of the street, at places nearly choking it closed, giving passage to only one wagon at a time while the waiting teamsters bellowed impatient curses and shook their fists at one another.

The timber had been hauled in by local sawyers, sold, and dumped, waiting to be cut and split for firewood.

A pig hung by its back feet from a wooden tripod outside a Chinese-run grog shop and opium den, which was a low-slung log shack with a canvas-covered front porch. It was one of the few businesses that hadn't changed much in the ten years since Tigerville's establishment, when the entire booming camp was no more than tent shacks like the Chinaman's, and the streets were choked with fur-clad frontiersmen who'd given up the beaver trade for gold panning. On open fires, pots had bubbled and meat had sizzled.

Back in those days, women were raped in the alleys, screaming, and men were shot and stabbed in the main street, their bodies left where they'd fallen to be stumbled over and trampled by horses and mules until they didn't even look human anymore. Eventually, they were dragged off by wild dogs or the wolves, wildcats, and bears that slinked into town after sunset, like ants converging on an especially succulent, honey-covered slice of buttered bread.

Indians were still rife in the Hills back then. Feeling sour over the breaking of the treaty that had forbidden such white settlements like Tigerville in the first place, a small party of painted Sioux warriors would sneak into town in broad daylight and smash tomahawks through the brain plates of men or women sitting down to supper or sipping a frothy ale in the street around a fire over which a venison haunch was roasting.

The warriors would quickly, handily slice away the trophy scalp and hold it high while the tobacco-colored savages went howling jubilantly through the streets on their way back to the tall and uncut, where they'd disappear, fleet as fawns and ephemeral as wood smoke.

And there hadn't been a damn thing anybody could do about it back in those lawless days.

Bringing Frank Stillwell in had been a

good idea. It had been Ludlow's idea after his geologists had found some promising-looking ore deposits in those hills just east of town and which were now honeycombed by Ludlow and Chaney's King Solomon Mine.

Stillwell and his men had done a good job of turning Tigerville into at least a rough outline of what a civilized town should look like. Women were no longer raped in the back alleys. At least, not as many. There were still killings, but weekly instead of daily, and the bodies were promptly hauled off to the local boot hill cemetery, where words were said over them before they were planted and even given a marker, crude as it often was. Men and women — even quite a few families — felt safe to live and work here now, and to spend their money here. There was even a school, and a couple more doctors were en route to build a hospital with Dahl, Ludlow and Chaney having donated a goodly portion to the Tigerville Hospital Fund.

Ludlow had a hard time believing what he'd heard about Stillwell from Max Chaney himself — before he'd led a contingent of men from the mine out to settle up with the Buchanon boys and their one-armed old ex-Confederate father. That the man had turned tail and run when Hunter Buchanon had bore down on him.

Hadn't even drawn his pistol until he'd locked himself away in his office. Then, when Buchanon had busted in, he'd thrown himself out a back window and hightailed it like a coyote that had just pilfered a beef loin from a fire grate.

Was even Frank Stillwell afraid of the Buchanons?

Just now riding past the sheriff's office on his left, Ludlow shook his head in wonderment. Then his thoughts were nudged back to the moment when he saw several men standing outside of a saloon on his right, staring at him incredulously and conversing in low tones. He frowned at them, puzzled. One of the men turned away, and then another and another did, as well, without so much as a smile or pinch of the hat brim.

What the hell?

Most folks in town, even those that hadn't been here long, knew him and Chaney by sight, them being the town's founding fathers and most prominent not to mention most moneyed citizens. Most folks waved or yelled a respectful greeting or at least gave a cordial nod.

But these men here had turned away without so much as cracking a crooked smile. Ludlow could see their lips moving but he couldn't hear what they were saying above the din in the street.

They were talking about him. He sensed that much from their furtive airs.

A sick feeling gripped him. It was as though he'd just taken a big drink of sour milk. Of course they'd learned about Annabelle's dalliance with that Grayback brigand, Hunter Buchanon. That's what they were talking about. About how yesterday she'd ridden out with the man who, along with his father and two wild, savage brothers, had laid waste to Tigerville's police force and disgraced its leader, the infamous and notorious Frank Stillwell.

How they'd run Stillwell out of town on the proverbial greased rail. Leaving Tigerville without a lawman once again . . . just like the wild old days.

Could those men talking behind Ludlow's back have already heard about Annabelle . . . Cass . . . and the burned barn? Heck, that foul bit of news must have spread as well. Ludlow could read it in the seedy, sneering eyes of other men he was just now riding past.

He felt as though he'd followed up that first swig of sour milk with another, larger one.

Forget it, he told himself, feeling that crab in his chest coming to life again, wrapping a claw around his ticker. *Just . . . take it . . . easy . . . Let them talk. Remember, you'll be the last one standing.*

And laughing . . .

At the south end of Tigerville and on an outlying street, Ludlow turned the dun up to a hitchrack fronting a large, sprawling, somewhat rickety-looking but fairly new saloon and pleasure palace identified by a large sign spread across the face of its second story — THE PURPLE GARTER. The Garter, as the place was locally called, served when needed as the Tigerville hospital, since the town did not yet have a bona fide one and the Garter sat next door to Norton Dahl's office in the second story over a law office.

Ludlow climbed heavily down from his saddle. He was here to see Chaney. They had to discuss their next plan of attack against the Buchanons. Ludlow considered Chaney the warrior of their partnership. The strong arm.

Also, Max had many friends and relatives in these Hills, having come here himself several years before Ludlow arrived. Ludlow tended to keep to himself and see to the ranch more than the mine. He left the mine mainly to Chaney. After all, the mine was Max's primary business interest here in the Hills, so he spent the bulk of his time here in Tigerville overseeing the daily mine workings as well as the ore shipments to Cheyenne.

Max knew men who knew men who could handle the Buchanons. Ludlow didn't want to involve his own ranch hands. Not yet. Not that they weren't capable. He'd hired them, after all, because they were very proficient in many endeavors, not the least of which was range justice. But the Hills were now in the territorial jurisdiction of the U.S. Marshals, and he didn't want to venture too far into the field of lawless acts — beyond hanging rustlers, shooting claim jumpers, and hazing off squatters — unless he absolutely had to.

Max Chaney was far more daring in that regard. Chaney was, after all, an old outlaw himself and really knew no other way of life. Besides, he liked killing Graybacks, as he'd been in Lawrenceville when Bloody Bill had come calling.

Ludlow slung the tired dun's reins over the hitchrack. Mounting the boardwalk, he stumbled slightly. His boots still felt heavy. He pushed through the batwings, cursing, then, letting the louvered doors slap back into place behind him, he doffed his hat and mopped his brow with a sleeve of his wool shirt.

"I'll be damned — look at that," said a pensive voice in the room's deep, smoky shadows ahead and on his right.

"Jesus, that's a lot of blood," said another voice from the same direction.

Ludlow stepped forward, scowling into the shadows beyond several vacant tables and ceiling support beams from which lanterns and/or bleached wild animal skulls hung. The bar was straight ahead, running against the far wall, and no one was back there as far as Ludlow could tell in the dim light.

There were only a few men in the room — three, to be exact. Two were standing in the shadows near the front end of the bar, by a table at which a beefy, bearded gent in a black immigrant cap sat smoking a pipe and holding a big mug of dark ale — Angus Buchanon's ale, no doubt.

Brewing ale was the only thing the old, one-armed Rebel was good for.

The only other person in the saloon's main drinking hall was a small, blond, scantily clad whore. She sat in a chair one table away from the three men, her head and hair both pale, bare arms sprawled across the table before her. Her left cheek was flat against the scarred tabletop.

Her little, plump, pink lips pooched out through the tangled strands of her hair. She snored loudly for such a delicate thing, Ludlow absently opined.

As the rancher approached the three men, he followed their gazes to the ceiling above them. Something dark stained the ceiling's four-inch-wide, soot-encrusted slats between the stout beams. Whatever dark substance Ludlow was looking at, it was dribbling in thick, intermittent streams from between the slats and onto the floor about five feet beyond the table at which the two men stood and the bearded gent sat.

It had formed a pool.

Ludlow winced as the realization came to him that he was looking at fresh blood. The pool of it shimmered redly in a slender sunbeam slanting through a window on the room's far side.

CHAPTER 21

As Ludlow stared down in shock at the blood on the floor, he became aware of quick footfalls in the ceiling — throughout the second story, it seemed. Many muffled voices speaking all at once pushed through the ceiling as well.

Most of the voices seemed to be those of women, but Ludlow thought he detected a man's voice up there too.

"What in God's name . . . ?" the rancher inquired.

All three men standing around or sitting at the table before the rancher jerked their heads toward him, startled.

"Christ almighty, I didn't see you there, uh . . . Mr. Ludlow!" said the man standing nearest the rancher. He was a mule skinner named Logan, and he worked up at the mine. Quickly modulating his tone, his eyes flickering sheepishly, he said, "Gave me a start's all." He gave a nervous chuff.

"Whose . . . whose . . . blood is that . . . ?" the rancher inquired, staring up at the ceiling again where another drop formed thickly and then dribbled onto the floor, adding to the ever-growing pool.

"Prob'ly Riley Tatum's blood," said the other standing man, whose name Ludlow didn't know but thought he worked at the mine as well. The mine superintendent did all of the hiring and firing, and men came and went all the time. "Tatum took a bullet to his leg and another one to the liver. Both wounds been problematic for the poor sawbones. He was workin' on Tatum all night, tryin' to get him to quit bleedin'.

"Just when he thought he got the blood stopped, an' came down for a quick drink before heading back to his digs next door for some shut-eye . . . though he took Miss Loretta along to help calm his nerves" — the man grinned and winked at Ludlow before quickly becoming sober again — "Tatum burst open again and started bleedin' all over the place. He been bleedin' off an' on like that all mornin'. Seepin' right through the floor up there. We been watchin' the blood an' hearin' the doc cussin' a blue streak for over an hour now."

"I for one didn't know a man of a sawbones' education could sport such a blue tongue," said the man smoking his pipe at the table. He gave a wry snort and lifted his schooner of coffee-colored ale topped with dark foam.

"At least he quit screamin' finally," Logan said, giving his head a relieved shake, as though the wounded man's screams had been quite the ordeal. "Jesus!"

"Any word on Chaney?" Ludlow asked.

The rancher hadn't seen Max Chaney since he'd returned, wounded, from the 4-Box-B, helped back to town by his two sons. From the sons, Ludlow had learned that Chaney had taken a bullet to the face. The slug had burst when it had cored into the bone of his eye socket, laying waste to his left eye and his left ear as well as making one hell of a mess of that cheek.

Logan merely shrugged, shook his head. The other two men followed suit.

Ludlow swung away from the three and headed over to the bar. Since there was no bartender, and he'd been yearning for a drink since that crab had come devilishly alive in his chest to crowd his ticker, he walked around behind the bar to serve himself. He found a dusty bottle of labeled bourbon on a high shelf, popped the cork, and filled a shot glass.

He drew a breath and tossed back the

entire shot, tipping his head back and squeezing his eyes closed as the bourbon warmed and soothed his insides, taking the hump out of the neck of that crab in his chest.

Logan was eyeing him from where he now sat at the table with the two other men. "You don't look so good, Mr. Ludlow."

"You look kinda pale," said the other man. "You feelin' all right, Mr. Ludlow?"

The rancher stared back at them, suspicious. He wasn't sure, but he thought he glimpsed a faint glint of mockery in their eyes, as though they, too, knew about his daughter and the Grayback, maybe even about what Annabelle did to Cass . . . and her burning the barn . . .

Hastily, Ludlow splashed more whiskey into his glass. Again, he threw back the entire shot. "Don't you boys waste your time worryin' about me," he said, slamming the glass down on the bar and scowling through the smoke-laced shadows at the three men now watching him uncertainly. "I couldn't be better!"

He ran the back of his hand across his mouth, then, with a caustic grunt, he walked out from behind the bar and mounted the stairs at the back of the room.

As he lumbered up the unpainted board

steps, two whores came down, brushing past him, also eyeing him with a vague incredulity he did not like. Or did he imagine it?

The first girl, a brunette, was carrying a large metal tray filled with bloody water and several grisly-looking medical instruments. The second girl, a pale, heavy-breasted redhead, carried a large bundle of blood-sodden bedding straight out before her in both hands, tipping her head away from the parcel and making a face.

Ludlow continued up past the second landing and into the second-story hall, where more doxies were moving in and out of rooms at the behest of Dr. Norton Dahl, yelling at them from an open door midway down the hall, on Ludlow's left. Another man, likely one of the several wounded who'd fled the Buchanon ranch late yesterday afternoon, was moaning and groaning loudly from behind a closed door on Ludlow's left.

Another man behind another closed door was yelling for whiskey.

Ludlow poked his head into the room from which Dahl had been yelling orders.

"Doc?"

The sawbones, looking sweaty and harried in his shirtsleeves, his arms and white shirt and wool vest nearly as blood-sodden as the

273

bedding the whore had been carrying, snapped his head toward Ludlow. "What the hell is it?"

He was standing over the still figure of a man on the bloody bed before him. The man appeared dead, mouth open in a silent scream, wide eyes glaring at the ceiling.

"Oh . . . uh . . . sorry, Mr. Ludlow," Dahl said, moderating his tone. "I've, uh . . . just had a long night is all."

"Did he expire?" Ludlow glanced at the obviously dead man before him.

"Yes — finally, thank God," said Dahl through a long sigh, staring at his bloody arms raised before him. "I didn't know a single man could hold that much blood, much less lose it and retain his ghost for so long."

"Who is he? I don't recognize him in death."

"Fella named Tatum. Riley Tatum."

"Ah, Tatum." Ludlow remembered now. Tatum had been an ore guard — a good one, as Ludlow recollected. He gave a satisfied half smile. "He was well-liked, has quite a few friends in town, I believe."

Friends who would no doubt eagerly sign on to another posse formed in the pursuit of exacting both revenge and justice for those murdered by the Buchanons. There were only two Buchanons left — the middle boy whom Annabelle was improbably sweet on, and the old man, who'd taken a bullet. How hard could it be to finish the job out at the 4-Box-B? How many men would it take?

The doctor turned to the rancher again, frowning curiously.

"Never mind, Doc. How's Chaney?"

Dahl jerked his chin. "See for yourself. Two doors down on your left."

Ludlow had just started walking toward the door indicated when a girl's shrill scream rose from a door on his right. The doctor ran out of the room behind the rancher, and threw open the door just beyond it.

"What the hell is going on in here?" Dahl yelled as he slammed the door behind him.

"Lousy cur bit me, Doc!" the girl cried.

The commotion continued as Ludlow moved on down the hall and knocked on the door the doctor had indicated. He didn't wait for a response but opened the door and poked his head inside. The room was small. Like all the other rooms up here, it was a crib where the Purple Garter doxies plied their trade.

Max Chaney sat on the edge of the room's sole, single-size bed. He was clad only in balbriggans. His bulbous paunch sagged over his lap like that of a woman eight months pregnant. He was around the same age as Ludlow, in his sixties, but his long-ish, curly hair was still black, and he had a long, drooping mustache on his craggy face, which was the washed-out color of a sun-bleached adobe.

Chaney's right side faced Ludlow standing in the doorway. The only indication of the man's injuries was a thick white bandage wrapped around his forehead. The right side of his face appeared unmarred.

It was when Chaney turned his head to face the rancher that Ludlow winced.

"How do I look, Graham?" Chaney lifted a brown paper quirley to his mouth and took a deep drag. In his other hand he held a bottle of whiskey atop his thigh. Another, empty bottle lay at his feet. The whiskey in the current bottle had been taken about two inches down.

"Christ," Ludlow muttered. He wanted to add that he didn't look all that worse than his son Cass, but did not.

Chaney's blood-splotched bandage angled down over his left, heavily padded eye socket. It dropped down to cover that ear as well. Blood shone over the ear. Or where the ear had been, rather. Chaney's cheek resembled freshly ground beef bristling with sutures.

Ludlow moved into the room. He removed his hat, held it before him, and nudged the door closed with his boot. Chaney took another drag off the quirley as he dropped his gaze to the hat.

"Christ, Graham, I ain't dead yet." Chaney gave a caustic chuff and exhaled smoke through his nostrils.

Ludlow glanced down at his hat, drumming his fingers on the brim. He looked at his business associate again, feeling the burn of irritation. He didn't like Max Chaney. He never had. Having to pretend he did strained his nerves. But then, he'd often suspected the feeling was mutual. They'd joined hands several years ago because at that time they happened to be the only two men around with money burning holes in their pockets, though Ludlow had come by his (relatively) honestly, while everyone knew that most of Chaney's had come from sheer thuggery — claim-jumping, rustling, and selling firewater to the Sioux.

"I just came to pay my respects, Max. No need for the nasty tone. I wasn't the one who shot you."

Chaney lifted the bottle. The air bubble at the bottom lurched toward the neck several times. When Chaney had taken down three more inches, he lowered the bottle to his thigh, smacked his lips, and ran a grimy longhandle sleeve across his mouth.

He turned again to face Ludlow, his lone eye rheumy from drink, his torso swaying on his hips. He was more than a few sheets to the wind. Sagging slowly backward, lifting his legs and bare feet onto the bed, he said, "Nah . . . but you might as well have." He badly slurred his words, and he seemed to have trouble keeping his lone eye on his visitor standing in front of the closed door.

Ludlow moved forward, his anger burning hotter. "What're you talking about, Max?"

"This never would have happened if you'd kept a shorter leash on Li'l Miss." Lying back on the bed, his head carving a deep valley in a sweat-stained pillow, Chaney wrinkled his nose. "You know who I mean. That girl of yours. If you'd have seen fit to let Luke marry the harlot, none of this ever would have happened."

Ludlow opened his mouth for a harsh retort, but Chaney interrupted him.

"No, no — you thought you were too good for us Chaneys. You thought *she* was too good for *Luke*! You don't mind my money and my expertise in *certain matters* . . . the kind of men I know."

Chaney shook his head, flaring his nostrils as he glared up at Ludlow through his one rheumy, dung-brown eye. "But your Li'l Miss is far too good to marry up with a Chaney. So, instead, she drops her underfrillies for some no-account Rebel scalawag. Runs off with the Grayback!"

He laughed loudly, hoarsely, and without humor. "And there ain't a thing you can do about it! Even after she pummels your useless son and burns down your barn! That's right — defies you, works over your son, burns down your barn, and throws in with a Grayback! Oh my God, if that ain't the richest thing I ever heard! Haw! Haw! Haw!"

Ludlow glanced back at the door, wondering how far away Chaney's tirade had penetrated, how many others had overheard his lashing words. The rancher walked up close to the bed, his jaws hard, his eyes dark with menace. "Shut up, Max! Keep your damn voice down! That's not how it was!"

Through his loud guffaws, Chaney yelled, "She was too good for my son! You were savin' her for some dandy from back east! But instead, she lets some louse-ridden Grayback have his unholy way with the — *ah, achhh!*"

Ludlow had grabbed the nearly empty

bottle from Chaney's hand. He'd turned it over and shoved the lip into his business partner's wide-open mouth. Gritting his teeth, the fires of fury burning more hotly inside him than the flames that had consumed his barn, he rammed the bottle as far down Chaney's throat as it would go.

The liquor chugged as it flowed down through the neck and out the lip into Chaney's throat.

Chaney choked and gagged, struggling wildly, throwing his hands up over Ludlow's arms, trying to pry free the rancher's fury-fueled grip on the bottle. He kicked up with his legs. Weak from the wound as well as drink, none of his thrashing packed much of a wallop.

Ludlow held the bottle fast, overturned in Chaney's mouth, pinning the man's head down hard against the pillow. Chaney kicked and gargled and spewed the whiskey out his nose and over Ludlow's hands and arms and into his face. Each time he tried to draw a breath, he inhaled more of the whiskey, a portion of which spewed out his nose. His lone eye was wide and bright with terror.

The rancher turned his face away, squeezing his eyes closed against the burn of the spraying whiskey, until he felt the last of the busthead leave the bottle. He could tell by the way Chaney convulsed, his chest swelling, that most of the whiskey had rushed into his lungs. When the rancher opened his eyes again, Chaney was staring up at him, his face set in a mask of frozen horror, his body lying limp and unmoving.

Whiskey filled the broad, dark "O" of his mouth, spilling over his lower lip and dribbling down his chin, like water from an overfilled stock tank.

Chaney's hands lay to either side of his head, the fingers curled toward his palms.

Ludlow dropped the bottle and stumbled back against the dresser. The room turned around him. The crab in his chest was stirring. The rancher gripped the edges of the dresser, drew a deep, slow breath, tried to relax. He drew several more slow breaths. Gradually, the crab returned to its slumbers. The pain abated, though his heart was still thudding from exertion.

Ludlow rubbed his arm across his forehead, stared at Max Chaney in shock and horror at what he'd done. The shock abated quickly, however, and he found himself chuckling. Nervously chuckling but chuckling, just the same.

Quietly, he said, "By God, I've been wanting to do that for a long time." He flared his nostrils in renewed anger. "A harlot, eh? Maybe. But only I have the right to call her that, you swine!"

The doorknob clicked.

Ludlow jerked his head to see the door open. Doctor Dahl stepped slowly into the room, frowning, casting his befuddled gaze between Max Chaney lying dead on the bed, and Ludlow standing back against the dresser. Dahl had washed his arms but a lot of blood remained — stubborn, dried streaks of it around his fingernails and clinging to the hair on his pale, slender arms.

"What in God's name . . . ?"

"Heart stroke." Ludlow shuttled his gaze to Chaney. "Poor Max. We were just having us a chat — you know, two old friends gathering wool. He made a strangling sound and died. Spilled whiskey all over himself." He shook his head. "Poor Max."

Ludlow looked at Dahl. Dahl looked back at him.

The doctor walked into the room, held a finger to Chaney's neck. Finally, he turned to Ludlow. "Poor Max."

Ludlow stooped to retrieve his hat from the floor. He set it on his head and walked to the door. As he passed the sawbones, he gave the man's shoulder a reassuring pat. "You did the best you could, Doc. No hard feelings."

Ludlow opened the door and stepped into the hall.

CHAPTER 22

Ludlow was heading back down the hall toward the Purple Garter's stairs when a door on his left opened. A copper-skinned girl clad in virtually nothing and touting nearly all of her wares — which were not half-bad by a long sight — stepped into the hall, nearly running into Ludlow.

"Easy, young lad— !"

The rancher's admonition was cut off by a man's petulant, sleep-raspy voice saying, "And bring back a bottle of something from a higher shelf than the one on which you found the last one! Good Lord — my head is . . ."

The speaker's voice trailed off when he saw Ludlow standing in the doorway, staring into the room from over the young doxie's bare left shoulder. The young man kneeling on the rumpled bed, beside yet another doxie, this one totally naked and lying belly-down and sound asleep under a honey-blond tumbleweed of sleep-mussed hair, was none other than Kenneth Earnshaw.

Earnshaw was as naked as the day he was born, a fact he immediately tried to compensate for by drawing up a badly twisted sheet from the bottom of the bed. Naked, he was even more unimpressive than he was clothed — small and bony and fish-belly white with an unseemly potbelly for a man so young.

"Earnshaw!" Ludlow exclaimed.

"Uh . . . uh . . . hello there . . . Mr. . . . Ludlow, uh . . . I was . . . I was . . ."

"Yes, I see what you was." Ludlow looked at the doxie standing before him, to one side of the open doorway, staring up at him with her full lips drawn up with amusement. She was a severe-looking, black-eyed half-breed. Probably more Sioux than white, with a ripe, buxom body and coarse, blue-black hair spilling across her shoulders.

Earnshaw scrambled down from the bed, taking the sheet with him, ripping it off the bed and wrapping it around his nakedness. "Look, Mr. Ludlow —"

"Oh, I know, I know, Earnshaw," the rancher intoned, trying not to sound sarcastic but knowing he was failing. "You were

285

just distracting yourself from a broken heart."

"Well, uh" — Earnshaw glanced at the girl sound asleep on the bed and then at the mostly naked half-breed in the doorway before Ludlow — "I guess you could . . ."

"Look, Earnshaw," Ludlow said, placing his fists on his hips and squaring his shoulder commandingly at the younger man, "do you still want to marry my daughter? She'd be quite a catch for you." The rancher let his eyes flick across the younger man's embarrassingly unimpressive body once more. "Quite a catch for you, indeed!"

Earnshaw's mouth moved several times before any words made it past his lips. "Uh . . . well, of course. Of course, but I, uh . . ."

"A woman like Annabelle is like a wild-assed bronco filly — don't you know that, Earnshaw? She wakes up with her tail arched and her neck up, and she goes to sleep the same way. But, my God — isn't she magnificent?"

"She is, indeed, Mr. Ludlow, but . . ."

"But nothing! The magnificent wild filly that is Annabelle Ludlow needs to be run down and tamed. *Broken,* by God! Buckled to harness! You don't take her first no for an answer. You don't even take her second or third no for an answer. Each one of those no's is merely her saying — 'How bad do you want me? How hard are you willing to fight for me?'

"That's how it is with a bronco like Annabelle. If you want her, you set your hat for her and you ride out and throw a loop on her at all costs. You don't let any other stallion stand in your way. If you do, you aren't working hard enough and you don't deserve her. You're not stallion enough for her. Hell, you aren't *man* enough for her! Do I make myself clear, Earnshaw?"

Ludlow didn't wait for an answer. He swung away, pinching his hat brim at the half-breed whore, and strode on down the hall, leaving Earnshaw staring wide-eyed and hang-jawed after him.

As he descended the stairs, the rancher chuckled, silently opining that it would be interesting to see how *that* played out. It was only right, though, really, that the man who wanted to marry Annabelle fight for her at least half as hard as Hunter Buchanon was fighting. You had to give that much to the Grayback. He was willing to fight and even die, it seemed, for Annabelle's hand in marriage.

Die it would be. Graham Ludlow wouldn't have it any other way.

"Mr. Ludlow, I didn't know you were here."

The speaker was Lon Avery, one of the Purple Garter's bartenders — a slight, hawk-beaked man in his late twenties with a pronounced limp. He'd once worked for Ludlow and Chaney until a rattlesnake had spooked the mules in the traces of the ore wagon he was driving to Cheyenne. The frightened mules ran themselves, the wagon, the ore, and Avery into a shallow ravine, breaking the mule skinner's left ankle in half a dozen places.

Now he wore a brace on the limb and served busthead in the Purple Garter, which he would likely be condemned to do for the rest of his ill-fated life.

He limped around back there now, removing corked brown bottles from a wooden crate and aligning them on various shelves in the back bar. He peered over his shoulder at the rancher, his weary eyes cast with curiosity. His face appeared a little more drawn and paler than usual. He'd likely been up all night, running whiskey upstairs to the doctor's ailing patients.

"Came to see my business partner," Ludlow said. "Toss me one down — will you, Lon?"

"Sure, sure, Mr. Ludlow." Avery popped

the cork on a bottle and set a shot glass on the plain pine bar fronting the rancher. "How is Mr. Chaney doing this morning?"

"Not very well, I'm afraid."

Avery arched a brow. "Oh?"

Deciding not to elaborate but to change the subject, Ludlow sipped down half his whiskey and then asked, "Lon, you got any idea where Sheriff Stillwell ran off to?"

He was of a mind to give the sheriff a good dressing down for running with his tail between his legs when the chips were down. Not only that, but he wanted Stillwell to turn his badge over to him, Ludlow, personally. The man's cowardice had put Ludlow in one hell of a bind, and he wanted Stillwell to know it.

The rancher still had a battle to fight, by God, and now he was going to have to bring in more help from only who knew where. Stillwell had come highly recommended. Turns out he was nothing more than a chicken-livered confidence man.

Badge for hire, Ludlow's ass!

"I sure do."

Ludlow arched both brows in surprise at the gimpy apron. "You do?"

Avery jerked his spade-like chin toward the front of the Purple Garter, indicating the large hotel and saloon, the Dakota Ter-

289

ritorial, looming largely on the other side of the street. "He's sitting over there in the saloon, playin' solitaire. Calm as you please. I just seen him not a minute ago when I was scrubbin' blood from the front boardwalk. He's sittin' up close to the front window. Even gave me a big grin and a two-fingered salute."

"Pshaw!"

"Odd, ain't it? After he lit out like that . . . like he done the other day?" Again, Avery turned his incredulous gaze toward the Territorial and smoothed his little caterpillar mustache with the first two heavily calloused fingers of his right hand. "I never expected to see him again. Not after he disgraced himself like he done. But there he sits. Two-fingered salute an' everything!"

"Big grin and a two-fingered salute, huh?" Ludlow threw back the last of the whiskey, ran his hand across his mouth, and started toward the door. "Well . . . we'll see about that."

Sure enough, Frank Stillwell was sitting right where Avery had said he was — at a table near a front window in the broad, carpeted saloon of the well-appointed Territorial Hotel. He was, indeed, playing solitaire while sipping a cream-topped dark ale and a shot of whiskey.

What's more, he had the gall to wear his five-pointed sheriff's badge on the lapel of his black clawhammer coat.

His dark brown hair, parted in the middle, shone with pomade, and his mustache was freshly brushed. He looked amazingly well rested for a man who'd lit out of his office as though the devil's hounds had been nipping at his heels.

Ludlow stood just inside the broad arched doorway leading into the saloon from the hotel lobby, silently fuming while trying to keep the crab in his chest sedated. Unclenching his fists at his sides, he walked over to stand beside the sheriff's table, glaring down at the man. Stillwell did not look up at Ludlow until after he had set a three of deuces on a four of hearts.

"Well, Mr. Ludlow — what a pleasant surprise." Stillwell smiled and laid down another card.

"You comfortable?"

Stillwell set down another card and looked up at his employer again, one brow arched. "What's that?"

"I asked if you were comfortable. Is there anything I can bring you? I see you have a pair of drinks before you though it is not yet noon . . . and a fresh deck of pasteboards. Your clothes look freshly brushed, you yourself freshly bathed after a good night's sleep and a little slap-'n'-tickle with Jane Campbell. Perhaps a chicken sandwich from the bar, a cigar, maybe a velvet cushion for your ass?"

"Ah," Stillwell said, setting down another card, "you're angry."

"Angry?" Ludlow said, frowning down at the maddeningly calm lawman setting down one card after another. "No, anger is for when someone steps on your toe or kicks your dog for no good reason. I'm not sure I can describe how I feel about you — sitting here as relaxed as a whiskey drummer waiting for a train — after the stunt you pulled the other day.

"After that embarrassing, humiliating display of cowardice on the field of battle. You do realize, don't you, that Hunter Buchanon not only ran you into the brush like a chicken-thieving dog — after he and his two brothers and one-armed father massacred every deputy in your employ — but that he also turned loose all of your prisoners. They're likely crowing about what a coward you are right now in every parlor house between here and Deadwood!"

If Stillwell had heard what Ludlow had said, he wasn't letting on. The disgraced lawman was nibbling a corner of the seven of hearts in his hand while scanning the other cards arranged in neat columns before him. You'd swear he'd gotten the upper hand on Buchanon and not the other way around. "Ah, there we go," the lawman said, and snapped the seven down on an eight of spades.

Ludlow sat down in the chair on the opposite side of the table from Stillwell. He extended his hand across the table, palm up. "Your badge."

Stillwell glanced up at him. "What for?"

"You're fired, you fool. You will never work as a so-called lawman-for-hire again. You're a charlatan. A confidence man. A *coward.* Everybody in the Hills knows it by now."

"Good."

Ludlow scowled, pinching one eyelid nearly closed. "Say again."

"Good. I'm glad they think I'm a coward. That's what I was going for."

"That's what you were going for?"

Stillwell took the card deck in both his hands and held it against his chest as he leaned back in his brocade-upholstered armchair. "Correct."

"Oh, I see, so there was a strategy to you throwing yourself through that window."

"Correct."

"Pray tell!"

Stillwell smiled. He set the card deck down and reached inside his coat pocket for a cigar and a single match. "I saw I was outnumbered and that all my men were down. If I had drawn my gun, I'd be just as dead as they are right now. Just as useless. Just as unable to perform my duties — which, I'm satisfied to inform you, I did. Yesterday. I'm sorry about your daughter, but, well . . ."

"What the hell are you talking about?"

"You'll know soon enough." Stillwell smiled. "Part of it you're going to like. Part of it" — he shrugged — "maybe not."

"You're not only a coward, you're a mad coward!"

The sheriff fired his lucifer to life with his thumbnail, touched it to the end of the long nine in his mouth, and inhaled, making the flame leap and causing smoke to billow.

Blowing a long plume across the table and over Ludlow's head, Stillwell leaned still farther back in his chair and said, "My men turned out to be utter fools. At least the ones who thought it was a good idea to try to open up on those three rifle-wielding killers — Southern Graybacks known for their outlawry as well as their cold-steel savvy — who had the high ground and beads drawn on our briskets."

Stillwell took a shallow puff from the cigar, blew it out his nostrils, wreathing his pale, mustached, brown-eyed face in smoke. "Damn fool move. When he drew — I think it was King — the rest drew, as well, and each one of them was dead within the minute. They didn't have a chance. They were being fired upon by surrounding rooftops, for screaming in the Queen's ale!"

"Yes, and you let them die without offering a hand. You didn't fire a single shot until after you ran inside your office. That's how I heard it told!"

"Exactly." Stillwell smiled, slitting his eyelids with a self-satisfaction Ludlow found intolerable.

Ludlow laughed and slapped the table. "Do you really think I'm fool enough to believe your act of cowardice was actually part of some strategy?"

"You can believe whatever you want to believe." Stillwell took a sip of his rye and followed it up with a deep drag from the long nine. When another plume was webbing in the air over the table, he scraped ashes from the cigar into a tray and said, "But I'll bet you silver certificates to chili peppers that none of the Buchanons are worried about me just now. At least, not the one still alive. Angus Buchanon probably ain't even thinkin' about me at all. I just want you to know, Ludlow, I'm sorry about your daughter. But she was with him, and, well, a man can't control all the outcomes."

Ludlow screwed up his face. "What the hell are you talking about, Stillwell? If you think Hunter Buchanon is dead, you have another think comin'!"

All the blood appeared to drain out of Stillwell's face. "What?"

Ludlow slammed his fist down on the table. "Like I said, you're a bloody coward. And a mad one at that!"

Stillwell's eyes drew inward slightly and one side of his upper lip curled. "Don't say that again."

"Why not? It's true. Everyone knows it, Stillwell. I just now rode out with a party of men to retrieve the bodies from yesterday's attack on the 4-Box-B. Hunter Buchanon was very much alive — standing out on the veranda of the Buchanon house with . . . with . . . my very own daughter." He'd let his voice trail off sheepishly with those last few words, raking a thumb angrily along his jaw. "Damnit all!"

Stillwell looked constipated, deeply befuddled. "Hunter Buchanon *and* your daughter . . . you just saw them, you say — both of 'em . . . this mornin'?"

"Yes, just this morning, you cowardly fool!"

Stillwell turned to stare out the window for a time, as though digesting the information, which appeared to be going down like fresh-baked crow.

"Why would you think otherwise?" Ludlow asked him.

Stillwell turned back to him, ignoring the question. "They and you can think what you want. But if there is any man in these Hills better equipped to bring Hunter Buchanon's head to town in a croaker sack, that man is me . . . and the three other men I sent for."

He added under his breath as though mostly to himself, "Started to think I wouldn't need 'em after all, but . . . but I reckon I was wrong . . ."

Ludlow thought he might as well play along. "Who'd you send for?"

"Wouldn't you like to know," Stillwell sneered, and drew another sip from his shot glass.

"That's it." Ludlow had had enough. He placed his hands flat on the table and hoisted himself from his chair. "I've indulged your bull long enough. You can leave the badge in the office. Make sure you lock the door on your way —"

"Dakota Jack Patterson," Stillwell said, cutting the rancher off.

Hands still on the table, half standing, Ludlow frowned at the sheriff.

"Weed Zorn," Stillwell continued, "and Klaus Steinbach."

Ludlow straightened, lifting his hands from the table. He stared curiously down at Stillwell smiling up at him again, like a snake confidently scouting a den full of cottontails. "Where in the hell did you find Dakota Jack? Steinbach, did you say?"

"And Weed Zorn, decorated ex-cavalryman. You remember Dakota Jack, do you?"

"Sure."

Two years ago, Ludlow and Chaney had hired Dakota Jack to take care of some irritating business involving a man — a wealthy Irishman from a prominent family — contesting the mineral rights of the King Solomon and threatening to bring in Pinkerton mine regulators as well as U.S. Marshals to investigate the matter. Dakota Jack was just the man for the job, leaving Stillwell and his deputies with their hands clean and keeping inconvenient attention away from their employers.

No one ever knew Jack was here in the

Hills — except the Irishman, of course. But, lying at the bottom of a deep ravine where only the wolves and wildcats could find him, and scatter his polished bones from here to kingdom come, he wasn't talking. His mine claim had been used as kindling to start a fire in Ludlow's big fieldstone hearth.

"Sure, sure, I remember Jack," the rancher said, his interest growing. "Not a very forgettable fella, Dakota Jack. Definitely leaves an impression. Where'd you find him? I didn't know he was still around."

"I heard in one of the saloons that someone had seen him and Steinbach and Zorn in Bismarck. They were tidying up some business for a steamboat outfit. I sent a telegram and was surprised but pleased when Jack wrote right back, thanking me for giving him and the others a reason to take their leave of the cesspool that Bismarck and Mandan have become now that they got the railroad."

"What reason did you give him?"

Stillwell chuffed a laugh as he absently riffled through his card deck with one hand. "Your old brain is muddled, Mr. Ludlow. Should talk to a sawbones about that. Haven't you been following the track of our conversation?"

"The Buchanons?"

"Isn't that who we been talkin' about? Ain't Hunter the one you just said you seen just this morning . . . with your daughter . . . out at the 4-Box-B?"

"True, but that Hunter . . . he's a handful."

"Oh, I know. Don't I know! Got him nine lives too!" Stillwell laughed without mirth. "Don't underestimate that Grayback just 'cause he swore off shootin' irons after the war. The only reason he done that is because he killed so many men — Union soldiers — that he sickened even himself. But knowin' how to kill, once you know how to do it, and are as good at it as I heard tell he was — *scary good* — you don't forget."

Stillwell took a pull off the cigar and blew three perfect smoke rings toward Ludlow.

The rancher grimaced his distaste, and waved the rings out of the air before him. "Well, well — maybe you're worth something after all, Stillwell."

"What I want to know, Mr. Ludlow, is what Hunter Buchanon is worth to you."

"What are you talking about?"

"I'm talking about what Hunter Buchanon is worth to you. Please concentrate so you're not losing me every other sentence."

Anger flared hotly into Ludlow's chest,

causing his heart to quicken and prodding that crab again. He winced against a nettling lance of pain creeping up from beneath his breastbone and into his left shoulder as he bunched his lips and said, "You're the sheriff of this county, Stillwell. The Buchanons massacred your men. Turned you into a laughingstock."

Stillwell pointed his cigar at the rancher, snarling, "I told you to quit sayin' that. I told you how it was."

"Oh yes, yes, of course — wait, what are you doing?"

Stillwell had unpinned his badge from the lapel of his frock coat. Now he tossed it onto the table where it clattered belly-up before the rancher.

"There's the badge you asked for. Now, how much for Hunter Buchanon's head in a croaker sack?"

Ludlow opened his mouth to speak, his eyes glinting angrily, but Stillwell stopped him with a wave of his hand. The sheriff leaned forward, snapping out his words like prune pits. "I figure it's probably worth a pretty penny to you, seein' as how your lovely daughter ran off with the man. Not only ran off with him but badly burned her brother and set fire to your barn. All because she wanted to run off with that Grayback."

Stillwell gave a jeering smile. "Let me remind you that everyone in town saw her ride off with him the other day. Saw them leave town together, practically arm in arm."

"I wonder what they're talking more about — my daughter or your cowardice."

"Your daughter." Stillwell laughed. "Bet on it!"

As he glared across the table at the smug sheriff, Ludlow drew a breath against his rage. "Half of the men in this county will be after Hunter Buchanon and that old man of his. The Chaneys have many friends. One of them will get him. If they don't, I'll throw my own Broken Heart boys at 'em."

"One of them might get him. For the right price, I will get him. Me, Dakota Jack, Steinbach, and Zorn. We'll fetch her home to you. After all, that's gotta be what you really want, ain't it, Ludlow? Why, a man like you can't walk around with folks knowin' how your daughter married up with a Grayback — one you strictly forbid her to see. One who killed damn near all the lawmen in this town. You can't let your daughter and that no-account Grayback get the better of you, have everyone laughin' . . . now, can you?"

Ludlow drew another breath and released it slowly, tightening his lips against the crab stirring in his chest. "How much do you want for you and Dakota Jack to go after him?" He hardened his voice. "To kill him?"

"I'm sure Jack and Klaus and the others will settle for a thousand apiece. That's what I'll settle for."

"Five hundred."

"A thousand. An extra thousand for her."

Ludlow glared down at him, brushed his fist across his nose, and gritted his teeth. "Another thousand for *her alive*. Unharmed!"

"Oh, of course, of course. Alive." Stillwell threw his arms out and grinned. "I wouldn't have it any other way." His grin broadened as though he was inwardly chuckling at a joke he shared with only himself.

Ludlow swung around and headed for the door, Stillwell laughing softly behind him.

CHAPTER 23

"Damnit, Hunter — get your big bear paws off'n me! I'm gonna stay here and fight for the ranch we carved out of these Hills or die in a blaze of holy glory, whistling Dixie, as they burn it to the ground!"

Old Angus tried to wriggle out of the arms of Hunter and Annabelle, who were half carrying and half dragging the rowdy old Rebel toward the supply wagon parked in front of the Buchanon cabin. He twisted around, trying to turn and stride back to the cabin out of which every window had been shot when Chaney's men had attacked the previous day.

"Pa, stop fightin' us, damnit!" Hunter scolded the old man. "You're gonna jerk Annabelle's stitches loose an' start bleedin' again. I am not letting you stay here, an' that's final. Stayin' here is sure suicide."

"What're you talkin' about — suicide?" The old man stopped and turned to his much younger and much taller son, scowling up at him. "We built that damn cabin to withstand a Sioux attack. A cyclone. Hell, the only thing that could pester that timbered fortress is —"

"Fire," Hunter finished for him. "With Shep and Tye dead, and you laid up, there ain't enough of us to defend all four sides against attackers running a burning wagon of brush up and setting fire to the place. Even if they didn't burn us out, they could starve us out. We don't have enough food and ammunition. I was going to refill the larder the other day in town, but as you'll remember, I had a change of plans."

Old Angus opened his mouth to refute Hunter's argument, but he checked himself. Doubt flickered in his washed-out eyes bleary from all the whiskey he'd drunk to dull the pain of his bullet wound. He slid his crestfallen gaze to the stalwart lodge, its wide timbered front porch trimmed with bleached-out animal skulls and old traps and other implements hanging from spikes in the thick, chinked walls.

A water gourd with a gourd dipper hung from the rafters of the veranda's pitched roof. At the moment, a mountain bluebird — as blue as any blue had ever been — was perched on the edge of the gourd, bobbing its head forward and dipping its beak to drink.

Angus glanced at Annabelle standing to his right. He turned to Hunter and, with a tear dribbling down his leathery cheek, said, "Just leave me here, boy. Leave me here to burn. I'll die where Shep and Tye died. It's my time. I'm old . . . an' I'm tired!"

Hunter grimaced, shook his head. "I can't let you do that, Pa. You see, if I left you here, I'd have to stay too. And where would that leave Anna? When she threw in with us two Graybacks, she pretty much burned her bridges."

Angus made a pained look and turned to Anna, who said, "Please, Angus. Come with us. You want to live to see your grand-children, don't you? To rock one on your lap?"

Angus drew a deep breath and turned back to Hunter. "Our chances are slim, boy. Damn slim. But, okay. All right. I'll go where you go. I reckon I'm outnumbered." He cast a fleeting, dry glance at Anna, who smiled at him. Then, turning back to his son, he hardened his jaws, and anger sparked in his eyes as he said, "But, by God, you better have my guns loaded in that wagon. Pistols, Yellowboy, both bowie knives, and double-barreled gut-shredder!"

"Don't worry, Pa," Hunter said, "I've packed all your toys."

He and Annabelle continued leading Angus to the old buckboard to which the mule was hitched. Hunter's grullo, Nasty Pete, and Annabelle's buckskin, Ivan — both saddled — were tied to the wagon's tailgate. Chaney's men had run off the Buchanons' other horses, housed in two separate corrals, but the mule had been stabled in the barn.

Annabelle had filled the wagon box with what few foodstuffs she'd found in the kitchen — mostly potatoes, a ham, fatback, some flour, cornmeal, sugar, and coffee. With animal skins, she'd made a comfortable nest for Angus, and at the top of the nest were two thick pillows upon which he could rest his head.

His weapons and his rucksack stuffed with ammunition were piled in a corner, near the water barrel Hunter had filled at the well. Bobby Lee sat atop the water barrel, on the thick wooden lid, licking his front paw like a cat and using the wet paw to clean behind his ear.

When Hunter and Annabelle got Angus settled in the wagon, Hunter helped Anna back down to the ground. Hunter turned to face the lodge that he and his pa and brothers had built by hand, by the sweat of their brows. He glanced around at the barn and the corrals, at Angus's brew barn and at Shep's blacksmith shop out front of which the finely churned dirt of the yard was still stained with the eldest Buchanon brother's blood.

Hunter looked down over his right shoulder. Anna stood close beside him, her arm against his, the back of her hand resting lightly against his own.

She'd been following his gaze, the breeze gently brushing her hair back against her cheeks, as he'd studied all that he and Angus were leaving behind. The loss he felt not only for the ranch headquarters but for his beloved brothers was a rusty knife in his belly. At the same time, it felt good to have this beautiful, smart, brave young woman standing beside him.

In some crazy way, despite all the terrible things that had happened in the past two days, something still seemed right with the world for the simple reason that Anna was in it with him. She would stand beside him, fight with him, to the end. Hunter Buchanon was a tall, broad-shouldered man. But with this woman beside him, he felt just a little taller, just a little broader.

As though curious about the turn of her

man's thoughts, Anna looked up at him, frowning quizzically.

"Thank you," he said quietly.

She gave him a slow blink, and the corners of her beautiful mouth drew up with a smile. "We'd best light a shuck," she said. "We're burning daylight."

Hunter walked around to the wagon's left front side, and climbed up over the wheel. Anna walked around to the opposite side, and climbed over that wheel, settling herself on the leather-padded wooden seat. Behind her on the water barrel Bobby Lee gave an anxious moan, bending each ear forward in turn and tilting his head, anxious and puzzled.

Anna reached back and patted the coyote's head reassuringly.

Hunter released the wagon's brake. He clucked to old Titus, getting him started, then, the mule braying with characteristic incredulity, swung around to head southwest, powdering the sage off the cabin's west rear corner. He followed a slight crease in the land, fragrant pines falling in around the wagon, and headed straight south through the buttes.

"Is that my boys' graves up there?" Angus asked behind Hunter and Anna, above the wagon's rattle and squawk.

Hunter glanced back at the old man, then followed his gaze to the rise on which Shep's and Tye's graves were mounded, shaded by a large, sprawling fir.

"Yeah," Hunter said. "That's them, Pa."

Angus hardened his jaws again. A muscle in his cheek twitched.

"Rest easy, sons," he bellowed. He sobbed and then raked out hoarsely, "You will be avenged!"

Bobby Lee lifted his long, pointed snout and yammered fiercely in agreement.

They'd crested the first hill south of the 4-Box-B fifteen minutes after leaving the headquarters, when Hunter turned to his left, staring at a young ponderosa pine standing like a sentinel at the crest of the rocky ridge. The wind was blowing hard up here, blowing cones out of the trees.

Hunter glanced at Annabelle. "Take the reins for a few minutes, will you?"

"What are you going to do?" she asked, reaching for the reins.

"One last thing."

As Annabelle took control of the wagon, Hunter leaped to the ground.

When Nasty Pete came up beside him, Hunter tugged the slipknotted reins free of the steel ring in the tailgate and stepped into the leather. He looked at Angus. The mossy horn appeared especially old and shrunken beneath the quilts and blankets that Anna had pulled up to his chin, covering most of his long beard.

Angus's eyelids were squeezed shut. Deep lines cut across his saddle-leather forehead mottled with liver spots. More lines than normal. Angus was sound asleep, his frail body rocking with the wagon's pitching and jerking as it clattered over the ridge crest and started down the other side, not following any trail but cutting cross-country. Angus's lips moved as though he were having a conversation with himself in his sleep.

Or maybe a conversation with the men who'd killed his sons. A bitter one.

The old man may have been dozing, but he was in misery — in both mind and body.

"Let Titus pick his own way down the ridge, Anna," Hunter said. "I'll catch up to you by the time you reach the next valley." He saw Bobby Lee watching him expectantly, ears pricked, getting ready to leap off the barrel to the ground. "Stay with the wagon, Bobby."

The coyote groaned and lay belly-down atop the barrel, crossing his front paws.

Annabelle looked at Hunter again curiously, vaguely troubled, then nodded and said, "Hurry."

Hunter touched spurs to Nasty Pete's flanks and trotted eastward along the crest of the ridge, weaving around shrubs and small rock outcroppings. He pulled up about twenty yards from the young ponderosa, and swung down from Nasty Pete's back. He dropped the reins and Pete stomped his left front foot, working some brome grass free of a small rock snag, and began grazing.

Hunter looked at the young pine. He and his brothers had brought it from their north-Georgia farm nearly eight years ago. Back then, it had been a slender seedling. They'd wrapped the dirt-sheathed ball of its tender roots in wet burlap and, keeping the burlap wet, hauled it all the way here to the Black Hills of southern Dakota Territory.

The tree had grown from a seed on their mother's grave. While they hadn't been able to move their mother's body out here with the rest of her family, they'd been able to move the next best thing, the seedling they'd believed represented her spirit, so she could reside with them here in their new home, watching over the boisterous all-male family from the crest of this rocky ridge in much the same way she'd done in life back in Georgia.

The only difference was that in life Emilia Buchanon often had a spoon or a cast-iron skillet in her hand, both of which she'd wielded threateningly when the need arose, which it often had — the boys being the rowdy trio they were, fathered by the wild old mountain catamount, Angus Buchanon himself.

While beautiful in her younger days, before the years of tough mountain living and then disease had eroded away her youthful vivacity and tempered the sparkle in her eyes as well as the flush in her cheeks, Emilia Buchanon had been as tough as an oak knot right up to the day she'd succumbed to her affliction.

Annabelle reminded Hunter of his stalwart mother. Emilia had been a tough Southern mountain woman, hailing from hardy Scottish stock from a boggy hollow to the west of where Angus had grown up. As tough as Emilia had been, she hadn't cottoned to men killing other men, whatever the reason. She'd disdained guns beyond their usefulness in supplying meat for the larder.

For that reason, on one of his rare visits home during the war, Hunter had promised her, a badly ailing woman by that time, coughing out her lungs in bloody bits, that as soon as the war was over he'd rid himself of his shooting irons — all but the rifles he used to hunt game. He'd also promised his mother that he would never again kill another man. Not for any reason.

That's why it was with a heavy heart and sinking feeling of dread and even fear that he walked slowly over to a pile of rocks not far from the tree that memorialized Emilia Buchanon. Before the cairn, he stopped and faced the tree.

He ran his tongue along the underside of his upper lip, drew a deep breath, and said, "I'm sorry, Momma. But when I made that promise, I hadn't expected this."

He dropped to a knee and removed the rocks from the pile two at a time. Beneath the rocks was a shallow hole filled with dirt. He used his hands to dig up the dirt and gravel and toss it aside until he'd dug up the old Confederate gray rucksack, badly faded, a gilded eagle stitched on its flap. He shook off the dirt and brushed off the rest.

He opened the flap, reached into the pouch, and pulled out an old, battered, and timeworn Confederate campaign hat. He shaped the hat as best he could, removed his newer Stetson, and set the old campaigner on his head. It molded right to it. Inside the hat had been a necklace of grizzly claws — a trophy he'd attained himself when he'd killed the grizzly that had stalked him back in the mountains of his Georgia home, when he'd been hunting a wildcat that had been feeding on their cattle. He'd strung the claws on a long strip of braided rawhide and worn the necklace during the war, having been told by an old north Georgia mountain man once that the spirit of the bear brings luck to young warriors.

He dropped the necklace over his head, letting it hang down across his broad chest, over his linsey-woolsey tunic, beneath his knotted green neckerchief.

Again, he reached into the sack. This time, he withdrew a worn leather holster and cartridge belt. The belt loops still shone brightly with brass .44-caliber cartridges. On the left side was attached a sheathed bowie knife with a hide-wrapped handle and brass knuckle haft. Shep had built the handsome pig-sticker himself, before Hunter had left for the war. The gun holster attached to the cartridge belt's right side was so worn it was nearly the texture of ancient buckskin, and it formed the shape of a sharp-nosed V.

Hunter drew another breath and unsnapped the keeper thong from over the hammer of the stout, heavy, long-barreled pistol residing in the holster. He wrapped his hand around the glistening pearl grips, as smooth as polished marble, and slid the gun from the holster.

He held it before him — a silver-washed LeMat with a seven-and-a-half-inch-main .44-caliber barrel and a shorter, stouter twelve-gauge shotgun barrel tucked underneath. The beautiful weapon — as fine a piece of shooting equipment as Hunter had ever seen — was hand-engraved with tiny oak leaves and a breech lever in the shape of a miniature saber.

His own initials, HB, had been carved into each side of the long, sleek main barrel by the man who'd gifted him with the gun after Hunter had saved the man's life from a sharpshooter's bullet. That man had been none other than the Confederate general Pierre Gustave Toutant-Beauregard, or "Little Creole" as he'd been known . . . even though there'd been nothing little about G. T. Beauregard's fighting spirit.

The LeMat had been his own, designed by himself and fashioned on commission by a French gunsmith in New Orleans. After Hunter had saved the general from a sharpshooter's bullet at Shiloh, taking the bullet himself, Beauregard had ordered a crafty gunsmith to change the monogram. He then gifted the handsome piece to the young

Georgia Rebel who'd saved his life and whose own fighting spirit had already made Hunter Buchanon something of a legend, his name spoken nightly in admiring tones around Confederate cook fires.

G. T. Beauregard, a dusky-skinned little man with dark eyes and a dark mustache, had handed the weapon over to the starry-eyed young warrior late one night in a hospital tent on one condition — that Hunter recover from his leg wound and continue killing the venal Yankees.

Hunter had vowed he would.

And he'd done just that.

More than his own fair share, even — at least, to his own mind.

He'd killed so many Yankees that killing had sickened him to the point that, following his mother's wishes, he'd buried the gun here under rocks, as a totem of sorts to his mother's will. He'd wanted to bury the gun back in Georgia, soon after he'd returned home from the war, but something inside him had prevented him from doing so. That something in him had worried and frightened him.

Was the killing spirit inside him so strong that he'd never be able to part with it completely?

He'd had plenty of time to ponder the

matter on the way west with his father and brothers and the spirit of his mother enshrined in the pine seedling. Right after he and his father and brothers had planted the tree, Hunter had stolen up here to the ridge — secretly, under cover of darkness — and buried the LeMat under the rocks. He'd prayed to the spirit of Emilia Buchanon to forgive him for his reluctance to part with the instrument of so much death.

He prayed to her spirit again now, beseeching her forgiveness for digging it up.

He strapped it around his waist, trying to ignore the fact that the big popper felt good and familiar there against his thigh. He tied the holster thong around his leg, just above the knee.

He said, "Sorry, Momma, but I know you'd understand . . . given the circumstances. There's one more war this Buchanon has to fight."

Hunter swung back up onto Nasty Pete's back and galloped down the ridge toward the wagon.

CHAPTER 24

Frank Stillwell had to shake the dew from his lily.

Or so he told himself.

The truth was, he was feeling a little shaken again this morning. Not fearful. At least, not fearful in the way he'd so shamefully displayed just days ago by running inside his office and locking the door, then leaping out a window when Hunter Buchanon had followed him inside, bloody murder blazing in his Rebel eyes.

No, not fearful in that way. But fearful of the fear. Of the fear coming back.

Fear of the way people in Tigerville were looking at him these days. Not really looking at him but sort of glancing at him sidelong so that he could see them peeking at him out of the corner of his eye but when he turned to face them straight on, they'd already turned away and were going about their business as if he wasn't even there.

As if they'd never given him that quick, skeptical, vaguely jeering gaze, wondering what kind of sand the man really had or if he had no sand at all. Maybe he was the faker that Graham Ludlow suspected he was.

Of course, Stillwell himself knew he wasn't a faker. He'd had a momentary lapse, was all. A fleeting loss of nerve. Deep down, he was a brave man. A cold-blooded killer who ran from no man. At least, he would run from no man ever again.

Or so he told himself. Now, as he finished his breakfast in the Dakota Territorial's saloon — at the same table near the front window at which he'd been sitting when Ludlow had joined him yesterday — he finished his third cup of coffee spiced with a healthy jigger of rye and slid his chair back. That fear of the fear coming back, his revulsion at his own actions and of the looks the townsfolk were giving him, were making his insides twist around the bacon and eggs and fried potatoes he'd just eaten.

It was pressing on his bladder.

Time to shake the dew from his lily. Maybe to sit down for a spell, take a good long dump, and have a long think over the privy hole.

His consternation hadn't been tempered

by his learning that somehow Hunter Buchanon and Ludlow's daughter had survived the cave-in. It truly was as though Buchanon wasn't quite human. Or something more than human, maybe.

How could he and the girl have survived? There must have been a rear exit to the mine shaft, the sheriff figured, frustration raking him hard. Humiliation at how they must have laughed at him blazed inside him.

He'd only known that they would be out there together because someone had left him a note the previous night at the Dakota Territorial's front desk, and the clerk had slipped the note under the door to his room. An unsigned note.

There is an old prospector's cabin at the base of Crow Ridge, five miles west of town. H. Buchanon and his Yankee sweetheart will be there early tomorrow morning.

Stillwell had figured the missive had been penned by some concerned citizen who'd wanted to remain nameless to protect himself. Or herself. Stillwell had no idea who'd penned the note, but the penciled scribbling had appeared decidedly masculine.

How the writer had known about the tryst, Stillwell couldn't fathom. He wasn't in any position, however, to look a gift horse in the mouth. He had been suspicious of a trap, and that's why he'd ridden out there well armed and extra cautious. He'd wanted to wound Buchanon and drag both him and Annabelle Ludlow to town, so the town could watch Buchanon hang. But Stillwell just hadn't been able to pass up caving the mine down on top of the two lovers.

He'd relished the idea of them dying together, slowly suffocating or starving . . . together.

Of knowing that kind of bone-splintering fear not so dissimilar from what the sheriff felt the day before he had enacted the gruesome scheme . . .

The Grayback and Graham Ludlow's uppity daughter, too good for any other man in the county. But not for the former ex-Confederate, Hunter Buchanon.

Now Stillwell scrubbed the napkin across his mustache, set his hat on his head, and started to turn toward the back door at the end of the dark little corridor flanking the horseshoe bar. He stopped suddenly with an incredulous grunt, grimacing as he stared at the morning barkeep, Clancy Becker, who stood behind the bar polishing the inside of a thick schooner with a bar cloth.

Stillwell squared his shoulders at the rail-thin, dour-faced, and balding Becker, and set his fists on his hips with an air of open confrontation. "What the hell were you looking at, Clancy?"

Becker, who had done his best to jerk his critical gaze from Stillwell when the sheriff had gained his feet and turned toward him, now feigned a look of surprise and indignation, jerking his head back and furling his thin, fawn brows. "Wha— *huh?*"

Ignoring the handful of other men around him taking their breakfast in the saloon instead of in the formal dining room on the other side of the lobby, Stillwell strode stiffly toward the barkeep. "I asked you what you were staring at just now, Clancy."

"What're you talkin' about, Frank? What's it matter to you what I was starin' at? I can stare at any damn thing . . ." Becker let the sentence trail to silence, for he saw the dark cast to the sheriff's eyes as Stillwell drew up on the other side of the bar from him.

"You think so, do you?"

Clancy stared back at the peeved lawman, wariness and consternation growing in his gaze. He was remembering the veritable bloodbath that had occurred not long ago, near the arched doorway to the lobby.

"You're talkin' pretty sharp to me these days, Clancy. What makes you think I'll let you get by with it? Did I let Jackson and Wise get by with it? What makes you think I won't cut off your ugly head, dry it, and wear it on my vest as a watch fob?"

Clancy swallowed. A single sweat bead popped out on his left temple and trickled down the side of his face. "Look, Frank, I . . ."

"Sheriff Stillwell, Clancy."

"All right, all right — *Sheriff Stillwell,* if you must know, I was starin' through the window *beyond you.* Not *at* you but *beyond* you. I was starin' at the Purple Garter across the street, where poor Mr. Chaney expired yesterday — murdered by them Buchanon butchers. I was thinkin' to myself about his poor boys, Billy an' Pee-Wee and what a tragic week it's been for them two. First they lose their brother Luke and then they lose their father, succumbing as Mr. Chaney did to his wounds.

"I was thinkin' what an awful tragedy it is. Then, with one thought followin' another the way they often do, I got to wondering what's gonna happen to this place, since Mr. Chaney was part owner. *That* thought led to me pontificatin' on how maybe I should go over to the undertaker's place, where I hear Mr. Chaney's laid out, and pay my respects to him and Billy an' Pee-Wee. I heard several other fellas talkin' about how they was gonna do that before the day heated up and the poor man started attractin' flies not to mention collecting gas and smelling bad. I got me a sensitive sniffer."

Clancy placed a finger beside his nose to indicate the organ of topic.

When Stillwell only stared at him, Clancy, growing even more uncomfortable under the heated lawman's dark scrutiny, added, "Forgive me, Sheriff Stillwell, if my eyes strayed to you. I assure you they did not do so with the intention of giving offense."

Stillwell kept his glaring eyes on Clancy for another several beats.

Finally, he drew a breath, curled his upper lip with disdain, and said, "I'll be danged, Clancy, if you ain't the windiest son of a gun who ever blew through Tigerville. It's a wonder you ever get anything done around here."

With that, Stillwell turned and strode stiffly on down the side of the bar. At the rear of the room he pushed through the curtained doorway. Once in the silence of the dark corridor that ran under the stairs slanting up on his left and the kitchen on his right, Stillwell drew another deep, calming breath and told himself quietly, "Calm, Frank. Just stay calm, for chrissakes. If you ain't careful, the town's gonna switch from thinkin' you're a coward to thinkin' you need to be carted off to a loony bin."

Stillwell pushed through the hotel's rear door and tramped across the pine planks extending from the door to the single-hole privy flanking a long, tall pile of split cordwood. The pine planks were to help keep boots clean during rainstorms, there being little grass but a lot of dirt in Tigerville.

The sheriff followed the planks to the privy constructed of vertical whipsawed boards and with a slightly slanted, shake-shingled roof and a half-moon carved into its door, near the top.

He grabbed the steel handle, pulled.

Locked.

"Occupied," sounded a gravelly voice from inside.

Stillwell cursed, grabbed the handle with both hands, and gave it a fierce pull. The door snapped open as the nail and steel locking ring clattered onto the privy's wooden floor.

"Hey!" bellowed the stout gent sitting inside. He glared out from under the narrow brim of a shabby bowler hat from the band of which a hawk feather protruded, and yelled, "I told you it was occupied!"

"Poop or get off the pot!" Stillwell lifted one boot over the threshold, grabbed the man by his shirt collar, and jerked him up off the bench.

"Hey, you can't . . . !" Tripping over his canvas trousers that were bunched around his ankles, the stout gent went stumbling through the privy door like a bull through a too-narrow chute, tripping over his own boots and dropping to his knees just outside the privy.

"Yes, I can," Stillwell said. "I'm the sheriff in these parts. Now, if you wouldn't mind, I'd like a little privacy!" He reached for the door as the stout gent cast him a russet-faced, indignant glare over his thick right shoulder, then pulled the door closed, absently lamenting that now he couldn't lock it.

"Occupied!" the sheriff bellowed before adding, "*Pee-YOU* — it stinks in here!"

Stillwell dropped his pants and made himself comfortable. Outside there was much growling and cursing as the stout gent got himself together and stumbled away, likely off to find another Irish shanty.

Stillwell drew another deep breath.

Perched there over the hole, he managed to relax.

However, he'd no sooner gotten his mind to calm down, the demons in his brain to scurry back to their hidey-holes, when something hard smashed against the privy door with a near-deafening *bang!*

A rock. Had to be . . .

"Who the hell was that?" Stillwell yelled, sitting there over the hole with his whipcord trousers bunched around his boots.

Outside there was only silence except for the piping of birds in the brush behind the privy, and the ratcheting of crickets. Distantly, he could hear the usual daily din of the main street, but back here there was nothing.

Then there was something as someone threw another rock against the privy door with an even louder *bang!* than before.

Stillwell's heart thumped with rage. "Who's out there?"

Another rock smashed against the door, causing the door to jerk in its frame, dust sifting around it. Stillwell gnashed his teeth together, enraged.

"It's Stillwell in here!"

Yet another rock barked against the door. The sound inside the privy was like a pistol shot. The concussive report was like two cupped hands slapped against the sheriff's ears.

"Is that you, fat man? Come back to get even?"

Stillwell cursed again, wiped himself quickly with pages from a catalog, and pulled up his trousers. His anger made it a clumsy maneuver. His entire body trembled with exasperation. When he got his suspenders pulled up over his arms, he strapped his Colt and cartridge belt around his waist. He left his frock coat and hat hanging from a peg on the wall to his left.

He paused. The rocks had stopped slamming against the door, but he thought he could hear muffled laughter and someone moving around out there. He peered through a gap between two vertical planks, but he couldn't see much for the grit crusted between the boards. He looked out through the half-moon.

Still, nothing.

Someone was playing a joke on him. They were mocking him.

Kids? Maybe one of the town's whores' wild urchins.

Stillwell's heart was thudding heavily. It beat so hard that he felt the painful throbs in his temples. Fury was a wild bronc inside of him.

He unsnapped the keeper thong from over the Peacemaker holstered on his right hip. He slid the long-barreled piece from its holster, thumbed the hammer back.

No one around here had any respect for him anymore. Well, he'd see about that . . .

Again, he heard a muffled snicker.

Stillwell stepped back against the bench, lifted his right leg, and thrust it forward, kicking the door wide with the bottom of his boot. He took one step forward, and as the door ricocheted off the privy to slam against his left shoulder, he extended the Colt straight out in his left hand.

A man stood before him, about ten feet away. Vaguely, Stillwell was aware of three others, but he drew a bead on the man straight ahead of him and, hearing one of the men shout, *Frank!"* he squeezed the Colt's trigger.

It kicked like a branded calf as the bullet flew from the barrel in a burst of smoke and bright orange flames to drill a neat round hole through the forehead of the man straight out in front of him. The man screamed and flew back, hitting the ground hard in the dirt to the right of the pine planks.

"Frank, stand down, fer chrissakes! Stand down! It's Jack an' the boys!"

Squinting against his own peppery powder smoke, Stillwell looked at the man who'd spoken. Dakota Jack Patterson stood to the right of the man Stillwell had shot and who now lay flat on the ground on his back, jerking wildly, eyes rolling up in their sockets. Patterson was a tall *hombre* as broad as a barn door and with thick, curly yellow hair tufting out from under the brim of his broad-brimmed black Plainsman hat, his long, pitted, ugly face framed in muttonchops of the same color. He stared at Stillwell, thick-lipped mouth hanging wide in shock.

He turned to where the down man was fast dying — a short, stocky man with Indian-dark skin and wearing a necklace of bear claws, which splayed out now on his worn calico shirt. Patterson turned back to Stillwell and said, "Stand down, Frank! Stand down! Willie's one of us, for the love of Pete!"

Stillwell had clicked the Colt's hammer back for another shot, but now he depressed the hammer and slowly lowered the piece to his side. Bewildered and flustered, he scowled at big Dakota Jack, and said, "J-Jack . . . ?"

"It's Jack," Patterson repeated, nodding his head. He gestured at the dying man who looked dead by now, no longer jerking. "That's Willie Cruz. Half-breed Mex from Arizona. Willie's one of my men, Jack. He rides with me an' Klaus an' Weed."

Patterson nodded at each of the other two men as he'd recited their names. Weed Zorn, a snaky gunman from Missouri, was crouched over the half-breed, Willie Cruz, hands on his thighs. Klaus Steinbach, a cobalt-eyed, black-bearded killer from west Texas, stood off to Zorn's right, a faint smile on his thin-lipped mouth, as though the scene amused him. He slowly shook his head, lifted a smoldering quirley to his lips, and took a long drag.

Weed Zorn looked at Patterson. "The bean-eater's dead — just like that." Zorn slid his flat, darkly accusing gaze to Stillwell.

Anger flared once more in the sheriff, and, holstering the still-smoking Colt, he snapped, "Well, what the hell was he throwin' rocks at the privy for?"

"That wasn't Willie," Patterson said, suddenly grinning, showing an uncommon number of large, yellow teeth and one silver one, which winked in the morning sun. "I was just funnin' with ya, was all. The barkeep told us you was out here."

"Well, I hope you enjoyed yourself," Stillwell said. "Now you got a man to bury."

"Christ," Zorn said, looking down at the unmoving half-breed. "Willie was a good man too. That's too bad." Zorn looked at Patterson. "I wonder what Lupita's gonna say about this."

Patterson filled his heavy lungs with a fateful sigh.

"Who's Lupita?" Stillwell asked.

"Willie's sister. Zorn's girl over in Laramie." To Zorn, Patterson said, "We'll make somethin' up between now and when we see her again. We'll make up a good story about how Willie died in an honorable way — maybe shootin' it out with lawmen or some such." He glanced snidely at Stillwell. "We'll make somethin' up."

Stillwell gave a caustic snort. "I don't care if you do or not."

"What're we gonna do with him?" asked the black-bearded Klaus Steinbach.

"Good question," Patterson said. He turned to Stillwell. "Any ideas, Frank?"

"Hell, I don't have any ideas. I was the one who had to shoot the sidewinder. That's as far as I go. You're the reason he's dead."

Patterson studied Stillwell, wrinkling the skin above the bridge of his nose. It was almost as though he sensed the turmoil behind the sheriff's own eyes. The scrutiny made Stillwell uncomfortable. Patterson must have realized it, because he suddenly returned his attention to the dead man.

"Well, this is a tragedy, right here. It sure enough is. Willie was a chili-chompin' half-breed, that's true, but you wouldn't know it by the way he carried himself. Honorable as any white man, and that's a fact."

Patterson turned to peer around Stillwell and the privy flanking the sheriff, gazing off toward scattered houses, woodpiles, and stock pens shaded by occasional cotton-woods and sheathed in sage. "As I recollect, some old woman has a hogpen back there somewheres. I mean a real hogpen. Not a whore's crib."

"Still does," Stillwell said. "The Widow Bjornson. That's her white house and red barn back yonder."

"Hell, Willie might've been a half-breed," said Weed Zorn, "but that don't make it right to feed him to hogs."

"You gonna bury him in this heat?" Steinbach asked Zorn. "Or pay to have the undertaker bury him?"

"Undertaker's done booked up for the foreseeable future," Stillwell said. "Him and his idjit son been sawin' wood to build wooden overcoats day an' night." He glanced meaningfully at Dakota Jack. "It's that trouble I wired you about. In spite of that fool trick you pulled on me, I'm glad you made it, though I doubt your dead friend here would feel likewise."

Stillwell chuffed an ironic laugh, satisfied how the old, notorious trickster Dakota Jack had gotten the tables turned on him. Jack flushed. That made Stillwell feel even better, made him stand up a little straighter, grin, and tuck his thumbs behind his cartridge belt.

Dakota Jack glanced at Steinbach and Zorn. "Hell, Willie ain't gonna know what happens to him. I liked Willie, too, but he was still a half-breed. In fact, I heard he was three-quarters Lipan Apache."

Steinbach's cobalt eyes snapped wide in shock. "That right?"

"That's what I heard tell." Dakota Jack gestured with his arm. "Haul him over to the hogpen. Hell, it all amounts to the same sooner or later. If he's buried in a hole, we're all smorgasbords for the carrion-eaters in the end."

"No truer words have ever been spoken," agreed Weed Zorn, crouching to grab the dead man's ankles. "Help me here, Klaus."

Dakota Jack turned to Stillwell. "While you two are disposing of Willie, Sheriff Stillwell and I will head inside and talk business. I for one am a mite curious about your so-called venture here, Frank." He smiled shrewdly. "And any money that might be involved. Bismarck is a literal cesspool these days. Do you know that I passed out drunk in a whore's crib and woke up the next mornin' stripped clean? Why, I'm poorer than Job's cat!"

CHAPTER 25

Hunter crossed the slope of the ridge at a hard gallop and drew Nasty Pete up close to the wagon's left side.

Annabelle had heard him coming. She gazed at him now over her left shoulder as she held Titus's reins in her gloved hands. Bobby Lee gave a couple of low yips in greeting as Hunter stepped off Pete's back and into the wagon's driver's boot. He tossed his Stetson into the box, then took the reins back from Anna, who was eyeing the floppy-brimmed campaign hat on his head, the grizzly claw necklace hanging down his chest, and the handsome pearl grips of the big LeMat jutting above the soft leather holster strapped to his thigh.

She slid her gaze back to Hunter's eyes but did not say anything. She pulled her mouth corners down and then turned her head to stare out over Titus's long ears. Hunter leaned toward her and gave her cheek a comforting kiss. She did not turn back to him but kept her eyes straight ahead, harboring her own dark thoughts about the coming storm, likely wondering about its outcome.

Who would live and who would die?

Hunter glanced over his shoulder at old Angus. The old man still slept in the same position as before, that troubling grimace still twisting his mouth.

As they reached the bottom of the long slope and Hunter put Titus up the opposite incline, Nasty Pete following along to one side without needing to be tied, Annabelle said, "How much farther? All this jostling can't be good for Angus."

"Top of this next ridge." Hunter shook the reins over the mule's back and said, "Come on, Titus — no stopping to graze, you old cribber!"

The next rise was as long as the first but not as steep. Still, to make the ride less jarring and to go easy on Titus, Hunter steered the mule on a gradual switch-backing route, ploddingly making his way toward the crest unseen beyond a thick stand of trees that started about halfway up the slope.

Hunter let Titus pick his own way through the trees, and when they couldn't go any farther because of thick brush and snags,

Hunter drew back on the reins and the wagon squawked to a rocking halt.

"Looks like this is as close as we're gonna get." Hunter set the brake. "That's all right. I wanted a place that's hard to get to."

"How much farther?"

Hunter nodded to indicate where the trees thinned just ahead and he could see some boulders of various sizes and a wall of crenelated limestone rock. "Up there. Fifty, sixty yards."

Hunter climbed out of the driver's boot and walked around to the back of the wagon. He opened the tailgate and leaped inside, dropping to a knee beside Angus. He touched the old man's shoulder and was relieved when Angus immediately opened his eyes and looked around.

"Where in hell are we?"

"Where I was headed."

Anger turned the old man's cheeks dark russet. "Don't run me around the dogwood tree, boy! Where's where you was headed?"

Hunter smiled. The old man still had his gravel. That was a good sign. "I'll show you in a minute, you old catamount. Do you think you can walk or do I have to carry you?"

"I'll walk, by God!"

Angus tossed the skins and blankets off of

him, and Hunter took his arm, helping him stand. When Hunter had the old man on the ground, Annabelle said, "I'll grab a few things and be right behind you."

"Grab Shep's Henry — will you, Anna?" Hunter would no longer be far from a long gun, and he thought it fitting that he'd appropriated Shep's handsome repeater, which he would use to avenge not only Shep but Tye as well.

"Got it," Anna said, reaching into the driver's boot for the rifle housed in Shep's leather scabbard and tucked beneath the seat.

Hunter took the bulk of his father's weight against his own right side as he helped the old man up the slope, tracing a wending path through the columnar pines. The wind made a near-steady rushing sound in the highest branches, though the air was still down here on the forest floor. It was quiet except for a squirrel giving the intruders holy hell from a near aspen branch, and for the bellows-like sawing of Angus's old lungs.

"Christ, Pa." Hunter couldn't help scolding the old man. "That pipe of yours and your consarned coffin nails are going to be the death of you yet!"

"You don't have a quirley on you, do you, son?" Angus quipped, wheezing. "I could sure use one." He coughed a raking laugh. Hunter glanced over his shoulder at Anna, who chuckled. Hunter shook his head.

At last they moved up out of the trees. Before them was a steep wall of limestone gouged here and there by the various erosions of time. The deepest gouge was a low, egg-shaped cave at the base of the formation and up a steep bank flanking several scattered, wagon-size boulders.

"That's your new home, Pa," Hunter said, nodding at the cavern. "For now."

"What the hell?"

"Home sweet home."

"Hellkatoot!"

"Come on."

Hunter had to nearly carry the old man up the steep, gravelly incline beyond the boulder and onto the crumbling shelf of dirt and gravel fronting the cave. While the old man leaned back against the mountain wall, loudly raking air in and out of his lungs, Hunter investigated the cave, having to doff his hat and duck his head to compensate for the low ceiling, which at its highest wasn't much over six feet.

Hunter knew the cave was often occupied, for he'd smelled gamey, wild smells and scat in here on several occasions when he'd visited the cavern on hunting trips and had needed a handy place to spend the night or to build a coffee fire. However, the presence of a wildcat or bear or a family of wolves had made it none too handy a time or two in the past, and Hunter had quickly lit a shuck.

No animals appeared to have made the cave home lately. There were a few deer and rabbit bones tufted with bits of remaining fur near the back, but they appeared several months old to Hunter's practiced eye. The cave, being roughly ten feet wide by twenty feet deep, would provide adequate cover for Angus and Annabelle while Hunter was off doing what needed to be done.

Hunter stepped back out of the cave as Annabelle came up carrying a buffalo robe over one arm, two canteens slung over her neck, and Hunter's Henry in her right hand. She ducked her head to peer into the cave, then gave a Hunter an ironic look.

"Just like the Morris House in Philadelphia."

"What's the Morris House?" he asked.

"Never mind."

They got Angus settled inside the cave. He was badly worn out from the climb and didn't say much except, "How in hell did you know about this place, boy?"

"You'd know about it, too, if you ever left

the ranch yard."

"How can I leave the ranch yard, you ungrateful pup?" Angus retorted. "I got beer to brew!" He rolled his eyes around. "Say, I hope you thought to bring a jug of ale."

"Bet on it," Annabelle said. She'd laid out some spruce and pine boughs for a bed, and she was tucking the buffalo robe and blankets over the needles. "I brought whiskey and ale."

Angus furled a brow at Hunter. "Tell me again how come you ain't married her by now?"

"I been holdin' back because I was worried you might steal her away from me."

"I still might." Angus winked at Annabelle.

She winked back at him.

Hunter placed his hand over his father's forehead. "How you feelin', you old reprobate? You pullin' a fever, are ya?"

"Hell, it's a hot day."

Hunter glanced at Annabelle kneeling beside him.

"How do you feel?" she asked Angus.

"Fine as frog hair split four ways."

"Go easy on the whiskey," she told him. "And no smoking."

"Shee-it. Purty as Christmas mornin', but this one's a harpy too!"

343

Annabelle laughed.

Hunter stared grimly down at him. "You heard the nurse, Pa," he said gently, worriedly.

"Don't sass me, boy!"

Hunter was about to respond, but Angus snaked his lone hand out from under the buffalo robe and wrapped it around Hunter's forearm, cutting him off. "Don't worry, boy — I won't die until those who killed Shep and Tye are kicked out with a cold shovel."

His fingers, surprisingly strong, dug into Hunter's arm, and his eyes blazed with fiery passion.

Hunter and Annabelle spent a good portion of the afternoon outfitting the cave with supplies they carried up from the wagon. They unhitched the mule and unsaddled their horses, and tied all three animals to a picket line strung between trees not far from the cave, close enough that the horses and Titus would alert them of possible interlopers if Bobby Lee, who was off hunting rabbits, did not.

Hunter doubted that anyone would find them way out here in the high and rocky, but he wasn't taking any chances. He doubted any other white man knew of the cave, but a good tracker could follow the wagon's tracks from the ranch.

He was sure that men from town would soon pay the 4-Box-B headquarters a visit. Maybe as early as tonight but by tomorrow night for sure. Not finding anyone in the yard, they might follow the wagon, but if they arrived late enough there wouldn't be enough light with which to pick it up. Hunter was always aware of the moon, a habit he'd gotten into during the war when he was customarily sent out on night raids or reconnaissance missions, and knew there would only be a late sickle moon this evening.

He built a fire just inside the cave, with a ring of flame-blackened rocks he'd arranged a couple of years ago and in which old ashes remained. He mounted an iron spider over the leaping flames, and Annabelle set a coffeepot on it. While the water in the pot gurgled and ticked, she made fatback sandwiches with cheddar cheese on crusty wheat bread.

Meanwhile, Angus snored in the cave behind her and Hunter, waking occasionally to take a painkilling pull on the bottle Anna had set close beside him. Down the steep decline from the cave, the horses quietly grazed. The sun shone on the face of the mountain in which the cave had been carved, but the forest below the cave was in deep, foggy green shadow.

From his vantage by the fire, Hunter sat and, sipping a cup of the hot black coffee and eating one of Annabelle's sandwiches, stared out over the forest and beyond the next ridge. He couldn't see the 4-Box-B headquarters from here, because it sat too low in the valley beyond that next ridge, but he thought that if the buildings were burned at night, which they likely would be when the men from town came and found the place abandoned, he would see the glow.

That's when he would make his first move.

He felt Anna's eyes on him before he turned to see her staring at him, her own untouched sandwich in one hand, a steaming cup of coffee in her other hand. Her eyes were soft and touched with fear.

"What is it, honey?" Hunter asked her.

"What . . . what are you going to do, Hunter? How are you going to fight all those men . . . alone?"

Hunter opened his mouth to speak but she cut him abruptly off with, "No. Let's not talk about it." She turned to gaze down the slope into the cool, dark, quiet forest. "Let's just sit here . . . enjoy the time we have."

They did just that.

Between the necessary chores of tending the stock and seeing to Angus's needs, they sat together by the fire, sipping coffee, not saying much but just being together, appreciating every second.

Hunter cleaned and loaded the LeMat and Shep's Henry rifle. He sharpened his bowie knife. He cleaned Tyrell's Winchester saddle-ring carbine and left it leaning against the cave wall for Anna, in case she should need it. Hunter cleaned Angus's Livermore twelve-gauge shotgun, his Yellowboy rifle, and his old cap-and-ball pistols, as well, loading them all and setting the four weapons near where the old man lay on his bed of buffalo robes and spruce branches.

Angus gave a dip of his chin in acknowledgment, then asked for a cup of ale.

That night, Hunter kept the fire very low. He wouldn't have built one for himself and Anna, but Angus needed to be kept warm, for nights in the Hills grew chilly. Anna leaned back against Hunter, between his raised knees, as he stared out over the dark forest toward the ranch, waiting.

Bobby Lee lay nearby, curled nose to tail

in sleep, yipping softly in rabbit-rending dreams.

The glow Hunter expected did not come that night.

But the second night, just after he'd poured himself a fresh cup of coffee and had returned the pot to the spider, Annabelle gave a soft, low gasp.

Hunter jerked his head to her. She stared out over the forest, her mouth slowly widening.

He followed her gaze to the southwest. A stone dropped in his belly. A light shone there — a soft, orange glow pulsating above the hollow in which the 4-Box-B lay.

Hunter slowly set his cup down beside the fire. His hand shook, causing some of the coffee to slop over the sides of the cup.

"That's it, then," he said, and turned to Anna. "You stay here with Pa. You stay here until I come for you." He looked at the coyote eyeing him expectantly, ears pricked. "You, too, Bobby Lee. You're of more use here than you would be with me, against a whole passel of men with guns."

Bobby Lee mewled softly in protest.

Annabelle repressed a sob but her eyes were shiny in the firelight as she gazed at her lover. "When will you be back?"

Hunter gathered his weapons and his

saddle. "I'll be back as soon as I know I won't lead them here."

He looked over his shoulder as he moved farther and farther down the slope and away from the fire's dim glow.

"But I will come back to you, Anna. I reckon I can't make any promises. I been through this before. But I sure am going to try!"

Then he was gone.

Soon, hoof thuds sounded in the forest below the cave. They dwindled quickly, and then there was just the starry sky pressing down low.

Anna sat back on her heels and lost the fight to hold her tears at bay.

Bobby Lee chortled longingly.

CHAPTER 26

Sitting in a wicker rocking chair on the front veranda of his sprawling ranch house, Graham Ludlow took a deep drag from his stogie and blew the smoke out into the night beyond the veranda rail.

The rancher had come out here to get away from the screaming and yelling issuing from his son Cass's room upstairs. But now that the doctor, Norton Dahl, was here, changing Cass's bandages and adding salve to the burn, the screaming had followed Ludlow out here to his sanctuary.

Ludlow was a tough man, but he couldn't take the screaming. Not that the screams made him squeamish. What bothered Ludlow was that a man shouldn't carry on that way. Hell, he'd been around ranch hands who'd been gored by bulls in unmentionable places or been thrown from horses into prickly pear thickets and even into barbed wire, half their skin peeled off, and they'd done little more than curse a few times through gritted teeth.

Ludlow had once known a man who'd lost a thumb to a lariat. It had taken several hands to restrain that man, to keep him from merely wrapping up his bloody hand, climbing back into his saddle, and getting back to work.

As another shrill scream vaulted out from the lodge's second story, Ludlow winced, shook his head, and took another drag from the stogie.

He supposed this would make its way around the Hills, as well as everything else that had happened — his daughter and the Grayback, his daughter burning down the barn, burning down her brother, and now, to top it all off, Cass's screaming like a girl with a frog down her dress.

Ludlow wanted to know what he'd done to deserve this patch of bad luck. All he'd ever done was try to make an honest living and give his children comfortable lives. For his troubles, his daughter turned out to be a trollop, her brother a nancy boy. Or worse — if what Annabelle had accused Cass of doing to her was true.

That turn of thought further soured Ludlow's mood.

He found himself welcoming the distraction of hooves thumping in the darkness west of the ranch, growing gradually louder in the otherwise quiet night. A rider was approaching.

Frowning curiously, Ludlow rose from his chair, took another drag from the stogie, then, exhaling smoke through his wide nostrils, moved down the veranda steps to follow the path down the slope toward the yard. He was nearly to where the yard leveled at the two iron hitchrails standing near a stock trough in which dark water reflected the lights of the bunkhouse on the yard's other side, when the rider appeared — a silhouetted figure checking his mount down to a trot as he entered the yard, shadowy dust curling up behind the horse's arched tail.

The metallic rasp of a rifle being cocked reached Ludlow's ears, and he saw a slender, hatted figure separate from the shadow of the burned barn rubble that still came to smoldering life now and then.

"Who is it? Who's there? Name yourself!" barked the picket.

The rider stopped several yards away from the sentinel Ludlow had been in the habit of posting nightly ever since the Sioux trouble. The Sioux themselves might have had their horns filed down by the U.S.

Army, but the Hills were stitched with desperadoes not above robbing remote ranch headquarters or assassinating rich and powerful men who'd stepped on the toes of others of their own ilk. A man like Ludlow, with lots of money and various sundry business dealings, some not so popular, had to have eyes in the back of his head.

Also, there were the friends and family of the men he'd hanged on his range . . .

"It's George Andrews from town," said the rider as the horse rippled its withers and shook its head. "I got a message for Mr. Ludlow."

"It's all right, Lowry," Ludlow said, stopping at the bottom of the slope and resting his left hand on the hitchrack.

Lowry turned toward the rancher, pinched his hat brim, let his Winchester's hammer click benignly down, then turned and continued making his rounds along the headquarters' perimeter.

George Andrews, an odd-job man from Tigerville, booted his calico mare over to the hitchrack, near where the doctor's shabby single-seated buggy sat behind a beefy zebra dun. Andrews drew back on the mare's reins and said, "Evenin', Mr. Ludlow."

"What's the message, George?"

"You said you wanted me to let you know when the Chaney boys rode out to the 4-Box-B."

"That's right."

"They rode out about an hour ago, Mr. Ludlow. They got liquored up after they laid their pa to rest, an' then they asked for volunteers to ride out to the Buchanon ranch. There's a whole bunch of 'em signed up. Boy, you get the liquor flowin', an' everybody's a pistoleer!"

Ludlow himself had attended Max Chaney's funeral, of course. It wouldn't have looked right if he hadn't, though he had to admit being a little worried lightning would strike him there on Cemetery Hill, especially when purple thunderclouds rolled in from the north. He thought he'd done a pretty fair job of impersonating a genuine mourner, however, and he'd managed to get down off of Cemetery Hill before the rain had started.

He hadn't talked to either of the Chaney boys — Billy or Pee-Wee — about their plans regarding the Buchanons. He knew they would get around to calling on the Buchanon ranch sooner or later. There was no way either of Chaney's sons would let their father's and brother's murders go unavenged . . . of course they didn't realize who had actually killed Max Chaney.

No one except Ludlow himself knew that, but he also knew that Doc Dahl had his suspicions. Anyway, Chaney would likely have died from that nasty head wound if Ludlow could have kept his temper on a leash. Well, he hadn't, and that was that.

Over and done with. Water under the bridge.

As the fog of his distracting thoughts cleared, Ludlow saw George Andrews staring incredulously up at the big house standing back against the hills behind it with most of its windows lit. Another of Cass's shrill screams caromed across the ranch yard from the young man's second-story bedroom. Ludlow had closed the window earlier, not wanting the hired hands to be privy to his son's inelegant caterwauling, but the sawbones must have opened it to let out the stench of rotting flesh.

"Ohhh, Jesus, help meee!" Cass shrieked in a high-pitched, girlish voice, sobbing. *"Please, Doc, you gotta give me somethin' stronger to kill the pain! It hurts so god-awful baaaddd!"*

More wailing.

"Jesus, Mr. Ludlow," said Andrews, staring up at the house. "Is . . . is that Cass?

355

Jeepers, he sounds like he's in a powerful bad way!"

"Yes, yes," Ludlow said, "I couldn't have put it better myself, George. Cass is in a powerful bad way."

"Is it true what they say?"

"Is what true and who's sayin' it?"

Andrews was a heavyset man, none too bright and with a penchant for the bottle, when he had the money, most of which he earned running errands for men like Ludlow and swamping out whorehouses and saloons when he wasn't butchering Mrs. Bjornson's pigs. He flushed now as he turned to the rancher, realizing he'd made a mistake by shooting his mouth off.

"Uh . . ."

"Go on," Ludlow insisted. "Is what true and who's sayin' it?"

"I just meant —"

"Is what true and who's saying it?"

"Never mind, Mr. Ludlow — I spoke outta turn!"

"Yes, you did, and make sure you don't do it again, George. Here or in town. Understand? If I get word you're spreading nasty rumors about me and my children, I will send a man to town to cut your ears off. Do I make myself clear?"

"More than clear, sir!" Andrews backed

the frightened mare away from the hitchrack.

"Hold on, George."

Reluctantly, Andrews stopped and turned back to the rancher. "Yes, s-sir?"

Ludlow glared up at him with seething menace, his cigar smoldering in the right hand he held down low by his side. Andrews stared down at him, mouth open, waiting in dread. Slowly, Ludlow shifted his cigar to his left hand and dipped his right hand into a shallow vest pocket.

"Oh, please now, Mr. Ludlow — !"

Ludlow pulled a coin from the vest pocket and flipped it into the air. Andrews squealed, recoiling as though from the der-ringer blast he'd expected, then caught the coin awkwardly against his chest, nearly unseating himself from the mare in the pro-cess.

The mare turned a full circle before An-drews got it back under control.

"What's the matter, George?" Ludlow said through a caustic laugh. "You don't like my money?"

Andrews stared at the coin in his hand, drew a deep, relieved breath. "Oh, uh . . . thank you, Mr. Ludlow! No, I like it just fine! Well, I'd best get back to town, sir! Good night, sir!"

Andrews turned the rattled mare and booted her back in the direction from which he'd come.

"Don't forget about our little talk, George!" Ludlow called after him.

"No, sir!" came the shuddering reply just before the mare galloped under the ranch portal and thudded off into the darkness.

Ludlow stood staring off after the man, puffing his stogie. A man cleared his throat behind him. Ludlow gave a start and wheeled to see the doctor, Norton Dahl, standing just up the hill from him, holding his medical kit, the lenses of his glasses glinting in the starlight.

"Jesus, Dahl! What the hell are you doing sneaking up on a man in the dark?"

"I wasn't sneaking," the doctor said. "I was taking my leave. You were talking with George."

Ludlow gave a wry chuff. "You're lucky I'm not armed. I might have shot you."

"I don't doubt it a bit."

Ignoring the sawbones' sarcastic tone, Ludlow said, "Well, how is he?"

"How did he sound?"

Ludlow just now realized that Cass's screams had died. "Christ, what were you doing to him up there?"

"I was changing his bandages, redressing

the wound. I'm too busy in town now to ride out here every day, and I have a feeling business is going to do nothing but improve, what with those Chaney brothers leading another gang out just as I was leaving town."

Dahl's tone was crisp, not so vaguely accusing. "I left carbolic acid, salve, and a week's worth of bandages for Chang. He's going to have to tend your son for the foreseeable future. I'm going to send a man out with more medicine. Something stronger to kill the pain, though I warned Cass it's highly addictive."

"What is it?"

"Night oil. Dragon wind. Hair of the spider." The doctor paused, blinked. "Opium."

"Christ, he's in that much pain?"

Dahl brushed past the rancher as he continued toward his horse and buggy. "You heard him."

Ludlow grabbed Dahl's arm. "Hold on, Doc!"

When the sawbones had turned back to face him, the rancher said, "How is he? I mean, is he going to . . . is he going to look like that . . . forever?"

"He was badly burned, Mr. Ludlow. She badly burned him, though I hear she was merely defending herself. That said, I'm afraid he's never going to be much to look at. If he lives through the infection, that is. The burn will heal to an extent, but there will be much scarring. His hair will not grow back, and neither will his ear."

Dahl started to walk away again but turned back once more when Ludlow said, "So . . . you heard, eh?"

"What's that?"

"You heard that it was Annabelle."

Dahl averted his gaze, looking a little incredulous. "Yes. I heard. It's a small town, Mr. Ludlow. Everyone in town seems to be very interested in you people out here."

Ludlow drew a deep breath, pensively puffed the stogie. Aware of the doctor's coldly incriminating gaze on him, the rancher's thoughts took an even darker turn.

He took another puff from the stogie, and said, "Doc, about what occurred in the Purple Garter . . ."

"What about it?"

"I don't know what you think you saw, but —"

"What I saw was that I left Chaney alive in that room, and when I returned, he was dead. And you were standing over him. A bottle that had been nearly full only a few minutes before was empty, and Chaney's lungs were filled with whiskey."

Ludlow stared at the man, narrowing his eyes as he took another puff of the stogie. "Best keep that under your hat, Doc. No real loss to civilization, do you think?"

"No. Chaney was a bully. He was a bully before you came along and went into business with him, and all the more after you got here and legitimatized him."

"Well, ain't I just the devil!"

"And then you killed him. Which is fine. We don't have a sheriff in this county. We never have and it will likely be a long time before we do. Not a real one, anyway — one that isn't here merely to watch over your and Chaney's interests, to keep peace in the town so you can make money here."

"Like I said," Ludlow repeated, quieter, "ain't I the devil?"

"The problem is, Mr. Ludlow, the Chaney brothers think their father died from the wound he suffered at the hands of Hunter Buchanon. That's why they rode out there — a good twenty or more Southern-hating Yankees. Most are from the mine. Some are relatives of those who were killed earlier at the 4-Box-B. They're all liquored up, most wanting to get in good with the Chaney boys. And the Chaney boys are riding out there to settle up for what they believe is the killing of their father."

"They would have ridden out there, anyway. You saw what Buchanon did to Max."

"I saw what you did to him too."

"You'd best keep that under your hat, Doc."

"Or what? You'll kill me, I suppose. Have one of your men do it. Have Stillwell do it. Shoot me in the back."

"However it gets done, it will get done. You best be mighty good at keeping secrets."

Dahl glared up at the taller, broader man, his spectacles glinting now as though from a fire burning in his eyes. "How long is this going to continue, Ludlow? All this killing?"

" 'Til justice is served."

"Justice, my kidney plaster! Justice for whom? Luke Chaney? Max Chaney? Stillwell's men? You, maybe, because your daughter happened to fall in love with the wrong man, and you feel betrayed?"

Dahl shook his head, gritting his teeth. "This is all nonsense, Ludlow. This is all about revenge. Nothing more, nothing less. Revenge for you, revenge for the Chaneys, revenge for the men killed out there for very justifiable reasons on Buchanon's part, I might add."

"Revenge is a valid reason, Dr. Dahl. Get down off your high horse. This isn't Philadelphia or Boston or New York, or wherever in hell you come from."

The doctor chuckled. "Boston, my ass. I was born and raised on a little farm in Iowa. Went to medical school in St. Paul, Minnesota. I'm from here. You're not. This is just your playground where, because you have money, you get to make the rules. And when those rules get broken, you exact revenge because revenge is all part of the game. Just don't ever call it justice, Ludlow."

"That's fine, Doctor. Revenge then. I'm fine with the term."

"Yeah, well, you know what they say about revenge, Mr. Ludlow."

"What's that?"

"When a man sets out for revenge, he'd best dig two graves."

Ludlow scowled at the insolent sawbones. "You've worn out your welcome here, Doctor."

"I was just going."

Dahl swung around, removed his horse's hitching strap from the hitchrack, then climbed into the buggy. As he released the brake, Ludlow said in a threatening tone, "You just remember to keep our secret, Dahl. Don't make me lose any more patience with you than I already have."

Dahl glared at him, then swung the dun around, shook his reins over the horse's back, and spun out of the yard, the wheels clattering softly along with the clomping of the horse's hooves.

Ludlow took another pensive puff from his stogie, following the doctor's retreat with his gaze. "Dig two graves, my ass."

CHAPTER 27

Hunter's heart was on fire.

It burned as hotly in his chest as did the blaze causing the red glow in the sky to his left as he rode cross-country in the direction of the main trail to Tigerville.

He'd tried to prepare himself for the burning of the 4-Box-B headquarters. He'd known there was nothing he could do to stop the Tigerville men from burning it. There'd be too many of them and they would have come expecting a fight. As much as he'd wanted to try to hold them off, he'd forced himself to face facts.

He was only one man, after all. He couldn't do Angus or Annabelle any good dead. He couldn't exact revenge for his dead brothers and wounded father if he was dead.

Still, seeing that pulsating glow in the sky off his left shoulder now, roughly a mile and a half away, his heart burned and his blood boiled in his veins. Hatred and rage seethed inside him more strongly and more poisonous than it ever had during the war. Somehow, the war hadn't felt personal. This, however, was personal. Very personal, indeed.

He sucked back his rage, his fury, knowing he had to keep it down where he could control it so he could think clearly and use it to his best advantage. He ducked under an aspen branch hanging low over the slender, pale ribbon of trail he was following.

He intended to cut the marauders off on their way back to Tigerville, when their defenses would be down. He knew a shortcut that meandered around through the bluffs east of the headquarters and then followed a dry wash north, toward a spot where the main trail on which the Tigerville men were riding cut sharply south — toward him.

It should bring them nearly right up to him.

It was a mild night without a breath of breeze. Hardly any night birds murmured in the pine-clad bluffs around him. The moon, a slender sickle dipped in lemon yellow paint, peeked through a thin cloud above a stony ridge to the southeast, ahead of him now and to his right.

Nasty Pete's hooves clomped softly on the slender trail, and the bridle chain jangled. He was making too much noise. During the war, he often ran barefoot behind enemy lines, with only a knife and a rifle, drinking water where he found it. If he rode, he straddled a horse wearing only a rope halter, its unshod hooves padded with burlap.

Those precautions would be lost on the buffoons who'd burned the ranch. They'd likely left town drunk, galloping hard. Their horses would be tired by now, and they'd likely be riding slowly, talking loudly, maybe bragging about their handiwork, and passing bottles. A raw recruit could ride up on that bunch unawares.

Or so Hunter confidently opined.

He learned only a few minutes later that he'd been right. Lying belly-down atop a low butte beside the trail, he heard them coming. First he heard the slurred voices of several drunken men. Then he heard the thuds of slow-moving horses, the squawk of saddle leather, and the jangle of bit chains.

One man laughed, mockingly. Then another.

A horse whinnied.

Presently, Hunter saw the shifting, bobbing, man-shaped shadows coming along the broad trail through the buttes on his left. Slowly, they passed before and below him. He could hear their voices, smell their unwashed, sweaty bodies, and the whiskey on their breath and oozing out of their pores. By the time the last man had passed, moving from his left to his right along the trail before him, he'd counted twenty-two.

As a large mass of riders often did, they were riding in separate groups of various sizes, separated by at least twenty yards. The last group that had passed was a pack of six led by, Hunter thought, none other than Pee-Wee Chaney. He thought he'd recognized Pee-Wee's drunken voice.

Now he turned his head to the right and watched Chaney and the five other men at the end of the pack disappear around a bend in the trail.

Hunter's heart was racing.

His surging blood sang in his ears.

Quickly, he scampered down the butte and ran over to where he'd left Nasty Pete silently grazing in the shallow wash. He removed his boots and socks, grabbed the Henry repeater, and dashed off afoot, following a course parallel with the trail.

"Hey, Pee-Wee," one of the pack members called. "When we gonna go back and look for that Buchanon? He killed my cousin, Earl, an' that means he bought and paid for a bullet from me."

Pee-Wee heard the slosh of beer as Leo Turner, riding abreast with two other men behind him, hoisted one of the crocks they'd found in the Buchanon house before they'd burned it.

Pee-Wee said, "We're gonna sober up in town tonight and then we're gonna ride out on fresh horses tomorrow and track him from the ranch. Him, that old Rebel devil of a father, and that Ludlow girl who thought she was too good for my poor dead brother, Luke — dead on account of her!"

Pee-Wee sobbed. It was like an injured coyote's gurgling cry. He lifted the bottle he was carrying in his left hand, tipped it back. Only a single drop dribbled onto his tongue. He cursed and threw the bottle down hard, shattering it on a rock beside the trail.

"Leo, get up here with that jug — I'm outta whiskey!"

Leo chuckled, then booted his horse up close beside Pee-Wee's mount, on Pee-Wee's left side. "That old mutt might be useless in most ways, but he does make good ale. I'm gonna miss his ale . . . when I'm through killin' both him an' his boy *real slow*. Once that's done, I'm gonna drag

Ludlow's ripe an' sassy daughter into the brush. I'm gonna make her moan like a ten-cent whore!"

Pee-Wee hoisted the jug high and threw back a big drink of the dark, malty Scottish ale. Lowering the jug, he laughed and said, "When I'm done givin' it to her, she's prob'ly gonna wanna marry up with *this* Chaney anyway! Maybe her an' me — Ludlow's high-and-mighty woman — will marry up an' move to San Francisco or some such."

He laughed again and turned to glance at the men riding behind him. "What do you think o' that, boys?"

They all laughed and said they wanted a turn with her too.

Laughing, Pee-Wee turned his head back forward and raised the jug again. He frowned as the thick, tepid brew washed over his tongue. He'd spied movement out the corner of his right eye.

It was a pale, ghost-like figure moving fast, dropping down from a high point above him and onto the trail before him.

His heart quickened. He'd just started to lower the crock before his horse jerked with a start, and then something unforgivingly hard and fast-moving slammed into the crock. The big jug was smashed savagely against Pee-Wee's face, his mouth taking the brunt of the blow, pulverizing every tooth in the front of his jaws and hurling him backward off his horse in a rain of beer and flying stone shards from the crock.

He hit the trail hard on his belly, spitting teeth and crock shards from between his bloody lips, hearing himself moan . . . though he was so stunned that the moans might have been coming from some wounded animal beside the trail.

Lifting his head from the blood-muddy dirt, he saw who he thought was Leo writhing on the trail to his left just as Leo's horse — a large dark bulk in the darkness — ran buck-kicking forward, screaming shrilly.

The ghostly pale figure was hunkered low in the middle of the trail, about ten yards ahead of Pee-Wee and Leo. Just as the men behind Pee-Wee began shouting, one man yelling, "What in the hell was *that*?" a bright orange flash of flames lanced over Pee-Wee's head.

It was followed by the explosive report of a rifle and the instant fetor of rotten eggs. The rifle roared again, again, and again, setting up a loud ringing in Pee-Wee's ears. The bright flashes were blinding.

The men behind Pee-Wee screamed, their horses whinnying shrilly. There were several hard thuds of bodies smacking the trail. The men ahead were shouting now, as well, as the rifle continued its everlasting thunder over Pee-Wee.

When it stopped, and there was only the din of screaming men and horses, Pee-Wee found himself lying belly-down on the trail, his face in the dirt, arms drawn up over his head. His bloody mouth was on fire. He wasn't sure if he'd taken a bullet from the attacker's rifle. If he hadn't been hit, he was sure the situation would change in a second . . .

He lay there, moaning, feeling more bits of tooth and crock jug slither out of his mouth on a continuous stream of blood.

Suddenly, a foot was thrust against his left side. A bare foot? He grunted sharply as he was kicked onto his back. He howled and lay staring up at a pale face hovering over him. He held his crossed arms in front of his face, as though they could shield him from a bullet.

Moon- and starlight glinted off the barrel of a rifle. The end of the barrel was shoved into Pee-Wee's mouth, between his raw, bloody lips.

Pee-Wee gurgled against the metallic taste of the hot iron in his mouth. He stared up in horror at a shadowy, gray-hatted head and two eyes blazing down at him from the side of the rifle. White teeth shone as the shooter stretched his lips back from his teeth.

"I ain't gonna kill you, Pee-Wee. Not yet. It's too damn easy. But soon, Pee-Wee. Soon."

The rifle barrel was thrust back out of Pee-Wee's mouth, and then, just like that, the shooter was gone.

The men who'd been riding ahead of Pee-Wee's group were galloping back toward him now, several shouting at once, one man sawing back on his horse's reins and yelling, "Pee-Wee — where is he? Where the hell is he?"

It was Pee-Wee's brother, Billy.

Pee-Wee rose onto his knees and thrust his right hand straight out toward that side of the trail, which was the direction he assumed the shooter had gone. Billy and several other men neck-reined their horses sharply and thundered off into the darkness.

Another drew rein in front of Pee-Wee, shouting, "Who was it? Who was it? Did you see him?"

Pee-Wee's head was reeling. He was still seeing blasts of orange light in his eyes. He looked around. Several men lay in the trail behind him. Leo lay to his left, arms thrust out, ankles crossed. He wasn't moving.

"Did you get a look at him?" the mounted man before Pee-Wee asked again as other riders thundered off into the darkness south of the trail.

Pee-Wee spat blood and bits of teeth from his lips. He hadn't gotten a good look at the man who'd thrust the rifle into his mouth. But he'd seen the gray Confederate campaign hat and the long, blond hair tumbling onto thick, broad shoulders clad in buckskin. And he'd recognized the handsome Henry rifle that had once belonged to the eldest Buchanon brother, Shep.

"Hunter Buchanon," Pee-Wee said, though he doubted the rider before him could make out what he'd said. With his mouth so full of blood, he hadn't been able to understand it himself.

Hunter Buchanon!

The name rocketed around inside his head, though, clear as a church bell on a cool autumn morning.

Hunter Buchanon!

CHAPTER 28

Billy Chaney galloped around a tall, broad cottonwood and then drew his gelding to a skidding stop. Several other men drew their own mounts to stops behind Billy, horses blowing, saddle leather squawking.

"Where is he?" asked a man to Billy's left. "You see him?"

"Shut up!" Billy rasped, violently slashing down with his arm.

Holding his reins taut in his right hand, holding his Winchester across his saddle-bows with his other hand, he looked around, listening. Trees pushed down close to the trail. Beyond the dark webbing of branches, stars shimmered. The sliver moon was kiting over the blunt peak of a distant ridge.

A silence too silent lay heavy over the trees and the slopes rising to each side of the crease Billy was in.

Suddenly, hooves thundered and the silhouette of a horse and rider bounded out from behind the dark shoulder of a slope maybe thirty yards ahead of the Chaney pack, and went charging on up the trail.

"Hi-yahhh!" the man bellowed. *"Hi-yahhhhh!"*

Hunter Buchanon. Had to be . . .

"There!" Billy shouted, crouching low over his horse's head and ramming his spurs into his gelding's flanks.

He whipped his Winchester up and snapped off a shot. The bullet screamed off a rock somewhere wide of his target. As the gelding lunged on up the crease between the buttes, Billy drew the Winchester across his saddle again. He had to pull his head down nearly to the gelding's mane as a low-hanging branch swept over him, brushing the top of his horse's head.

Behind him, a man screamed as the branch unseated one of the half dozen or more riders giving chase behind him.

Billy stared over his horse's laid-back ears at the dark crease ahead of him, and the misty gray shadow of the rider pitching and swaying maybe forty yards beyond. The crease through which he was leading Billy and the other riders was brush-choked in places. Choked with rocks and fallen trees in other places. More branches hung low from the slopes to each side of the trail.

Billy ducked another one just as the branch swept his hat from his head. Behind him, another rider screamed. The scream was followed by the crashing thud of yet another rider smashing to the ground.

Ahead, the pack's quarry rose and fell violently as Buchanon's horse leaped a deadfall pine. Billy's gelding cleared the pine. A second later, a horse behind him screamed and then its rider screamed as horse and rider, apparently not making the leap as cleanly as Buchanon and Billy had, took a nasty tumble.

"Where the hell's he leadin' us, damnit?" yelled a rider behind Billy. Billy recognized the voice of a Chaney cousin, Ed Landers, who worked as a guard at the mine. "That rascal's trying to kill us!"

"Shut up and ride, Ed! I am not losin' that devil! He killed Luke an' my pa!" Billy ducked another low branch. "Might've killed Pee-Wee, by the look of the poor soul back on the trail! Savage rat!" he bellowed, lifting his head high to direct the insult at the man riding like a wind-blown tumbleweed ahead of him.

"Crazy to be ridin' this hard at night!" a man far back in the pack shouted. "Damn reckless, you ask me!"

Another horse and another man screamed.

377

More crunching and thrashing as the terrain took down another rider in the Chaney pack.

Another man cursed.

Ahead, the crease turned sharply to the right. Billy followed it around a wall of broken rock. Two eroded, brush-stippled stone walls now rose to each side, pushing down close to the trail Billy was following, which had suddenly become a dry creek bed, it appeared, though it was hard to see much of anything in the darkness relieved only by the starlight and the light of the sickle moon angling down through the trees.

Billy slowed the gelding, then stopped it, holding up his hands for the other riders to follow suit. They came storming up behind him, jerking back hard on their horses' reins. Billy glanced over his shoulder. There were five . . . now six men behind him, checking their nervous, skitter-stepping mounts down.

Billy turned his head forward, squinting his eyes, probing the nearly impenetrable darkness closing down around him. The sudden, inky darkness was why he'd stopped the gelding. Ahead, a horse whickered. Billy snapped his Winchester to his shoulder, loudly pumping a live cartridge into the action.

With his knees, he urged the gelding slowly forward.

When his horse had taken maybe four steps, Billy saw another horse standing just beyond him, maybe fifteen yards away. The horse, staring toward him, eyes like dim lamps in the darkness, was saddled. Sweat foam glistened on its withers and in wind-blown streaks across its jaws. Its bridle reins were wrapped around its horn. Peering beyond the riderless horse, Billy saw nothing but a high rock wall. Atop the wall were the dark columns of pines and firs.

"Holy cow," exclaimed a man close behind Billy. "He's led us into a box canyon!"

"Trap," raked out a man sitting stiffly to Billy's right, his voice pitched low with dread. "It's . . . it's a trap!"

The silence closed around them. Billy sensed the fear of the other men. It was growing as palpable as his own. His heart thudded heavily against his ribs.

"Oh . . . darn," said a man to Billy's left.

Billy kept his Winchester pressed to his shoulder, his cheek snugged up against the stock. He swung the barrel left, then right, then left again, looking for a target, waiting in silent terror for a bullet.

"Where is he?" he said, quietly but anxiously. "Anyone see him?" He raised his voice. "I know you're here, Buchanon!"

Stretched seconds passed.

A disembodied voice came out of the darkness, a rich Southern accent, slow and self-assured, sounding near yet far away. "You fellas don't realize that when you tangled with the Buchanons, you dipped your hand in a sack filled with cottonmouths. You tangled with the wrong damn passel of Graybacks!"

Billy screamed and triggered his Winchester at where he guessed the voice had come from, the rifle bucking hard against his shoulder, bright red flames lapping from the barrel. He screamed as he fired again, one-handed, holding his jittery mount's reins taut with his free hand. The other men raised their own rifles, and they fired into the darkness at the top of the canyon wall.

The din was deafening, the screeching of the reports vaulting around the canyon to chase their own echoes toward the high-floating moon.

One terrified horse bucked, screaming, and threw its rider back over its arched tail.

The hammer of Billy's Winchester clicked benignly down against its firing pin.

Shortly, the hammering of the rifles dwindled, replaced by the clicks of empty chambers. The man who'd been thrown from his horse gained his feet, grunting and cursing under his breath.

The silence descending over the smoke-foggy canyon was even denser than before.

"Did we get him, you think?" asked the man to Billy's right.

The answer came from the darkness, the voice slow, steady, deadly.

"Nope."

The only thing more satisfying than killing men who'd wronged you in the worst possible way was doing the job with your big brother's prized rifle — the big brother whom some of these men or their raggedy-assed brethren had killed gutlessly from ambush.

Lord help him, as Hunter squeezed the Henry's trigger and watched Billy Chaney punched back off his horse. Hunter cut loose with a wild, involuntary Rebel yell, an ear-rattling chortling wail that would have impressed even Bobby Lee — the coyote, not the Confederate general, though the latter likely would have sat up and took notice as well.

Guffawing loudly, Hunter rammed another round into the Henry's action and fired down into the box canyon before him, at the horseback riders sitting their horses like ducks on a millrace.

Damn hoople heads had ridden straight into his trap.

Hunter fired again, again, again, and again, flames geysering from the Henry's barrel and the empty, smoking cartridges arcing back over his right shoulder as he opened the breech and seated yet another round that sent yet another Chaney-sympathizing SOB wailing to his reward.

He was disappointed when only six riderless horses were bucking and pitching and screaming loudly down there beyond the webbing fog of powder smoke. Nasty Pete was down there, as well, but he was acting far calmer than the other six mounts, who were wheeling in the darkness and finally galloping out through the bottleneck-like entrance to the box canyon, on the canyon's far side.

Pete had just turned and was starting to follow them when Hunter, rising from his prone position behind a low rock and a thick cedar root, stuck two fingers in his mouth and whistled. Pete whinnied, looking up at Hunter, who approached the lip of the canyon.

"Stay, Pete."

The horse bobbed its head and remained in place.

Quickly, adroitly, Hunter clambered down the canyon wall, leaping the last five feet to the canyon floor and swinging around to face the chasm littered with sprawled, man-shaped silhouettes.

One man was moving, moaning.

Hunter walked over. The only man who appeared not to have given up his ghost was Billy Chaney. Chaney was holding a hand to his neck, groaning and cursing and pushing up into a sitting position. He heard Hunter's quiet barefoot tread, saw his tall shadow angle over him.

Chaney looked up, sidelong, raising one brow, saw the broad-brimmed Confederate campaign hat on his assailant's head, the grizzly claw necklace splayed across his broad chest.

He looked at the Henry rifle in Hunter's right hand.

"Ah hell," he said.

"Fittin' place for you, Billy."

Hunter aimed the Henry casually with one hand and drilled a neat, round hole through the dead center of Billy Chaney's forehead.

His rifle report rocketed around the canyon before dwindling toward the stars.

Silence settled.

It was short-lived.

As Hunter looked around, making sure

none of the other Chaney riders was still moving, a horse whickered beyond the canyon's entrance. It was followed by a man's hushed voice. Another hushed voice answered the first one.

Quickly, Hunter made his way over to the narrow canyon entrance, the thick, calloused soles of his bare feet absorbing the pinch of sharp rocks and thorns. He dropped to a knee at the entrance's left side and peered out into the dry creek bed down where he'd led his foolhardy pursuers.

Maybe sixty yards back down the cut, two horseback riders were moving slowly toward him, riding abreast. Hunter could see only their shadows, which occasionally melded to the shadows of large trees and rocks as well as to the cutbanks on each side of the wash.

The men kept coming, the horses taking slow, plodding steps toward the canyon, one of the horses bobbing its head, likely smelling the coppery odor of fresh blood and powder smoke.

"You see anything?" one rider asked the other when they were roughly thirty yards from Hunter's position.

"Hell, it's so damn dark I can't see my hand in front of my face."

"The shots came from just ahead. You

think maybe they got him?"

"If they did, where are they?"

Hunter straightened. He stepped forward, his left arm and his rifle wide, showing himself and saying, "They're in the canyon yonder," Hunter said. "They're as dead as Sunday's pig."

"Nuts," one of the men cried, jerking back on his horse's reins.

Hunter racked a round into the Henry's breech, snapped the brass butt plate to his shoulder, aimed quickly, and triggered two quick rounds, emptying both saddles. The horses reared, clawing their hooves at the sky, whinnying crazily, then swung around and galloped back the way they'd come, kicking one of the two fallen men.

The other one grunted as he heaved himself onto all fours and began crawling after the horses.

Hunter walked up to him.

He kicked the man over on his back. The man looked up at him. It was Wilbur Brown, a man who mucked out livery barns in Tigerville and was a known Chaney friend and Confederate-hater.

"Rebel trash!" Brown spat.

Hunter responded with Shep's Henry.

CHAPTER 29

Hunter raised the Henry, the octagonal maw smoking in the darkness. He rested the rifle on his shoulder, held up his left, gloved hand.

As still as stone.

He looked down at the man he'd just killed. The man's eyes were half-open, dimly reflecting the moonlight. Blood bubbled darkly from the round hole just above his right brow.

Hunter's nerves were customarily calm in the face of killing. He wasn't sure what bothered him worse — that he'd killed again or that he felt little to no emotion about it. At least, no emotion in its aftermath. A few minutes earlier, however, the bloodlust had literally howled out of him, as it had in the early days of the war, when he'd found himself not only uncommonly adept at making war but being thrilled by it.

Like a savage. Which he supposed a very

large part of him was despite his efforts to deny that aspect of himself. He had a good dose of the warrior blood of his Scottish ancestors, forever at war with the wild blond hordes from across the North Atlantic.

He felt no emotion. No guilt. No regret. If he and his family had been left alone, he wouldn't have had to take up arms again. But they hadn't been left alone. His brothers had been killed, his father wounded.

All he really felt about the entire nasty mess was a firm resolve. He hadn't started this war. But he was damn sure going to finish it.

He could hear men yelling farther back along the dry creek bed — likely those injured from the breakneck run along the wash, who'd had the misfortune of finding themselves astride less sure-footed and night-savvy mounts than Nasty Pete — and those men gathering the injured as well as the dead. Hunter felt compelled to go back and finish them all off — one after another.

Why not?

They'd burned his ranch and some had probably been in on the earlier ambush that had killed Shep and Tye.

He nixed the idea. He'd killed enough men for one night. When more came after him, he'd kill them. He'd kill as many as he had to. He'd like to kill Stillwell, as well, but he had a feeling the man had taken the gold — Hunter and Annabelle's stake — and lit out for Mexico. Maybe someday Hunter would meet the gutless thief again, and he'd settle up for the thievery and the cave-in.

He'd done enough here for one night. Besides, he wanted to check on Annabelle and his father. These men wouldn't track him tonight. They'd had a belly full of Hunter Buchanon.

He whistled for Nasty Pete. When the horse had trotted up to him, blowing and shaking his head, Hunter shoved the Henry into the saddle scabbard, mounted up, and rode off down the dark draw, past the entrance to the box canyon filled with corpses. He took a roundabout way back toward the cave.

He knew this part of the Hills like the back of his hand, and Nasty Pete did as well — even at night. Some horses were better night travelers than others, and Nasty Pete was the best night horse Hunter had ever ridden.

Nearly an hour later, he rode up the final ridge through the trees and saw the small, flickering orange fire that Annabelle had kept burning against the night's chill. From somewhere, Bobby Lee gave a low howl. Nasty Pete took only two more strides before there was the loud scrape of a Winchester being cocked.

"Who's there?" Anna called. "Name yourself!"

Hunter smiled. He could hear her but he couldn't see her. She'd obviously heard him coming and moved away from the fire, knowing the flames would compromise her night vision and allow her to be seen by a rider coming up on her like Hunter was now.

"It's me, honey."

Hunter kept Nasty Pete moving up the steep incline, hearing the crackling of the flames now in the cool, quiet night. Bobby Lee ran up and then around Hunter and Pete, yipping softly in greeting. Hunter heard the soft ping of the Winchester's hammer being set down against the firing pin. Anna stepped out of the darkness to the left of the cave and into the small sphere of flickering light encircling the fire.

Anna leaned the rifle against the cave wall, then strode down to where Hunter stopped Nasty Pete near where Anna's buckskin was tied and wildly switching its tail, happy to have Nasty Pete back, Hunter reckoned — as Nasty as Pete was.

"Thank God," Anna said. "I heard the shooting."

Hunter swung down from the grullo's back.

Anna gazed up at him, her eyes wide with concern. "Are you all right?"

Hunter nodded, wrapped his arms around her, and hugged her tightly against him. She hugged him back. She lowered her gaze to his feet and then smiled up at him. "My barefoot warrior."

Hunter looked down at his feet and chuckled. "I reckon I forgot to put my boots back on."

"You're as wild as an Indian."

He grinned as he crouched to pat Bobby Lee. "Wilder."

"Hunter?" Anna's voice was suddenly grave. "It's Angus. Come up and take a look."

Hunter's heart thudded. He grabbed his boots and socks out of his saddlebags and followed Anna up the slope past the fire and into the cave. Angus lay at the edge of the firelight, under the skins and blankets. A kettle of water in which a red rag floated lay nearby. Angus lay on his back, another damp rag resting across his forehead.

The blankets quivered as Angus shivered beneath them, his eyes twitching. His forehead glistened with sweat.

"Fever," Anna said as she and Hunter dropped to a knee beside the old man. "I've been trying to get it down all night."

"Pa . . ." Hunter rested the back of his hand on Angus's left cheek. He turned to Anna. "He's burning up."

"I know. I'm worried."

"Has he been conscious at all tonight?"

"He's in and out. When he's awake, he talks gibberish. A few times he called me Emilia."

"Ma."

"He was telling me how sorry he was that he was off in the war when she died. He said he should have been home." A thin sheen of tears shone in the young woman's jade eyes.

Hunter rolled onto his butt and began pulling his right sock onto his foot. "I'm gonna fetch Dahl."

Annabelle placed her hand on his arm. "Hunter, you can't ride to town!"

"I don't know what else to do, Anna. I'm not gonna just sit here and watch Pa die. I have to do something."

"Your riding into Tigerville and getting yourself shot isn't going to do Angus any good."

Hunter pulled on his left boot, then his

right one. "If I don't fetch the doc —"

Just then Angus said, "Emilia, honey!"

Hunter whipped his head around, as did Anna. Angus's eyes were wide open and bright with anxiety. He slid his gaze from Annabelle to Hunter and said, "Oh, Shep, it's you . . ."

"No, Pa," Hunter said, scuttling over to his father, placing a reassuring hand on Angus's spindly shoulder. "It's Hunter, Pa. Do you know where you are?"

Angus stared up at him, his cheeks flushed with fever. "No . . . no . . ." He frowned, shook his head. "Hunter's off fightin' the war." He gave a crooked, proud grin, slitting his eyes. "A real Rebel devil, I hear too." He snickered, then quickly sobered. "Shep, fetch your ma for me, boy. Hurry along now. I got somethin' I have to tell her."

Hunter glanced at Annabelle kneeling beside him.

"It's okay, Pa," Hunter said. "You don't need to tell her. She knows. She forgives you, Pa."

"Oh, Emilia!" Angus cried, tears rolling down his craggy cheeks. "I'm so sorry I wasn't here for you!"

He squeezed his eyes closed and sobbed for a time, his head jerking. Slowly, he rested his head back against the pillows, sobbing quietly. As Anna removed the cloth from his forehead and soaked it in the pot of cool water, Hunter said, "He's deep in fever, Anna. If I don't fetch the doc, he'll die. He might die anyway, but I have to do something or I'll never be able to live with myself."

Anna dabbed at the old man's forehead and turned her worried eyes to Hunter, nodding. "I know." More tears glazed her eyes and she choked back a sob of her own. "I know . . ."

"I'll reach town before light. No one will see me. I'll have Dahl back here pronto."

Hunter kissed her cheek and then walked out of the cave. He walked past the fire, stopped, then reached down and plucked a couple of small pine branches off the pile beside the fire ring. He set the branches on the fire, building up the flames a little.

Annabelle strode quickly out of the cave and into his arms. He drew her to him again, hugging her tightly, sensing the fear that gripped her. She had every right to be afraid. They were at war.

She pulled away a little, looked up at Hunter. "Where will this end?"

Hunter grimaced, shook his head. "No tellin', Anna. But we're gonna make it, you an' me." He glanced into the cave. "You an' me an' Pa. We're gonna make it. We're gonna make a go of it . . . somewhere."

Anna stared up at him, smiling and sobbing at the same time.

Hunter kissed her cheek and squeezed her shoulders. "I'll be back soon."

She placed a hand over his on her shoulder.

He pulled away, walked back down to where Nasty Pete grazed. Hunter picked up the horse's dangling reins, stepped into the leather, and rode away.

Annabelle stood by the fire, hugging herself as though deeply chilled, watching the gray-hatted warrior disappear into the shadows of the forest.

Hunter could have made it to Tigerville from the cave in less than two hours, but while Nasty Pete had deep bottom, he was not bottomless. Hunter had to stop and rest the horse several times, let him graze and drink from creeks.

Still, despite the frustratingly slow travel, Tigerville appeared on the horizon before him around dawn, haphazardly spread across the broad bowl bordered by pine-bearded buttes. The King Solomon Mine was perched on the craggy peak to the east, which was still in deep shadow now before sunrise, though Hunter could hear the ever-present thunder of the stamping mill.

He'd approached the town from the southwest, having avoided main trails and roads. Now he halted Nasty Pete at the base of a low bluff littered with strewn rocks and tufts of sage, ground-reined him, fished his spyglass out of his saddlebags, and climbed the knoll on foot.

Near the top, he dropped to his knees, removed his hat, and crawled to the crest, keeping low. He raised the spyglass, tele-scoped it, thrust it between a rock and a small cedar shrub, and twisted the cylinder until the town a quarter-mile away swam into magnified vision.

He couldn't see much except the backs of the buildings on the town's near side. Even those were obscured by the murky, pale blue light of the early dawn. He couldn't see much, but, nearly as importantly, he couldn't hear much, either, especially the commotion he'd half expected to find if the surviving marauders who'd burned his family's ranch and paid for the transgres-sion with his own hot lead had made it back to Tigerville by now.

Either they were still out in the tall and uncut, making their painful ways back to town, or they'd already made it back and been taken off the street for tending. Hunter hoped they hadn't made it back. If they had, it was going to be damned hard getting Dahl out of town unseen.

He'd soon find out how hard the job was going to be.

He'd just started to crab back down the bluff when something touched the nape of his neck. He jerked around with an audible start. Bobby Lee pulled his long snout back from Hunter, sat down on his bushy gray tail, and gave a low, whimpering squeal of sneaky delight.

"Bobby Lee, I swear you scared a good seven years off my life!"

The coyote slitted his long yellow eyes and lifted his black lips above his small, sharp white teeth in a delighted grin. No one could tell Hunter coyotes didn't grin. Bobby Lee grinned.

Hunter blew a deep sigh of relief. He'd expected to see a man aiming a Winchester at his head, though it was damned hard for anyone except his devilish coyote friend to steal up behind him. Hunter chuckled, gave the coyote a brusque, affectionate pat, and crabbed on hands and knees back down the butte.

Rising, he said, "You stay here with Nasty

Pete, Bobby Lee." He dropped the spyglass into a saddlebag pouch and shucked his Henry from its scabbard. "Town ain't exactly a haven for you an' me, as I'm sure you profoundly remember from the other day."

Bobby Lee sat, curled his thick tail around himself, and groaned.

"Stay, Pete," Hunter ordered, patting the grullo's long snout.

The grullo gave an anxious whicker and switched its tail.

Hunter crouched low as he made his way around the base of the bluff and, keeping his eyes skinned for movement ahead of him, began making his way through the tall, dun grass toward the backsides of the main street business buildings. He made his way through the jumble of old, mostly abandoned log cabins, stock pens, trash piles, and leaning privies as well as small garden patches and stacks of split firewood.

Fingers of morning breakfast smoke poked up from a few of the shacks, but he saw no one out and about except a lone man in the far distance chopping wood near the woodpile flanking a tumbledown shanty. There was also a collie dog chasing mice around a pile of lumber behind the mercantile, but the dog was too distracted to pay Hunter any attention.

Hunter made his way through a break between two tall business establishments, careful to avoid kicking discarded airtight tins and bottles, and paused at the mouth of the break, which let out on Tigerville's main drag. He scanned the street stretching away to either side. A few shopkeepers were either sweeping the boardwalks fronting their shops or hauling out displays, but they were too far away to make him out in the weak dawn light.

It was getting lighter though. He couldn't dally.

The doctor's office lay above the law office directly across the street from the breakout where Hunter was making his reconnaissance. Hunter made for the two-story office building, letting the Henry hang low against his right leg, keeping his head down so his hat brim hid his face. He neither walked nor ran but kept his pace somewhere in between, wanting to hurry but not look overly conspicuous should someone be peering out a street-facing window.

As he walked, he saw a saddled horse standing to his right. The horse wasn't tied. Its reins were hanging in the street as the horse drew water from a stock trough. It hiked a rear leg to scratch its side, and

Hunter saw the muddy-silvery lather bathing the mount that had been ridden hard recently.

Keeping his head down, Hunter strode up the stairs that ran along the office building's right side and knocked lightly on the door at the top. There was no answer, but he could hear voices on the other side of the door. He tried the knob.

It turned.

CHAPTER 30

He swung the door open and poked his head into the doctor's office outfitted with a desk and several glass cabinets as well as a bookshelf spilling books and papers. There was a heavy medicinal odor. The desk was a mess, littered with papers, thick reference books, and an array of medical utensils and stoppered bottles as well as trays of bloody water.

"Doc Dahl?"

The doctor was speaking to someone behind one of the two closed doors flanking the desk. That someone was cursing and grunting and speaking around what sounded like rocks in his mouth.

Pee-Wee Chaney must have made it to town. The saddled horse outside must have been Chaney's, though Hunter hadn't recognized it in the darkness on the trail.

He went in and closed the door behind him. He walked around behind the desk and tapped lightly on the door behind which Dahl was tending Chaney. He leaned the Henry against the wall to his right and unsnapped the keeper thong from over the hammer of his holstered LeMat.

"Doc Dahl?" Hunter called, pinching his nose closed to disguise his voice. At the same time, he slid the LeMat out of the holster.

He had to call two more times before the doctor yelled, "What the hell is it? Can't you hear me tending another man in here?"

"Big trouble, Doc," Hunter yelled, keeping his nostrils closed, in case Pee-Wee recognized his voice. "Better come quick!"

Dahl sighed. There was a clink as he tossed an instrument into a metal tray. A footstep, and then the door opened. Dahl stared out through the four-foot gap between the frame and the door. Hunter thrust the barrel of the big LeMat against Dahl's soft belly and clicked the hammer back. With his left hand, he grabbed a flap of Dahl's shabby, age-silvered, bloodstained, food-encrusted vest, and drew the man brusquely into the office.

Dahl's face twisted in anger. "What the hell is — ?" He stopped when he saw the cocked LeMat poking his belly.

Hunter pulled the door closed, making

the latch click.

Dahl stared up at Hunter, who stood a good head taller, nearly twice as broad. The doctor's face flushed with anxiety, and his lower jaw loosened.

"Sorry about this, Doc," Hunter said. "But I myself have more pressing business than that hog-wolloper in yonder."

"You're . . . you're . . ."

"Hunter Buchanon." Hunter and Dahl had never been formally introduced, but Hunter had seen the sawbones around town, heard him called by name.

"Holy Jesus," Dahl said, glancing at the closed door and keeping his voice low, "what are you doing in town? That man in there . . ."

"Is likely missing a few teeth, I know."

"He has a busted jaw and a busted nose to boot. Possibly a fractured skull."

"There'll be more where he came from, some in a whole lot worse shape, I'd imagine." Hunter scowled down at the pill roller glaring up at him. "Chaney burned my ranch. He was there when my brothers were killed from bushwhack. I'm here to take you out to where I got my pa holed up. He's been shot, and he's out of his head with fever."

Dahl pulled his head back in astonishment. "I can't just leave that man —"

Hunter shoved the LeMat harder against the sawbones' belly. "Yes, you can. And you will. Or I'll feed you a pill you can't digest." He dipped his chin to send those words home in a neatly wrapped, menacing package. He wasn't sure he'd really shoot the man just standing innocently before him, but he didn't want Dahl to doubt it a bit.

The sawbones appeared to buy it. The muscles in his pasty face sagged and a red flush rose in his jowls.

"What . . . what am I supposed to do about *him*?" Dahl canted his head toward the door behind which Pee-Wee Chaney was moaning and sobbing. He sounded like a deep-throated infant wailing for its mother. "I can't just leave him. Not like that. I'm sewing . . ."

"You're gonna leave him just like that, Doc. It's better than what he deserves." Hunter pulled the LeMat out of Dahl's belly and waved it at the room. "Quick, now! Gather up what you need. We gotta split tail outta here fast. My pa is burnin' up with fever."

Dahl glanced at the door again. "Christ!"

"Doc!" Pee-Wee Chaney cried, though the garbled plea was nearly indecipherable. "Doc — where'd you go, Doc?"

403

Dahl stared up at Hunter, deeply con-flicted.

"Forget him, Doc. Get your stuff together — *now!*"

Dahl jerked into action, stumbling around his office and anxiously rubbing his hands on his vest, trying to get his thoughts in order. Finally, he found his medical kit under a coat on his office chair and moved around the office, gathering bottles and tins and instruments he thought he might need.

Finally, he grabbed a sack of cut cloth bandages, closed his medical kit, and grabbed his hat off a peg by the door.

"All right . . . I think that's everything I'll need," he said, breathless, glancing around his cluttered office.

"Let's go."

Hunter opened the office door and ush-ered Dahl through it.

"My buggy's over at the Federated," the doctor said as he dropped down the outside stairs.

"No time for a buggy, Doc," Hunter said. "We're gonna find you a saddle horse. We'll be traveling cross-country."

"Ah, hell," the doctor complained. "I haven't ridden a horse in years. The damn beast is liable to snap me like a wishbone!"

"Keep your voice down, Doc," Hunter

said as they gained the bottom of the stairs.

Hunter led the sawbones around to the back of the lawyer's office and then moved down an alley toward a livery stable at the very south edge of town. Black Hills Livery & Feed was an old place run by Cleve Flowers. It was a tumbledown barn with a couple of split rail fences housing a dozen or so livery cayuses — mostly cavalry culls whose next stop would be the glue factory.

Cleve Flowers was an old friend of Angus's and a fellow ex-Confederate hailing from Alabama. He and a friend had come to the Hills illegally before the war to dig for gold but had ended up buying and running a livery and feed barn. Cleve's partner had died several years ago when shot by a drunk prospector in one of the saloons. Cleve himself was getting too old these days to keep the place up himself but was too tight to hire help.

"Why . . . Hunter Buchanon," Flowers said when Hunter woke the old man in his side shed sleeping quarters. Cleve gazed up at him, blinking sleep from his watery brown eyes. An empty whiskey bottle lay beside him on his canvas cot. "Good Lord, boy . . ."

Obviously, Cleve had heard about the trouble. He might have even witnessed the shoot-out near the sheriff's office the other day, seen the death dances of Stillwell's deputies.

"No time to waste, Cleve," Hunter said. "I need a horse. And you gotta keep quiet about it. Can you do that?"

Cleve ran a gnarled paw over his nearly bald skull and stared at Hunter as though still half-asleep and dreaming. "Yeah . . . yeah . . ."

"One more thing. I can't pay for it. I don't have a dime on me."

"Don't worry about it, boy." Cleve placed his hand against the back of Hunter's neck and squeezed. "Them goddamn murderin' Yankee scum! I seen what Stillwell did to you the — make you wipe your feet on the ole Stars an' Bars."

He twisted his mouth in a delighted grin, exposing his wreck of tobacco-rimmed teeth. Last night's supper was crusted in his grizzled gray beard. "I seen what ole one-armed Angus an' Shep an' Tye did to his deputies too — and how you made Stillwell howl like a wolf with its leg in a trap!"

The oldster snickered through his teeth. His breath smelled rotten-sour. Hunter's eyes watered.

"They got us back, Cleve."

"I know they did."

Hunter straightened, stepping back away from the cot, as the old liveryman tossed a horse blanket off his spare, bony physique clad in pale longhandles so wash-worn they were nearly see-through, and dropped his bare feet to the floor. "You can have all the hosses you want, an' I'll even saddle 'em fer you!"

"I just need one," Hunter said, swinging around and heading out into the morning-shadowy barn where Dahl waited. "And I've already saddled him myself!"

Hunter had picked out the best horse in Cleve's meager lot. None looked younger than ten; they were all either overweight or bony. Most were good only for pulling a widow's buggy to church of a Sunday morning, as long as she didn't live far from the church.

The sorrel Hunter had chosen was ewe-necked and knock-kneed but with only a modest layering of excess tallow padding its ribs. A glimmer of an old fire still flickered in its eyes. Hunter thought it had a fair chance of not having a heart attack before it reached the cave.

"Ah, hell," Dahl wheezed out as he settled himself in the saddle. He hooked the handle of his medical kit and tied the drawstring of his bandage sack around the saddle horn.

On foot, Hunter led the sawbones and the ewe-necked sorrel to the town's nearest edge, looking cautiously around, relatively certain that no one saw him. There were a few people out in the street now as the sun lifted its lemon head above the eastern horizon, beyond the mountain on which the King Solomon perched, but most of the folks he saw were all distracted with morning chores.

Once on the town's outskirts, Hunter made a beeline back toward the knoll where he'd left Nasty Pete and Bobby Lee. He jogged, the doctor keeping pace behind him but looking none too fleet in the saddle. He manhandled the sorrel's reins so that the horse fought the bit and ringed its eyes with white.

"Easy, Doc," Hunter said as he ran around the backside of the butte to see Bobby Lee and Nasty Pete where he'd left them. "Lighten up on the reins or that broomtail's gonna throw you!"

"I told you it's been many days since I've sat a saddle!" Dahl reined up behind Hunter and pointed, frowning, at Bobby Lee. "Buchanon, those beasts carry rabies!"

Bobby Lee growled his indignation at the man.

"All Bobby Lee carries is a grudge, so

watch your back, Doc." Hunter reined Pete around and put the spurs to him. "Come on, Doc — try to keep up!"

Standing on the balcony outside his second-story room in the Territorial Hotel, Sheriff Frank Stillwell tensed, grabbed the balcony's wooden rail, and crouched defensively. A long nine smoldering between his lips, Stillwell stared over the top of the rail through a break between two buildings directly across the street.

"I'll be damned."

"What's that, honey?" a girl said in the room behind him.

Stillwell blinked against the smoke curling up over his nose to pepper his eyes. "I'll . . . be . . . damned."

The woman giggled. "What's that all about, honey? You get the notion to take me out to breakfast, treat me like a lady for a change?"

She giggled again.

Stillwell's heart chugged. Blood surged in his veins. He swung around and walked through the open French door into his suite of rooms. A large, canopied bed lay before him. A girl lay on the bed, barely concealed by a thin white sheet.

Jane Campbell worked here in the Dakota

Territorial. She prided herself on being a saloon girl and dancer, distinct from a whore. Still, she was Stillwell's favorite whore. She was young and pretty and she sported nearly a full set of teeth. She wore some scrapes and bruises on occasion, but there wasn't a saloon girl/dancer in Tigerville or anywhere in the Black Hills who didn't wear the usual scars of the trade.

Best of all, Stillwell liked how she treated him. She was special in that way, Jane was. She was known for the finer arts. That's why Stillwell had started courting her.

What Stillwell liked nearly as much as how Jane treated him in her own talented way was how easily he forgot about her after he'd set his hat on his head and left, knowing that the girl herself would be gone within the hour, making her way back to her own, crib-like room at the end of the second-floor hall, where she'd sleep and while away the hours until it was time to head downstairs to work.

Knowing that he wouldn't see her again until he felt the burning need for a woman, and he sent a boy to fetch her.

Another thing he liked about her: Her red hair was nearly the same texture and shade as Annabelle Ludlow's. That was all that Jane had in common with Annabelle, but when you mixed in some whiskey-fueled imagination, it was often almost enough.

"Frank, you're grinning like the cat that ate the canary," Jane said now as Stillwell walked into the room, exhaling a plume of smoke toward the stamped tin ceiling.

"I just saw something . . . or *someone* . . . I never expected to see in this town again. Leastways, I think it was him."

Frowning, dressed in only his balbriggans and a plaid robe and socks, Stillwell glanced over his shoulder. "Sure enough. Had to be. Big fella with long blond hair tumblin' down from a Confederate gray hat. Sure enough. That was Hunter Buchanon . . . leadin' the doc out of town. I recognized Dahl for sure — little guy with his black medical kit. Buchanon likely fetched him to tend old Angus."

Jane sat up in bed and widened her eyes, letting the sheet drop low. "Hunter Buchanon?"

"That's what I said." Stillwell laughed, shrugging quickly out of his robe and reaching for his whipcord trousers draped over a chair arm.

"You best be careful, Frank," Jane warned, drawing the sheet up to cover up, looking suddenly fearful. "If that really was Hunter Buchanon, like you think it was, he might've come back to town to finish what he started."

Stillwell pulled up his pants, then froze. He lifted his head to frown over at Jane leaning back against the bed's brass frame, her red hair hanging in mussed and tangled tresses to her pale, slender shoulders.

"What're you talking about? 'Finish what he started.' " Stillwell's eyes darkened and drew together a little, the old, gnawing anger returning. "Finish what?"

"What?" Jane said. It was just a little peeping sound, like the sound a startled mouse makes.

"Finish what, Jane, dear heart? What did Hunter start and didn't finish?"

Jane stared at Stillwell standing there about six feet beyond the foot of the bed, facing her, his pants pulled up, suspenders hanging down against each leg. Jane frowned. Then humor sparked in her pale blue eyes and her plump cheeks flushed and she chuckled throatily as she slapped a hand across her mouth.

"Why, you know . . . the other day?" She laughed again, dropped her hand to her lap, then, her smile stiffening before disappearing altogether, she turned her head slightly and curled a lock of hair around her right index finger.

"No, I'm unclear as to your meaning, Jane. What do you mean about the other day?"

Jane flinched. The flush in her cheeks turned a deeper shade of rose. Another smile, even stiffer than the last, tugged at the corners of her ripe, full mouth.

"You know, Frank. Why do you want me to say it? You know . . . the way he ran you into your office, and . . . how you ran out the back. I mean . . . you know . . . I'm not sayin' anyone else in your place wouldn't have done the same thing. I just mean — Frank, please don't come over here now, honey. You know how I hate it when you get that look in your eye. Oh, please, Frank, get back . . . *stop . . . stop or I'll scree— !*"

CHAPTER 31

Hunter pulled Nasty Pete up to the edge of the creek, then loosened the reins to let the horse drink. Pete was tired. Hunter could feel the weariness in the tightness of the muscles beneath the saddle. He hated pushing a horse as hard as he'd pushed Pete the past several hours, stretching from last night into today with damn few breaks, but he had no other choice.

If any horse could take the wear and tear, however, that horse was Pete.

Bobby Lee took a long drink, as well, then flopped down in the shade of a sprawling box elder, tongue drooping over his narrow jaw, bright eyes narrowed.

Hunter glanced over his shoulder. Dahl was riding up on the ewe-necked sorrel. Hunter wasn't sure which one looked the worse for the wear — the sorrel or Dahl. The doctor had opened his collar, for the day was heating up. Sweat basted his shirt and shabby wool vest to his torso and against his sides, under his arms. The doctor's face was as pink as a doxie's rouge, and sweat dribbled down his cheeks and soaked his scraggly, light-red mustache and goatee. His spectacles sat crooked on his nose; sweat speckled the dusty lenses.

"Lord!" Dahl grunted as he threw his right leg over the sorrel's rump. He dropped abruptly to the ground and stumbled backward, nearly falling.

When he regained his balance, he lifted each foot in turn, placing his fists on his hips and turning this way and that, stretching. "I'm not cut out for this kind of abuse."

"You've got it easy, Doc."

"Do I?" The sawbones glared up at Hunter. "I'm the one having to doctor the men you send back to town half-alive!"

Hunter laughed caustically. "Too damn bad! Luke Chaney and Stillwell started this whole damn thing."

"You can end it."

"I'll end it, all right. I'll end it when every last man who ambushed my father and brothers is dead. I saw most of 'em up close. I know who they are. I won't rest 'til they're dead. 'Til the men who sent them are dead."

Hunter was only vaguely aware of Bobby Lee pacing in the brush nearby and mewling anxiously.

"Eventually, you're going to play out all your aces, Buchanon. Could be today, could be tomorrow."

"Maybe." Hunter nodded, staring off with a cold expression.

Dahl walked over to the edge of the creek. He dropped to his knees, looked at Hunter over his shoulder. "Why don't you just leave? Take your father and go. Go to Wyoming. Hell, go up to Montana. I hear there's still plenty of unclaimed range up there. Beautiful country. Green grass stirrup-high, and plenty of wild horses along the Missouri River breaks."

"I've got a nasty habit of facing my troubles square on."

Dahl laughed without mirth, then dipped his hand in the stream, cupping water to his mouth, drinking. "Isn't that just so damned noble?" He gave another caustic laugh and removed his spectacles and lowered his face to the creek, turning his head this way and that and blowing, making both horses jerk their heads up with whickering starts.

Water dripping down his face to further soak his vest and shirt, Dahl turned to Hunter again. "You'll die. Your father will die." He paused then added, "*She'll* die."

"It might not be official, but Annabelle's a

Buchanon now. Buchanons stand together. If it comes to that, we'll die together."

"If Stillwell himself doesn't run you down, her father's men will. You probably haven't seen what she did to her brother. It's not pretty."

"He deserved what he got."

"Nevertheless, there'll be a price to pay for that. And for her siding with you, a Grayback who killed Ludlow's business partner's son and wreaked holy hell across these hills. If Stillwell doesn't run you down himself, he'll bring in U.S. Marshals. Hell, maybe the cavalry from Fort Meade."

"Stillwell?" Hunter gave a sarcastic snort. "Hell, Stillwell's likely in Galveston or New Orleans by now. With my thirty thousand in gold dust. He thinks I'm dead — both me and Isabelle. Dead in the mine he caved in on top of us."

Dahl scowled up at him, shaking his head slightly, as though trying to decipher the strange language he was suddenly speaking in now. "What are you talking about? Stillwell's still in Tigerville. I just saw him last night. He's brought in more men from Bismarck. Killers."

The doctor's gaze drifted beyond Hunter, and he narrowed his eyes. "In fact, I think they . . . might be headed this way right now . . ."

Just then, Bobby Lee yapped three times sharply from where the coyote sat beneath the box elder, staring back in the direction of town.

Hunter whipped his head around. Six or seven riders were heading toward them. The men were riding single file around the base of a finger of high ground sloping into the grassy valley. They were maybe two hundred yards away, trotting their horses, holding their reins high against their chests. Their backs and shoulders were set with rigid determination.

As Hunter stared at the pack, the lead rider suddenly threw an arm up and forward, pointing. He and the others spurred their mounts into lunging gallops.

"Gol-darnit!" Hunter leaped out of his saddle. "Get back in the hurricane deck, Doc." Dahl gave a yelp of indignation as Hunter grabbed him by the scruff of his neck and the waistband of his broadcloth trousers and hurled him up onto the sorrel's back.

"Good Christ — what in the hell are you —"

"You head straight across this creek, Doc. Then up and over the next ridge. In the next valley, you'll find an old horse trail. Take it southwest, following the valley floor. After a couple of hundred yards, you'll see a cave on the slope to your left. That's where Pa and Annabelle are. She'll likely hail you!"

Bobby Lee was wailing now, lifting his long, tapering snout toward the sky.

Hunter swung up onto Nasty Pete's back, and the grullo sidestepped anxiously, arching his neck and tail. He needed more of a rest, but he wasn't going to get one.

"What're you going to do?" Dahl asked.

"I'm going to lead them away from the cave . . . and kill 'em!" Hunter slapped the sorrel's rump. The old horse whinnied angrily as it lunged off its rear hooves and splashed into the stream, nearly throwing its rider, who hung down the side for several perilous seconds before regaining his seat on the saddle.

Dahl glanced anxiously back over his shoulder at Hunter, who yelled, "Keep goin', Doc! Get the hell out of here!"

Hunter swung Pete around and booted him back through the spare fringe of brush and aspens lining the creek. At the edge of the trees, he saw the riders closing on him now at full gallops, leaning low over their horses' buffeting manes.

Hunter snapped the Henry to his shoulder, ramming a fresh round into the breech, and triggered off two hasty shots. Both bullets plumed dirt to each side of the string of riders now roughly a hundred yards away, evoking a couple of audible curses and flinches.

Giving a high, raucous Rebel yell, Hunter swung Pete hard left and put the steel to the tired stallion, who gamely churned up the ground as he headed straight west toward a pine-clad slope. Bobby Lee was a dun gray cannonball with a bushy, smoke-gray tail shooting off through the tall grass ahead and to Hunter's right, as though leading the way.

Hunter followed the coyote, swinging Nasty Pete out into the open, where his pursuers couldn't help but see him and give chase, ignoring the doctor, who was likely now heading up the southern mountain. All Hunter could think about was keeping those men away from the cave, about leading them up into the high country and killing each and every one — starting with Stillwell.

He glanced over his shoulder. Had the doctor been right? Was Stillwell still around? He must have had the gold. Why hadn't he lit out with it? Apparently, his pride had been so battered in town the other day, when he'd leaped out his office's back window, that after learning that Hunter and Annabelle had survived the cave-in, he'd decided to stay and finish the job he'd started.

Hunter thought the lead rider was likely Stillwell himself, the man in the dark-brown Stetson crouched low over his claybank's pole, holding his reins up close to his throat in one hand, a Winchester in the other hand. The claybank was gradually closing the gap between it and Hunter's weary grullo.

Hunter could hear Pete's lungs working like a worn-out bellows.

Silently Hunter cursed as Pete galloped up an incline through aspens and firs. Another glance over his shoulder told him that Stillwell was still closing on him quickly. Several other men behind him were branching off and appeared to be heading around the base of the incline, apparently intending to cut Hunter off on the other side of the mountain.

Again, Hunter cursed. If Pete had been fresh, he'd be able to keep climbing into the large boulders and towering ponderosas that he knew capped the very crest of this ridge — which was called Black Mountain, a favorite hunting spot of his — but Pete just didn't have any more fuel in the firebox.

As he crested a shoulder of the ridge,

Hunter put Pete straight out across it, the horse chugging and blowing hard, tossing its head against the bit, warm wet froth blowing back from his snout to stripe his neck and withers.

There was little cover here atop this grassy flat. Hunter had to get down into the gorge on the other side, where he'd at least have a chance. There was cover there — trees and rocks. Maybe afoot, he could gain the high ground against his pursuers and lay into them with Shep's Henry.

The lip of the gorge appeared dead ahead.

"Just a little farther, Pete," Hunter wheezed into the ailing bronc's right ear. "Just a little farther."

Pete's front legs folded.

The bronc whinnied shrilly as it hit the ground on its knees maybe twenty feet from the chasm yawning below. As it started to roll, Hunter kicked himself free of the stirrups and flew forward to hit the ground on his right arm and shoulder, feeling the Henry kicked out of his hand by one of the bronc's flying hooves.

Hunter rolled and rolled, flinging his arms out, trying to stop himself before he went over the lip of the gorge.

"Noooo!" he cried as he suddenly felt himself dropping through the air.

For two or three mind-numbing seconds he was weightless. He watched the steep gray slope rising in a blur around him. Then it smacked him hard, talus and gravel and powdered sandstone punching an indignant *whufff* of air from his lungs.

"Ah, Jesus!" he cried and then cursed again, more severely, as he began to roll.

It was as though he were a single craps die thrown by the fist of an angry god. He rolled . . . rolled . . . and rolled. Brush slowed him and then a boulder stopped him with a bone-jarring jolt.

His ears rang from the blow. He fell forward. After a good thirty seconds of trying to draw air back into his battered lungs, he managed to suck down a teaspoonful of the stuff and push up onto his hands and knees.

He shook his head, trying to clear the lambs-tail clouds from his vision.

A bullet screamed off a rock not two inches from his right hand. Half a blink later a Winchester's rocketing belch resounded from the ridge crest above.

Hunter jerked his head up, and as enough clouds cleared from his retinas, he saw Stillwell down on one knee beside a wagon-size boulder maybe ten feet down the slope from the top. His horse stood on the ridge above him, near Nasty Pete, who was back on all fours and calmly grazing despite the bad tumble he'd taken.

Hunter was vaguely aware that Bobby Lee was nowhere in sight. The coyote, being no fool and always a fair judge of the odds, had taken cover.

Smoke and flames stabbed from the barrel of Stillwell's Winchester again, the bullet curling the air over Hunter's left ear. Hunter reached for his LeMat, but the pretty popper wasn't in its holster. He must have lost the gun when Pete had fallen. He wouldn't have been able to use it, anyway, for just then the rock he'd found himself perched against suddenly gave way.

He pitched over backward bellowing, *"Ohhhh shiiitttttt!"* just before he hit the slope on the back of his head and shoulders and continued rolling ass over teakettle.

Again, he rolled . . . rolled . . . and rolled.

Suddenly, he was weightless again. The world became a chalky gray and fawn-colored blur with a glint of sunlight reflected off tea-colored water.

Water?

As if to answer the question, he hit the stream with a cold plunge, dropping quickly beneath the surface to hear the gurgling of water closing over him and seeping into his ears. He remembered that a stream, dry most of the year, ran along the base of Black Mountain. That stream, likely fed by recent mountain rains, had found him now. The most Hunter could say for it was that it was cool and refreshing and it had broken his fall, though it couldn't be much over three or four feet deep.

Lying belly-down in the water, he shoved his splayed fingers into the gravelly bed. Coughing water from his lungs, he shoved up on his hands and knees, the water streaming off of him, his long hair hanging in dark wet bands over his face. The sliding water of the stream was up to about halfway between his elbows and shoulders.

He remained there, more stunned than sore, though he knew he'd be feeling the soreness soon, when the sound of several sets of galloping hooves reached his ears. He whipped his head up, and his thudding heart jounced.

Four men were galloping toward him along the stream's left bank, which was nearly even with the floor of the narrow gorge. Its right side was banked by the steeply looming ridge down which he now saw Stillwell leading his horse, following a cautious, slanting course, both horse and man taking mincing steps.

Hunter jerked his head back to his right when he heard splashing. The riders were galloping into the stream, heading straight toward him.

"Get that Grayback son of a mule skinner!"

CHAPTER 32

Hunter automatically slapped his holster, but of course the LeMat wasn't there. He'd dropped it on the ridge.

The four riders galloped toward him, closing fast, whooping and hollering, water splashing up high around them, the beads glittering like diamonds in the sunlight. Hunter swung around and ran, looking for cover. There were trees and rocks up the bank to his right, but he'd never reach them before his pursuers were on top of him.

He tripped over a submerged rock and fell, the water closing over him once more. Hot dread pooled in his belly when he looked up to see the horses stepping around him, circling him. Two more men rode toward him from behind the others. In their brush-scarred leggings and billowy neckerchiefs, they had the look of local tough nuts. So did one of the four men circling Hunter now, moving in close.

But three of the others weren't merely local troubleshooters. They had the cold, dark eyes and grim mouths of professional, wide-ranging cold-steel artists. Their guns attested to this as well — the number of them and the way they were positioned on hips or thighs, in oiled holsters, for quick draws. These three wore large knives as well.

The biggest man appeared the leader of these three. He had blond, curly yellow hair oozing out of a shabby black Plainsman hat, and muttonchop whiskers of the same color framed his long ugly, amber-eyed face. He fit the description of the notorious regulator, Dakota Jack Patterson.

That meant the other two hardtails were likely Patterson's partners — Weed Zorn, small and poison-mean, and Klaus Steinbach, a tall, slender, blackbearded man with flat cobalt-blue eyes dressed in a long, black duster and high, black boots. He wore two big pistols on his hips and held a Winchester Yellowboy across his saddlebows.

Slowly, Hunter climbed to his feet, his soaked clothes hanging heavily on him. He stood crouched slightly, holding his hands away from his sides. They had him boxed in, trapped, but he wasn't a man who'd give up until he'd exhaled his last breath. He looked at the guns glinting in the sunlight

around him, bristling on the four men surrounding him, and felt the palpable urge to
get his hands on one of those hoglegs.

The blond man sat facing Hunter straight
on from the back of a steel-dust stallion, the
horse bobbing its head anxiously, champing
its bit. Dakota Jack spread his thick lips in a
grin. He raised his own Henry repeating
rifle one-handed, clicking the hammer back
with his thumb.

The others were also aiming their rifles at
him, staring at him darkly, a cold delight in
their eyes, like wolves that had run down
their quarry and were eager for its blood.

"Bye, bye, Rebel-boy," said Dakota Jack.

"Hold on, Jack!" This from Stillwell, who
was near the bottom of the ridge, leading
his horse by its bridle reins. "Hold on! Hold
on, now, Jack!"

Dakota Jack. Sure enough.

Jack was said to be like a shadow in the
night. But here he was in broad daylight,
grinning with bald menace now at Hunter
as he aimed that deadly Henry one-handed,
gloved thumb resting on the cocked hammer.

"Jack!" Stillwell barked. "Hold on, Jack.
Not so fast!" Stillwell had found a relatively
gentle incline on the grade, and now he led
the horse down off the incline and into the

429

stream, the claybank sagging back on its rear legs and loosing sand and gravel in its wake.

Once in the stream, Stillwell climbed up onto the clay's back.

Dakota Jack glanced behind him at Stillwell. "You want the honors, I s'pose — eh, Frank?" He chuckled wryly. "S'pose you deserve it." He glanced around at the others, who swallowed their laughter.

A small log slid downstream to nudge Hunter's right leg. It careened over to bounce off the leg of the horse standing to Hunter's right. The mount gave a start, whickering and sidestepping. The man in the saddle raised his rifle to grab the reins with both hands. As he did, Hunter moved quickly, taking two quick lunging strides toward the rider on the startled horse.

He rammed his right shoulder against the side of the horse. The horse whinnied as it sidestepped again and, getting its feet tangled beneath it, began to fall, hooking its head around toward Hunter and loosing another, furious whinny.

"Whoa, there!" bellowed Dakota Jack. "Check your horse, Weed!"

When the horse was halfway to the water, the rider cursing and jerking back on the reins, Hunter grabbed the barrel of the man's Winchester rifle with his left hand and easily jerked it out of the man's hands, which had a stronger grip on the reins.

Hunter fell backward against the side of the horse as well as against the rider's left leg. But as he did, he swung around, taking the Winchester in both hands and working the cocking lever, ramming a cartridge into the action. He raised the rifle, curled his index finger through the trigger guard, and started to aim it.

Dakota Jack bulled his big steel-dust straight into Hunter, throwing him backward over the flailing rear legs of the horse beneath him. The rifle flew up in his arms and he inadvertently triggered the shot skyward.

And then he hit the water, stunned by the merciless force of the bulling steel-dust. The flailing horse beneath him kicked his right side as it scrambled back to its feet, adding an extra, agonizing ache to the whole nasty ordeal.

Hunter found himself belly-down in the water again. Quickly, the fight still in him since a breath of life was still in him, he thrust himself up off his hands and knees, sucking air down his throat as water cascaded off of him. He was vaguely aware of something dropping down over his head.

He looked down just as the loop of a lariat was drawing closed around his chest. Panicking, he thrust his arms up and out of the noose, but before he could then grab the noose with both hands, to thrust it off of him, someone behind him drew it painfully taut against his upper torso, just beneath his shoulders.

It ground against him, a burning, grinding misery.

A horse whinnied loudly.

"Let's go, Mort!" he heard Frank Stillwell bellow. "Time to give this damn Rebel a Dutch ride over rough rocks!"

Hunter raged as he was pulled savagely straight back off his feet. His hands were free so he was able to somewhat cushion his fall back into the water. But the slack was quickly taken out of the lariat with a jerk and he found himself being pulled violently through the water, head forward.

He was pulled past two riders, one to each side of him, both men laughing and watching as he was dragged downstream on his back, the water pushing against the top of his head to curl over his face, threatening to drown him.

Kicking his legs and gasping, Hunter twisted around, turning belly-down in the water but keeping his head raised above its surface. The rope ground up against his armpits, and he gritted his teeth against not only that misery but the misery of being pulled through the water, the water splashing back over his face with more being kicked up by Stillwell's claybank's galloping hooves.

Stillwell howled and laughed, giving his own mocking version of a Rebel yell as he spurred the clay-bank up the stream bank and onto dry land, pulling Hunter along behind him. Hunter reached up and grabbed the taut rope before him, trying to ease the pressure under his arms.

Meanwhile, sage clumps and rocks and stiff tufts of buck brush came up to rake him mercilessly. He was thrust askance against a large clump of wild currant. The shrubs punched him over onto his back until he managed to heave himself back onto his chest and belly, so he could see what was coming and maybe avoid having his neck snapped.

He gripped the rope with both his burning hands, squeezing his eyes shut as dirt and sand flew at him from the clay's hooves. The ground raked against him with a steady, unrelenting violence, clawing at him, burning him, gouging him, hammering his knees and hips. A sudden plunge over a mound of gravelly ground ripped off his cartridge belt, which was a relief since the ground was grinding the buckle against his belly.

Dirt and gravel and bits of grass were forced down behind the waistband of his buckskin breeches. His shirtsleeves were torn to ribbons. Blood oozed from dozens of scrapes and cuts. Pain-racking bruises bit him deep. He felt as though he'd been hammered with tomahawks.

Bobby Lee shot out of the trees to Hunter's left and ran along beside Stillwell, barking angrily and leaping up as though to nip the sheriff's leg.

"No, Bobby," Hunter raked out through gritted teeth. "Get away!"

Stillwell palmed his pistol and fired two shots at the yipping, snarling coyote. Bobby Lee yelped and then turned and ran back into the trees.

"You mule fritter," Hunter said. "You better not've shot my coyote, you low-down dirty dog!"

He put his head down and endured another twenty or thirty raking, hammering yards.

Suddenly, mercifully, he stopped moving.

He let his head sag forward, knocked silly by the pummeling, choking on the dust that had been forced down his throat.

"You still kicking, you Grayback devil?"

Hunter looked up to see Stillwell grinning down at him, the clay's dust catching up to him. The man and the horse were only a few feet away. The rope hung slack against the ground.

"So . . . you're human, after all." Stillwell laughed. "I thought after you escaped the mine you might've been a ghost!"

Hunter cursed under his breath, through the dirt and mud and bits of grass and sand clinging to his lips. He tried to climb up onto his hands and knees, intending to make a run at Stillwell and possibly pull him off his horse. But his head was swirling.

He felt drunk. Sick. He felt as though he were still in motion.

Stillwell was breathing hard with excitement. "You've got game, I'll give you that. Let's have another go-round. What do you say? The boys are waiting back at the stream." He paused. "But don't you die on me, you son of a Rebel bitch. You hear? I don't want you to die 'til I get you back to town. I'm gonna hang you from that cottonwood growing out in front of the lumberyard. Dead center of Tigerville! I'm gonna hang you right there . . . for all to see!"

The sheriff gave a grunt and then kicked

savagely at the clay's flanks with his spurs.

Hunter gave a howling cry of outrage, bracing himself, as the clay galloped out away from him. Suddenly, the slack was jerked out of the rope. Hunter screamed again as the noose bit him hard against his armpits, and then he was being raked once more against the ground, through the valley outside of the gorge in which the stream curled.

Through the dust and gobs of turf the clay's hooves were throwing at him, he could see the brown water at the base of the stony ridge maybe a hundred yards away. The other men, five or six of them, sat their horses in a line along the stream, at the gorge's mouth, watching the entertainment.

Stillwell gave another raucous Rebel yell, laughing at the tops of his lungs.

Finally, Hunter came to another grinding halt, breathless, his body on fire.

He let his face sag against the ground. He coughed and groaned, writhing.

Hooves clomped up close to him. He could hear a man breathing hard, a saddle squawking as that man, Stillwell, leaned out from his saddle to get a good look at the victim of his torture.

"Hell, he's still in good shape," the sheriff said. "Let's have one more run an' then we'll head to town for the necktie party!"

"Horn toad," Hunter said with a groan, lifting his head and shaking his mud-caked hair from his eyes. His entire body was on fire with raking burns.

The other men, whom he glimpsed sitting their horses straight ahead of him, laughed. A couple were smoking. Dakota Jack sat with his right leg hooked around his saddle horn, like a man enjoying a Fourth of July rodeo parade.

Stillwell laughed, then swung his claybank around.

"You ready, Grayback?" he asked Hunter, grinning over his shoulder at him and dallying his end of the riata around his saddle horn.

Hunter glared back at him. As he did, he saw a moss-stained rock poking up out of the ground about ten feet ahead of him and slightly right. Blond grass poked up around it. It appeared to be solidly set.

Hunter shifted his gaze back to Stillwell, and, despite the rusty railroad spikes of pain grinding into every bone socket, feeling as though three layers of skin had been scraped off of him, he somehow got his lips twisted into a smile. "Sure. Why the hell not? That all you got, Stillwell, you nancy-boy coward?"

Hunter glanced at the other men astride their horses ahead of him. "You fellas should have heard how Stillwell screamed like a little girl with her pigtails on fire when I stormed into his office the other day!"

The others laughed. Most laughed uneasily. All except Dakota Jack. He threw his head back on his shoulders and roared.

Stillwell glared at Hunter over his left shoulder. A russet flush rose into his dusty cheeks. He slid his eyes toward the other men, then returned that flat, ominous gaze to Hunter. The sheriff tightened his jaws and whipped his head forward.

He stabbed the clay with his spurs.

CHAPTER 33

Hunter had made the decision to make his next move while not really believing he had the strength to attempt it. But just as the clay lunged off its rear hooves and shot back out across the valley, quickly taking the slack out of the riata, Hunter heaved himself to his feet with a great, raucous Rebel yell fairly vaulting out of his strained lungs, and ran ahead and to his right.

His feet were heavy and numb, and his bones seemed to clatter together without benefit of cushioning cartilage.

Stillwell and the claybank barreled forward. Only a little slack in the rope remained.

"What the *hell* . . . ?" bellowed one of the men sitting their horses behind Hunter as they all jerked up their rifles.

Hunter dove over the rock, hitting the ground on the other side of it and quickly, aware that the rope was nearly taut, wrapped the fast diminishing slack around three sides of the rock. As the rope jerked taut as a bowstring, Hunter screamed as it cut into his sides, crushing the air out of his lungs. It held fast to him and the rock, which quivered a little but held. For a few seconds, Hunter thought the loop would cut him in two.

A high, wailing shriek was wrenched out of the claybank. The horse jerked sharply to its right, twisting its long neck to the left. Stillwell screamed and threw his left arm up and out like a rodeo rider. The horse dropped back onto its right hip, screaming shrilly, and then onto its side . . . and onto Stillwell's right leg.

Again, the sheriff screamed.

There was enough slack in the rope now that Hunter, gaining his knees, lifted it up and over his head, tossed it away.

"Get him!" shouted one of the men sitting their horses behind him.

He heard Dakota Jack roar again with laughter. Hooves thudded behind Hunter as he lunged to his feet and ran toward where Stillwell lay pinned under the clay's right side while the horse flailed around, trying to rise and only increasing Stillwell's agony. Hunter wanted to get his hands on Stillwell's rifle. He wasn't going to be able to kill all of these men, but by God he wanted to kill Stillwell before he himself became crow bait.

He may have underestimated his ability a moment ago, when he'd first sprung into action. Now, however, the note on the energy he'd borrowed from deep inside himself just after he'd spied the rock was being called due.

He'd run maybe half a dozen yards, each step growing heavier and more uncertain than the one before, when his knees buckled. He hit the ground with a grunt, and flopped onto his back. Hooves drummed behind him. The other riders circled him while Stillwell bellowed and cursed, the clay screaming angrily as it finally scrambled to its feet.

Hunter looked up. Dakota Jack was laughing while extending his Colt's revolving rifle straight down at Hunter, one-handed, his other gloved hand holding his reins. "You had your chance, Frank," Dakota Jack bellowed, tears of humor dribbling down his pocked and pitted cheeks carpeted with a curly, sun-bleached blond beard. "Now it's my turn!"

Jack closed his eyes suddenly.

His head jerked so sharply to his left that his hat flew off. His torso sagged out over that side of his saddle. At the same time, his right hand opened, and the Colt's revolving rifle dropped to the ground six feet away from Hunter.

The blast of the rifle that had just blown a hole through Dakota Jack Patterson's head reached Hunter's ears as the notorious gunman himself sagged farther out from the side of his horse, which was sidestepping now, startled.

All the other men sitting their horses around Hunter stared at Dakota Jack in mute shock. As Jack dropped to the ground and his horse reared, whickering, the same rifle that had ventilated Dakota Jack belched again, again, and again. The men around Hunter cursed, raising their rifles in one hand while checking their frightened horses down with their other hand.

Bullets thumped into the ground around them.

One slammed into a rifle stock, evoking a sudden yelp from Weed Zorn, who cursed and dropped the rifle with the cracked stock.

"Ambush!" one of the other riders bellowed.

"Pull out!" another yelled. "Pull out! Pull out!"

Hunter reached for Dakota Jack's blood-speckled rifle. It was just out of reach. He rose to hands and knees and crawled toward it, hearing the dwindling thuds of the fleeing riders.

He finally reached the revolving rifle and lifted it in both his rope-burned hands, raising it, but by then the riders had fled — all but Stillwell. The sheriff had gained his feet and was hopping on his good leg, trying to climb into his saddle and casting frantic, wide-eyed looks in the direction from which Dakota Jack's killer had fired.

Hunter wanted desperately to dispatch Stillwell, but the dragging had cost him most of his strength. The rifle weighed a ton in his hands, and the ground was spinning around him so quickly that he was having trouble getting the rifle's hammer cocked back.

Stillwell swung up into the leather, batted the heel of his good leg against the clay's flanks, and galloped after the other men. As he did, he glanced back over his right shoulder at Hunter, as though in his haste to flee he'd suddenly realized he'd left alive the one man he'd wanted dead after all the trouble he'd gone through to kill him.

"Next time, Buchanon!" Stillwell bellowed, then turned his head forward and galloped up and over a grassy rise.

Hunter dropped to a knee. Then to his butt.

"I'll be here, Stillwell," he yelled as loud as his pinched lungs would allow. Which was barely loud enough for he himself to hear the threat. "I'll be here," he repeated.

He was sitting there, letting his marbles roll back into their rightful pockets, taking slow, deep breaths, when he heard the thud of galloping hooves. He turned his head to see a rider gallop out from behind a low, rocky scarp on the other side of the stream. Dark red hair bounced on slender shoulders clad in a red-and-black-checked shirt, beneath a brown Stetson.

Hunter watched Annabelle splash across the creek on her buckskin. She galloped toward him, concern in her eyes.

"Hunter!" Annabelle checked the buckskin down to a skidding halt and leaped out of the saddle. "Oh God!" She threw her arms around his neck, sobbing.

"You must have some Scot in you," Hunter said.

Annabelle pulled her head away from his and ran her horrified eyes across his torn clothes and bloody, dirty, grass-covered body. "How bad?"

"Looks worse than it feels. But, then . . ." Hunter tried a weak smile, showing his relief at seeing his girl out here, saving his bacon, which he'd thought for sure was about to be thrown to the wolves. "But, then . . . I'm not sure I can feel all of it . . . yet . . ."

"Is anything broken?" She ran her hands down his arms, down his legs. "Can you stand?"

"Not sure how that's possible, but I don't think anything's broken."

A yip sounded from the trees and then Bobby Lee came scurrying out, head and tail low. The coyote ran up to Hunter and placed his front paws on his master's knee, sniffing him and mewling.

"I'm all right, Bobby. How are you? That mossback didn't . . ." Hunter let his voice trail off as he found a bloody furrow across the top of the coyote's back. "Burned you, didn't he?"

Bobby Lee yipped when Hunter ran his finger across the shallow gash.

"You'll live." Hunter sandwiched the loyal coyote's head in his hands and brushed his thumbs over the pricked ears. Bobby brushed his rough tongue over Hunter's lips. "We'll both live to fight another day, Bobby," Hunter said. "Next time, we'll kill that son of a bitch. Just as soon as . . ."

Hunter turned to Annabelle and placed his dirty hand on her arm. "Pa . . . Did Doc

445

Dahl make it to the cave?"

Annabelle nodded. "Just after he arrived and went to work on Angus, I heard the shooting. I threw a saddle on the buckskin and . . ."

She let her voice trail off as she stared down at the dead man.

Hunter heaved himself to his feet, wincing and grunting at a million sundry pains both little and large. "Meet Dakota Jack."

Annabelle gasped, closed a hand over her mouth. "That's Dakota Jack?" She looked at Hunter. "The killer?"

"One an' the same. You might've made yourself some money. I believe he has a hefty bounty on his head."

Annabelle's cheeks turned pale as she stared down in disgust at Dakota Jack Patterson, who lay twisted on his side, a hole in his head just behind his right ear. As it had taken its leave of the killer's head, the bullet had blown out a goodly portion of the man's left temple. Still, Dakota Jack appeared to be smiling as he stared up past Hunter and Annabelle through heavy-lidded eyes.

"I didn't think I could hit him from that distance. I've only shot deer and antelope before." Annabelle looked at Hunter. "Never a man." She clutched her belly. "I think

I . . . I think I might be sick."

"The first one's always the hardest," Hunter said grimly, drawing her against his side, squeezing her. "Don't look at him anymore. He'll just haunt your dreams, an' he ain't worth it."

Annabelle drew a deep, bracing breath and turned to Hunter. "We have to get you cleaned up." Her eyes swept him. "You might need stitches, and we can't be sure bones aren't broken. I'd be surprised if they weren't, the way that madman dragged you behind that horse!"

"Nah," Hunter said, turning and walking heavily, tenderly toward the stream. "All I need is a little bath in the creek. Then I'll be ready to ride."

Bobby Lee dogging his heels, Hunter walked down the sloping bank. He strode out into the stream. In the middle, he turned back to face Anna standing on the bank, Bobby Lee sitting beside her, both watching Hunter with concern. He flopped backward into the water, holding his breath as the cooling creek closed over his head, at once burning and soothing his many cuts and bruises.

Bobby Lee yipped at the sky.

Annabelle reached down to pat the coyote's head. "I'll fetch Pete — I saw him on the ridge," she said to Hunter, stepping up onto the buckskin's back. She turned to stare off in the direction in which Stillwell and the others had fled. "We'd best light a shuck before someone else comes." She turned back to Hunter and shook her head. "I don't think I can kill another man, Hunter. Even . . . even one like him."

"Yeah," Hunter said, lolling in the stream's cool, gently swirling currents. "I used to think that too."

As the surge of emotion dwindled in the minutes following the confrontation with Stillwell, Dakota Jack, and the others, Hunter felt more and more like he'd been run over by a runaway freight train dead-heading on a long downhill stretch of open rail with a firebox filled to its brim.

His torn and battered body sagged in the saddle as Nasty Pete followed Annabelle and the buckskin along an old Indian trail back in the direction of the cave. Every lunge and lurch felt like a nasty wallop from a drunk and angry miner's axe handle. He was glad indeed when he saw the cave's dark, egg-shaped maw reveal itself at the base of the ridge as he and Annabelle surfaced from the thick pine forest beneath it.

Bobby Lee, who had been trotting along beside Hunter, stopped suddenly, growling and showing his teeth as he stared toward the cave. Hunter stopped Nasty Pete and slid his hand toward the LeMat holstered on his right hip. Annabelle had retrieved the pistol and Shep's Henry when she'd fetched Nasty Pete from the ridge. Hunter was glad to have both prized weapons back in his possession, where he sure as hell hoped they remained.

"It's Dahl," Annabelle said, drawing the buckskin to a stop beside him.

Hunter saw the doctor then too. Dahl was down on his knees beside the small, crackling fire at the edge of the cave, washing his hands and arms in a pot of steaming water. He looked grimly down the slope toward Hunter, Annabelle, and Bobby Lee still lifting his hackles and growling at the sawbones.

"Stand down, Bobby. The doc's here to help Angus."

Bobby Lee let his lips fall back down over his fangs but continued to give the sawbones the woolly eyeball. Bobby Lee had had his fill of strangers for one day.

Hunter swung heavily, achingly down from his saddle. Annabelle looked up at him darkly, complicit in his dread at hearing

449

what the doctor had to say about his father, then took Pete's reins. "I'll tend both mounts, Hunter. You go up and talk to the doctor." She rose onto her tiptoes and kissed his cheek. "I love you."

Hunter moved slowly up the steep grade to the cave. The doctor eyed him incredulously, raking his torn, bloody clothes and the bruises on his face with his critical gaze. "Looks like you asked the wrong wildcat to dance."

"Who says I did the askin'?" Hunter quipped. "How is he, Doc?"

Dahl dried his hands and arms on a towel. "Not good. Alive but not good. Annabelle did a fair job of suturing the wound, but he was bleeding beneath the stitches."

"Must've been the ride up here."

"I drained the blood and infected fluid out of the wound, and cauterized it. His fever is still high. It might go higher. If it does, he'll probably die."

"Isn't there anything else you can do, Doc?"

"No." Dahl straightened, shaking his head. He adjusted his round, dusty spectacles on his nose. "Not out here, anyway. Maybe not even if you got him to town. Now you just need to keep bathing his face with cold water and pray, if you're so inclined. The rest is up to God and Angus, I'm afraid. It all depends on how tough he is, how badly he wants to live."

"All right."

"I guess you're the next Buchanon I'd better have a look at. My God, man . . ."

"I'm all right, Doc. Just scraped and beat up some."

"You'd best hole up here for a while. Rest up. Both you and your father. Don't try to move him for a couple of days, at least. And then don't move him far, but it would be wise to get him into a clean cabin, a comfortable bed."

Dahl returned bottles and instruments to his medical kit and snapped his bag closed. He set his hat on his head. "I'll be going."

Hunter grabbed his arm. "Doc?"

Dahl turned back to him. "What is it?"

"Someone must have seen us leave town together."

"I gathered that. Is Stillwell still alive?"

Hunter nodded. "He might be a problem for you."

The doctor shook his head. "Don't worry. Neither he nor anyone else will learn from me where you three are holed up. I won't be responsible for more bloodshed."

"They could get rough."

"I'm the only doctor in town." Dahl gave

451

a cooked grin.

Hunter returned the smile with a wooden one of his own. He turned to peer into the cave. Angus lay beneath the skins, atop the bed of spruce boughs. He looked small and frail and pasty. He looked dead. Hunter felt hollow inside. Cold.

"If it's any consolation," Dahl said, "most men in his condition, having suffered the kind of wound your father suffered, would be dead by now. Even much younger men. It amazes me he's still going. Still fighting."

"Not me." Hunter turned to the doctor. "He hasn't gotten payback yet for Shep an' Tye."

CHAPTER 34

"Ouch!"

"Did that hurt?"

"Of course it hurt — that's why I said 'ouch.'"

"Some Rebel warrior — crying when a girl cleans a little cut on his arm. A Yankee girl, no less." Annabelle glanced wryly up at him from under her dark red brows, then continued gently swabbing a deep gash on the underside of Hunter's left arm.

It was late in the afternoon, the sun tumbling westward and turning the forest below the cave dark. Hunter lay naked on a buffalo robe beside the low fire on which a pot of coffee gurgled. Angus lay nearly silent in sleep, still shivering with fever but not as violently as before. Annabelle checked on him often.

Bobby Lee sat on the far side of the fire, watching Annabelle clean Hunter's wounds with cool cloths and then, once she had all the sand and grass and other grit out of the bloody gashes, she smoothed arnica into them from a tin that the doctor had slipped her before he'd mounted up and ridden away.

Hunter had minor scrapes and bruises over much of his large, heavily muscled body, but the primary cuts were the gashes on his elbows and knees, which had taken the brunt of the dragging. There were a few shallow cuts and abrasions on his cheeks and chin, as well, from the brush he'd been pulled through and from the rocks Stillwell's horse had kicked into his face.

"That's more than a little cut," Hunter corrected the girl, glancing down at the deep, long gash that she was dabbing at tenderly with a corner of her damp cloth. "And I wasn't cryin'." He grinned. "I don't cry, I roar, you silly little Yankee girl."

She smiled up at him again, coquettishly. "Yes, I've heard you roar."

"Now you're talkin' dirty to me."

"Hush. Your father's only a few feet away."

"Sound asleep."

"Watch that hand, sir."

"I'm watching it, all right."

Annabelle giggled and scuttled slightly sideways, away from the reach of his frisky free hand.

"I reckon it is a rather nasty cut," she said after a while in a mock conciliatory tone, glancing up at him again, this time her eyes cast with dark gravity. "You're damned lucky, Hunter. So far, you've been lucky."

"Yeah, well, so has Stillwell."

Annabelle wrung the bloody cloth out in a tin pot, frowning at Hunter. "I thought you figured Stillwell was long gone from here. That he'd likely headed to Mexico with your gold dust."

"With *our* gold dust. I panned that for both of us — remember?" Hunter shrugged as Annabelle went back to work on the cut on his arm. "I can't figure it. If he's got the gold, why is he hangin' around? He must figure revenge is worth as much or more than thirty thousand dollars. Maybe that's what his pride is worth to him."

"Maybe it's not him who has the gold."

"If not him — who?" Hunter looked at her, pensive. She continued to dab the cloth at the cut, pressing the tip of her tongue to the underside of her rich upper lip in concentration.

She looked up at Hunter. "Remember how Bobby Lee was acting the day you first showed me the gold?"

"Yeah."

"Someone must have followed us out from

town. I doubt it was Stillwell. He was probably still licking his wounds . . . his injured
pride." She frowned, shook her head.
"Someone else . . ."

Hunter thought about that.

Finally, he said, "Nah, it was him, all right.
He's got the gold. Before I kill him, I'm
gonna find out where he hid it. He probably buried it somewhere outside Tigerville,
close to town."

Annabelle set the cloth aside and then
picked up the arnica tin. "That gold isn't
going to do us much good if we're dead."

"It's not gonna do us much good if we're
not free to spend it either."

Annabelle gently rubbed the arnica into
Hunter's cut. She didn't say anything for
over a full minute. Then she looked up at
him again, gravely, and said, "Maybe it's
time we pull foot. After Angus is well
enough to move, I mean."

"We've talked about this, honey."

Annabelle pressed the lid onto the arnica
tin and set it aside. She set her hand on
Hunter's flat washboard belly and ran it up
his broad chest, through the light blond hair
nestled in the valley between his broad pec-
torals.

She rested it gently on the side of his face.
"Hunter, you're at war with a whole army

of men. Stillwell's going to go back to town and bring back more. More and more. We can't last out here. We have provisions for only a few more days."

"Tomorrow, I'll go hunting."

"A shot might be heard."

"I have other ways to hunt."

"My point is, Hunter — when are you going to have accounted for enough?"

"When I get the last man who burned our ranch." Hunter placed his hands on her shoulders and looked at her directly. "I didn't start this war, Anna. But like we both said before, we're damn well gonna finish it!"

Annabelle swallowed, kept her tone low and controlled. "When . . . and if . . . you get that last man, more will come. More men like Dakota Jack Patterson. You're the lone Confederate out here, Hunter. Against a whole passel of Yankees who stick together."

She paused, licked her lips, then leaned closer to him, pressing her face up close to his, a deeply worried, anguished look carving deep lines across her forehead and around her eyes.

"These hills can never be our home now," she said. "Not after all this bloodshed. We can never live here in peace. We can never raise a family here in peace. My father won't allow it. He's a very powerful man with deep pockets. If you kill the men he will eventually send, he'll hire more . . . send more. He'll kill you and Angus and he'll drag me back to that house of his, which will be condemning me to a living hell."

Annabelle looked down for a time, pondering.

Slowly, she raised her gaze once more to his. The worry and anguish was suddenly gone.

Now the lines were gone from her forehead, and her eyes were flinty with resolve. "But if this is what you want . . . if war is what you want . . . revenge for your brothers . . . I will fight beside you. We'll fight until we're out of food and water and bullets and too many men come for us to fight them off any longer — and then we will die together. We'll die fighting. Together."

Hunter stared at her for a long time, his thoughts racing.

Finally, he let his hands slide from her arms, and he leaned back on his hands. "Ah, hell."

"What is it?" she asked quietly.

"It's hopeless." He turned away. Suddenly, it was all coming clear. He turned back to her. "You're right, Anna. They'll just keep throwing more and more men at me — bounty hunters, lawmen — until I'm dead. Until we're both dead. There's no point to it. No point to more killing . . . dying. As for the gold — well, it's just gold. If Stillwell wants it so bad, let him have it."

He paused, glanced toward where Angus lay on his makeshift pallet, mumbling in his sleep.

"As soon as Pa is out of the woods, we'll pull our picket pins. We'll shilly-shally on out of these hills. I don't know where we'll go or what we'll do, but living is better than dying. Better than killing. I knew that once. I guess it just took more killing to make me learn the lesson all over again. I guess it took you. I hope it's the last time I have to learn it."

"Oh, Hunter."

Annabelle lay her head upon his chest. "We'll make do," she said, pressing her lips to his chest. "Wherever we go, we'll make do. We'll have each other, we'll have your father, and that will be enough."

"It will be more than enough." Hunter kissed the top of her head but slid a worried glance at Angus. "Keep kickin', you old Rebel."

He lay back against the pallet. Aside from his concern for Angus, he felt as though a great weight had been lifted from his shoulders.

Frank Stillwell reined his horse up in front of the Dakota Territorial Hotel in Tigerville, where the horses of the other five surviving members of his party were already standing, heads hanging, tails switching at flies.

Those men were Dakota Jack's two partners Weed Zorn and Klaus Steinbach, as well as three close friends of Pee-Wee Chaney — Mort Rucker, Henry Kleinsasser, and Bill Williams. Stillwell had seen Rucker, Kleinsasser, and Williams in the Territorial earlier that morning, just after he'd spied the doctor leaving town with Hunter Buchanon, and had invited them to throw in. "The more the merrier."

Besides, Graham Ludlow was offering a sizable bounty on Buchanon's head as well as for the man's daughter, though only if she was brought back to him alive.

Rucker, Kleinsasser, and Williams were fighting men who often worked for area ranchers "resolving" range disputes. They'd ridden along with Stillwell this morning for the challenge of a good fight as well as to exact payment for the killing of Max and Luke Chaney.

Now, however, all three men as well as

even such hardened killers as Weed Zorn and Klaus Steinbach had seemed to have had a little starch taken out of their drawers by the killing of such a formidable regulator as the legendary Dakota Jack Patterson. On the way back to Tigerville, they'd ridden on ahead of Stillwell, who'd taken it slow due to the nasty bruise and cut his right leg had suffered when his horse had fallen on top of it.

He wasn't sure if the leg was broken, but it had definitely incurred a nasty gash from a pointed rock that needed tending.

He wasn't sure what he was going to do, however, with the doctor likely still running hog-wild around the hills with none other than Stillwell's worst enemy, Hunter Buchanon. First things first. He needed whiskey. And maybe Jane was still up in his room feeling sorry for herself from his having had to bring her under rein earlier. He'd have her clean it up and bandage it for him. He'd ply her with good whiskey, promise to buy her something special when all this damnable dust had settled.

Stillwell stepped gingerly down from his horse.

"What happened to your leg, Sheriff?"

Stillwell turned to the young boy sitting on the Territorial's broad front steps. The

461

kid wore a watch cap and knickers. He was drawing in the dirt at the bottom of the steps with a forked stick.

Stillwell had seen him around town before. A strumpet's bangtail. He made pocket change by running sundry errands and building fires for crippled widows and doxies down with the clap.

Indignant rage welled up in Stillwell. "None of your damn business, boy!"

"Sorry, Sheriff."

"Take my horse over to the livery barn. Give him a good rubdown."

The boy cast away his stick and rose from the step, dirty little hand extended. "It's gonna cost ya."

"What?" Most of the fatherless urchins around town had always run Stillwell's errands for free. Their payment had simply been the honor of running an errand for the highly respected . . . and feared . . . sheriff of Pennington County.

Stillwell considered backhanding the kid. But then he looked around. There were too many other people on the street, a good many staring his way, likely wondering, as the kid was, about his leg.

Grumbling, Stillwell dug into a pocket of his whipcord trousers and pulled out a coin. He flipped the nickel to the kid, who caught it expertly out of the air. He looked at it, muttered with some disappointment, "This'll do . . . I reckon."

He grabbed the clay's reins and led it off in the direction of the livery barn. Supporting himself on the step rail, Stillwell watched the kid tramp northward along the street. He caught several snide glances tossed his way by passersby. By men who'd once respected and feared him.

The only way to get that respect and fear back where it belonged was to drag Hunter Buchanon to town and hang him from the cottonwood. By God, he would do that if it was the last thing he ever did. He would leave the body to hang there until the crows had devoured all but the bones. Then he'd let the bones hang there until the sinews between them became so brittle they fell one by one into the street to be carried away by stray curs.

Somehow, he had to locate the man's hideout.

Stillwell cursed and made his slow, plodding way up the hotel steps. He stumbled through the lobby, ignoring the skeptical glance of the old lady, Mrs. Merriman, manning the front desk. He stumbled through the arched open doorway and into the saloon. The men he'd ridden into town with

463

were all standing at the bar, throwing back bracing shots of whiskey backed by frothy schooners of Angus Buchanon's ale.

Pee-Wee Chaney sat alone at a round table between the entrance and the bar. None other than Stillwell's dear Jane was crouched over Pee-Wee, extending a balled cloth to the man, whose face resembled freshly ground beef. A whiskey bottle stood on the table in front of the big Pee-Wee, whose hamlike left fist was wrapped around it.

"Hold this against your face, Pee-Wee," Jane was saying to the man. "It's a poultice of fresh mint and mud. Should bring the swelling down for . . ." Jane's gaze had drifted over to Stillwell.

Stillwell winced when he saw her face straight on. A corner of her mouth was badly swollen, as was her left eye. The eye, the color of a ripe plum, was swollen nearly closed. All the color drained out of her face as she squatted there, glaring back toward Stillwell standing in the doorway.

"There's my girl," the sheriff said, sheepishly clearing his throat and limping forward. "Bring me a bottle of the good stuff, will you, darlin'?"

All eyes were on Stillwell now, including those of the men who'd ridden out to hunt Buchanon with him. The day barman, Hank

Mitchum, was glaring at him, hard jawed. Obviously, they knew who'd performed the handiwork on Jane Campbell's face.

Jane didn't say anything for a couple of beats. Then, crisply, obviously more than a little miffed — which Stillwell couldn't blame her for one bit — she said, "Sure, sure. A bottle of the good stuff. Coming right up, Sheriff."

She stood up, swung around, and marched over to the bar.

Feeling sheepish, Stillwell headed to a table near Pee-Wee and slumped into a chair. Pee-Wee was the only one in the bar not looking at Stillwell. Obviously, Pee-Wee was in more than a little misery. He sat slumped in his chair, staring down at the table, tipping his head back now and then to pour whiskey into his mouth without letting the bottle touch his lips.

His greasy, straight brown hair hung straight down to his shoulders.

"What happened to you?" Stillwell asked him.

Pee-Wee turned to him. Again, Stillwell winced.

The man's face was a swollen purple mask. His nose appeared to have tripled in size, and turned an especially sickly shade of yellow. It appeared to be trying to take over his entire swollen face. Both of Pee-Wee's eyes were black, and his lips were crusted with dried blood.

Pee-Wee stared dumbly at Stillwell for a full ten seconds, then curled his upper lip enough to reveal the bloody stubs of several broken teeth. Then he turned his head forward again, tipped it back, and poured more whiskey into his mouth.

Brisk footsteps sounded. Stillwell turned toward the bar out from behind which Jane was striding. She held a bottle in one hand a glass in the other hand.

Stillwell smiled. Just thinking about that whiskey soothed his aching leg. He didn't, however, care for the bitterness betrayed by Jane's dark, flat eyes and the pasty pallor of her cheeks. He liked it even less when she stopped about seven feet from the bar, just beyond Pee-Wee, and held the bottle up above her head and twisted her face into a specter-like grin.

"Want the whiskey, Sheriff?" she asked in a pinched, bizarre-sounding, singsong voice. "Come an' get it!"

CHAPTER 35

The men at the bar turned to face Stillwell. Klaus Steinbach elbowed Weed Zorn, chuckling. Zorn grinned as he slid his gaze from Jane to Stillwell then back again, and chuckled once more.

Even Pee-Wee took the trouble to turn his head and swollen, drink-bleary eyes to the sheriff.

Everyone probably saw the crimson flush in Stillwell's burning cheeks. He could feel a vein throbbing in his temple.

"Here's your whiskey, Sheriff," Jane chortled, wagging the bottle above her head. "Come an' get it!"

The men at the bar chuckled. All except the bartender, Hank Mitchum. Mitchum stared in exasperation at the saloon girl, who had surely lost her sanity.

"Jane!" Mitchum admonished.

"Jane," Stillwell said tightly, every bone and muscle in his body drawn with painful rigidity. "Bring . . . me . . . that . . . blasted . . . bottle."

"You want it? Come an' get it!"

"Jane!" both Stillwell and Mitchum croaked at nearly the same time again, the bartender digging his pudgy fingers into the edge of his mahogany bar top. At the bar, Mort Rucker and Henry Kleinsasser shared a sidelong grin. Williams ran a hand down his face, laughing.

"Sure," Stillwell croaked, wincing as he slid his chair too quickly back in rage that was quickly becoming an explosive boil. "Sure . . . sure . . . I'll fetch the bottle, you three-penny whore!"

He fairly leaped to his feet, no longer feeling the raw pain in his leg. Barely limping, he strode around his table, and, jaws set hard, clenching his fists at his sides, he made a beeline for the saloon girl grinning before him, still wagging the whiskey bottle above her head.

When Stillwell was halfway between his table and Jane, he stopped suddenly. Just then he saw the gutta-percha grips of a silver-chased, over-and-under derringer peeking up from the saloon girl's cleavage exposed by the bodice of her frilly, skimpy red dress.

The devilish grin slowly left Jane's face.

Her eyes hardened even more. Her right hand opened. The bottle fell to the floor to shatter, whiskey and glass flying in all directions. Jane's swollen lips formed a narrow line across the lower half of her face, and a flush now rose in her cheeks as she dropped her hand to her corset. She pulled out the derringer, clicking the hammer back.

"Here's what you really deserve, you sick toad strangler!" Jane screamed as she raised the pretty little popper cheek high and narrowed one eye, aiming down the stout double barrels.

"No!" Stillwell screamed, throwing up both hands palms out, tipping his head backward and to one side and screwing up his face as he squeezed his eyes closed.

The derringer made a menacing little *pop* that sounded hardly louder than that made by a snapped twig. Stillwell's left hand went numb.

"Jane!" Mitchum bellowed from behind the bar.

Smelling cordite wafting on the saloon's still air, Stillwell looked up to see blood running down the back of his still upraised, quivering left hand. The bullet had gone through the hand, opening a hole filled with blood, raw meat, and daylight in its exact center.

Stillwell pulled his hand down, howling and clutching the wounded limb with his right. He glared up at Jane, who gave a ferocious, animal-like scream as she pulled the derringer back, holding it with both hands as she cocked it again, engaging the second barrel.

Stillwell wheeled, his old enemy fear running off its leash inside him again.

"No!" he heard someone scream in a high, screeching wail. As he ran toward the front of the saloon, he realized with a thundering humiliation that the screamer had been none other than himself.

"Jane, no!" he screamed again, as though there were an impostor inside him, one that keenly new fear and wasn't afraid to express it.

He stopped and glanced behind him.

Jane was striding toward him, laughing, aiming the derringer straight out from her right shoulder, shifting the gun slightly from side to side and up and down, drawing a bead on him.

"Jane, no!"

Stillwell twisted around and threw himself into the big plate-glass window at the front of the room. The pop of the derringer was nearly drowned by the raucous shattering of glass. Stillwell flew through the window frame, through the rain of breaking glass, and landed on his back on the wooden floor of the veranda fronting the hotel.

He lay there for a time in shock, gasping like a landed fish. Dimly, gradually, he became aware again of the throbbing, burning pain in his left hand. By comparison, it made the ache in his leg little more noticeable than the bite of a fly.

Stillwell looked around. People on the street had stopped to stare at him. Even a couple of horseback riders trotting past the hotel now stopped their mounts, one nudging the other and then pointing out the sheriff lying on the veranda in a small sea of broken glass. A couple of dirty-faced street urchins peeked through the veranda rails at him.

The street had fallen silent. There was only the monotonous thumping of the stamping mill up at the King Solomon.

Stillwell's humiliation was now becoming the kindling building a fire of unbridled fury.

Again, that vein throbbed in his temple.

Ignoring the bites of the broken glass and the pain in his hand, he climbed to his feet. He stood and peered through the broken window.

Jane stood ten feet away, smiling at him victoriously, gray smoke curling from the barrels of the derringer where she held the little pistol down low by her right side, at the hem of her short skirt. Stillwell glared through the broken window at her.

Gradually, the smile left her battered face.

It was as though Stillwell himself was sucking the humor out of her, causing her lips to return to a straight if lumpy line across the bottom half of her face. His left hand bled against his left pants leg. He lifted his right hand and closed it around the grips of the .44 holstered on his hip.

Cold fear sparked in Jane's eyes.

"Bitch." Stillwell slid the long-barreled, ivory-gripped Peacemaker free from its holster and, holding it down along his left leg, he clicked the hammer back.

Jane screamed, "No, Frank!"

She whipped around and ran back through the saloon, toward Pee-Wee and the men standing at the bar.

Stillwell raised the Colt, extended it straight out from his right shoulder, narrowed his right eye as he aimed down the barrel, and fired.

Jane screamed. Not because she'd been hit. Just terrified. The bullet had been fired just wide of her head on purpose. It plunked into the egg-shaped ball atop the newel post at the bottom of the stairs.

Stillwell smiled. He stepped back through the window frame and began moving quickly across the room, following Jane's route toward the bar. He stopped, fired again, evoking another scream as Jane tripped over Stillwell's own chair sitting at an angle to his table, which he'd fired his second bullet into.

She hit the floor and rolled.

"Jesus, Frank," bellowed Hank Mitchum. "Stop it!"

Stillwell continued striding forward, wincing a little against the pain in his hand and leg. Jane scrambled to her feet, crying, moaning, and took off running again toward the stairs. The men at the bar were all crouching low, well aware that Stillwell's lead was being flung in their direction.

Jane ran around Pee-Wee, screaming, "Help me! Make him stop! Help me!"

She ran to where Klaus Steinbach stood crouched before the bar, both hands gripping the bar top behind him, ready to dodge the next bullet. Jane ran up beside him and tried to tuck herself behind him, between him and the bar, clutching his arm and yelling, "Help me! Please, don't let him kill me!"

The black-bearded gunman gave her a brusque shove away from him. "Sorry,

473

sweetheart. I reckon you should've aimed better!"

He and the other men around him laughed. Except for Hank Mitchum. He stood crouched low behind the bar, his own frightened eyes on Stillwell now as the sheriff stepped around the gruesomely grinning Pee-Wee, lips quirking a savage smile beneath his thick, brown mustache, as the sheriff made his way toward Jane.

The saloon girl screamed again as she swung around and dashed up the stairs, one hand on the rail, her long hair dancing like a red curtain across her back.

Stillwell gained the bottom of the steps and raised the .44.

"No, Frank!" bellowed Hank Mitchum.

Stillwell fired up the stairs until his Colt's hammer dropped with a dull ping against the firing pin.

Jane's bullet-riddled body rolled back down the stairs to lie faceup at Stillwell's boots. Dull with death, her eyes stared up at him. Blood oozed out one corner of her cracked and swollen mouth.

The room was silent for a good thirty seconds. Outside, the street was silent too.

Mort Rucker raked his shocked gaze from the pretty saloon girl to Stillwell, who was fumbling around with his gun, trying to reload, though the bullet-torn left hand made the maneuver awkward and painful. His own powder smoke wafted around him, stinking up the entire saloon.

"Stillwell, you're a crazy son of a bitch," Rucker said. "She didn't deserve that!"

Stillwell cursed as he continued reloading, the empty shell casings rolling around on the floor between his boots and Jane's bloody body.

"You hear me, Stillwell!" Rucker said.

Stillwell clicked the Colt's loading gate closed, spun the cylinder, turned, and shot Rucker through the chest.

Rucker hadn't expected it. He'd only had his right hand closed over the grips of his own pistol, but the Schofield was still in its holster. Now he jerked back with the impact of the bullet, his lower jaw hanging slack with shock. He glared at Stillwell, his face twisting in pain and rage. He tried to wrench the Schofield free of its holster, but then his knees buckled.

They hit the floor with a thunderous boom.

He fell straight forward onto his face and lay quivering as he died.

Stillwell slid the gun toward the other men standing to the right of where Rucker had been standing. He jabbed the still-smoking

Colt toward Rucker's partner, Kleinsasser.

"Any hard feelin's, Henry?"

Kleinsasser stared down at the pistol aimed at his belly, and made a sour expression. "No . . . no, I, uh . . . reckon not." He right eye twitched as he raised his gaze to Stillwell.

"How 'bout you two?" Stillwell asked Weed Zorn, standing a few feet away from Kleinsasser.

"Hell, I don't care who you kill, Frank!" He laughed.

Stillwell slid the Colt past Zorn to Klaus Steinbach, who raised his hands shoulder high, fingers curled toward his palms. He chuckled.

"Easy, Frank. Easy, now. We're friends here — you and Weed an' me. Heck, I hadn't knowed Rucker from Adam's off-ox before this mornin'. Now, the girl was right purty, but I reckon she was purtier before you messed her face up."

He shrugged, his broad smile in place. "No skin off my nose."

"Easy, Frank," Zorn said, frowning down at the gun in Stillwell's hand. "Easy, easy, easy." He gave a nervous chuckle.

Stillwell turned to Hank Mitchum glaring at him from the other side of the bar. "What do you say, Hank?"

476

Mitchum just stared at him, his round face creased distastefully. Finally, he said, "Christ!" He walked out from behind the bar, picked up the dead saloon girl, and carried her out through the arched doorway into the lobby, then out onto the veranda, heading for the undertaker, no doubt.

On his way through the arched doorway, he passed Graham Ludlow. The rancher/mine owner stood with his hat in his hands, staring stony faced at the dead girl in the bartender's arms. He turned to stare after Mitchum and Jane, then sauntered into the saloon.

Stillwell holstered his pistol and ripped a handkerchief out of his back pocket. He wrapped it tightly around his wounded hand and stumbled around behind the bar. He pulled a bottle of good rye off a shelf, grabbed two shot glasses off a pyramid atop the bar, and walked over to where Ludlow sat at the table at which Stillwell had been sitting and on which his dark-brown Stetson remained.

Stillwell cursed as he sat down in his chair. He set the bottle and the glasses on the table, then leaned forward, squeezing his left hand with his right hand in his lap, gritting his teeth against the god-awful pain.

Ludlow regarded the man with amusement.

Then he popped the cork on the bottle, poured them each a drink, and said, "Well, you've proven you can kill a saloon girl." He tossed back half his shot. "How 'bout now we discuss Hunter Buchanon?"

CHAPTER 36

Using a leather swatch so he wouldn't burn his hand, Hunter removed the pot from the fire and refilled his and Annabelle's coffee cups.

"Thank you, kind sir," Annabelle said as she chopped up for the breakfast skillet a bloody haunch from the deer Hunter had killed earlier that morning.

Hunter smiled at her as he returned the pot to the tripod's hook. "Don't mention it, milady."

"Lady. Mhmmm. I'm not sure many would describe me as a lady. Not after last night." She gave a raspy chuckle.

Last night, their second night together here after the doctor had tended Angus, they'd stolen off in the brush together for a "rascally hoedown," as old Angus himself would have called it. They'd acted quickly . . . though not to either one's dissatisfaction . . . so as not to leave Angus alone for too long.

Or to let their guards down against a possible attack from their enemies. Breathless but sated, they'd returned to the fire and snuggled down together, each with a cup of the old man's Scottish ale, to stare up at the black velvet sky flour-dusted with shimmering stars.

Hunter was recovering well from the dragging. He was still stiff and sore, but no Buchanon had ever let a little stiffness and soreness keep him from enjoying his lady.

"You'll always be a lady to me, Anna," Hunter said, gazing across the fire at the young woman with open admiration and affection. "A wild lady, maybe, but a lady just the sa—"

"Do you two think you could hold off on makin' goo-goo eyes at each other long enough to bring me a cup o' that mud? Smells powerful good!"

They both whipped their heads toward Angus in shock.

"Pa?" Hunter set his cup down and rose, hurrying over to kneel down beside the old man. Blue eyes stared up at him as clear as the morning sky. "You're awake." He placed the back of his hand across Angus's leathery forehead and turned to Anna. "Fever must've broke!"

"How long was I out, anyways?"

"Three or four days, Pa. You cut out on us just after we got you up here. I brought the doc out to have a look at you. He must be better than most folks give him credit for."

"Dahl was out here?"

"That's right, Angus." Annabelle had come over to kneel on the other side of the old man from his son. She held a cup out to him. "Here you go. Careful, it's hot."

Angus lifted his head and wrapped his gnarled, brown hand around the blue-speckled cup. "Thank you, sweet. I think it was the smell o' this that woke me. The only thing I like better than hot black coffee is cool black ale!" Angus smacked his lips. "Whoops!"

The hot cup sagged in his hand, some of the brew dribbling down the sides and onto his covers.

"Here, Pa — I'll hold it for you," Hunter said, taking the cup. He tipped it to Angus's bearded face. The old man blew ripples on it, sipped, smacked his lips again. "That's so good! Never even knew how good it was. One more."

Hunter tipped the cup again, and Angus sipped, slurping it over the rim and into his mouth.

"Do you think you can eat something?"

Annabelle asked him.

Angus frowned, thinking, then his gaze brightened. "You know, I think I could."

"I'll be hanged — you are getting better," Hunter said with relief. He hadn't realized how the dull, rusty knife of worry had been poking him. Now it was finally giving some ground.

"Good," Annabelle said. "I'm fixing venison stew with wild onions. I'll get back to it . . . let you fellas talk." She glanced at Hunter, meaningfully, then strode back to the fire.

"Venison. Mmmm," Angus said. "Where'd you shoot the deer?"

"Didn't shoot it. Snared it, cut its throat. I was worried the shot might be heard."

Angus smiled admiringly up at his son. "We named you right, your dear ma an' me." His gaze darkened. "Speakin' of huntin', you get that Chaney bunch yet? You get all them that killed Shepfield and Tyrell?"

"I got most of 'em, Pa. Those that aren't dead are wishing they were. Dahl told me Max Chaney's dead. Billy's dead. Pee-Wee is one o' them wishin' he was dead too."

"Well, hell, boy — we still out here on account o' me? Load me back into the wagon. I'm ready to go —"

Angus stopped. He gazed darkly up at his son. His mouth opened and tears glazed his eyes. His voice wheezed up from his sparrow-like chest, high and thin and forlorn as a death dirge. "They burned us out, didn't they?"

Hunter drew a deep breath.

"Ah, hell!" Angus rested his head back against his pallet and ground the back of his fists against the cave floor. "Ah, hell! We built that place from the ground up . . . by the sweat of our brows!"

"We'll get us a new place, Pa. Somewhere new. We'll make a fresh start."

"Fresh start?"

Hunter glanced behind him. He and Anna shared a look.

Turning back to his father, he said, "Me an' Anna . . . we think it's time to pull our picket pins, Pa. Time to pull out. Find another place to build a ranch. I was thinkin' of Montana."

"Montana, hell!" Angus was sobbing through his rage, tears pooling in his anguished eyes. "This was our home. We built it ourselves. We ain't gonna be run out, boy. A Buchanon don't run. Or, if he does, he runs *toward trouble*!" He spat the last two words out in an impotent fury, spittle flying from his lips, his face swelling up and turning red. A muscle twitched beneath his left eye.

Hunter placed a hand on the old man's spindly shoulder. "Easy, Pa, easy! Settle down, now, or you'll give yourself a stroke."

"Ah, prairie oysters," Angus lamented, turning his head from side to side, stretching his thin cracked lips back from his teeth. "My oldest and youngest boys dead. The ranch burned. Likely the stock all run off, maybe dead. And here I lay, useless as a hind-tit calf!"

Hunter pulled a whiskey bottle out of a sack beside him, near where Angus's double-bore, twelve-gauge shotgun leaned against the cave wall. He dribbled a little of the whiskey into the coffee cup. When he'd returned the bottle to the sack, he lifted the cup. "Here, Pa. Spiced it up for you. Good medicine."

When he'd helped Angus to a couple sips of the spiked coffee, he set the cup down beside the pallet. He gazed down at the miserable old man and said, "If we stay here, there'll be no end to it. We'll die, Pa. All three of us. We're gonna get you out of here. We're gonna build a new home elsewhere."

"Leave me here."

Angus had lost all of the vim and vinegar

he'd awakened with only a few minutes ago. Now he looked like a hollow shell of his former self once more, eyes drawn, cheeks sallow. The skin of his face was like that of a worn, empty leather sack. "I wanna die right here. You two go. Get married. Have you some kids. God knows I don't blame you for that. I want you to. Me? I just wanna die. Bury me with Shep and Tyrell."

"You'll feel better when you've eaten, Angus," Annabelle said gently, kneeling by the fire and stirring the stew hanging from the tripod. She looked deeply worried.

"I ain't hungry," Angus rasped. The words sounded like a small breeze caressing a slender reed before dying.

After they'd eaten and Hunter had helped Anna clean the dishes with water from the barrel strapped to the wagon, he set his hat on his head. "I think it'll be time to go soon. Maybe tomorrow. The next day at the latest."

"What about Angus?"

They both looked at the old man once again slumbering on his pallet, snoring softly.

"I got a bad feelin', Anna. That bullet might not have killed him, but I have a feelin' those peckerwoods burnin' the ranch did the job." Hunter shook his head, at war with his agony, his rage. "I don't think he's gonna make it. I think they killed him." He drew a breath, let it out slow. "I think we'll be able to pull out, either with him or without him, tomorrow or the next day, sure enough. A day'll probably tell."

Hunter grabbed his rifle and his saddle.

"What are you going to do?" Annabelle asked him.

"I'm gonna ride back to the ranch, see if there's anything worth salvaging." Hunter lowered his gaze in defeat to the ground, shrugged. "I don't know. I guess I'd just like to have one last look at the place. Maybe say a few words to Shep an' Tye."

He looked at the dark forest running along the base of the ridge, alive with chirping birds and quarreling squirrels. "I took a good look around earlier. Didn't see any sign of anyone. I think we're all right for now. Maybe Stillwell and the others from Tigerville came to the same decision we have — there's been enough bloodshed."

"You think that's possible?"

"I'd like to think so." Hunter leaned toward her, kissed her soft, pliant lips. "I'll be back soon. If there's trouble, fire two quick shots. I'll be back in no time."

"All right." Anna nodded, smiled weakly.

She seemed to feel as dour as Hunter did. After all, they were homeless, their future uncertain. "Be safe out there."

"I will."

"Hunter!"

He stopped, turned back to her. She ran to him and hugged him. They held each other tightly. When they separated, Hunter made his way down the steep slope from the cave.

Anna called, "Think ahead, not behind."

He smiled back at her and continued on down the slope toward where the two horses were picketed at the edge of the trees.

Bobby Lee lay in the shade of a giant fir. He was busily cleaning the bones of a recent rabbit kill, snarling scrappily, flicking his bushy tail.

"Come on, killer," Hunter said. "Let's take us a ride."

In an upstairs room at the Purple Garter Saloon in Tigerville, Dr. Norton Dahl said, "Prepare yourself, Minnie. And you might want to open that window a little wider."

"Why's that, Doc?"

Dahl was slowly, gently unwrapping a heavy cambric bandage from around the leg of Willie Heaton, who lay moaning and groaning on the small bed, pressing the heels of his hands to his temples. "I can tell from the discoloration around the bandage that . . ."

The doctor pulled the bandage free of the bullet wound, making a face against the stench of vituperating flesh. "Yes, just as I thought, gangrene has set in. Damn it all, anyway!"

"Phew!" said Minnie, who generally performed her function in the Purple Garter in this very room but in the bed and on her back. In the upright position, she often helped Dahl. Now she stumbled back against the window, waving a hand in front of her face as though trying to clear the sickly, musky stench from the air. "Boy, you were right, Doc." She choked, stifled a gag.

"What's goin' on, Doc?" Heaton asked. "Jesus God — what's that awful smell?"

Dahl glanced at Minnie, a pretty brunette with a heart-shaped face, her hair cut short just beneath her ears. She was a frail girl with a frank and open personality, which made her a favorite with the miners from the King Solomon. "You all right, dear?"

"I'm fine, Doc. Just caught me off guard for a second's all. Don't worry about me. I'm not about to run out on you. My pa was a sawbones back in Iowa, don't ya know, and I started helpin' him when I was half as high as our kitchen table."

Dahl was examining Heaton's open wound, still making a face. "Your pa was a sawbones, you say? So what got you into your current line of work?"

"Pa caught the Cupid's itch an' Ma shot him. Turns out he hadn't saved a dime. Spent whatever he made — and it wasn't much in the small town we lived in — on whores."

"So you became one yourself?"

"If you can't beat 'em, join 'em," Minnie said, chuckling. "That's what I always say!"

Dahl gave a snort.

"I hate to interrupt your cozy conversation with Miss Minnie, Doc," Heaton barked, "but what in the hell is that awful stink?" He was breathing hard and he was bathed in sweat, his short, curly blond hair matted to his head. He was twenty-six or -seven and worked as an ore loader up at the King Solomon.

"You, I'm sorry to say," Dahl said, straightening as he continued staring down at the man's leg. "Gangrene has set in, Willie. I tried to keep it out, but sometimes the damn affliction has a mind of its own. If you'd gotten to me sooner, I maybe could have done more for you."

"I was layin' out there for two days before

that prospector picked me up. If he hadn't come along, I'd still be out there." Heaton ground his teeth. "That blasted Buchanon!" He arched his back on the bed and scrunched up his face, causing the cords in his neck to stand out. "He's gonna die slow, I tell you! He's gonna die slow, that murderin' heathen!"

Dahl looked at the man skeptically, said in a patient, reasonable tone, "Well, Willie, did you not ride out there and burn the man's ranch? Weren't you of the same group that murdered his brothers and severely wounded his father?"

"No!" Willie wailed, panting against the pain. "I mean . . . leastways I rode with them fellas both nights. I might've sunk one bullet into the oldest brother, but it was some others that set the fire. I turned the stock loose that night. Pee-Wee Chaney wanted to shoot all the horses, but I couldn't set with that. So I opened the barn and the corral gate and chased all the horses out."

He ground the ends of his fists against the deep, soft mattress. "An' this is the thanks I get!"

"Yes," Dahl muttered, wryly. "Ungrateful yellowbelly, that Buchanon."

"Please tell me you ain't gonna cut off my leg, Doc!"

Just then the door behind Dahl clicked open. He glanced over his shoulder to see Sheriff Frank Stillwell limp into the room on his tender hip. His left hand was wrapped in a thick white bandage. "Got a minute, Doc?"

"Got a minute?" Dahl said, gesturing at the writhing Willie Heaton. "Does it look like I got a minute? This man has contracted gangrene in his leg!"

Stillwell shook his head as he closed the door behind him. "I'm gonna need a minute, Doc." He limped over to a brocade-upholstered armchair in the room's corner, sagged gently into it, wincing a little at the pain in his hip not to mention in his hand, then dug a long nine out of the breast pocket of his black frock coat. "Just a minute."

He scratched a match to life on his thumbnail and gazed steely-eyed through the flame at the doctor. "Gonna have to insist, I'm afraid."

CHAPTER 37

"Sheriff, I might very well have to amputate this man's leg!" Dahl said in exasperation.

"No, Doc!" Willie Heaton cried. "Please don't cut my leg off!" He bawled like a baby.

Stillwell took a drag off the long nine and blew smoke into the room. "I'll let you get right to it, Doc. Christ, that leg stinks to high heaven, don't it? Phew! I just need to know where Hunter Buchanon is holed up with his old man and Ludlow's daughter. Just tell me that, an' throw in some good directions, and I'll be out of your hair pronto. You can saw away to your heart's delight!"

"No!" Heaton wailed.

Miss Minnie knelt down beside him, cooing to the horrified patient while holding one of his hands and glaring at the sheriff.

"Forget it," Dahl said. "I'll never tell. Just so more men can be brought to me in this condition?" He gestured at the sobbing

Heaton. "Just so more men can die?" He shook his head adamantly. "Nope. Not going to do it. You're wasting your time, Stillwell. What's more, I'm not afraid of you. If you do anything to me, who's going to tend your own wounds?"

He dropped his chin to indicate the man's bullet-torn hand, which Dahl had sutured along with his hip. He turned to Minnie and said, "Dear, would you please fetch my surgical kit from . . . ?"

He stopped when he saw Stillwell rise from the chair. The sheriff moved toward the bed. Dahl stared at him, incredulous. Minnie rose, frowning curiously, as Stillwell stepped past her to stand over the bed and stare down at the sobbing Willie Heaton.

"Willie, I'm gonna do you a big favor, my friend. I'm gonna save you from a life of one-legged hell."

Before Heaton could say anything, Stillwell grabbed the pillow out from beneath the wounded man's head. He held the pillow over Heaton's face, shucked his Colt from its holster, and fired two rounds through the pillow.

Minnie screamed and fell backward against the dresser, dropping to her knees. She screamed again.

Stillwell triggered one more round through

the pillow. Again, Minnie screamed. Bloody goose feathers snowed down over the bed. Heaton's body quivered violently on the bed.

"Oh . . . oh God!" Minnie cupped both hands over her mouth and sobbed.

Dahl clawed his way out of his shock to say, *"Stillwell, you crazy chucklehead!"*

The sheriff turned to face the doctor. His eyes were dark. He raised the Colt, and, keeping his dark, threatening gaze on Dahl, extended the revolver out from his right shoulder and pressed the round steel maw against Minnie's head.

He cocked it loudly. "I'm gonna ask you just one more time, Doc!"

Riding into Tigerville bright and early the next day, Graham Ludlow drew back on his stallion's reins while raising his left hand, halting the dozen Broken Heart men riding behind him on their dusty horses.

As Ludlow and the other men drew up in front of the sheriff's office, the rancher shuttled his gaze to the sheriff dropping tenderly down his veranda steps. Stillwell winced with each movement. He held his bandage-wrapped left hand across his belly, as though it were an injured bird.

Two other men filed out the office's open

494

door behind him, saddlebags slung over their shoulders, Winchesters in their hands. Each man wore a five-pointed deputy sheriff's star.

"Good God, man," Ludlow said, frowning at Stillwell. "You're a sorry sight!"

Stillwell stopped and glared up at the older man, who wore two pistols on his hips and had his own Winchester Yellowboy repeater shoved down in its freshly soaped and oiled saddle scabbard. Likewise, his dozen riders were all armed for bear.

Or Graybacks . . .

"You ride all this way to take my temperature, Mr. Ludlow? You want me to turn around, drop my drawers, and bend over?"

Ludlow drew a lungful of air, beating down the anger rising inside him. He glanced at his foreman, C. J. Bonner, sitting his paint gelding to Ludlow's right. Bonner turned to Stillwell and started to reprimand the lackey for his insolence, but Ludlow cut him off with a raised right hand.

He jerked his chin toward the other two men dropping down the steps behind Stillwell, grinning at the sheriff's barb. He'd seen them in the saloon the day before, standing at the bar.

"Who're your new deputies?" the rancher asked. "I don't believe we've been formally

495

introduced."

Stillwell turned away from the rancher and stepped over to his claybank tied to a near hitchrack. "That there's Weed Zorn and Klaus Steinbach."

Tossing their saddlebags over their horses' backs or adjusting saddle straps and buckles, Zorn and Steinbach turned toward Ludlow and dipped their chins by way of a cursory howdy-do.

"Ah, I see." Ludlow knew both men by their names and reputations. He'd never been introduced to either, however. Again, he frowned, glancing around. "Where's Dakota Jack Patterson?"

"Jack had him a pill he couldn't digest," said the man Ludlow assumed was Zorn — shorter and wiry and with a gunman's hard stare. Steinbach was tall and black bearded, and he wore a long duster the same black shade as his beard and eyes. Probably the same black shade as his soul. "Just been a ton of misery all the way around." He glanced at Stillwell.

"Dakota Jack's dead?" Ludlow said, genuinely surprised at Stillwell's failure to inform him yesterday at the Dakota Territorial. When he'd absorbed the startling information, he turned his thoughts to the business at hand. "Speaking of pills, did you ask Dahl about Buchanon?"

Stillwell turned from his horse and, still holding his bandaged left hand across his belly, used his right hand to dig a long nine from his shirt pocket, inside his black frock coat. "Yeah," the sheriff said, snapping a match to life on his thumbnail. He gave an acidic grin.

"Tell me you didn't kill the town's only doctor!" Ludlow said with not entirely genuine exasperation and mainly for the benefit of the onlookers. Dahl had had valuable information that had needed to be extracted at all costs, even if it meant severe damage to the sawbones' person.

Stillwell grinned as he puffed the cigar, causing the flame to expand and contract in front of his face. "Nah, I didn't kill him. In fact, last time I saw him, he was getting good and drunk in the Purple Garter. Really crying in his whiskey. The whores were cooing to him like he'd just lost his best friend." The sheriff flicked the match into the street. "Stupid sot."

Stillwell turned to his horse. He removed the reins from the hitchrack and reached up with his right hand to grab his saddle horn. As he lifted his left boot toward his stirrup, his right hand slipped off the apple. He reached out automatically with his bandaged left hand to break his forward fall, and whacked it against a stirrup fender.

"Oh!" Stillwell turned to face the street, leaning back against his horse and cradling the injured appendage taut against his belly. The hand quivered. Stillwell closed his eyes, moving his lips but not saying anything, his face turning as pale as an onionskin.

"You okay, Sheriff?" Ludlow said, casting Bonner a quick, furtive half smile. "Maybe you better stay here in town. Rest up. Me an' my boys from the Broken Heart and your two eager deputies will put an end to the, uh, trouble" — he glanced again at his foreman — "and bring my daughter home safely."

Stillwell opened his eyes. They were cold and hard. A little color started to return to his face. "Your concern warms my heart, Ludlow. Your daughter ain't home yet, eh? I'd have thought she'd have come to her senses by now. I wonder what it is about that big Grayback she likes so much . . ."

He glanced over his horse at Zorn and Steinbach, who'd swung up into their saddles. They returned his grin, cutting their mocking gazes at the rancher. Ludlow's fleshy, deeply seamed face flushed, and his broad nose turned bright red in anger. "Let's go, Stillwell. We're burning daylight!"

Stillwell cast another conspiratorial grin at his deputies, then managed to successfully, albeit gingerly and awkwardly, climb onto his claybank's back. As Ludlow and the other Broken Heart men waited for him to take the lead, he swung his horse into the street and did just that, Zorn and Steinbach moving up to either side.

Ludlow glanced at Bonner, said, "All right . . . let's finish this damn thing!"

He booted his horse on down the street after the cocky sheriff and his two cocky deputies. As they neared the south end of town, heading for the western trail, Ludlow saw a badly disheveled man step out from a break between two buildings. It was Dr. Dahl. The man's thin hair was splayed across his bulbous forehead and down over his ears. He looked sweaty and greasy, as though he hadn't slept at all but only drank himself pie-eyed.

His spectacles sat crooked on his nose. He stumbled over some trash between the buildings and nearly fell onto the boardwalk before him.

"Stillwell!" he called in a taut, raspy voice. "Ludlow!" He sidled up to a post holding up the awning over the boardwalk. He slid off the post and wrapped an arm around it to keep from falling. "Don't do this! End it now! No more . . . no more killing!"

"Go back to bed, Doctor!" Ludlow called as he rode past the drunken sawbones.

"Please!" Dahl pleaded.

"Don't you worry, Doc!" Stillwell called, hipping around in his saddle to keep his gaze on Dahl as he continued on out of town. "After today, all the killin' will be done for a while, and you can stop pissin' down your leg!"

Zorn and Steinbach threw their heads back, laughing.

Nearly two hours later, Stillwell reined his mount to a halt between two haystack buttes. The others, including Ludlow, checked their horses down behind him, blinking against the dust catching up to them.

Stillwell looked around as though trying to get his bearings.

"Well?" the rancher said, impatient and generally annoyed with Stillwell. "Do you know where you are, Sheriff, or have you gotten yourself . . . and us . . . lost?"

Stillwell had proven himself a coward and a fool so many times that Ludlow wasn't even sure why he'd invited the man along on what the rancher hoped would be his final assault on Hunter Buchanon and the old man's father — if old Angus was even still alive. No, Ludlow did know why he'd invited him.

Dahl was the only man in town who knew where the Buchanons and Annabelle were holed up. Ludlow knew that Stillwell could get that information out of the doctor, if anyone could. Ludlow himself hadn't wanted to perform the grisly task and risk having folks in the town and the surrounding hills holding it against him if he had to get rough.

Stillwell, however, had played out his hand here in Tigerville. He no longer cared what anyone thought of him. Now he just wanted to finish what he'd started, exact some revenge for the humiliation he'd suffered, leave the hills to find some distant corner of the west that maybe hadn't heard of what had happened here, and get to work restoring his pride and honor to some semblance of its former self.

At least, that's all Ludlow *thought* the man wanted. It was hard to tell with Stillwell. The law-for-hire was as hard to read as the face of a flat boulder. He was that way now as he looked around, his back to Ludlow, ignoring the man's question. His shoulders were set stubbornly beneath the broadcloth of his black coat.

Finally, Stillwell glanced at Zorn and Steinbach both sitting their horses to his right and said, "Stay here."

He gave a quiet grunt in protest of the pain in his hip and hand as he swung down from the clay's back. He dipped a hand into his saddlebags, pulled out his field glasses, then started to climb the left-most haystack butte before them.

"I asked you a question, Sheriff," Ludlow said from his saddle.

Unless he'd suddenly gone deaf, again Stillwell ignored the question as he ambled slowly up the side of the butte.

Ludlow glanced at Bonner, who gave him a crooked smile.

"Stay with the men," the rancher said with a disgusted chuff.

He stepped down from his stallion's back, tossed the reins up to Bonner, then pulled his own field glasses out of his saddlebags. He followed Stillwell up the side of the butte. After only a few climbing steps, his lungs seemed to shrink, and he had to work hard, sucking air in and out of them, wincing against the raking pain. He felt as though a rat were in his chest, gnawing on his sternum.

By the time he got near the top, where Stillwell was dropping to his knees, grunting and sighing with his discomfort, Ludlow was breathing like a bellows and sweating through his clothes. The hot sun burned against the back of his neck.

Stillwell snugged himself belly flat against the butte, lifted his field glasses, and stared across the top of it toward the southwest. Ludlow spat, doffed his hat, and lifted his own glasses, directing them toward where the sullen sheriff was directing his own. The rancher adjusted the focus, sweeping the hills and forest with the single, round magnified field of vision, expecting to spy a cabin out there somewhere — something two men and a young woman might be holed up in.

All he saw was blond grass and the irregular angle of hills and mountains and blue-black forest shimmering in the midday sunshine.

"See it?" Stillwell grunted to Ludlow's right.

Ludlow glanced at the man and then peered through his glasses again. "See what?"

"Cave."

CHAPTER 38

Ludlow adjusted the focus, swept a deep fold nearly cloaked in shadows about a mile beyond, at the base of a steep rock wall and at the crest of a pine-choked ridge sloping up like a table lying on its side. As Ludlow stared, squinting through the lenses, stretching his lips back from his teeth in concentration, he saw the dark, egg-shaped feature at the base of the rock ridge.

"That's a cave?"

Stillwell pulled his own glasses down and stared straight ahead through his naked eyes. "Remember them three half-breed woodcutters from Deadwood I chased . . . for you . . . last summer?" The sheriff didn't wait for an answer; his tone made Ludlow bristle. "That's where me and Buck Fowler found 'em — happy as clams dinin' on one of your freshly butchered steers!"

He chuckled sneeringly.

"That's where you think . . . ?"

Stillwell quickly raised his glasses, gazed in the direction of the cave. "I know it is. Look there."

Ludlow raised his binoculars again. A human figure had just stepped out of the cave before which now Ludlow could see gray smoke curling from small, flickering orange flames nearly concealed by the cave's overhang. A slender figure capped in thick red hair walked out behind the larger, taller figure. As Ludlow tightened the focus, straining his eyes, he watched as Hunter Buchanon turned back around to face the cave and accept Ludlow's daughter into his arms.

Ludlow's heartbeat picked up.

It kept picking up as the two appeared to draw their heads together, likely kissing.

Stillwell lowered his binoculars and turned to Ludlow, shaping a mock heartfelt expression. "Ain't that sweet?" He pretended to brush a tear from his cheek with his bandaged hand.

Ludlow told him to do something physically impossible to himself and continued staring through the binoculars. Buchanon and Annabelle separated. Buchanon turned around and, picking up what appeared to be a saddle and a rifle, made his way down the steep shelf of rock fronting the cave and threw his saddle over one of the two horses standing at the edge of the dark pine forest.

"He's leaving," the rancher said through gritted teeth, turning to Stillwell. "That'll leave just my daughter and the old man — if Angus is still breathing — in the cave!"

Stillwell continued to stare through his binoculars. "It does, it does . . ."

"Now, you see how easy a thing like this can be when you actually think it through and don't go off half-cocked!"

Stillwell grimaced, turned to the rancher with fire in his eyes.

Ludlow grinned. Finally, he'd gotten the upper hand.

"Here's what we'll do. We'll —"

Bonner's voice cut him off. "Boss?"

Angrily, Ludlow turned to yell, "What is it? The sheriff and I are —"

Bonner and the other men were all looking along their back trail, toward something Ludlow couldn't see from his vantage. "Rider."

"What?"

"Rider comin'!"

"Well, who is it?"

Silence. All the men including Stillwell's two deputies continued to stare off in the direction from which they'd come.

Ludlow cursed and yelled, "Bonner?"

The foreman turned to Ludlow. "You'd

better step down here, boss. See this.''

Ludlow heaved himself to his feet, grunting and sweating with the effort. Stillwell did the same, sounding even older than the rancher, though the sheriff was his junior by a good twenty years.

Ludlow set his crisp, cream Stetson on his head and started down the slope. After a half dozen steps, he stopped.

A horse and rider were moving around the base of a low hill, coming into Ludlow's view now. The rider rode as though he were all loose joints and limbs held together by thin threads. The horse didn't look any more comfortable with the rider on his back than the rider himself appeared to be comfortable sitting the western stockman's saddle. Round spectacles glinted on the rider's nose.

At first, Ludlow thought: Dahl. The doctor had come to give them more grief.

But no. As the rider approached, the horse swinging its head to look warily at its rider, its eyes ringed with white as it fought the bit held too tightly back in its mouth, Ludlow saw the diminutive but well-dressed visage of his son-in-law-to-be. Kenneth Earnshaw wore riding trousers and knee-high riding boots. A round-brimmed beaver hat sat back at an angle off his pale, pimply forehead.

Around the outside of his tweed coat, which he wore over a white silk shirt with a ruffled front, he'd buckled a pair of the prettiest, pearl-butted, silver-chased Colt pistols Ludlow had ever seen. They appeared brand-new, as did the fancy, black leather, hand-tooled holsters that housed them. Both scabbards appeared as stiff as new boots fresh off the cobbler's bench.

"I'll be damned," Ludlow said.

Stillwell stood beside him. "Who the hell is that?"

"Kenneth Earnshaw."

"Who the hell is Kenneth Earnshaw?"

Ludlow didn't answer him. He stood scowling at the young man on the discomfited horse, who drew up now within ten feet and stopped, still fighting the bit.

"Kenneth?" Ludlow said, deeply incredulous. "What the hell are you doing out here?"

Earnshaw wobbled in the saddle, even though the horse was no longer moving. He held out a hand toward his would-be-father-in-law-to-be, palm out. Then he lifted the bottle he held in his right hand. It was a brandy bottle. Ludlow thought the label said Spanish brandy. Expensive stuff. Kenneth tucked the bottle's lip between his own, threw his head back, and took a couple of deep swallows.

"Why, he's three sheets to the wind!" Bonner said, chuckling.

The other men laughed.

"Who is he?" Stillwell said, his exasperation growing.

Ludlow vaguely heard Bonner mutter a response to the sheriff. The rancher watched Earnshaw pull the bottle down, ram a cork into its lip, and run a sleeve of his dusty tweed coat across his mouth. "Now, then" — he hiccupped — "let's get after her!"

"What?" Ludlow said.

"Mr. Ludlow, you said that if I wanted your daughter's hand, I had to fight for it. Well, I saw you men ride out of town earlier, and I suspected that you were on the trail of Annabelle and that . . . that . . . that lowdown, dirty, Confederate devil! Well, I am here to play my part. I am here to fight for the woman I love and wish to marry!"

"Christ, man," Ludlow exclaimed. "You're drunk as a lord!"

"I may have indulged in a wee bit much of the liquid courage, but courage it has given me, sir. As well as soothed the rawness in my arse." Earnshaw shifted around in his saddle, wincing. "These western range saddles are a bit rigid, are they not?"

"You'd best go back to the Purple Garter," Ludlow said. "You're liable to fall off that horse and kill yourself. I'd hate to have to share that bit of bad news with your father." He said to Bonner out the side of his mouth, "Might strain our business relationship, don't ya know."

He gave a wry chuff.

Bonner snorted a laugh.

"I insist, Mr. Ludlow." Earnshaw tossed the bottle away. It shattered on a rock. "There — I'm through! I am ready to split the wind and fog the sage!" He patted his holstered pistols. "I bought these two smoke wagons the other day from a traveling gun drummer. A fine pair, indeed, and I am ready to put them to good use."

He added in a mocking, badly overdone and stiffly manufactured western brogue: "This day, I'm a gonna kill me a yaller-bellied Grayback dog! Gonna fill him so fulla lead that rattlesnake's gonna rattle when he walks!"

He gave a hoot and slapped his thigh.

"Christ," Ludlow said with a sigh. "Well, all right. Have it your way. If you want to try to give a good accounting of yourself with the intention of winning Annabelle's hand — well, I reckon that's more honorable than lying around, diddling the doxies in the Purple Garter. I don't have time to worry about you, though, so try to keep up!"

Earnshaw grinned and gave an awkward salute.

Ludlow turned to Bonner. "It looks like Buchanon is headed west, possibly toward his ranch. I want you and the other men to cut him off. Take him down. *Burn* him down, you understand! This ends now. Right here today!"

He turned to Stillwell. "You and I and Earnshaw here will ride to the cave and get Anna."

"I wanna ride into the face of that devil!" Earnshaw exclaimed.

"You'll face devil enough in that cave," Ludlow told him. "If that one-armed old Rebel is still alive, he'll put up a fight. As will Anna." He glared at Stillwell. "Fight though she might, I want her unscathed, you understand? Any man who so much as musses a hair on her head will answer to me!"

He looked around Stillwell at Zorn and Steinbach, who grinned and hiked their shoulders, shrugging.

Stillwell turned to Bonner. "Take Buchanon alive. I want the final honors." He glanced at Ludlow. "I think I've earned that."

Ludlow thought it over. He turned to Bonner, said begrudgingly, "Take him alive if you can. Drag him back to the ranch. We'll be headed there once we've gotten my daughter on a leash."

"You got it, Mr. Ludlow."

Bonner swung his horse around. "Let's go, boys!"

He galloped off toward the southwest, the other twelve men falling into line behind him, putting the spurs to their mounts.

Ludlow turned to Stillwell standing beside him, staring after Bonner and the other riders. "I'd have thought you'd want to join them, Sheriff. I'd have thought you'd want to face Hunter Buchanon man-to-man . . . after all that's happened between you."

He'd threaded his tone with not-so-vague mockery.

Stillwell turned to the older man and gave an icy smile. "I got a feelin' that I'm still gonna have the chance. I got me a feelin' that your daughter's gonna be the bait that leads him into the final trap."

"Pshaw!" Ludlow laughed. "You think he'll go through all thirteen of my riders? Those are all tough men. Cold-steel savvy. That's why I hired 'em!"

"I'm just sayin'." Stillwell glanced at Zorn and Steinbach and then turned to his horse.

He grabbed the saddle horn and lifted his left foot to toe the stirrup but, being unable to use his left hand again, made the maneuver awkward if not downright perilous.

He missed the stirrup and fell against the claybank with a curse.

"You need help, Sheriff?" Ludlow said, swinging into his saddle and grinning smugly down at the gimpy lawman.

Stillwell cast the man a hard glare and swung into the leather with a pained grunt. He turned to the old rancher and said, "A thousand dollars when we've gotten your daughter back to the ranch. Another thousand for Hunter Buchanon."

"A thousand dollars for each of us," Steinbach said, wanting to make sure the terms were clear. He smiled with challenge at Stillwell. "An extra thousand for the one who brings down Buchanon. Uh . . . if your own riders don't, of course!"

He grinned through his thick, black beard.

"That's what we agreed to, gentlemen," Ludlow said, touching spurs to his stallion's flanks. "I'm a man who keeps my word. You don't last long in business by breaking it even once."

Stillwell nudged his horse over to where Kenneth Earnshaw sat his fidgety steel-dust, appearing as though he was having trouble keeping his head up. The pasty-faced young man's eyes were loose and red. "You really gonna make that girl marry this nancy boy?" he asked Ludlow. "Seems a shame to waste a filly like that on a stud like this . . . if you can call him that."

Kenneth jerked his head back as though he'd been slapped. He blinked hard. *"Pardon me?"*

"Yes," Ludlow said, gritting his teeth in anger. "Yes, I am. Now more than ever!"

He swung his horse around and booted it into a gallop.

CHAPTER 39

Hunter drew back on Nasty Pete's reins, stopping the horse off the ranch yard's southwest corner.

The hill on which he'd buried his brothers and where the tree honoring their mother grew rose on his right. The house and barn and corrals lay ahead.

He drew a slow, deep breath.

He'd thought he'd prepared himself for what he would find here, but there was no preparing yourself to see your home burned. His heart thudded heavily. A cold stone lay in his belly. He closed his eyes as though to wipe the images from his retinas, but when he opened them again, the scene was still there.

The house was all charred rubble and fire-blackened timbers. Two walls remained standing, but they appeared so insubstantial that the next slightest breeze would likely topple them. The stone chimney and hearth stood, as well, but as black as coal.

Bobby Lee sat on the slope to Hunter's left, moaning.

"Come on, Bobby, let's have a look," he said softly, dreadfully, and nudged the grullo forward. Nasty Pete lifted his head to sniff the air, twitching his ears. He seemed to be feeling as heartsick as Hunter was. After all, this had been the stallion's home as well.

Bobby Lee followed just behind the grullo, moaning and yipping softly, pausing now and then to sniff the charred rubble.

Hunter rode wide around the house, knowing without looking too closely — *unable* to look too closely — that there was nothing left. Nothing useable, anyway. Then, again, he'd known there wouldn't be. He'd only used that possibility as an excuse to pay a visit here. He'd had to see it for himself. He'd had to visit his brothers' graves one more time.

Trying hard to keep his sorrow and rage on a short leash, he rode around the house and then across the yard to the east, making a cursory inspection of the other outbuildings, including Angus's brew shed and Shep's blacksmith shop. All had been burned. The Halladay Standard windmill had been toppled. It lay like a child's giant toy lying across the stock tank — an accusing finger pointing toward town.

The buildings and the corrals were no more than rubble. At least the horses had not been shot and burned as well. At least someone in the group of cowardly cutthroats had valued the four-legged stock enough to have opened the gate and turned them loose. He could tell no stock had been in the barn, because he knew that smell from the war, and he didn't detect it here.

At the edge of the yard covered in gray ash, he turned and rode back over to where the blacksmith shop lay — or what remained of it. He glanced down and stopped the horse. His heart thudded again, harder this time. He swung down from the saddle, dropped to a knee off Pete's left stirrup.

Beneath the gray ash lay a dark-brown stain.

Shep's blood.

"Ah, hell," he cried, and lay his hand on the blood. He closed his hand, pulling up a wad of dirt mixed with the dried blood of his murdered brother, and squeezed.

Tears welled in his eyes.

"Ah, hell!" he cried again, louder, tears dribbling down his cheeks.

Squeezing the blood and dirt in his hands, he lowered his head and sobbed.

Nasty Pete whinnied, sidestepping away from Hunter.

Bobby Lee yipped and snarled.

The horse's whinny and the coyote's snarls were followed by the thud of a bullet into the ground to Hunter's right. The thud was followed a heartbeat later by the crack of a rifle.

Bobby Lee jerked with a start, then hunkered low, mewling.

Hunter dropped the blood and dirt and leaped to his feet, looking around. Horseback riders were galloping toward him from three sides — from his left and his right and from straight north of the ranch, beyond the remains of the blacksmith shop.

"Damn!" Hunter leaped for his rifle butt protruding from the sheath over Nasty Pete's right withers. "Run, Bobby! Hightail it!"

As Bobby Lee ran off with his bushy tail pulled down, Nasty Pete whinnied again as another bullet plunked into the ground near his prancing hooves, and sidled farther away, so that Hunter's fingers merely brushed the walnut stock.

"Damnit!" he yelled, falling to his knees.

As more bullets cut the air around him, rifles crackling in the distance but growing louder as the riders approached, Hunter lunged up and forward once more, throwing his right hand out for the rifle and wincing against the aches and pains in his battered body. He closed his hand around the stock and ripped the rifle free of the sheath just as Pete wheeled and bolted away from the oncoming riders.

As bullets screeched and whistled through the air around his head and thudded into the ground around him, Hunter dropped belly flat and pumped a cartridge into the Henry's action. He picked out one of the four men galloping toward him from the north, for that group was closing on him slightly faster than the ones to his left and his right, and fired.

His shot flew wide but it made its target flinch in his saddle, slowing his horse.

Hunter's next shot hit home, punching dust from the leather chap over the rider's left leg, making his horse scream and swerve sharply left and into the horse of the rider beside him. Both horses screamed as they disappeared in a cloud of billowing dust, throwing their bellowing riders wide, rifles flying.

As a bullet carved a furrow over Hunter's left shoulder and another nicked his left calf, Hunter hurled two quick rounds toward the riders galloping toward him from

519

his right. Swinging left, he fired three rounds toward the riders hammering toward him from that direction. His own bullets did not stop his attackers, but it slowed them some and spread them out.

In fact, a couple did stop, he saw now through his own wafting powder smoke. One man on his left curveted his mount, halting it, and rested his rifle barrel on his other raised forearm, aiming down the barrel, which promptly blossomed smoke and fire. That bullet carved a nasty burn from left to right across the middle of Hunter's back.

He sucked a sharp breath through gritted teeth, then heaved himself to his feet, looking around for cover.

All he saw around him were the hulking black ruins of the ranch buildings. He glanced south, toward the hill on which his brothers were buried. It was the nearest high ground.

Wheeling, he ran toward it, lunging forward, throwing his head back, scissoring his arms and legs. Hearing hooves thudding loudly behind him, he glanced over his shoulder. One rider was closing on him faster than the others.

Hunter swung around too quickly. He got his feet tangled. But that was all right. Falling, he'd avoided the bullet the closing rider had just flung at him and which would have drilled him a third eye if he'd still been standing.

Hunter slapped the Henry to his shoulder, quickly racking a fresh round in the action, and fired. The man's horse quickly became riderless, swerving sharply right in time to avoid trampling Hunter. The fallen rider rolled up over Hunter's left boot, groaning.

Hunter lowered the Henry's barrel to the man's forehead.

The man, hatless, saw the rifle barrel. He widened his eyes and his mouth. *"Nooo!"*

The Henry said yes.

Hunter emptied the saddle of the next horse barreling toward him. That man hadn't hit the ground before Hunter leaped again to his feet and resumed his run up the hill toward the minimal cover of the trees and rocks on the hill looming before him.

He'd taken only five more strides before a bullet slammed into his left leg.

He hit the ground and rolled, hearing the whoops and yells and thundering hooves of the man-wolves closing on him for the kill.

Standing outside the cave, Annabelle sipped her coffee and stared out over the forested slope in the direction of the 4-Box-B. A vague apprehension vexed her. She tipped her ear to the breeze. There were only the bird and squirrel sounds of the forest, the occasional soft plops of pinecones tumbling from branches.

Just nerves.

She threw back the last of her coffee, set down the cup, then walked into the cave's cool darkness. She dropped to a knee beside Angus, who'd fallen back into a deep sleep. Again, he looked deathly pale. His breath rattled in his throat, issuing out of his open mouth. The poor man sounded as though he were drowning.

Which she supposed he was in a way. Drowning in sorrow.

Anna had the depressing feeling that Hunter was right. Angus might have survived the bullet wound only to be finished off by the knowledge of what the men from town — the murdering devils from town — had done to the ranch.

Annabelle plucked the cloth from the basin on the ground beside Angus, wrung it out, and lay it across the old man's forehead. She gave his spindly shoulder a reassuring, affectionate squeeze.

Odd how she'd found herself feeling more tenderness toward this old Rebel than she did toward her own father. On the other hand, not so odd . . .

She rose and walked back out into the sunlight.

She stopped suddenly, gasped. Her heart skipped a beat.

Graham Ludlow stood at the edge of the forest below the cave, holding the reins of his vinegar dun stallion. He held his Winchester rifle on his right shoulder. He canted his regal head to one side and stretched his lips back in a sneering grin.

Annabelle blinked as though to clear the illusion from her eyes. Only, it wasn't an illusion. Her father stood right there in the brassy afternoon sunshine, his horse cropping the grass jutting up around his boots!

Annabelle swung around, reaching for her rifle.

A shadow moved up on her from behind, sliding past her.

"Uh-uh," said a man's low voice.

Arms engulfed her, drew her back away from her rifle, and lifted her up off the ground.

"No!" Annabelle cried. "Damn you!"

The man holding her chuckled. As she fought him, he said, "Ouch!" and tossed her violently down and to the left. She hit the ground and rolled, hair flying, dust wafting around her. She almost rolled over the edge of the shelf the cave was on, but she caught herself just in time.

She looked up at Frank Stillwell standing over her, cradling his bandaged left hand against his chest. The bandage was spotted with blood. The sheriff stared at her darkly, flaring his nostrils. His eyes were like two lumps of charcoal beneath the broad brim of his hat.

"Don't hurt her!" yelled Ludlow.

Annabelle turned toward her father. As she did another horse plodded up out of the forest flanking him. In the saddle was none other than Kenneth Earnshaw. Again, Annabelle blinked, still half believing she was hallucinating, or maybe she'd fallen asleep and was dreaming.

Leaning forward in his saddle, Earnshaw groaned. He slid down the saddle's left stirrup and gave a yell just before he hit the ground. He pushed up onto his hands and knees and promptly spewed his guts into the tall, blond grass, vomiting.

"The old man in there?" Ludlow called to Stillwell.

The sheriff turned to peer into the cave, shading his eyes with his good hand. He turned back to Ludlow, and grinned. "Yep!"

Ludlow turned and said to someone else.

"Finish him."

Two men were standing on the other side of the cave entrance. One was short and seedy looking, the other tall and black bearded. They'd been concealed by the mountain's shadow. Both men grinned as they cocked their rifles and stepped into the cave.

"Have fun, fellas," Stillwell said.

"Noooo!" Anna screamed, lunging to her feet.

As she scrambled toward the cave entrance, Stillwell grabbed her arm with his good hand and pulled her back.

"Noooo!" she screamed again.

The scream was nearly drowned by the near-deafening blast of a shotgun.

The tall, bearded man flew back out of the cave as though he'd been lassoed from behind, screaming. His black duster flapped around him like the wings of a giant bat.

The first blast was still echoing when it was joined by a second explosion.

The shorter, seedy-looking killer flew back out of the cave, boot toes barely raking the ground, and was thrown off the ledge and into the grass near where Ludlow stood with his horse. Near where the taller gent lay convulsing with his hands over the gaping, bloody hole in his middle, dying fast.

Stillwell slid his pistol from its holster.

"No, you don't!" Annabelle lurched up and dug her teeth into the man's right forearm.

"Bitch!" Stillwell backhanded her. It was only a glancing blow. Annabelle lunged at him, punching him, clawing at his face. Somehow they got turned around on the ledge, and then suddenly Annabelle felt herself falling over the edge toward the grassy ground beneath.

Stillwell cursed as he, too, fell, his legs entangled with hers.

The yellow-brown ground came up hard, smacking Annabelle about the head and shoulders. She groaned and rolled onto her side, the summer-cured grass crackling around her. Stillwell gave a yelp as he hit beside her and rolled several times down the grade toward Ludlow.

"Jesus Christ!" Ludlow said, dropping his horse's reins and walking toward Annabelle. "Stop it, Stillwell! I told you — !"

Stillwell came up clutching his bandaged hand to his chest, grimacing. His hat was gone, and his short hair was mussed, grass clinging to it. He turned to where Annabelle lay, butterflies dancing in her eyes.

"You bitch!"

Annabelle spat grass and sand from her

lips and pushed up onto her elbows. "Go to hell!" She turned to her father. "You go to hell too!"

"You bitch!" Stillwell repeated, rising, glaring at Annabelle with menace. "You're the cause of all of this — you realize that?"

Annabelle shook her head and heaved herself to her feet. "You got that wrong, you fool. You started this war in Tigerville. No one would be dead — except that idiot Luke Chaney — if you'd been smart enough and *man* enough to accept Hunter's word for what had happened on his way into town! Instead, you tried to humiliate him . . . and then you sicced your men on him. For no good reason. Now they're dead!"

"Shut up, you bitch!" Stillwell lunged toward her, slapped her hard with his right hand.

Annabelle screamed, spun, and fell.

"Stop!" This from the unlikely source of Kenneth Earnshaw. "Stop that, you brigand. That is my betrothed you're manhandling, sir!"

Kenneth had gained his feet uncertainly and was now moving slowly toward Stillwell, pointing accusingly with his left hand, closing his right hand around one of his fancy six-shooters.

"Shut up, you four-eyed sissy!" Stillwell

snapped out of the side of his mouth, keeping his eyes on Anna. "Stay where you are, or I'll gut you like a fish!"

"Hold on, Stillwell!" Ludlow said, aiming his rifle at the sheriff.

"Shut up, old man!" Stillwell moved on Annabelle once more. "I've about had enough of smart-ass women. Time to teach this sassy little filly a lesson she won't forget!"

Annabelle gained her feet and sidled defensively around Stillwell, who grinned coldly and drew his Colt.

"Stop!" Earnshaw strode toward Stillwell and drew one of his fancy pistols. "I say stop right now or —"

The Colt in his hand roared and bucked.

CHAPTER 40

"Oh!" Kenneth stared in shock at the smoking gun in his hand, then dropped it like a hot potato.

Stillwell jerked around to face Earnshaw. He took two stumbling steps backward. He looked down in shock at the blood bubbling up out of the hole in his upper left chest.

"Oh crackers!" he said, brushing his bandaged left hand across the wound. He looked at Earnshaw, aghast. "You . . . you killed me . . . you son of a bitch!" He turned to Ludlow and said with strange imploring, "I . . . I've been killed by . . . by a damn *sissy!*"

He dropped to a knee and then fell back on his hip, one leg curled beneath him. He was wincing, breathing hard.

Ludlow cut his shocked gaze between Stillwell and Earnshaw, who promptly dropped to his knees and began vomiting in the grass. Annabelle hurried over to Stillwell. She dropped to a knee and tugged at the front of the man's wool vest.

"Stillwell," she said. "Where's the gold? Where's Hunter's gold? What did you do with it?"

The sheriff rolled his glassy eyes up at her. "Huh?"

"The gold! Hunter's gold!"

Stillwell beetled his brows. "What . . . what the hell . . . you talkin' about, crazy b-bitch?" He wheezed out a bitter laugh. "You think that . . . that I'd be out here gettin' . . . *killed* by some damn nancy boy in a tweed coat if I had . . . *gold*?"

He choked out that last word. His face slackened. His eyes rolled up in his head. Annabelle let him fall back in the grass, dead. She looked around, frowning, deeply befuddled. "If . . . if he didn't have it . . . who does?"

"Get on your horse, girl!"

She'd been so distracted that she hadn't seen her father walk up on her. Ludlow stopped six feet away and aimed his rifle at her from his right hip.

"You're goin' home. And you're gonna marry that Nancy-boy if it's the very last thing I make you do. Not only that, but you're gonna have a passel of kids with that tinhorn!"

Still down on one knee by Stillwell's dead body, Annabelle looked up at her father. She hardened her jaws and an angry flush rose in her cheeks. "I'd rather die!" She cut her eyes over to Earnshaw, who was on both knees and slowly running his coat sleeve across his mouth. "No offense, Kenneth."

The dandy turned his head to glare at her.

"That can be arranged!" Ludlow walked over to her, grabbed her arm, and shoved her toward her buckskin. "Saddle your horse and get started back to the ranch! I won't listen to one more word of —"

"Stand down, you old fool."

Annabelle turned to see Angus standing on the ledge fronting the cave. The old man had gotten into his longhandles, baggy canvas trousers, boots, and battered gray campaign hat. He held one of his old Confederate pistols in his hand, aimed at Ludlow.

He gritted his teeth as he clicked the hammer back. "You turn that girl loose and head on home before I do what I should do and grease you right here! The only reason I won't is because whatever you are, you're still her father. I don't want her to have to live with watchin' you die." Angus gave his head a slow, ominous shake. "That don't mean I won't do it if I have to, you old

531

polecat."

"You go to hell, you Southern devil!" Ludlow lifted his arm and pointed an enraged, accusing finger at Angus. He strode stiffly toward him. "This is none of your affair! Why, you're nothin' but a . . ." He let the words trail off as he tensed suddenly and began issuing strangling sounds from his throat.

The rifle fell from his right hand.

He lifted his left hand, which curled toward him, claw-like, as though of its own accord. Standing behind him, Annabelle watched his thick neck turn beet red. His strangling sounds growing louder, Ludlow dropped to a knee.

Annabelle walked around in front of him, stood over him, her eyes stony. "Your heart?"

Clutching his stiff left arm with his right hand, Ludlow nodded. He cursed and groaned, wincing. Finally, he dropped forward onto his hands and knees, panting.

Annabelle turned to Kenneth Earnshaw, who stood facing her and Ludlow now, his face pasty, eyes glassy from drink and shock. "Get him on his horse and take him home," she said coldly.

Earnshaw stared at her, his lower jaw hanging. He turned to look at the dead Stillwell, then strode uncertainly forward. He knelt beside Ludlow, placed a hand on his arm, and said, "Do you think you can ride, Mr. Ludlow?"

He looked up at Annabelle uncertainly.

"He can ride," Annabelle said, grabbing her father's other arm, pulling the stout old man to his feet. "He doesn't have a choice in the matter."

She and Earnshaw led Ludlow over to the vinegar dun. It took some doing, but they finally got him mounted. He didn't say anything. He just sat leaning forward in his saddle, over the horse's pole, holding his left arm with his right hand. He stared glassily down at the dun's mane.

Annabelle stepped back, turned to Earnshaw, and tossed the dun's reins to him. "Light a shuck, Kenneth."

The young dandy climbed awkwardly into his saddle. He turned to Annabelle, hardened his jaws.

"This won't stand," he said primly. "I tell you, this won't stand. You think you won't marry me?" He laughed with menace, nearly dislodging his glasses from his nose. "We'll see about that!"

He booted his steel-dust ahead and nearly fell out of the saddle as the horse lunged off its rear hooves. He dropped the dun's reins as he desperately grabbed his own saddle horn, barely holding on. That was all right. The dun trailed him, anyway, eager to get back home to fresh hay and water.

Annabelle's father turned to glare back at her over his shoulder. His eyes were none-too-vaguely threatening. They seemed to say, "This isn't over."

When they were gone, Anna walked toward where Angus still stood on the ledge fronting the cave. "Are you all right?"

"Some better." Angus was staring off over the pine-stippled ridge behind Annabelle.

She stopped, frowned up at him. "What is it?"

"They wouldn't have come up here with so few men," Angus said darkly. "Not if they were out to run my son to ground. They would have sent another small army."

Suddenly, Annabelle knew it was true. Her heart thudded. She turned to stare down the slope through the trees, in the direction of the 4-Box-B. "Oh God!"

Hunter picked out a man scurrying up the slope before him and fired.

The man gave a shrill yell as he dove behind a cedar. A bullet smashed into the top of Shep's grave to Hunter's right, and the big ex-Confederate pulled his head down in the valley between his brothers' graves, scattered rocks and the grave mounds themselves offering his only cover from the killers climbing the slope around him.

Two more bullets hammered the rocks around him. Hunter lifted his head and rifle, picked out a target, and fired. His assailant flew backward, dropping his rifle and clutching his shoulder, screaming as he fell.

Hunter picked out another target — he thought he'd killed maybe five of them so far, wounded two or three more. But it looked like at least five were still trying to make their way up the hill around him, dodging behind rocks and trees.

Hunter squeezed the Henry's trigger.

The hammer clicked, empty. He'd fired all sixteen rounds.

"Oh Lordie!"

He set the rifle aside and drew the big LeMat as more bullets screeched through the air around him and tore up gravel and rock from the mounded graves. Straight ahead of him, two men were sprinting up the slope, deadheading toward him. In the corners of his eyes, he spied several more. He fired at one, missed, and drew his head down in time to avoid a bullet that would have cored through his left ear.

They were moving on him too fast now. He only had five more bullets in the LeMat, and the shotgun shell. His seconds were numbered.

He could hear Bobby Lee howling mournfully in the woods nearby. Even the coyote was aware his master's ticket was about to be punched.

Hunter thought he might as well take down as many of these hardcases as he could before he died up here, appropriately enough, to lie with his dead brothers . . .

Hunter heaved himself to his feet, loosing a loud, hair-raising Rebel yell. Crouching he looked around and extended the LeMat.

His own yell was answered by another, louder one:

"Yeeee-HAWWWWWWWW!"

It was accompanied by the thuds of galloping hooves.

Hunter whipped around, raising the LeMat, preparing to fire. He lowered the big popper when he saw the darkly wizened, white-bearded face and gray campaign hat of the man barreling toward him on an unfamiliar horse, grinning as Angus held a double-barreled shotgun in his lone hand, which also held the reins of his hard-charging claybank.

"Pa!" Hunter bellowed as the rider gal-

loped past him, raising the shotgun and discharging one barrel with an echoing, cannon-like blast.

One attacker screamed as he was punched backward down the hill.

Angus discharged the second barrel, evoking another cry.

As he stopped his horse and drew one of the twin Confederate pistols shoved down behind the waistband of his denim jeans, Hunter went to work with the LeMat, emptying the cylinder into the men around him who'd been taken off guard by the hard-charging old Rebel.

When he'd popped his last .44 cap, he flicked the LeMat's steel lever, engaging the twelve-gauge shotgun shell. He swung the pistol to his right just as an attacker in a weathered Stetson and flapping chaps ran toward him, cocking his Winchester and howling like a gut-shot lobo.

The LeMat leaped and roared, turning the man's face the color of a ripe tomato, throwing him backward down the hill.

Hunter turned toward where Angus was riding along the shoulder of the slope, emptying his twin Griswold & Gunnisons, one after another in his lone hand, into the wounded, howling killers, sending each one to his own reward.

Hooves thudded in the same direction from which Angus had so unexpectedly come.

"Hunter!"

He turned again to see Annabelle galloping toward him on her buckskin. She leaped down just as Hunter felt his left knee buckle and drop to the ground. He winced, clutching the bloody wound in the back of his left leg.

Annabelle dropped to a knee beside him, placing a hand on his shoulder. "How bad are you hit?"

"Where in the hell did you two come from?" Hunter said, staring at her in disbelief before cutting his eyes at old Angus then back to Anna again.

"We had visitors," she said.

"Stillwell? Your old man?"

Annabelle nodded. "Stillwell's dead. My father is heading home with his tail between his legs." Her eyes swept Hunter's big frame, noting the many bullet burns oozing blood. "Oh God!" she intoned. "How bad . . . ?"

"Not bad," Hunter said. "The leg here is the worst, but, hell, I've cut myself worse shaving."

"Oh, shut up and let me look at it!"

"How bad you hit, son?"

Hunter looked up to see his father stop the unfamiliar horse, which now Hunter thought he recognized as Stillwell's gelding, before him. The old man looked somehow both haggard and hale. "Pa . . ."

Angus swung heavily down, wincing against the pain of the wound in his side. He dropped to a knee beside Anna, spat to one side, and shook his head. "I may have been down," he said. "But don't count this old rascal out. Not yet."

Hunter smiled, wincingly, as Anna wrapped a bandanna around the wound in his leg.

"How bad's it look?" Angus asked Anna.

"He'll live," Anna said, nodding, her gaze cast with grave relief. She kissed Hunter's cheek. "He'd better. There's this Yankee girl he's gotta marry."

"Oh yeah?" Hunter said. "I hope she's not bossy."

"Well, she is." Anna crossed her eyes at him. "Very bossy!"

"And you got yourselves a ranch to re-build." Angus gave Hunter a direct look, then turned to peer down the hill at the burned-out ranch buildings.

Hunter smiled, nodded. "Our blood was spilled here, Pa. It's hallowed ground."

He glanced at the graves humping up

beside them, mounded with rocks. Some of the rocks had been scattered by flying lead. Angus looked at the graves, too, and a sheen of tears grew in his eyes.

"We have to rebuild. We have to stay." Hunter turned to Anna. "No one's gonna drive a Buchanon off his own land. Just won't happen."

"I wouldn't have it any other way!" Anna threw her arms around his neck and kissed him with all the passion in her wild heart.

A yammering sounded to Hunter's left. He and Annabelle and Angus turned to see Bobby Lee hiking his leg on the head of Ludlow's dead foreman, C. J. Bonner.

Angus chuckled. Then he brushed tears from his bearded cheeks and grimaced as he pushed to his feet. "I need to locate a jug of beer. I bet I still got one or two in the old cellar behind the garden."

The old Rebel ambled off down the hill, limping a little but otherwise steady, his stride proud and certain. He beckoned to the coyote. "Come on, Bobby Lee. Let's leave these two lovebirds alone. I'll buy ya a drink!"

Anna looked at Hunter, brushed her thumbs across his cheeks. "It's over. It's finished."

"You think so?"

Anna nodded. "We can build a home here now. Raise a family."

Hunter grinned. He tipped his head back, loosed another wild yell. Then he took his lady in his arms once more and kissed her with all the passion in his Rebel heart.

Neither he nor Annabelle were aware of the rider sitting atop the ridge above them, astride a fine paint stallion, staring down at them from behind a mask cut from a flour sack. The strange visage wore Spanish-cut bell-bottom trousers with silver conchas, and a short, elaborately embroidered leather waistcoat. A black felt Stetson capped his head.

"Congratulations, lovebirds," the rider said, smiling darkly behind the mask. He lifted a flat laudanum bottle, took a long drink. Smacking his lips, he said, "May I reward you with twin tombstones to help you celebrate this joyous occasion?"

He laughed, if you could call it a laugh. Some might call it a cackling demon's cry. "Soon," he said. "Soon!"

ABOUT THE AUTHORS

William W. Johnstone has written nearly three hundred novels of western adventure, military action, chilling suspense, and survival. His bestselling books include *The Family Jensen; The Mountain Man; Flintlock; MacCallister; Savage Texas; Luke Jensen, Bounty Hunter;* and the thrillers *Black Friday, The Doomsday Bunker,* and *Trigger Warning.*

J. A. Johnstone learned to write from the master himself, Uncle William W. Johnstone, with whom J.A. has co-written numerous bestselling series including The Mountain Man; Those Jensen Boys; and Preacher, The First Mountain Man.